MW00571299

YOKE OF WIND

LUKE COMER

The Aurignacian, Llc
Boulder, CO

ISBN 978-0-9848046-0-3
Library of Congress Control Number: 2011960600
Copyright information available upon request.

Typography: Palatino
Cover Design: Author
Interior Design: J. L. Saloff

v. 1.0
First Edition, 2013
Printed on acid-free paper.

In countless, upward-striving waves
The moon-drawn tide-wave strives.
In thousand far-transplanted grafts
The parent fruit survives;
So, in the new-born millions,
The perfect Adam lives.
Not less are summer-mornings dear
To every child they wake,
And each with novel life his sphere
Fills for his proper sake.

~ Ralph Waldo Emerson

PROLOGUE

"That fireboat is gone for sho," said Jake.

Awakened from his nap, Shaka watched the steamship, which had brought them to the island, sailing away into the approach of night. Puffs of smoke rose black and round from its chimney like holes shot through creation.

Waves churned into shore, eroding the island back into the gulf. And the sand, as dry as the ashes of bones, blew into the dunes and settled momentarily around the sea oats and scrub oaks, creating smooth, riblike patterns.

Although leaning back onto something stable—the only tree on the island—Shaka felt that this mound of land was floating cloud-like while slowly dissolving underneath him.

"We in trouble now," said Jake.

Ignoring him, Shaka looked into the sun that created molten, golden rays of light upon the waves while sinking into the horizon. While his flesh warmed euphorically in the remains of heat and his eyes flooded with mild but glorious light, he felt he could leap into the sky and soar back to his homeland.

"We stuck on this here pile of sand," said Jake, "like lizards floating on some log."

Shaka then turned to face Jake who was clenching his fingers around the thick, knobby roots protruding from the tree, saying, "When that log rolls, niggers drown."

Jake's gut convulsed, but empty after days of vomiting onboard the steamship, his stomach eructed nothing but vaporous and putrid wind as though some part of his soul, old and useless, was flushing from his body. "I caint understand nothing."

Shaka realized that Jake was trying to coerce someone to ask him questions. But the other three slaves scattered around the tree stared listlessly toward the gulf, ignoring him, hoping to deflect another one of his wild, trampling assaults of words. But Shaka was curious. "What you mean?"

"I mean I caint understand why Massa done dragged all his niggers to this pile of dust, nor how, neither, we all done got here."

"Go on," said Shaka.

Jake opened and stretched his lips yawnlike, displaying his mouth like some warrior brandishing his sword. "Before coming here, my life never changed. The bell done clanged at dawn, I trampled in them fields and plowed, planted and picked, stupid with boredom, watching the sun hurl across the sky like some rock chunked. I done all that so much, so long, that this rotten-boned, pumpkin-brained grandpa caint remember nothing that ever changed, except for shouting at the Lawd on Sundays.

"But then my whole life done gone rabid.

"I was snoozing in my shack before the clang of the bell, bit of the chill rattling my bones, hugging onto sacks of leaves cause my wife done died. Then come Massa hammering on my door, stomping into my shack, grinning and showing his teeth. What he wanting with some half-dead, already-rotting nigger like this Jake, I was wondering.

"Hallelujah, I thought, Massa done come to say, 'Jake, you toiled like the mule and populated the plantation with niggers as quick as watermelons on the vine, making your Massa rich. But now you is retired. But hurry and die soon lessen you break the bank.' For the rest of my days, I was reckoning on sipping the whiskey, playing with the grandchildren, waiting for the Lawd's Chariot to take me away to heaven.

"Instead Massa said, 'Come on.'

" 'Sho I's coming. But where's I going?'

" 'On an adventure.' "

" 'I aint never heard of that place before.'

"I followed Massa down to the river where our folk was loading the barge with cotton bales and wooden crates. Massa aint retiring this Jake, I knowed, wanting to whack him upside his head, but trading me for some hat-eating, broken-legged goat to some white trash, whip-loving Massa expecting his niggers to eat rats and shovel shit from his outhouse. Naw, I aint retiring but toiling clear through the dirt to my grave.

"But that aint happened neither." Jake paused.

Shaka noticed that the other slaves, prodded by this bombardment of words, were emerging from their lethargy. Sitting next to Jake but hidden from his sight was Shobuck, the surly and restless boy who was flicking twigs at Jake, who swatted around his head as though shooing away flies.

"So what happened?" asked Shaka.

"We all done got on that boat and floated away from all that I knowed. At the end of the river, we done switched boats onto the one out there now," said Jake, pointing toward the ship now fading into the horizon, "that's like some town that set fire to itself, growed fins and started to swim about the place. Then all I knowed my whole life—all them withering fields, dark forests and stomping and braying critters—just done fell off the earth like some mule that wanders so far off you caint see him no more. Aint nothing about the ship but water, clear, blue and fluffy like cotton but bitter was the taste, like piss. But I aint never tasted none, you know," said Jake, looking furtively at the other slaves.

"This Jake felt like some gnat, some tiny, flakey insect floating around in nothing but sky, up there, way up there, without places to land, lost and wearied and scared to hell." Looking disturbed, Jake gripped his fingers into the bark of the tree and pointed toward the gulf with the other hand and asked, "What is all that water that look like the sky done fallen to the earth." He looked directly at one of the slaves named Nomaw.

Who was slouched against the tree. The weariness of age and years of perpetual, grinding toil pulled her spine toward the ground so instead of sitting, she slouched on her side across the roots of the tree, splaying her flanks of fat. At first she gazed upon Jake incredulous, even fascinated as though he was speaking to something deep and latent in herself.

Suddenly aware that others were looking at her, she scowled and blurted, "That's just the ocean, fool, like the Bible say."

"I heard about that place. But I reckoned that was some muddy, smelly lake with a bunch of Jesuses, Abrahams and Ezekiels walking about and shouting at the Lawd."

"That just shows that you caint reckon," said Nomaw.

"I reckon you be right if I could reckon," riposted Jake. "But I sho aint studied on that ocean."

Once noticing that Nomaw was not responding to him anymore, Jake resumed with his story. "Scared as some gnat looking to land cause his wings done wore out, I looked behind our boat at that slither of land fading in the distance, starting to feel dizzy. My skin too was turning purply black while my stomach started to churn and gurgle like I done drunk some barrel of whiskey, except I aint having any fun. I upchucked, bits of pone, pork and turnips flung out my mouth, threaded down my chin, then come this drool that I reckoned I ate about last summer that looked like bird shit and bitter was the taste."

"Nasty," said Nomaw.

"You was seasick," said Shaka, "like all of us."

"Anyhow," resumed Jake. "Back on the plantation, bit of the chill was coursing through the air, the leaves on the tree was drying up and withering away. But on that boat the sky come hot all of sudden. I was mighty befuddled." Jake paused, the drone of the sea, of the waves lolling onto the shore, filled the silence for one moment before he resumed. "So what did this Jake do?"

"What?" asked Nomaw.

"I done all niggers can."

"What's that?"

"I scratched."

"You scratched?" asked Nomaw.

"I felt like my soul—all them useless nigger thoughts—done flung out my head and I was calm for once in my life. All I knowed and felt was gone, leaving nothing but this carcass of whipped-on, burnt flesh and grinded-down, crooked bones."

Shaka was piqued. Once sitting and leaning back on his arms, he lurched forward to place his hands around his knees, looking piercingly at Jake. "You felt dead?"

"Dead?" said Jake quizzically. With a slight but distinct nod of his head, he showed some glimmer of recognition. "I reckon. But not like I was in my grave feeding the worms. My heart was beating. I know, I checked. I mean that Jake, the slave, was dead. Floating around in all that blue, heaving space that went on forever, I felt free and, shit, I aint know what I is trying to say and..."

"That's the point," said Nomaw.

"But that aint the point," interrupted Shaka sharply. Shaka remembered experiencing the death of his identity as a child after his mother revealed his purpose in life. His mother also told him about the shamans in Africa who were expected to kill themselves ritualistically, usually through excruciating pain, to purge all they knew from their minds to attain the purity that would allow them to pass into the underworld. Even Christ was killed in body before ascending into Heaven. Shaka believed that Jake too was experiencing something like that. "You recollect, Jake, seeing them ducks that Massa keeps in his coop?"

"That he fattens up to eat," said Jake.

"They look like the ducks on the river that can fly," said Shaka. "But what happens when you take them ducks from the coup and they try to fly?"

"They flop about like they wings is broken."

"On that boat you were like one of them ducks taken from its coup and trying to fly."

"But I aint like ducks. Most say I be like mules."

"Sho you is. You wanting to fly but you aint never given the chance."

Shaka saw that one of the slaves named Pear was looking at him intently. Although shy most of the time, she now was balanced on her torso so that her spine, not yet tainted from the stoop and slump of the fields, rose upright, making her look feral and regal. But once Shaka smiled at her, she slumped her shoulders and once again stared at the gulf listlessly.

"We all know that you is the smartest nigger in the land," said Jake while smiling with some hint of recognition, however distant and vague. "I rather be like birds than mules anyhow."

"You aint birds," said Nomaw, "and you aint free. As for you, Shaka, if you keep teaching all this nonsense, you bound to cause some trouble for all of us."

Shaka was tempted to respond but hesitated.

"Anyhow," resumed Jake, "back on the boat, I was studying all them folks yanking on all them ropes—sailors they is called. They aint neither white, black or brown. They aint neither slaves, masters or nothing like that. Though most of them caint talk but made noises like beasts in the fields, one fellow pulled me aside on the deck; he was huge, his arms like stumps, his teeth like white rocks, some necklace hanging from his neck glimmered like trickles of golden field piss. This one could talk too.

" 'Come here, nigger,' he said.

" 'Sho,' I said.

" 'Men aint born to be owned by masters. They know that in England already. If I was you—and I am not, nigger, thank God—I'd kill your master and his family, kill them all, take their life worse and bloodier than they took yours.'

" 'What?' I said, shocked. 'Kill who?'

" 'Kill,' he said.

" 'I caint kill my master. He feeds us, clads our flesh. He don't sell our babies most of the time. At Christmas he gives us whiskey.'

" 'Well, that's how come you nigger and I aint.'

"I felt sick. I caint tolerate the thought of killing Massa. I knowed him since he was tiny and helpless. I sooner kill myself."

"You should of told Massa to whip that boy," said Nomaw. "He aint nothing but trash."

"I reckon," said Jake. "But that aint what I was thinking. Them sailors was free but not like whities. They lived out there like your birds, Shaka, soaring all over the ocean. And I got this notion that they was guiding this Jake—and all yawl too—toward this place called 'adventure.' Somehow this trip seemed like some kind of... well...what's the word?"

"Deliverance," said Shaka.

"Sho," said Jake. "Deliverance."

"But this here aint the Promised Land there, Shaka. But some pile of sand."

"Shaka," blurted Nomaw, "you don't make any sense cause you caint read so you aint learning about things from the Bible but Lawd only knows where, probably the Devil."

Shaka wanted to retaliate against Nomaw but remained silent once again. He allowed his words to pass without event, taking root in some minds and becoming blighted from others.

"I like his riddles," said Jake. "I am like them ducks. Quack... quack..."

"You like anything that makes noise," said Nomaw.

"But really," resumed Jake, easing the tension, "I knowed them sailors aint angels and that Massa, not them, was leading that ship. Since whities aint never taken me some place I was wanting to go, I figured we was heading for hell, not heaven. So I wandered over to Oakleaf, saying, 'Massa, excuse this butt-itching, mule-brained fool but I was pondering about this here adventure. Reckon that, in your kindness, you can educate Jake on this matter.'

"As usual I caint understand much about what he say, something about peril and glory and our destination, something called an island."

"So I asked, 'This here island, what's that?'

" 'An island, Jake, is a piece of land surrounded by water.'

" 'Well, where is this here island.'

"Massa started to look all strange and that was troubling to me. He walked across the deck and pointed over the water like he some hound smelling coons in the distance, his hair flaring in the sun like his brains afire. And he said, 'Yonder lurks our island, to the south.' And he just walked away.

"I squinted in the sun, searching for this island but seeing nothing until that vomit in my gut—stuff eaten about when I was twelve—was spewing out my mouth again, old, ruint pork fat threading down my chin. Feeling like some spooked rabbit, I finally figured why Massa aint saying much about our 'adventure.' Cause like his father before him, he was gonna settle some chunk of land in the wilderness. I was gonna spend the last of my days chopping down trees, sleeping in the dirt covered with leaves, digging up roots and killing rodents and bugs for something to eat—all to make the whitie richer. That island aint nothing but hell, I reckoned—some plot of dirt for planting more cotton.

"I was wanting to fling myself overboard.

"Instead I reckoned this here island aint wobbly like the boat, that the dirt was made from cookie crumbs, the streams from fine whiskeys, so we can gnaw on the ground like mules. And fine, young girls, their melons ripe for plucking, their loins moist and succulent like summertime peaches, was gonna wash my ol', tired body and suck and kiss on things so them dust balls down there that aint good for nothing nowadays but scratching, heat up, catch afire and spew about the place. Hoooooweeeee, that was deliverance for sho." Jake released his clutches from the tree and threw his hands in the air, relief on his face, the rotting knobs of his teeth showing through his smile.

"About sunrise this morning Massa done shouted," resumed Jake, his face instantly becoming forlorn. "I looked out over the water, seeing this tiny, round, white place like some pebble barely rising above a creek, except they was this one little tree on it. That aint nigger heaven, I thought, my hopes done ruint.

"But know what?"

"What?" blurted Nomaw.

"I rejoiced," Jake said. "Cause that whiteness was cookie crumbs and all that water, turning clear under the boat, was fine whiskey. After we done paddled them rowboats over here, I dropped on my knees and scooped up some of that sweet, white sand. But you know what?"

"Sho," said Nomaw. "You is ignorant."

"I is?"

"All this talk about girls," she continued. "You is whacked for sho. You's always thinking with the wrong parts of your body."

"I reckon so," continued Jake, "cause that sand sho aint taste like sugar. Tasted like rocks. Then I licked the water. Tasted like piss although, like I said, I aint never tasted none before. And I aint feel goofy at all." Jake stood from his stoop and reached above his head, grabbing some leaves which he put into his mouth. "And you know what? These leaves—they aint tasting nearly as good as turnips." Jake dropped back to his knees, scooped up some of the sand between the roots of the tree, which then spilled from his hands and blew away in the wind. "Yawl recollect the first of my hopes, that we going to some place that aint wobbly?

"I aint even get that hope. Study about this place. It aint nothing but sand blowing in the wind, here now but sinking before long, leaving us neck deep and half drowned in that there ocean, clinging to this tree while fishes and gaiters chomp on our legs." Jake was silent, which seemed to intensify his misery, so he spoke again. "And still I heave. I be wobbling like that boat, like we aint attached to the earth but floating around on some lily pad."

"I be wobbling too," admitted Nomaw. "Sho seems strange."

"And study on that," said Jake.

Shaka swiveled around the tree and pointed toward their master named Jonah who was standing atop one of the dunes. While his clothes were streaming in the wind, the sand was swirling from under his heavy black boots as though the island was dissolving beneath him. He would periodically stomp his boots into the sand to attempt to entrench his feet but to little, if any, avail, so he stood in resolute but futile defiance of the elements of oblivion like some farmer standing in his fields swatting the locusts devouring his crops.

Below him in the troughs of the dunes were supplies from the steamship—crates, barrels, bags, one large wooden table. And down on the beach was his wife, Eloise, and their two children wandering around collecting shells while also seeming as bewildered and disconcerted as the slaves.

"Massa aint like most white folks," Jake continued. "When little he was like some regular pickaninny playing around my shack, eating my pone, playing with my chilluns. But once he come of age, his father done beat all the nigger from his soul and like his son was just some regular ol' ox, done strapped the yoke about his neck, cracked the whip and reined hard on the bridle. Ever since that day, I aint never knowed that man no more—he there, you know, but he aint. He talks, sho, he breaths but he aint there.

"But once his father died, the yoke about his neck done broke and now he just stomping and braying around like some angry, confused beast. But all us niggers—and even Miss Eloise and his chilluns—is riding the wagon hitched to his haunches. And we just got dumped on this heap of sand in the middle of nowhere, knowing nothing, told nothing, and left to the mercy of some wild and braying beast."

CHAPTER ONE

Blowing from the south the wind was laden with warmth, stirring the tight, incipient buds of the trees. Hoe in hand, mud caked about her boots, Eloise was unearthing the brittle, brown corpses of plants dead from the winter to plant the seeds of spring. From the distance one horseman approached, arrived, dismounted and stood before her. He was black, dressed in some formal but wrinkled suit.

"For you, Miss Eloise" he said, handing her an envelope. Oddly, almost comically, he curtsied with the deliberate and strained effort of someone practicing what he had learned only recently.

Inside the envelope the paper was delicate, the calligraphy nicer than any she had seen before. The invitation was for a party at the Whiteoak Plantation. Scrawled in the margins looking awkward and brutish, without any signature, were the words, "Please Come." She knew nothing about Whiteoak but in town she occasionally saw his son, Jonah, who never approached her but always looked at her furtively but yearningly like he wanted something from her—maybe sex, though she knew nothing about that subject. She was intrigued by him but probably more frightened. He was handsome though and she could not help but wonder, while gently reprimanding her own vanity, whether those words scribbled in the margins were from what she imagined as his own heavy and crude hand.

Later she stood before her father who was hunched over his

desk amidst his book and icons, his long and disheveled beard falling onto the scrolls of paper on which he was writing. But when he raised his head, exposing his intense but haggard eyes which seemed to peer into her soul, she felt exposed for all of her vanities and conceits.

"Yes, Eloise," he said.

"Oh nothing, father," she said, turning to leave.

"What is that in your hand?"

Eloise turned and handed him the invitation.

While reading the paper, her father seemed concerned. "What do you know about this man, Whiteoak?"

"Very little."

Her father spoke to her as usual, by lecturing. "They say he's abhorrent to behold due to the mutilation of his face. He came to Alabama from the north with nothing but his horse and three or four starving, barely-clad slaves and managed to create one of the largest, most prosperous plantations in the land by working harder and smarter than other planters who came here already bequeathed with fortunes from their parents. They say he knows how to manage negroes better than any man on earth, probably because he lives like one himself. He still sleeps in some cabin much simpler and more primitive than our own.

"And he never comes to town, never attends church—is rarely if ever seen in public. This man does not care for Christ, nor for other people, nor for whiskey or carousing but only for expanding his empire."

"So why is he holding this party?" asked Eloise.

"I have heard that he's close to completing one of the largest and most luxurious mansions in these parts. I imagine the purpose of this party is simply to display his wealth."

"That seems odd," said Eloise.

"These people behave that way."

"Do any of his slaves come to our church?"

Her father became grave. "I've been writing that man for years now trying to persuade him to that end."

"And he refuses?"

"Yes," he replied. "All sorts of slave masters live around here. Some exploit the Bible to teach that slavery is justified and even beneficial—and therefore abominably deceive their flock. Some are indifferent to whether their slaves worship. And some, in the silent but ignored whispers of their heart, know that slavery is wrong in the eyes of God but lack the courage to take action. But Whiteoak is the worst. He denies his slaves any contact with Christianity and punishes them if they defy him. In response to my letters, he writes back the same every time. 'Don't need Jesus complicating the minds of my darkies.' Despite the advances across the county, that plantation remains impenetrable to the Word."

"So why would he invite me?"

"Does seem odd, considering I'm ostracized, if not despised, by many of the planters."

True, thought Eloise, her father was the gadfly of this community. They once lived on their farm in Massachusetts but after her mother died, her father got ordained as a minister to rescue himself from his grief and became involved with the Abolitionists in Concord. Soon after the two of them moved to Alabama to start the Church of All Men. But as shrewd as he was wise, her father knew that openly pursuing abolition would only get him imprisoned, if not lynched, so instead of pursuing his goals outright, he settled instead for simply trying to convert Negroes to Christianity which most slave owners, being Christian themselves, found difficult to oppose and which was the impetus for emancipation.

"I'm just as alienated as you," said Eloise. "I don't know anyone who associates with people invited to these parties."

"The fact is," her father said, "I doubt he invited you at all. He probably does not know who you are. The person who handled the invitations probably scribbled this note down here in the margin."

"But should I attend?"

"You know my thoughts, Eloise. These people are evil. But I won't shelter you. You must answer that question for yourself."

Later that night Eloise was looking into her mirror. Woolen and white, her dress was stained with mud from working in the garden. Look, she thought, I am not even pretty, certainly not glamorous. So why am I even interested in attending that wicked party?

Nearly twenty, she knew she did not want to stay with her father forever. So ever since coming to Alabama, she had attended picnics and even weddings, hoping to meet friends or even suitors but she always felt estranged from these southerners including the girls her own age—usually the daughters of planters and lawyers and merchants who always seemed so obtuse, so frivolous, so fawning toward men and who treated her, not necessarily impolitely, but as though she was obviously different from them, impoverished in some way. And the men were always smoking and drinking, bragging about how many acres and slaves they owned—all oblivious to the cruelty and sinfulness upon which their lives were founded. And worse, they entirely ignored her while lavishing their attentions upon the other girls. Upon coming home lonelier than ever, she would hide away in her bedroom weeping, angry at her father for dragging her into this demented and benighted land.

She tried to evade her loneliness by tending to her chores and reading the Bible, Shakespeare, St. Augustine and any novel she could find that was not banished by her father. She also toiled away for the church, for what her father called their flock: all those Negroes, mulattoes and mendicants—the meekest, most downtrodden people of the earth—and also the dirtiest and smelliest; she could not even converse with them about anything important to her. She tried to love them. Indeed, as she fed and listened to them and tended to their sicknesses, she sometimes felt in her heart something like the love of Christ, the sort her father preached about. But it vanished all too fast, leaving her saddened and even angry sometimes.

Why, she beseeched to God, must I abandon all my hopes and dreams to serve Your wishes?

So why was she still interested in attending this party? Those words, "Please Come," beckoned to her and offered her the hope, however irrational, that at this party, even amidst all its fake, nefarious glamour, she would meet someone—not yet calloused by the demands of slavery—who would find her beautiful and who would carry her away from the drudgery of her life. But when she thought of that strange, unsociable boy Jonah, she knew she was grasping only for disappointment.

Looking into the mirror again, she felt maybe she was not unattractive after all. Perhaps she was even pretty, maybe beautiful. Someone once said she looked like the women in the paintings of Botticelli, voluptuous with tousled wheat-colored hair. Looking at herself flirtatiously and even seductively, she felt the desire to rebel and defy the wishes of her father.

One week later she was riding in the wagon with her father silent at her side. When first seeing the mansion of Whiteoak in the glow of lanterns, she thought it resembled some kind of temple, some great, geometric, vaulting and white monolith that was beholden to darker, more secular powers.

Once arriving at the verandah, she turned and said to her father, "But I can't father. I'm afraid of these people."

"Go in pride, Eloise. Shine your light into the darkness of their lives."

The rooms inside were almost devoid of any furniture while the candlelight cast shadows on the bare, white walls. People were scattered about in cliques, forming circles with their backs turned toward her. They seemed hesitant and even dragooned amidst this display of wealth. Unanimated and joyless, their voices echoed from the walls, creating a drone broken only by the clinking of china.

Around one of the tables some slaves were pouring wine, others carving into the sides of some charred but bloody cow that covered half the table. Although seeming clumsy, as though more accustomed to handling only hoes and plows, the slaves also seemed curiously proud of this mansion built upon the suffering heaped upon their backs. Already Eloise felt alone and dejected so when at last recognizing someone, she felt relieved and walked in that direction. The girl was standing in a circle with other girls, their backs facing toward the crowd.

Eloise tapped her on the shoulder. "Hey, Mary."

"Can you believe," the girl said, turning only slightly, without addressing Eloise by name, "that Whiteoak hired Mrs. Withersby all the way from Mobile to arrange this party?"

"How glamorous," offered Eloise.

"But can you believe that the furniture never arrived, that the orchestra is lost out there in the wilderness still trying to find this place."

"How unfortunate," said Eloise, feigning startlement.

"And I happen to know," continued the girl, never turning all the way around to face Eloise as though afraid of losing her position amongst the other girls, "that half the women in here are wearing dresses beyond their means—purchased on credit and not paid for until after harvest. All to stand in this empty, musicless barn and eat cow?"

"How odd," said Eloise.

"But not my dress. Pappy said mine's paid for," said the girl, posing for Eloise in her bright, silken gown. "And I bet yours is too."

Suddenly becoming aware of her simple linen dress with the collar made from lace she wove herself, Eloise felt ashamed, even like a pauper. Since the girl never bothered to introduce the others to her, Eloise wandered off into the room by herself. She hated the south, these gaudy, fake people and wished God would bring his hellfire and fury down upon them now. And she was furious at herself for letting her silly imagination, fueled by her own vanity, to compel her to wish for things that would never come to pass.

Jonah came toward her quickly like some predator seeking his prey. She wanted to flee but realized that she was trapped in a corner. He looked handsome, she realized, with brooding eyes and hulking chest. His tie was ruffled and his hair was disheveled, taunting the formality around him. Breathing quick, he stared at her amazed but frightened.

"Dance with me," he said, wobbling.

He was drunk, she realized with distaste.

"Pardon me?" she said.

Grabbing her hand, he tugged on her.

"But there isn't any music," she said testily.

"Now there is."

As he pulled her into another room and motioned with his hand, music began to course through the air like cool, electric wind from a thunderhead, coming from a group of slaves beating on drums, strumming fiddles and blowing on their little fifes made from bamboo.

"The orchestra has arrived," said Jonah.

He began to dance and move without any discernable pattern, gyrating around and hopping almost rabbitlike—what she heard other whites describe as "nigger dancing" as though naming some disease. She looked around the room at the other people, some looking at them aghast, others snide, others just surprised. She was tempted to run away to hide in the bushes or even out in the fields until her father returned. But she stayed for some reason, perhaps only because she was paralyzed with embarrassment until she became so anxious that she started to move to the music herself, if only to release her energy.

She suddenly did not care about any of these people staring at her and wanted to defy them, spite them and rebel against them all. She started trying to mimic the motions of Jonah, awkwardly at first until her body began to flow effortlessly into the rhythm. Then some other couples—their smell pungent with the sweet wildness of bourbon—joined into the dancing. Many others were now coming into the room, moving away from their cliques, eagerly watching the dancing and gradually she saw their stiff and subdued demeanors giving way to aloof and friendly amusement and even smiles. Even Mary was pointing at her while turning quickly to chat with her friends. Enraptured into the music, Eloise felt all of this was for her—the mansion, the party, the music—so that she could come to know this strange, wild boy. And for once she saw beyond her attempts at humility and meekness and felt, without any hint of guilt, utterly beautiful.

His clothes now dark with sweat, Jonah never paused from dancing and continued on after she began to tire. Was he afraid, she wondered, that he would not know what to say to her if the motion ended? One of the Negroes soon jumped into the middle of the dancers, lilting and gyrating about, making the whites look tame by comparison. His mouth was agape with smiles and jutting with brown, knobby teeth.

The dancing stopped.

Jonah leaned toward Eloise, whispering, "One moment, my lady," before grabbing the Negro by his wrist and followed by Eloise, leading him gently toward the verandah and shooing him away into the fields, saying, "Not for you, Jake. Not for you," as though the Negro was some cute but lost puppy that needed help finding its way.

While outside Eloise saw her father already waiting on her much sooner than she expected, probably never having left. "I must leave," she said. "My father is here."

But Jonah pulled her back toward the house where she saw the man who she knew was Whiteoak standing in their way, looking menacing in his black suit with his scars visible beneath his top hat. Jonah swerved away from him, pulling Eloise, muttering, "The bastard, always trying to rule my life."

Although excited by his air of rebellion against his father, she slipped from his clutches and scurried toward the door until Jonah ran and caught her by the arm, imploring, "Can I come visit you, Eloise? Can I?"

She did not know what to think, stood there, feeling vague. "Yes, I suppose," she said while rushing away.

Days later, Eloise spotted him on horseback in the woods surrounding their fields. Only after she waved to him, he came toward her, dismounted, took her hand in his and kissed her knuckles as though he was practicing something he read about in a book. He smelled like gunpowder, leather and bark.

She tried to engage him in conversation but he was uncommunicative and at last flustered, took the hoe from her hand, saying, "Yawl women aint got to do the work of men."

As she watched amused then disappointed, he hoed one row after another until all of the garden was complete. He returned the hoe to her, nodded his head, mounted his horse and rode away into the woods.

He continued to visit, driven by an intense, virile and almost scary need for something she could see in the piercing cast of his eyes, the urgent slant of his body. Removed from the earshot of her father, they sat on stools made from logs while Jonah hunched tight into himself like the bud of a tree incipient with energy waiting to unravel its leaves. After sitting in silence at first, he gradually began to talk, his formal, stentorian voice, which sounded like he was reciting phrases from a book, slowly fading into staccato, backwoods jargon. As though he wanted to impress her, he talked incessantly about how his father, Whiteoak, wanted to become the largest landowner in Alabama before expanding into Florida and Texas so that he could bequeth his empire to his son upon his death. How she hated that pompous chatter. And how could he believe that she was impressed. But as she just listened to him, apathetic and unresponsive, that part of his personality beholden to his father began to feel increasingly staged and forced until he confessed, in an instance of liberation one day as though trying to exorcise his father from his mind, the words coming before he had the opportunity to censor them.

"I'm miserable out yonder with all those darkies, and my father hounds me all the time about my duties, keeping the ledgers and keeping Negroes in check. My only escape from the loneliness and drudgery is exploring and hunting in the forest and coming to visit you, Eloise."

"I feel that way too," said Eloise happily. "Nobody is out here but my father. Sometimes I don't see another white person for days. I dream all the time about traveling away from here over to Europe, maybe to visit all the churches and castles and dream too about dancing in fancy balls. Don't you think about those sorts of things?"

Jonah smiled awkwardly. "I reckon."

"What do you really want?" she continued.

"Nobody ever asked me that before."

"But I'm asking you now."

"To get the hell out of here," said Jonah, smiling broadly.

She laughed.

"And would you come with me?"

"Indeed I would," she said.

"Would you really?"

"Yes, I would."

After that day their relationship changed; they became free with each other, Jonah not any longer hunched into himself but open now like the leaves of the tree emerging bright green from their winter corpuscles. She began to teach him about the Bible, about all the books she read, about how God wanted man to live on the earth. And he took her on rides through the forests where they sucked nectar from honeysuckle and he plucked young purple irises to put into her hair; he even showed her the places where he liked to escape: the caves buried into the sides of hills already stocked with candles, firewood, blankets and smoked venison. "For emergencies," he said.

One day they were on horseback riding through the forest. Normally sodden and white during the summer, the sky was vivid and blue and the thickets were full of honeysuckle and the woods were flickering green and silver as the wind stirred the leaves of the trees. Arriving at a creek Jonah dismounted to gather water while Eloise sat under a canopy of vines clustered with muscadines, some of which had fallen to the ground.

Startled she saw Jonah moments later walking toward her, his clothes bundled in his hand, naked except for his underwear that sloshed about his glistening, wet legs. He sat next to her and she leaned forward, wrapped her arms around her knees, folding into herself.

"I was ruminating," he said nonchalantly, "about what you said about the Bible. About how Adam and Eve before eating the fruit and catching some scorn and knashing their teeth, lived free in the garden not even worried about their privates. Sometimes when wandering about, I feel that way too, like Adam. All that stuff back in what we call civilization just seems like some trouble caused by all of us wanting to eat more and more fruit until we all get sick with ourselves."

"This forest is as lovely as Eden. And somewhere in all of us, we're still the children of God as unsullied as we were before the fall."

"I was hoping you felt that way. Out here we don't need to pluck that fruit."

Unlocking her arms from around her knees, Eloise leaned back. She felt the spirit of Christ was inside them and the forest was alive with his majesty. Jonah was blossoming as the fulfillment of her dreams—gentle, thoughtful and ripening with the Spirit. Perhaps Jesus was rewarding her for her years of loyalty to her father, allowing her to find fulfillment while remaining in his service. She felt at ease with Jonah even now as the wind ruffled her dress and stirred the sweet, tart scents of muscadines.

"Yes," she said. "We can live this way. God intended us to live this way."

So when Jonah twisted his face toward her and touched her arm awkwardly, then leaned forward and kissed her cheek, she felt shameless. A current of warm pleasure flowed along her spine. Eve must have felt this way around Adam, she thought, when Jonah kissed her neck and her lips then leaned her back, pressing her against the muscadines spread about on the ground and kissed the bare, delicate spot above her breasts before pulling her dress down and kissing her small, pinkish and tumescent nipple. She was still thinking of Eve too when something hard and protrusive touched her through her clothes on that spot that seemed to engorge and peel open to him like fruit as he heaved gently back and forth, each time whispering to her, "I love you, Eloise," as the muscadines under her dress burst their tight, purplish testicular skins, emitting their slippery and viscous meats.

Once the pleasure faded, Eloise was gradually overcome with shame and flustered, she rose to her feet, mounted her horse and fled through the forest while Jonah went in pursuit. Arriving back at her house, she quickly dismounted and rushed into the house weeping while momentarily stunned to see her father inside. She passed him quickly, heading to her room.

"What's wrong," he asked.

"Nothing Daddy," she said as nonchalantly as possible, realizing that he could now see the stigmata of the splattered, purplish stains.

Later her father spoke to her in her study, his voice not gentle as usual but stern, even threatening. "I know not this boy. But I know the lives of these men. Even those who are graced with kindness and refinement on the surface are hard and callous underneath. But this man, Whiteoak, and his son, even lack refinement. That place is dark and they are tyrants, worshiping not the Lord but the golden calf, squandering the lives of men in the process. They are men accustomed to taking and violently, if necessary, while damning the consequences."

When her father looked at her piercingly, she acted as never before: She looked away ashamed. Outside in the darkness the vibrating, electric chorus of the crickets chided her for her sins. She never attempted to conceal her outings with Jonah from her father but fearing his concern, never volunteered any information either. She remained silent.

"That boy may want you, Eloise, and he may think he loves you. But I know this. He will drag you onto that plantation, intertwine you into his dark, sinful life and make you powerless to resist. You will become his vassal like one of his slaves. Flee, Eloise, flee from him now.

"You cannot serve the Lord by walking into the den of hell."

"Yes, Father," she said, looking into her lap.

Later that night Eloise was lying in bed upon her back. A draft was coming from under her window and her candle, dimly wavering, flickered light and shadow across the room. Her mind was cleaved with schism, her body tense, her breathing short and erratic. Why am I, she thought while addressing both God and herself, defying my saintly and infallible father to court this man who opposes all of our values? How ungrateful. Am I only trying to defy my father? And is my father not right that Jonah was exploitive, waiting all the while for his opportunity to seduce me, to almost deflower me, to fulfill that dark, urgent need in himself? Maybe he thinks of me as his chattel, there for his pleasure.

But I succumbed to his seduction, she thought, writhing around on her bed, pleasure and shame churning inside her. How could I believe that it was with the blessing of God? Turning onto her stomach she buried her face in her pillow to muffle her scream while kicking her feet into the bed, feeling all the tension draining from her body. She felt relaxed afterward, her breathing becoming slower and deeper. Maybe Jonah was not wicked, she thought, maybe their actions were not shameful. Maybe underneath his façade, he was full of gentleness and light as she always suspected, yearning to replace his father with guidance from Christ. Maybe they both yearned to be free of their fathers to seek life and meaning—and service to God—on their own terms.

At once the candle ceased to flicker and the chatter of the crickets now became a chorus of angels, heralding something divine and motherly inside herself. The schism dissolved away, her mind becoming whole as she acknowledged what she knew but never really admitted from the beginning. She reached over to the table beside her bed, gathered her pad and pencil and sketched this note to her father.

"Father,

"In my prayers I was visited by God who led me to my path. As you, Father, were called south to serve the Negroes, I am called to love Jonah, to save his soul by bringinig Christ into his life. If he asks me to marry him, I must and I must then go and serve on his plantation and preach the gospels to the slaves to prepare them for that impending, glorious day. Together we will turn those lost African Negroes into the legions of the Lord.

"I am meant like you to walk into the den of sin to shine the light of Christ. The wicked more than the righteous need our love."

"Eloise"

She left this note in her father's study and upon waking in the morning, found this note slipped under the door.

"Eloise,

"Since your mother died, you became all the light and joy in my life. The Lord has indeed revealed your purpose and you are blessed for that. But like mine, your life too will become woeful as you travel even deeper into the territory of the sinful. My love for you conflicts with His divine will. But as always, I deliver you into His hands and pray for His guidance. Thy will be done.

"Your Father."

Soon Jonah apologized for seducing her in the muscadines, bending chivalrously on one knee, saying he never meant to "besmirch the virtue of his lady." His manner was contrived but his earnestness was touching. But now knowing the power she exerted over him, she would at times brush her breasts seemingly inadvertently across his back while gently breathing on his neck, delighted when he almost shivered with desire, fumbled with his words and stormed off into the woods. The need in him, she knew, belonged to her and she was not surprised when Jonah asked for her hand.

For months after the wedding—a small, quick ordeal designed to avoid the awkwardness of intermingling their families—they traveled to New Orleans where they slept and dined in plush, luxurious hotels. They traveled afterward along the coast not far from Mobile and stayed in a small inn where Jonah spent his days fishing and she reading. After eating roasted fish on the beach in the evenings, they moseyed off into the white, sensuous dunes glowing in moonlight, blankets and wine in hand, their clothes molting away from their bodies like remnants of the past. Away from the plantation Jonah seemed renewed and spontaneous while embracing the world around him with a sweet and childlike curiosity.

But soon their travels were interrupted by a message received from Whiteoak.

"Must we return?" implored Eloise, dreading this day as she watched some militant, almost hypnotic energy descend upon her husband as he quickly prepared for their trip.

"Profits are dwindling away back home," he said. "Lots of folks overfarmed their lands and is suckling on some dried-up, dusty teat like starving piglets. Now they're abandoning their lands, heading west. But not us. We've protected our fields and stashed some heap of cash and we gonna buy their land for cheap. Raise some cows to shit all over the place until the cotton is eager to grow again."

"But surely many of those people are near starving," said Eloise. "Must you exploit their desperation and underbid them."

"The reason for their starving aint us but their own greed. And if we was in the mind to offer charity, then we'd sooner or later become as poor and destitute as them, unable to help even ourselves."

"But God's law of love for your neighbor," said Eloise, "is greater than profit."

"I aint never seen God pluck any cotton from the ground and put clothes on folk's back. So from here on, you let me tend to business and you just carry on with your womaning."

"My what?"

"Your womaning."

Eloise felt tears welling but sealed them away. Jonah was ordinarily sensitive to her teachings about Christ but now she felt she was losing him to some force which she neither understood or controlled.

She composed herself. "But why must we return now?"

"Cause Father wants to ride out to Texas before the others, find him some deals.

"Truth is," continued Jonah, "I got the chance to prove my mettle. Father said that if I can manage the plantation by myself during these crucial months he might throw me some bone of my own, another plantation, maybe even out west. This is our chance to get the hell away forever."

After returning to Whiteoak they moved into a bedroom upstairs and while his father was away, Jonah worked unrelentingly from dawn to dusk eager not only to maintain but also improve the performance of the plantation. Eloise was left alone after breakfast in the mansion with one slave named Nomaw, an older, solitary woman who was docile and perfunctory unless she was ranting about the ignorance of other slaves. At first timid and even avoidant around Nomaw for fear that God might judge her for using the services of a slave, Eloise tried to maintain the house herself but Nomaw, evidently uncomfortable with this, began to finish most of the chores before Eloise could even start. Before long she was without any occupations and surprised to find that she rather enjoyed the leisure after tending to her father and his congregation for all those years.

She even learned to supervise Nomaw in the making of lavish, exotic meals—recipes and spices for which she gathered in New Orleans—so that in the evenings she and Jonah dined languidly together amidst candlelight, the sipping of wine dissolving their minds into the mesmerizing shrill of crickets, the hoots of owls, the occasional howl of coyotes and the dissolution into the warm, moist bedroom.

During the days she read sometimes and other times wandered into town to shop for their dinners. She realized with difficulty that she enjoyed her freedom from men: from her father, from Whiteoak—from all those fathers, even God the Father. Back in Concord when her mother was alive, they attended church, prayed and turned to God at times for guidance and consolation but otherwise went on about their business without thinking about Him all the time. But once her mother died, she adopted the God of her father—all consuming, all demanding, ever present—only to try to please him. But removed from all that now, she realized that she liked the God of her mother more—the more maternal, relaxed and forgiving God.

Whiteoak soon returned and somehow secretly, hardly without detection, established his dominance over the household. Although bounding with energy, he rarely if ever spoke—expressed nothing but bare and studied efficiency in the way he ate, walked and rode his horse—all of which seemed to give him pleasure but which made it difficult for her to feel even slightly comfortable around him. Every time she passed him in the hallway, which she tried to avoid, she could hardly look at him without cringing, the mutilation of his face disturbing to behold. As though describing the habits of a monarch, Jonah explained that his father would not tolerate any of that fancy European cooking in his house so their evenings—the only time she really spent any time with Jonah—changed for the worst. When she might slip her arm around Jonah's waist or touch his hand, he suddenly began to stiffen, to resist almost, as though not wanting his father to see that he was desirous of affection. In the evenings they retired to bed early and feigned sleep until hearing the creaks in the boards as Whiteoak ascended the steps into his own bedroom. And even then their fear of him hearing was so great that their lovemaking was reduced to one final, efficient, almost breathless expenditure of energy before both of them fell to sleep.

Sometimes while riding through the fields and watching the activities of the slaves, she thought about her divine mission—not her father's but hers. She realized most of all that she must keep her purpose secret from Whiteoak for she believed he was beyond conversion. She tried talking to Jonah about the slaves, usually through hints, saying things like they were in her prayers, that maybe she could tend to their souls someday—but he responded as he did at the beach with this sort of amused but sweet condescension. If she persisted he quickly turned surly and even shockingly wrathful and would scorn and humiliate her without any shame, usually concluding with some remark about her womaning.

When confiding in her father about her predicament, he only admonished her by saying that he predicted that sort of outcome. Then he would try to instruct her like she was some foot soldier of the Lord about the ways to combat evil at Whiteoak and begin to minister to the slaves. She loved her father and still respected him but he never really tried to understand her feelings—did he ever, she wondered? Besides, she perceived in him some kind of secret ambition to sap power from Whiteoak for stealing his daughter from him, causing her to feel lost and disoriented in the frontline of some kind of spiritual and psychological battle between patriarchs.

So since her relationship with Jonah already seemed fragile, she decided that for the moment she should not pursue the matter directly but concentrate only on converting Jonah to Christianity. He did at least attend church once per week even against the will of his father and tolerated her teachings about the Bible, although with an amused but aloofish satisfaction. Yes, she thought, save the soul of her husband then naturally the slaves would follow. Thus her hope was that once Jonah proved his mettle and inherited his own lands, she could work exclusively through him.

Although Jonah successfully proved his competence, his father only spoke of rewarding him land in the future. When Eloise questioned him about this, he responded as usual by insulting her for meddling in the affairs of men. Before long Eloise began to picture Jonah as a mule hitched to his father's wagon and as he plodded along, his father dangled before him a carrot tied onto a stick.

Regardless of how hard Jonah pulled, driven onward by unquestioning loyalty or utter fear or perhaps both, the carrot stayed the same distance, just removed from reach as the bridle cut into his flesh then deeper into the bone.

One evening Eloise was at dinner with the overseer, Tote, and his wife, Molly. During that day they had just slaughtered numerous heads of cattle, Eloise hearing their distressed, panicked calls from the mansion. Later in the evening as the cold and damp drafted through the windows, the predators were outside excited by the scent of blood, the coyotes with their wild, piercing shrills and the wolves with their somber, dreary howls, both wanting to reclaim the plantation back into the wilderness. Although some of the men who worked for Tote fired their rifles to drive the predators back into the woods, Eloise felt that she was surrounded by something dark insinuating itself into her soul—something from which she needed to protect herself.

As the men talked Eloise felt as usual—as though she was but some adornment, some example of feminine beauty and virtue for display and she retreated as usual into sadness. She was losing Jonah to the dominance of his father, her influence upon him fading away into something that was merely formal.

As the others ate in silence, Eloise looked at her plate—the bloody, almost raw slab of beef with potatoes and greens—food which she did not even like but which she was served anyway. I am not only losing Jonah, she thought, but myself. I am not only losing the God of my father but my God as well. As my father predicted I am becoming lost into the darkness of this plantation. Deep in her stomach she felt something rupture—something dark, bilious but calm.

She listened as the men started to talk about the management of slaves. To avoid feeling ignorant and humiliated when she spoke to Jonah about business, she had started to study books, newspapers and anything she could find on the subject of commerce on plantations. Motivated by her own panic, by her desire to reclaim herself, Eloise found herself foregoing all her strategies and preparations and speaking out loud, her voice sounding even distant and weak to her.

"I read in the paper the other day that increasingly many slave owners are allowing their slaves to worship. Many claimed that productivity was increasing. And they all spoke about the joy in their hearts as they rode along their fields, hearing their slaves singing hymnals as they plucked King Cotton from its stalks."

The faces around the table stared at her in disbelief which somehow motivated Eloise onward, her voice now becoming stronger.

"They all believed they had rescued the Negro from darkest Africa and their animal gods and saved their souls by bringing them to Christ."

Whiteoak was now scowling at his son scornfully. Tote and Molly had stopped eating while looking into their laps.

"Imagine," concluded Eloise, her voice quaking. "We could have that here."

All was silent. Then astonishingly close to the mansion, she heard the crack of a rifle, then a yip. Some wounded, small-sounding animal whimpered. Men shouted, sounding childish in their excitement to exert pain.

"As I have explained to you, Eloise, countless times," said Jonah, "the balance on our plantation between master and slave is delicate. We don't want that disturbed."

"But their souls—what about their souls?" Eloise heard her voice carry weakly through the room.

"I have explained this to you before. We don't want our slaves thinking they got souls. They will get uppity and feel entitled to our rights and leisure and that will make them—and about this, I am certain—indolent and intractable. Productivity will go down and the less we shall have to spend on clothes, blankets, shoes and food for our charges, until all our slaves will be reduced to the same condition as many other slaves around here, wearing tattered threads, shivering in their cabins, having their children ripped from their arms in the middle of the night. And Tote will be forced to uncoil his whip. Do you, Eloise, want to be responsible for that calamity?"

"But...," stammered Eloise.

"Do you?" blurted Jonah.

"No, of course not."

"I thought not," said Jonah, sighing with relief. "Tell her, Tote."

Tote looked momentarily confused. "Yessir," he said, seeming to understand. "Trick is dispassion. Some folks starves and beats their darkies sometimes out of malice, thinking that's the way to manage. But not us. We got our covenant with them. Rewards and punishments are given strictly according to rules that everybody understands. Transgressions aint tolerated. We set the line, they cross that line by one toenail, they is punished so they aint got the chance to get their foot across. Results are that our darkies are the most productive in the land. And all that profit, yessum, profit allows us to feed and clothe them well, prevents us from needing to sell them off. I aint whipped any darkies around here in nearly one year."

Eloise was faint, even dizzy. "Their souls—what about their souls?"

Again there was silence, not even any wailings from the predators, until Whiteoak spoke. "We could always shut down that little ramshackle of his."

All three men rose quickly and walked toward the den, leaving Eloise behind stunned, lost to the meaning of Whiteoak's words.

"I aint educated like you," said Molly, who was sitting across the table from Eloise. "But I know this. Before Tote was hired, we was digging for roots, eating whatever he could shoot out in the woods. But now we got our own house, good food, respect in the community and schooling for our children. And we is thankful to Whiteoak and his son for that. As thankful as we can be."

As Eloise listened dully to Molly, feeling herself fading, she slowly came to realize, more stunned than angered, that the "little ramshackle," referred to by Whiteoak was her father's church.

"And Tote does good work, yes mam, he does," Molly continued. "He feels right by his work. And many of them darkies, they seem thankful to..."

Without even excusing herself Eloise walked from the room then up the stairs and into her bedroom, shutting the door behind her. She lay upon her bed not moving, hearing Jonah down below in the den as he sipped his bourbon and smoked his cigars, his voice this disconcerting mixture of vaulted diction and backwoods slang that made him sound intoxicated by his own power. He seemed to mock her as though knowing she was listening, saying I will love you but only if you obey me. But she also sensed that he was hurting—that he himself knew he was falling even deeper into darkness.

The threat from Whiteoak was real, she knew. Ever since she left her father had become more outspoken about emancipation and many planters were eager to see him extradited from the state or even thrown in jail. Paradoxically, she suspected that Whiteoak was protecting her father, not from any sense of loyalty but rather to keep the comity in his son's marriage; he probably also felt that her father was so pathetic that he ultimately posed little or no threat to slavery throughout the region. But if Whiteoak ever changed his mind, she knew he could persuade the sheriff to shut down the Church of All Men or resort to other more secretive means of enacting his will, probably with one letter and maybe some extra cash on the side.

Outside in the darkness she heard the howls and yips of the predators but when not hearing the crack of the rifle, she imagined the beasts moving closer to the plantation, even sniffing around the windows. Something slow and menacing was insinuating itself into her soul, perhaps even the devil, entering now without resistance. She clasped her hands together to pray, raising her head from the bed but for once she sensed that God was not with her, even suspected that this God who told her to marry Jonah was nothing more than some symbol for her naïve hopes and childish vanities. She imagined one of those predators from outside somehow slipping into the foyer, passing the men in the den unheeded and loping up the steps toward her bedroom.

She wanted to leave Whiteoak. Maybe she could return to her father, older, wiser, more empowered to shape her own life in his world. Maybe she could move into town, any town, become a seamstress and fade away into spinsterhood, rejected by other men for fleeing from her first husband. Best of all, maybe she could return to Concord. But she suspected that all these options, while beckoning to her, were merely hopes not possibilities because of her blood, her blood that would not flow.

CHAPTER TWO

Many years later, Eloise, having come from Whiteoak, was riding in her carriage toward her father's church which she now saw in the distance: the barn-shaped, unpainted ramshackle with the cross above the door. In front of the church was the garden full of orange and yellow gourds amidst brown and withering stalks. After her carriage stopped, her father walked out to greet her. The young slave, who was steering the carriage, unloaded the carcass of beef—which was not even butchered, just disemboweled, hacked into quarters and wrapped in burlap—and delivered it inside the church.

"Thank you for the contribution," said her father begrudgingly but with the humility to know that his congregation desperately needed the food.

They strolled toward the cabin where they once lived and while Eloise sat on the porch, her father retrieved some food from the kitchen—a stew of beef, corn and squashes which they ate eagerly as though trying to avoid the unease between them.

Wiping food from his beard, her father said, "I don't see you much anymore, Eloise."

"I'm sorry, Father. The children and all keep me busy." Her voice sounded distant like she was hearing herself speak from afar.

Truth was that she felt increasingly distant from her father, not any longer his adoring, unquestioning daughter. But Eloise was specifically invited to visit this time.

"How are the children?" he said sadly. "I was hoping to see them today."

"They're fine. Visiting with our neighbors again."

After her last visit with her children, James, her oldest, returned to Whiteoak and started telling everyone, even the slaves, that slavery was "abominating" to the Lord. Jonah exploded in anger, chiding Eloise about exposing their children to her father. So now she was hesitant about bringing them back.

Her father nodded his head knowingly. "I understand. How are the slaves?" he asked. "What are you doing about the slaves?"

"The what?" asked Eloise.

"The slaves?"

"What do you want to know about them?"

"You told me all those years ago that you intended to save their souls."

Eloise was startled. Soon after she was married, her father quizzed her about her mission at Whiteoak but she felt his questions were intrusive like he was trying to control her from afar. She tried to answer him at first as truthfully and patiently as possible until one day both of them exploded into fits. Wanting to punish her father afterward, she did not visit him for months. And he never asked again.

Eloise thought about her answer. She had concluded that the mission to save the slaves, which she had thought was revealed by God, was in fact the illusion she used to rationalize falling in love with the likes of Jonah. What other stupid and ruinous decisions were made by people who think they are talking to God?

Instead she just parried. "The slaves are just fine," hoping that her father would stop his questioning.

"What do you mean 'fine'? "

"I know myself now that the balance at Whiteoak is precarious and delicate. Jonah believes that introducing the slaves to Christ too quickly could upset the balance and result in suffering for all involved. Whiteoak would lose much of his fortune and the slaves would find themselves jobless and drunk. But Jonah occasionally comes with me to one of the churches in town; he dresses well, prays and takes communion—says he likes the taste of bread and wine. I foresee that he himself someday when at last converted will turn the spirit of Christ upon the darkies."

"But I asked about the slaves," her father said, "not your husband. Are you offering them guidance?"

Eloise studied her father. Ever since she left he had stopped taking care of himself: his clothes were unraveling into shreds and his beard, left ungroomed, was now an unruly, nappy nest of gray. He looked feral and maniacal like John the Baptist. Maybe he was even eating honey and wild locusts. As the years passed he seemed to become more openly radical in his beliefs about abolition so that now even the most liberal slave masters were not allowing their slaves to attend his church and as such his congregation was shrinking, frequented now mostly by freed blacks, mulattoes, derelicts and lunatics.

Maybe he at last needed some truth, some dose of reality to clear his thinking. She proceeded sheepishly, watching his face for his reaction.

"Do these Negroes suffer as much as you think? Our slaves are not sold but provided with clothes, rest and all the food they can eat."

Her thoughts feeling alien, she continued to talk. "I believe like you in the abolition of slavery. Negroes cannot live forever in bondage. But Jonah believes that by introducing the slaves to Christianity they'll think they're equal with their masters—and the harmony on Whiteoak would collapse, resulting in suffering for all involved, most of all the blacks."

"But that's our goal. To make the blacks acknowledge the truth: that they're equal, that all men are equal. Once believing that they shall seek equality and even emancipation eventually. Freedom is our mission and the desire of God. Besides, the slaves already suffer as much as any people who ever existed on this earth."

His disappointment was obvious but she continued to speak,

diverting her eyes, just exchanging information as efficiently and impersonally as possible like her husband.

"Compare that to the hoards of immigrants in the cities up north. All crowded together in filthy apartments crawling with rats—sometimes whole families stuffed into small rooms without windows. Everyone in the family, including the children, working from dawn to dusk in factories. And their jobs and wages snatched away from them at any moment because their bosses, unlike slave masters, aren't responsible to their employees beyond their work.

"But our slaves are our responsibility at Whiteoak from birth to death and are thus sheltered from many of the cruelties of life. Slavery too keeps them honest and away from trouble. Compare that to all the freed black and mulattoes in town, many of them drunk most of the time while getting into brawls and loitering about the streets. Whereas our slaves—you should see them, especially on Sundays—their minds are so untroubled and so childlike, free of responsibility, and so quick to joy and humor. I sometimes wish I could live as them.

"Is it not wondrous too that through this relationship we have tamed the wilderness and civilized the world with Christianity? Think of Thomas Jefferson, George Washington. Were they men of sin? Is my own husband a man of sin?" Suddenly Eloise became angry. "And won't teaching them the Word only simply result in more futile, meaningless and painful struggles like the one you've forced me to endure throughout most of my life in this hated and uncivilized backwoods?"

While regurgitating the words she had heard from Jonah, she was convinced of the strength of her reasoning and elated by her anger, believed she was crushing her father, perhaps showing him the absurdity of his life: that all of this—coming to the south and snatching her away from her life in Massachusetts—was just to help him escape from his own grief at losing his wife. But when looking at him contritely and even with compassion, she saw that his face was blank, not disappointed, just blank, except for the tension which she had never seen in him before, witnessed by the quick, tight thumping of his fingers on the table.

He spoke calmly. "I asked you that question in the beginning for this reason. I have been told that whole families are vanishing from Whiteoak in the middle of the night. Children are being sold from their parents. Your slaves are horrified that they're next at any moment. I was hoping to alleviate their suffering by imploring you to ask your husband to stop his actions, assuming that you could sway him after all these years."

"We never sell our slaves at Whiteoak," Eloise said, shocked. "Our profits are strong. For that reason we can keep the families intact."

"This is the truth," he said calmly.

"But are you sure? Have you examined and verified your sources? Negroes are prone to lies of this sort to win the pity of the whites."

"Eloise," her father said, remaining calm but with an ominous, almost scary tone in his voice. "Like all men except for those who walk the path of righteousness, you see in life what you need to satisfy your own selfish, base needs. You're so estranged from the truth that while this atrocity is happening before your eyes you are blind—although you claim some knowledge of the souls of Negroes. Go forth and witness for yourself."

Eloise felt manipulated by her father, that when at last confronting him she was utterly undermined. "But I know this isn't happening."

She was shocked by some loud, jarring noise and looking upward, saw that her father had slammed his fist into the table. Wrath on his face he stood at his desk, looking like Moses after hurling the stone tablets at those dancing around the golden calf.

"You blasphemer! Have you become so enamored with the ways of sin, so lost in the ways of darkness, that you doubt the veracity of your own father. Your security and pleasure, your rationale and deceit—these are but fleeting and mortal. Profit and loss—these are the motives of the weak and venal, here now, gone tomorrow. But truth—the everlasting and only truth—for which legions have suffered throughout the history of mankind, for which the earth and all of humanity was created, for which your Lord hung upon the cross. This, you child of wickedness, you who have lost her way, is supreme."

Shame, fright and anger collided in her soul but becoming entwined, got choked, leaving her numb. She rocked in her chair, staring at the ground almost catatonically until she jumped from her chair and ran from the porch as he shouted, "Go forth and witness. And never return to my home again unless the Word of God, not the chatter of infidels, ushers from your tongue. You blasphemer!"

After she climbed into her wagon without looking back toward her father, her driver was awakening from his nap and soon they moved onward. On the way to Whiteoak she stifled her tears—something she had learned after years of practice—while feeling disturbed by something ominous but nameless in her soul. Once passing the gates into Whiteoak, Eloise looked down from the wall of radiant trees to the fields where the slaves were moving along the glebes like locusts, plucking the plumes of cotton from their prickly, brown carapaces, leaving behind them nothing but the skeletons of plants. But unlike locusts, she thought, they were not getting any sustenance.

While the wagon passed along the slave quarters, Eloise noticed that one of the shacks looked abandoned: nothing at all was on the porch. Once Shobuck halted at her behest, she peeked into the window: inside was empty without furniture, without anything at all and the floor was swept clean. At the shack next door was one slave who too ancient to work anymore, was slumped in her chair which was made from branches strapped together with twine and which balanced precariously on the verge of collapsing. Her mouth was toothless, her lips sucking the remnants of sinew from some bone.

"What happened to the slaves in this cabin?" asked Eloise.

"They aint there no more," said the woman.

"But why?"

"Spooks got them."

"Spooks?"

"Sho nuff." The woman removed the bone between her lips, peered at Eloise then spit something from her mouth. "Is you one of them spooks? Come stealing niggers in the night?"

Eloise fled back to the wagon. As they moved toward the mansion, she looked at her driver who not much older than her children, wore this suit that dwarfed him, made him seem frail and delicate. Through the clanking of the hooves, she said, not seeing his face but only his back, "Shobuck?"

"Yessum."

"What happened to the folks back in that cabin?"

Shobuck hesitated. "I don't know, Missus."

"I believe you know the truth. And you should never lie to me. It might make my husband angry."

"I aint know, Missus. All I know is that one night I heard all this racket and scruffing around that shack. In the morning it was empty, them folks gone. Most folks reckon Whiteoak got them to sell them yonder in Montgomery."

"I see," said Eloise.

They continued down the road but before arriving at the mansion, Eloise heard what she thought was whimpering, soft, muffled and spasmodic while noticing that Shobuck's back was hunched, his head quivering.

"What's wrong?" she asked.

"I'm scared."

"Of what?"

"That yawl is coming to get me. Take me away from Maw and Paw."

"Who is 'yawl'?"

"All yawl up yonder in the big house," said Shobuck between his whimpering. "Maw say, unless I behaves myself and keeps my mouth shut, yawl can come snatch me from my shack, take me away some place I aint even heard of before."

Eloise realized that Shobuck perceived that all white folks were his enemy in some ways, including herself. Even when they thanked or praised her or delighted in her company, she was perceived as their enemy—the one who could wreck their life on whim without even caring. As her father suggested she was perhaps blind to the secrets of their souls and to the cruelty inflicted upon them, blind, as she once thought all slave masters, to her own wickedness.

"I'll never let that happen," she said.

"Sho," he said, sounding unconvinced.

"Trust me."

"Yessum," he said, "I reckon I might try."

Later that evening Eloise was lying next to her youngest, Josh, his back against her stomach, her arms wrapped around his small and bony chest that heaved gently and almost imperceptibly with his breaths, the life in him seeming so delicate that at any moment his breaths might stop. She frequently sought solace amidst the cold, damp mansion with her children, usually not admitting that she needed the comfort more than they did. She imagined Shobuck's mother and others like her out in the quarter holding desperately onto their children, the chill of autumn seeping through the chinks in the boards, their ears alert, their bodies, though mostly asleep, jolting to every squeak and shuffle and gust of wind rustling through the dying, withering leaves—all of them terrified that starting with some furtive command from her own husband, something would intrude into their house, violently break the hold of their arms and drag their sons forever away from them into the darkness of life.

How did her life come to this, she wondered? Alienated from her father. Raising her children in her own loveless, miserable marriage. What were the series of compromises, each so small that she could hardly notice them, that made her complicit in the ways of sin?

She turned her head sideways and not wanting to wake her children, buried her face into the pillow to muffle her weeping, dampening the fabric with her tears. Once finished she wanted to pray for the first time in years, not formally as she did at church but from something deep and hurting and damaged inside of her. But what did she want to pray for? For the soul of her husband? For the children separated from their parents? She did not want to pray for any of that. She only wanted to thank God with some kind of blind, almost cruel desperation that her own skin was not black.

Eloise descended the stairs into the den where Jonah was sitting in his large leather chair in front of the fire which was casting large, menacing shadows behind him on the white and bare walls. When facing him she saw that he was leaning into one of the armrests, both arms wrapped around his chest as though he was trying to console himself. He did not even look at her but stared into the flames hypnotically, seeming to want to blight something from his mind.

"Jonah."

He did not respond. She walked closer to him and not having anywhere to sit, looked down upon him while the fire refracted from the reddish, silken weave of her dress.

"I have heard."

"Heard what?"

"That whole families of slaves are disappearing in the middle of the night."

Jonah sat upright, retrieved his glass of bourbon from the floor, sipped. "Where'd you hear that?"

"Here and there," she said. She waited but he did not speak. "Is it true?"

"Don't intrude into matters you don't understand."

"As a mother, I understand this. And I demand to know."

"They're being sold, Goddamnit. We are forced to sell some of our slaves."

"But I thought that never happened."

"That was back then. Conditions have changed."

"And what changed?"

"I don't have to tell you anything. You know our agreement. You manage the children, I run this plantation."

"But I demand to know."

"All right," he said. She detected in him the desire to confess. "We're short of cash for covering our operations. All this investment in cattle—and in lands, seeds and slaves to make this land produce—has drained our tills. Some of our lands are only now beginning to produce and may not become profitable for years in the future.

"We need cash. And the best way to raise cash is to sell slaves. Since the African trade is abolished and since the frontiersmen need hands, slaves are fetching high prices.

"We get them in the night so nobody witnesses them getting dragged away in shackles. Whenever we can, we sell the whole family. Gives them the hope that maybe they will stay together. Besides, we don't want the stragglers torn from their families moping around the plantation or running away or otherwise damaging the morale of the other slaves. By selling the whole family, we purge all the problems. Because all the other slaves are afraid they're next, their behavior is exemplary. All works well.

"You need not worry. We'll hunger for nothing and soon we'll be high on the hog."

"You are destroying these families. And you think I care about living high on the hog."

"Oh," said Jonah, sarcastically. "I forgot you were so saintly there, wearing your dress that cost as much as one of my darkies on the block."

"Which I will happily sell to prevent this from happening."

"We do the best we can." Jonah stared at the fire, quaffing his bourbon.

"And what does happen to them at the market?"

"I don't know. We can't control the outcome."

"Now do you see?" she asked.

"See what?"

"The wickedness of this institution."

"Goddamnit, woman. Life is wicked. All of creation is hell," said Jonah, throwing his glass of whiskey into the fire, succumbing to anguish, tears even coming from his eyes. "I've tried all these years to never sell any slaves from this plantation unless for reasons of discipline. All these years tried to not separate sons from mothers. All these years, gone against the wishes of my father. And now that this is done, you turn against me—who has tried with all my power."

"But you could have sold land or..."

"Enough," he shouted, desperately. "Please, Eloise. I can't endure this."

Confused by the intensity of his grief, Eloise was silent. Jonah slumped into his chair and stared again at the flames, the tension flowing from his body as she seemed to disappear from his awareness.

Eloise walked toward the stairs but before leaving the room, she turned and spoke, her voice whispered but threatening. "Don't you dare, Jonah, sell anymore slaves from here, not one. If you do, I and my children will run from here, flee as far as possible, where you will never find us."

In the morning Eloise awoke still wearing her dress from the night before. Below the window outside, she heard surprised but muffled voices and heard the door from Whiteoak's bedroom opened then slammed shut. Unraveling herself from her son, she walked to the window and looked down. A crucifix jutted upward rising almost as high as the window, made from crooked, knobby limbs covered with bark and strapped together with twine. Some slaves were standing around excited but bewildered while off in the fields whole hoards of them were staring and pointing toward the mansion. Axe in hand, Whiteoak barged from the house shirtless, his skin thin and pale like parchment, exposing the purplish maze of his veins in the glow of the dawn. Violently he hacked at the cross, pieces of wood chipping into the air, as though he was uprooting some great, terrible weed. As the cross began to tilt and fall, she thought of mustard seeds for some reasons—the ones that fell upon dry ground.

For days afterward these crosses appeared across the plantation, infuriating Whiteoak while Jonah seemed more befuddled.

Crudely made from limbs and twigs strapped together with twine, the crosses—some she saw, others she heard about—appeared in front of the slave quarters, in the outhouses and even smeared with mud into the windows of the mansion. At first she felt stigmatized by the crosses like they were heralding the wickedness of the mansion and shielding those on the outside: not too dissimilar from the talismans that she knew the Negroes used to protect themselves from harm. Fearing for her soul and the souls of her children, she began to pray while alone in the kitchen or the barn or even in her own closet, sometimes bringing her children along with her, begging the Lord for forgiveness and asking Him to cleanse the darkness from her heart. Before long she began to see something other in those crosses—a sort of beckoning to something deep and still alive within her.

Several days later she received a note from her father delivered to her in person by one of his minions. At the top was a crude sketch of a cross, resembling the ones appearing across the plantation.

> *"Dear Eloise,*
>
> *"You are the light in my life—the promise of the future. Forgive me for my outburst. Never are you wicked in my eyes, never are you but angelic. Please come to the Church of All Men on Sunday, for our service.*
>
> *"Your Father."*

Eloise quickly hid the note in her dresser. She felt tears seeping from her eyes, the relief of forgiveness. But why does he want me to attend? she wondered, feeling both manipulated and suspicious.

On Sunday she climbed into the wagon, wearing one of her simpler linen gowns and with Shobuck at the reins, they moseyed toward the church. She intentionally arrived late and not wanting to interact with anyone, she skulked inside but was surprised to find that the church was packed, some even sitting on the floor in the aisles, so she was forced to stand and lean against the back wall unseen by just about everyone except for her father who nodded his head in greeting. As usual most were Negroes, some dressed in cheap, black suits, many of the women wearing colorful scarves about their heads, others in the filthy, soiled tatters that they wore in the fields, filling the room with the stench she remembered from serving with her father.

Ahead in the pulpit was one Negro preaching and reading from the Bible while her father looked on approvingly. At last she realized the reason her father wanted her to come: to show her the advancement of his congregation to restore his dignity in her eyes. But she thought the man seemed ridiculous, almost comical: He was dressed in one of the suits that once belonged to her father, which was pressed stiff so that his shoulders looked square and oversized. Although the room was chilly, sweat oozed through his skin as though pushed by the strain of his effort and beaded upon his forehead. The man would speak nervously then pause to read from his Bible, the words broken down into monosyllables so that she could hardly discern his meaning, while others from the congregation would shout "Amen" to goad him along and her father would nod his head in delight.

Because her father was watching her, she stood poised and pretended to listen, even trying to feel inspired. Mostly she felt impatient, however, not only for the preacher but also for her father who although as erudite as any man on earth, chose to while away his time teaching these folks to read. She soon stopped listening, not wanting to strain her ears to decipher the words anymore. Despite her compassion for the slaves, she still was not motivated like her father so she decided to just endure this to the end and afterward say some words of encouragement to her father to avoid any conflict then mosey on her way.

Beneath these thoughts was a well of sorrow and longing, however. Something was still beckoning and calling to her from years of isolation and callousness, calling her away from herself.

"Someone in our congregation today has been tricked by his ways..."

She was roused from her reflections to see her father now at the pulpit, preaching.

"Tricked by the darkness," the congregation shouted.

"Though I know their heart remains one with Christ," her father preached, "they have been led astray from the path by others."

"Like lambs led to slaughter," someone shouted.

"Today, I'd like to invite that person back to Jesus."

Eloise was relieved to see that one of the Negroes in the church stood, saying. "I done sinned, sir. Been drawn so deep into the dark that I caint even see my own ugliness anymore. Deliver me from the dark, Oh Reverend."

Drawn from the flow of his rhythm, her father seemed disconcerted before smiling and saying, "I'm not talking about you, Tyrone. We'll forgive your sins later."

"All right then."

"I proclaim today about someone who for years now was deaf to the voices in their heart—someone who traveled into the den of abomination hoping to enlighten but losing their way."

"Show us this lost sheep, Oh Lord, so we can guide them back to the path of righteousness."

"Someone who veiled her heart from her own father."

"Oh my God," said Eloise, startled, realizing her father was talking about her. Her mind swirled; her body went weak.

"Someone who we've prayed about for months now."

Eloise lowered her head. Although wanting to walk from the room, she was palsied with fright, not in control of her own body. Now many of the Negroes were turning their heads to look around the room.

"Show us the lost lamb, Reverend."

"Here she is," said some older woman sitting in the back pointing at Eloise with joy on her face. "Mrs. Whiteoak."

Everyone turned in their seats and gaped silently at Eloise with both awe and incredulity in their eyes like they were about to witness some miracle. Though feeling struck as though grasped by the hand of God, Eloise looked to the floor.

The woman whispered to Eloise over the silence. "You just trotted away with the wrong shepherd. Come on back to Jesus, Missus, come on back."

The voice sounded kind and melodious. Was it from heaven? Eloise wondered. Eloise raised her head, shyly glancing at the faces; some looked familiar. Maybe they cared about her, she thought.

"Come on back," echoed across the room. "Come on back to Jesus."

Eloise felt she was hovering above her body in mind alone while something inside of her—some kernel of purity and goodness that was normally subdued and muffled—began to pulse as though wanting to find expression. Her identity back at Whiteoak—of feeling powerless and hopeless and even afraid—seemed to fade away from her like something unreal along with all her attempts to rationalize and explain away the wickedness of her life. While looking at her feet to avoid the stares, she felt that kernel, once packed tight, rupture and spread throughout her body and she knew she was crying from watching the tears staining her dress.

She was then being held by someone swaying her back and forth while whispering melodiously in her ear. "Don't worry now, you just coming on home, coming on home. We never forgot how you was back then, Miss Eloise. How you used to take care of us. We loves you, always did."

"I'm sorry," Eloise said, looking at the woman almost unaware that anybody else was in the room, recognizing her faintly as someone she cared for in the past.

"It's all right," said the woman. "You just aint had nobody to cry on, is all. Come on and cry as much as you want."

Then another woman was at her side and both of them were supporting Eloise and moving down the aisle toward the pulpit. The slaves were singing something slow and sorrowful but liberating—the words of which she did not even attempt to understand. While they sat her down at the altar, she looked above at the wooden and splintered crucifix holding the figure of Jesus with his face in anguish as blood oozed from the nails driven into his hands and feet. She suddenly understood his suffering—knew his suffering as her own. Her father was at her side, his face calm and confident.

"Let us pray.

"Thanks to you, oh Lord, for delivering my Eloise back unto You. Please direct her back unto the path of…"

But while he prayed Eloise genuflected on her knees before the crucifix while feeling all the tightness and numbness once in her soul dissolving into even more tears. "Oh, Jesus," she kept saying to herself over and again, "forgive me...forgive me...for I have sinned," as her soul left her body and merged harmoniously with the sorrowful and redemptive singing of the congregation.

When awakening later Eloise was in her father's study collapsed in the chair in front of his desk. She felt exhausted but her soul was not any longer in conflict but harmonized. What happened to me? I was saved, she realized, my soul purged of evil by the great and merciful hand of the Lord. Unfettered by clouds the sun outside slanted toward the forest, the leaves of the trees flickering gold and red like God was strafing and purifying the earth with some great, heatless blaze. In the fields she saw the congregation surrounding yet another fire while roasting slabs of beef upon skewers. She saw not Negroes, not whites or blacks, not fat or thin, smart or dumb, rich or poor but only souls momentarily encased in the flesh of this world. Last of all she noticed her father sitting across from her, the sunlight shining on his frizzled gray hair creating a slight nimbus around his head.

"God told me it was time," he said.

"I understand."

"Forgive me, Eloise, for allowing you to stray while watching you flounder without helping you. Perhaps I was angry that you married that boy even if you did follow God's will and I spurned you. But I suspected that like us all you must suffer in darkness before truly finding God."

"You were always right, Father. What you said all those years before about losing myself to their world. I was too weak and too afraid. I was angry at you too, thought you responsible for the misery in my life."

"Perhaps I was. I knew your life here was difficult. But I could not deny God."

"I suppose we can never deny God," said Eloise.

"I forgive you. And you forgive me. And the Lord, both of us. And now much work is at hand."

"Work?"

"At Whiteoak. We must continue our assault."

"What do you mean?"

"Did you not suspect, Eloise?"

"Suspect what?"

"That this church was behind all the events at Whiteoak?"

"You mean all the crosses?"

"Yes. And much more."

"I suppose I suspected, Father."

He became grave, frowned. "Forgive me for questioning you, Eloise. But since lives—the dear, delicate lives of my disciples—are at risk, I must ask. My revelations to you today can never be told to anyone ever without my permission. Betrayal would ruin us, ruin this church."

Eloise knew what her father needed to ask. While reflecting back on her life at Whiteoak, she felt the enervation, bitterness and selfishness as already some distant and tainted memory.

"I will never return to that life."

Her father smiled. "We have been infiltrating Whiteoak for years now. Our accomplishments are greater than you imagine. Many of the slaves have already been saved and are meeting amongst themselves in the middle of the night. Nothing can stop us before long."

I am resting in the hand of God, she thought. Through all the years she was lost, the Lord had carried on her mission without her awareness. Her father was not this misguided and ineffectual man as she once believed but powerful and cunning and unflinching before Whiteoak.

"The Lord is wondrous," she said.

"But you shall learn shortly and painfully why those who do the work of the Lord are called soldiers."

"I'm ready to serve."

"You must reveal nothing about the events here today. I talked to the boy who drives your wagon. He never came into the church, knows nothing about your conversion. He is also friendly to the movement at Whiteoak. But say nothing to him either. Trust nobody. When returning to Whiteoak, act normally. Do not make any attempts to contact our people.

"But they shall contact you next week on Saturday at midnight. You shall meet one of our men at the well behind the slave quarters at the edge of the forest. Many nights I gazed from there while wondering about you inside that mansion. Do you know the place?"

"Yes."

"I won't come to the meeting. You shall come in my place. Be careful not to be followed and once contacting them, stay subdued. For now only show them your support—and that will strengthen the movement."

"Yes, Father."

"So not to arouse any suspicions, you must return home. Your wagon is waiting out front. Go forth, Eloise, and behold the work done at Whiteoak."

"Yes, Father."

Her legs feeling weak Eloise rose slowly to her feet and embraced her father. She walked away toward the wagon and sat behind Shobuck and though both of them were silent, she sensed that some invisible but powerful strand connected them across the distrust to the heart of Christ.

CHAPTER THREE

On Saturday at midnight the mansion was silent and dark and cold and Jonah and Whiteoak were sleeping after spending the evening besotted on whiskey. Carrying her Bible and festooning her crucifix around her neck, Eloise skulked down the steps into the kitchen and out the door. The sky outside was cloudless and limpid and the color of deep and rarefied purple and the sliver of moon provided only enough light to reveal the shape of things. After checking to see if anybody was following her, Eloise walked to the well and waited until someone appeared hesitantly and even reluctantly from the forest, wearing a bag to mask his face with holes cut for his eyes.

"Come," he said flatly, almost disdainful.

"To where?"

"Come," he said.

They walked behind the slave quarters then along the margins of the fields until they swerved into the forest, their feet rustling through the thick, crackling mulch of leaves. Like the swooping and gentle hand of God, the breeze at times stirred the desiccated leaves in the trees while the limbs groped upward like ancient and chilblained fingers toward the heavens. In the distance, above the wan, clarion cascade of the river, she heard other noises becoming distinguishable as shouts, mumbles, shrieks—some great tumult of noise—coming louder as they moved. Soon through the shafts of the trees came the glow of light.

"Wait," said her guide.

He walked ahead into the forest and moments later returned with a boy she recognized from around the plantation, who seemed excited but unable even to look at her. Together they proceeded into the hollow by the river where she saw what appeared to be a shelter made from quilts tied onto trees, designed to contain the noises within. While light filtered through the sides which looked like the skein of ghosts, the top was open, funneling some great torrent of energy—of fire, smoke, sparks and noise—into the heavens.

Eloise heard that some inside the tent were speaking words of praise—but above that she heard other, stranger noises that resembled birdcalls—squawks, tweets and piercing shrieks. Frightened she grabbed the arm of her guide unknowingly then walked closer and peeked through the crack in the quilts which were dripping with water. In the middle of the tent was the fire, sparks whizzing through the air, flames leaping toward the quilts, smoke roiling the darkness above, casting huge shadows that flickered around like nervous ghosts. The tent was crammed with Negroes, many dangerously close to the flames, some pacing about on their feet and squatting at times, others sitting on the ground rocking back and forth—as though all of them were trying to expurgate their bodies of their anguish. But standing on a stump and rising above them all was the strange Negro they called Shaka who was known to be unusually and even excessively silent and docile around whites. But now his presence was beatific, rage and euphoria mixed on his face while he glanced at the Bible he held in his hands pretending to read.

"Rise up, brethren, from your binds and soar with Jesus."

"Rise up, oh brethren," chorused the congregation.

"Rise up from your persecutors."

"Rise and see the light."

"Rise," shouted Shaka, "with your soul as light as wings and soar, my brethren."

Birdcalls—everything from the calls of mockingbirds, whip-poorwills, to hawks—pierced the room. Shaka then turned around to face the crucifix towering above him and Eloise noticed, gasping, that some bird was strapped onto the crossbeams with this long and thin beak that darted and stabbed about as though trying to impale something while its wings extended the length of the cross-beam and struggled against its bindings.

"Jesus suffered so that we might soar to the heavens."

Shaka then pulled a blade from his belt, turned toward the bird and began to cut the fetters away from its legs then its wings until the bird fell to the ground and stumbled and flopped around.

"Rise, brethren, rise," shouted Shaka. "Break your bonds and soar to the heavens."

Shaka raised his arms like wings and shrieked. Mimicking him the congregation also rose to their feet and called and shrieked like birds and flapped their arms around the fire while building in intensity until the bird, after stumbling around on the ground, out-stretched its own wings at last and with one leap launched into the air, soared above the flames of the fire, becoming occluded momentarily in the puffs of smoke before vanishing into the darkness.

"Rise up, brethren, and witness the nigger Jesus," shouted Shaka messianically.

All the slaves collapsed back to the earth, some sitting while others sprawled across the leaves looking entirely vacuous and spent, not moving except for the heaving of their chests.

"Lord help me," whispered Eloise, aghast.

She wanted to flee away but could not defy the trust of her father again, nor retreat from her mission. Was that the spirit of Christ in there, she wondered? But even if they were tricked by the devil, she must try to protect them and steer them toward the light. She stepped away from her guide into the space between the quilts, brandishing her Bible before her.

Seeing her first Shaka bolted out of the tent, running straight through the quilts which were not tethered to the ground, shouting, "Run, brothers, run," while some of the others followed him.

But most of them turned their heads toward her without making any attempt to flee, looking so dazed that they were not even capable of understanding the gravity of her presence. Some remained in their trances while squirming around the fire, mumbling and whimpering.

"Shut them niggers up," somebody shouted.

A child stood from the morass and threw cups of water over those still in their trance, awakening them, so that they stared at Eloise, mouths agape, eyes squinted, until all was silent except for the crackle and sizzle of the fire.

"What the hell's she doing here?" someone asked angrily.

"I come bearing the Word," said Eloise while holding her Bible before her chest.

"Caint hear you."

"I come bearing the Bible," proclaimed Eloise, her voice now louder but quaking.

"Whities use that Bible to beat niggers over the head."

"I come in the name of my father, the Reverend at the Church of All Men. I thought you knew I was coming."

In the back of the room, another man with wild, graying hair stood above the others, saying, "I told them you was coming. But they aint believe me. They said they aint want any whities about and for long Shaka done took hold of they minds and they went deaf and blind."

"Don't be afraid," said Eloise.

"She comes with Christ," confirmed the man. "She's our friend."

"We all bound for the whipping post now," someone shouted.

"No," said the man. "She aint gonna turn you to the gibbet."

Eloise gazed around at the faces, hoping to see understanding and acceptance. Instead she saw anger and distrust and in some the possibility of belief. Still frightened, feeling the tension in the room mounting, she held her Bible outward from her chest shield-like and while retreating from them, said, "You'll see that I won't betray your cause."

Once outside the tent she proclaimed, "Let it be said now, when you gaze upon the mansion, that the spirit of Christ is inside and alive even in that tomb of sin."

She turned and, panicked, ran as fast as she could through the woods back toward what she thought was the direction of the mansion, tripping at times and rising and tripping again while imagining some flock of Negroes chasing behind her, shrieking, coming to snatch her from the night like some small, wounded rodent in the clutches of their talons. Before long she was lost in the forest and not until dawn was she able to find her bearings and skulk back into the mansion unnoticed.

That day she wrote to her father about the events she had witnessed then sent Shobuck to deliver the message. She stayed inside all day for fear of upsetting the slaves with her presence but even in her own home she sensed or imagined—which, she could not tell—furtive and fearful glances from the house slaves. Did they even know what was happening late at night, she wondered? She overheard Jonah telling Whiteoak that the slaves seemed unusually subdued for a Sunday. Jonah surmised that since it appeared that some of the slaves were turning to Jesus, they might now consider their Sunday ritual of song, dance and drink sinful in the eyes of the Lord.

On that same day she received a note from her father delivered by Shobuck.

"Eloise,

"I attempt to train as many as I can, frequently in the middle of the night, which is the only time they can escape. I try to teach them to read, to quote the Scripture, to understand the difference between sin and virtue, between Christ and Satan, to recognize the false gods. But with His spirit now spreading like the wind across the plantations, I am responsible for the training of hundreds of souls. I am not equal to the task, being but one weak old man. The result is that many of the Negroes, such as the ones

you saw the other night, are but infants in Christ, most of them unbaptized and groping toward the Spirit as well as they can.

"The other night my man was there of course, slated to preach that evening the sermon that I taught him. As is the case frequently, however, he was overcome by another who, however misguided, was more charismatic and excitable. When this happens sometimes their sessions go astray. And sometimes the gods from Africa, which I consider harmless in the face of Christ, become infused into their worship. Most of these gods are deities resembling animals, including birds. During these fervors, their behavior sometimes becomes incomprehensible and intractable.

"But fear not. Though these events are frightening to behold, I am certain that the spirit of Jesus is ablaze in their hearts, even though their rituals seem corrupted. Judge not too harshly what at the moment is beyond our comprehension. His way is mysterious.

"But be careful and vigilant. For false gods and Satan himself may insinuate themselves into our flocks. You will know when this happens for they become enslaved to pleasure, sloth and sin— even willing to murder for their purposes. We are all vulnerable.

"Do not take any action yet. Someone will make contact with you soon. At that point follow my instructions listed below. Above all, do not allow Whiteoak or your husband to detect your actions or intentions for that would ruin us all.

"Strive to teach them scripture which is short, easy to grasp and potent so they can commit the words to memory and spread them around to their family and friends. Avoid quotes that are open to interpretation or that suggest freedom in any way for they become too excited, act too quickly and get themselves into trouble. Be gentle and gradual with their souls as you are with your own children.

"Use your example. Now knowing that you are one of His soldiers, they will look to you for guidance and will be eager to please.

"God is alive and overtaking the darkness through our actions.

"Your Father."

Several nights later over dinner, having finished his meal of rabbit carcass roasted on the outside but slightly raw inside, Whiteoak was picking his yellowed teeth with the thin, brittle bones from his plate. In his seventies he now looked even more gaunt than usual, his cheeks becoming concave. At times he coughed—the sound like an axe hacking on wood—but despite his attempts to stifle the spasms, he could not as the malfunctions of his body slowly overcame his will. But between his coughs, he looked pointedly and approvingly at Jonah who was now talking.

"Yes, Father. We've hired patrols—the usual, mostly the stragglers from town. They're wandering around until dawn looking for Jesus meetings. On account of their drinking whiskey and all, they're not carrying guns for fear they might kill somebody, even themselves. But they do carry whips. The other night they flushed this meeting in the hollow by the river. But these slaves are organized with wards hiding in the woods giving warning whenever the patrol approaches. So by the time they arrived, the tent was abandoned, the fire doused with water—all the slaves gone.

"We tried checking the shacks in the middle of the night to see who was missing. But that proved ineffective and too disruptive to the slaves who were nodding off in the fields.

"And we can't root out the source. Not certain there is one anymore. I suspect that most of the slaves are involved. This contagion of crosses spreads like lice—perhaps you can expel them but you got to kill them in the process. Production remains constant so far, says Tote, but he doesn't hold any promises for the future. He suspects that the slaves are behaving well because they know they're under suspicion.

"My recommendation is that we maintain the pressure on them but nothing beyond that. I think attempting to expurgate Christianity from the plantation might possibly result in more harm than good. Over time we should allow the slaves to worship legitimately. Bend for now, in other words, but don't break. After all, slaves are worshipping on other plantations and not causing any harm.

"Hell, before too long, we can open some little nigger church of our own here at Whiteoak. Then you and me, we can get up there and sermonize, praising Jesus, telling our darkies that Jesus aims for them to serve their master. Might even improve productivity."

Whiteoak snickered.

"All this was bound to happen, given the amount of activity on the other plantations."

Whiteoak nodded toward Eloise.

Chagrined, Jonah turned toward Eloise, saying disdainfully, "Your father got anything to do with this?"

"To do with what?" she asked.

"Instigating our niggers?"

Eloise paused. She noticed that she was not afraid or anxious. And she spoke without any hint of remorse, her voice not quaking but confident. "As you know my father is meek and passive. Not one to instigate, cause trouble. Only opens his door to all men, does not foment rebellion or ignite conflict."

"Eloise," Jonah pressed, his voice resentful. "Are you sure? We got some reason to believe."

"I answered your question."

"You know we could close down that degenerate Jesus shack of his," said Jonah. "We know he's teaching darkies to read. We could have that place razed by Sunday."

Eloise stood from her chair without even looking at Jonah but straight at Whiteoak, not fazed anymore by the grotesquery of his face. "You do that and you'll never see me and my children again."

That evening Eloise walked along the fields not far from the shacks where the slaves lived. She was tempted in the past to pray for Whiteoak's death—but resisted. If Whiteoak overcame whatever ailment was afflicting him now, he might remain alive for decades and continue to dictate all the policies for the plantation and to control Jonah and her own family by extension. Most of all she feared for her sons, knowing that soon their forefathers would come for them, sunder them away from her, indoctrinate them into their Godless, venal way of life while she watched helplessly.

She stopped resisting her death wish for Whiteoak and prayed, her heart determined and malicious. "Please allow Whiteoak to die, oh Lord, so I can free all of Your children from the torment of his reign. In exchange for his death, I shall deliver unto You the souls of my children and husband—and the souls of all the Negroes upon this plantation. I shall turn this land of darkness, now infiltrated by Your light, into heaven upon earth. Amen."

For many weeks all signs of Christ had disappeared from Whiteoak and her father revealed that for the moment the slaves had stopped congregating in the woods but were still praying in their shacks at night and Eloise somehow sensed that the light of Christ, though not visible, was burning strong nonetheless. One evening she was in the kitchen checking on dinner when a girl came to the back door with several ducks in her hands, their necks wrung.

"Here's yawl's dinner," the girl said sweetly.

Eloise turned away, grabbed a basket from one of the counters then returned. After dropping the ducks into the basket, the girl traced the outline of a cross across her chest so quick as to seem imperceptible, then walked away.

Eloise was startled while holding the basket, doubting what she saw. "Missy," she called.

The girl stopped, hesitated then turned, looking afraid. "Yes-sum."

Slowly yet definitively, Eloise traced the outline of the cross across her own chest.

The girl smiled.

"Jesus loves you," whispered Eloise.

The word evidently had spread afterward because Eloise noticed that other slaves in her presence were making these almost unseen traces of the cross on their chests; and she would then do the same and whisper short words of scripture into their ears. When strolling along the shacks or in the fields, she saw more of these symbols as the trust developed—all this eerily reminding Eloise of the fish used by Christians during Roman times. Christ was burgeoning across the plantation, she knew, the wordlessness and serendipity of his presence only seeming to enhance his power. Knowing that everybody was under suspicion, however, she did not take any action beyond those signs and waited patiently until Whiteoak and her husband could not any longer deny His presence.

Weeks later around midnight Eloise lay in bed alone while Jonah was downstairs around the fire, having drunk himself to sleep to avoid the noises coming from his father's bedroom: the spasmodic hacking and cracklings of lungs full of blood and phlegm that sounded like something inside was dissolving and shredding away. God had answered her prayers for surely Whiteoak was moribund but He also was tormenting her with guilt. But on this night God wanted her to redeem herself by going forth, speaking to Whiteoak and trying to save his soul from damnation.

She placed her feet into her slippers and wrapped her robe over her nightgown and walked into the darkness of the hallway. Faint and wavering light emanated from the crack beneath his door. As instructed by the doctor, she placed her handkerchief over her mouth and nose and opened the door without knocking.

One dim, flickering candle provided light inside. The room was devoid of furniture except for one chair and the long, narrow bed where Whiteoak lay—his thin, emaciated body wrapped in sheets and quilts—looking embalmed already. Not seeing her he was hanging over one side of the bed appearing to scribble on some paper on the floor.

After coming somewhat closer and sitting in the chair, she saw the splotches of blood expectorated all over his sheets, his own body, even on the walls across from the bed. Whiteoak suddenly turned toward her, his head looking small and gaunt when appearing from the quilts, his pale eyes full of scorn. He turned quickly and coughed away from her on the floor with his chest crackling. Eloise was disturbed to see this once fearless and vital man reduced to this condition, sickened with herself for ever wanting to curse anyone to such fate.

He looked back at her, wiping blood from his mouth.

She dropped to her knees on the floor, genuflecting, proclaiming, muffled through the handkerchief. "For the Love of God, Whiteoak, open your heart to salvation. Plead for forgiveness so you can pass into the Kingdom of Heaven."

Whiteoak lay there impassive, staring at the ceiling.

"I'll forgive you. Forgive you for forcing my family to live in your Godless, vacuous home, forgive you for stealing the soul of my husband, forgive you for spurning my father. I'll forgive you everything and God will do the same. Such is promised through his son Jesus Christ."

He did nothing, only breathed.

On the other side of his bed, Eloise noticed the scrolls of paper also splattered with blood scattered amongst some overused, cracked quills.

"Have you confessed your sins, begged for His mercy? Given instructions for Christ to prevail here on your plantation?"

Again he said nothing.

"The Lord's afoot even here at Whiteoak winning the hearts of your slaves. The time of your death…"

She suddenly heard this clamor—and saw that Whiteoak was ringing the bell sitting next to his bed. She was enraged at him for spurning her again and after he dropped the bell on the floor, exhausted, she came closer to his face, seeing the veins threading under his skin like worms gnawing into him.

"I've now tried to save you, you withered, sinful man. Now go to the gates of Hell knowing that in this kingdom of yours, your reign of torment is over, that Christ at last is burgeoning through the workings of me and my father. I'll swear to you that after your death He will prevail in the hearts of your slaves, of your grandchildren and of your only child."

When the slave who attended to Whiteoak appeared at the door, seeming confused and yawning, Eloise looked back at Whiteoak and saw in him the terror of someone bound infirm and helpless before his enemy waiting to be slain. And she walked away.

Months later, after coming from his father's bedroom, Jonah announced the death without emotion, almost disdainfully, saying that his father had drowned in his own blood. Moments later some slaves with bandannas around their faces ascended the stairs, carrying the casket made from unpainted, rough-hewn pine. That evening Jonah worked on the eulogy while locked in his study, scribbling furiously, then wadding and pitching the pieces of paper into the fire and starting over again, as though trying to sort through his own feelings. For the funeral the next day, Eloise stood beside the grave holding the hands of her children. Scattered around her were many of the people who dealt in business with Whiteoak: the overseers, merchants and some dignitaries from town. Behind them were the slaves attending less to show their respects but more to avoid working in the fields.

Looking tired but commanding, Jonah stood elevated above the fields at the pulpit and spoke only these words. "Whiteoak came and conquered the wilderness. Unto chaos he brought order, unto shiftlessness, purpose."

The casket was lowered into the earth. As Jonah threw dirt into the grave, Eloise studied his face expecting to see…what she could not say: remorse, grief, respect? His face instead seemed to relinquish tension as though some yoke, once harnessed tight about his neck, was broken and he realized for once the freedom of his existence. She saw him bite his lip, perhaps to purge the urge to smile.

She whispered to herself, "Is he free? Oh Lord, is he free at last?"

Against her hopes he became more intense and commanding after the funeral, determined to prove the strength of his reign across his plantation. He worked as usual from dawn to dusk and once returning home at night, disappeared into his father's study to review papers and study ledgers and after dinner, retired to his chair and fell asleep. During this time he revealed little, if anything, about his thoughts or feelings but rather seemed to retreat into himself.

One evening he disappeared from the plantation without any forewarning. After looking around the next day, all she noticed was that his canoe was missing from the landing by the river and that his favorite rifle was gone from the pantry.

"He's checking on some of his properties," she told the others, hoping to hide his flippancy.

She suspected that he was out there in the wilderness, doing what, becoming what, she could not quite imagine, although she felt some inkling of hope.

Several nights later Eloise lay in her bed unable to sleep with all her sheets thrown back. Her windows were open but the night was motionless without any breeze. Coming from the walls of the forest was the wail of the crickets, their frenzied, pulsing friction seeming to create heat that hovered over her even late into the night like some saturated but rainless cloud.

Light flickered into the room almost indiscernibly, followed by a muffled grumble of thunder moments later. Leaves rustled outside the window and the breeze wandered into the bedroom, cooling the mist of sweat that made her nightgown cling to her skin. She imagined Jonah out there in the forest crouching next to his fire as the rain extinguished the flames, leaving him soaked in the dark as God baptized him and washed him free from his past. Was he once again becoming the man liberated from the influence of his father, whom she loved all those years ago? The man who she knew in the wilderness?

All the way to the cusp of sleep, she repeated the prayer over and over. "Lord, please guide him back to you...back to himself."

She awoke later into the dark. The rain outside poured from the sky and propelled by gusts of wind, swashed into the sides of the mansion and splattered into her bedroom. Someone was inside the room, she sensed. Alarmed she raised upward and over the drone of rain, heard someone scruffing next to her bed. As light pulsed through the room along with the concussion of thunder, she saw the hulking and hunched silhouette of her husband.

"Is that you, Jonah?"

She heard him breathing and smelled his scent of pine smoke, charred venison and wet leaves. After hovering over her, he crouched low on the bed and then she felt his face on her stomach, his stubble rough upon her flesh.

"What are you doing?"

"Please, Eloise, please."

He was kissing her around her navel then lower, licking her like some dog trying to extract nourishment from the excretions of her body. How long had it been since he touched her in this way, she thought? Was this right in the eyes of God? But when he came to her unannounced like this in the middle of the night, she always discovered some distant and fallow yearning seeping forth underneath her surprise and even her repulsion. She just lay there deleting the sensation of his tongue, slightly scared and captive, feeling preyed upon by her own husband.

As her thoughts flushed away into the sounds of the downpour, she seemed to meld into the shrill, passionate clamor of the crickets—and her resistance faded away. Once rigid her body softened and her legs went slack and she offered herself to him and when light flashed into the room, she saw him undulating on top of her with his hair streaked about his forehead. Afterward, as he rolled from her and lay on his back, she felt her thought return as she wondered why she always succumbed to the madness of that ungodly and crude passion?

They lay there for some time without speaking, although Eloise could tell he remained awake, until she asked while hoping her voice did not sound too cold, "Where did you go?"

"Just away," he said.

"I want to know, Jonah."

"I just went to walk down by the river at first. But when coming back to our house, I saw our children standing in the window of the dining room." He spoke in a tone of voice which she had not heard for years: gentle, hesitant and searching. "They were dressed for bed. Above them I could see my father's portrait—with all his scars blotted away, he looked almost benevolent but he was still lording over them, holding them fixed in his vision. But they weren't looking at the portrait, just staring bewildered into the darkness and hoping perhaps for something or someone to help them. Looking for me perhaps.

"I thought of stepping into the light from the window. But I wanted to remain invisible so that I would not inflict anything upon them. I wanted them to mold their own destinies without my hindrance or help. Free yourself, I thought, from the life I've known.

"I thought oddly that I wasn't their father, they not my children. It seemed that I didn't own or even know the house around them. The lands and slaves, the shacks and shovels—none of that was mine. Even you seemed strange and distant, Eloise. All my life seemed illusionary and unreal. That person in the dark, alone, powerless, invisible, was the real me, waiting perhaps to emerge."

"Jonah," she said.

"Yes."

"James and Josh in that window—they were looking for you, wondering where you were. You said you would read to them before they went to bed. Then you disappeared. They were waiting for you to come back inside."

"Oh," said Jonah gently, disappointed with himself. "I forgot. They were searching for me. But I had nothing to show them."

"But you do. You're their father."

"All I can show them is misery," Jonah said. "I decided to leave for that reason. I snuck into my own house like a thief, grabbed my rifle, some supplies, went to the river and drifted away from here, away from the life that was not mine."

"What did you find out there?"

"Nothing other than freedom. I drifted downstream through the forest while passing other plantations. Camped in the evenings on the banks of the river, stared at the stars as the water lulled me to sleep. I felt free, unfettered, living as God intended. But I knew I must return.

"One morning I traded my canoe for some old horse and rode

upriver, stalking deer along the way, skulking across other plantations like some fugitive. But once getting back here to Whiteoak, I stayed out there in the woods. Watched the slaves toiling in the fields. Looked at this house from the distance, amazed that this was my home. Walked this evening secretly amongst the slave quarters, listening to them, smelling their food—they of course oblivious to the man who owned and lorded over them. I couldn't own all of this, I thought, not the souls of these people. I was not that man.

"Later tonight I camped in the forest and cooked venison for dinner. In the rain I got cold and wet and wanted to come back to you, Eloise. I snuck back into my own house, feeling like a ghost of myself. I came up here, saw how beautiful you are, your body, so soft and pale, flashing in the lightning. And I needed you. Of all this, Eloise, you seemed closest to me. You brought me back."

Eloise sensed that now in the middle of the night, while cleansed by the rain, Jonah was able to reveal himself to her. And though enchanted and moved by his story, she was also worried. Was he losing his mind? But she felt the old, almost lost love rekindled and she prayed softly to herself. "Guide him, Oh Lord, guide him."

Then she asked, "Are you all right?"

"Yes," he said, though his voice was unconvincing. "I just feel that I'm on the brink of...of...."

"Of what?"

"I don't know."

They were silent as the rain faded into a drizzle and the lightning flashed dimly, followed by the grumble of thunder seconds later.

"Remember riding through the forest before our marriage," said Jonah, "free from our fathers, from the world?"

"I long for those days."

"Do you really?"

"Yes."

"I do too," he said.

Moments later Jonah continued. "I know how we can make that happen again, not just with you and me but the children also."

"What do you mean?"

"I'll show you." After lighting the candle next to their bed, Jonah donned some clean trousers and left the room carrying the candle in his hand. He soon returned and sat next to her, revealing some scrolls which he unrolled onto the bed. "When looking through my father's papers, I discovered this map along with some deeds from the state of Florida. He usually kept me uninformed about most of his deals, probably to keep me from having too much control. Anyway, he purchased this island off the coast of Florida."

Eloise studied the map, the broken, jagged coastline woven with rivers and inlets. Off the coast and out in the gulf were hundreds of islands—sinewy, convoluted things. Beyond that was the place where Jonah was pointing—a circular, solitary island.

"And you want to go to this island?"

"Yes."

"But what do you know about it?"

"Most of the islands and the coastline are thick with these ugly, twisted trees called mangroves. But the lawyers said this island is devoid of mangroves and is covered with sand and dunes and one old giant tree for shade."

"Why did your father purchase this island?"

"Nobody knows. But this area was rumored to shelter pirates once. Perhaps he intended to search for the treasure he believed was buried there. Anyway, these islands were once inhabited by hostile Indians. But our militia destroyed most of their camps—killed them off with guns and smallpox.

"Now the island is deserted, an Eden waiting for our touch. We can bring along James and Josh, some slaves to tend to the chores. I thought we could stay about one month. I can tell all my associates that we're heading south to overlook some lands purchased by my father."

"But why to this island?"

"To hunt and fish. The waters are teeming with fish, the skies with birds. But mostly to flee from the imprisonment of my life. To live with my family in the purity of this paradise as I lived for days out there in the forest on my own."

His excitement, so childlike and innocent, reminded her of her sons as they planned to build forts in the woods and catch rabbits in their traps. He was emerging anew and expres-sing parts of himself which she had not really witnessed for years so she did not want to dampen his enthusiasm for fear he would withdraw. But she was also worried about being alone on this island with him and her children.

"But this is wilderness. Nobody is around for miles. What would happen if we became sick, if we were attacked by some faction of Indians hidden away in the swamps?"

"All the Indians are gone or living on reservations. And if we encounter problems, we can send one of the slaves for help. A settlement of some sort is about forty miles away."

"But what about mosquitoes, storms, bugs or predators," she said, keeping her voice gentle. "Is this best for our children? Befitting to someone in your position? Why don't we travel to Boston or even to Europe and show our children the wonders of Christendom?" Her voice rose with irritation. "Why to some scrawny, sun-scorched, wind-battered island in the middle of the ocean?"

He usually reacted with anger whenever she challenged him but now Jonah looked hurt and defeated.

"I'm sorry. Maybe something good could happen there. Perhaps you need this."

"So you'll come, Eloise?"

"Perhaps. But you cannot force me, nor our children."

"I want you to come of your own volition."

"We'll come on this condition."

"What's that?"

She felt almost paralyzed with disbelief that after all these years, she was about to reveal her secret to Jonah: "That you allow my father to minister here at Whiteoak."

"To minister where?" he said, flaring with anger.

"You heard me."

He looked at her as never before, scrupulously, as though examining his rival. "I thought you were involved all these years. But I really didn't want to know, didn't want to be forced to shut down your father's church. But you were involved, weren't you, your father too, with the crosses, the meetings, with converting the slaves?"

"Yes we were," said Eloise.

"So you lied."

"Yes I did to save my father. I'll lie again for that purpose, if necessary. So don't place me in that position."

"But God says 'Thou shall not lie.' "

"God knows the world is imperfect, that sometimes we must sin for the sake of goodness."

"I can understand that."

"I suppose you might understand that," said Eloise.

Jonah ignored her comment.

"So what's your decision?"

"You think you outfoxed us," said Jonah, "but in fact we planned on making Christianity legitimate once it was too entrenched to uproot. If your…"

"I don't care about who outfoxed whom. I don't need you to acknowledge your defeat. I just want you to be good."

"Well," said Jonah, startled. "I suppose he can come and minister. But he must respect our rules."

"Then we've decided," said Eloise.

"We shall go to the island," said Jonah.

Jonah walked toward the window and she came and stood at his side. Outside the thunderstorm was gone. Revealed in dim, gray light, fog hovered around the fields. The porches of the shacks were empty, the Negroes still asleep.

"Maybe we'll discover something at your utopia," she said reassuringly.

"I hope so."

After she watched in silence, the light remained un-changed. "Is this light from the moon," she asked, "or is dawn aborning?"

"I hope so," said Jonah, touching her hand.

On the following Sunday Eloise waited in anticipation while standing on the verandah of the mansion, wearing one of her simple linen dresses from her childhood and clasping her Bible to her chest. In the distance, through the misty and bluish haze of the morning, she saw her father dressed in his robe marching past the gates of Whiteoak, holding his giant, wooden cross before him. Behind him was his congregation of slaves, both free and emancipated, both black and mulatto, of the smattering of mendicants, derelicts, madmen and fugitives of all colors—all of whom found their home in the Church of All Men. As they marched onward, the slaves of Whiteoak emerged from their shacks and lined the road in greeting, singing hymns, playing little songs on their fifes, drums and fiddles, many breaking into shouts of "Hallelujah" and "Praise the Lord" and some weeping in joy while the children ran around frenzied in the excitement.

Standing on the porch next to Eloise was Jonah dressed to hunt, oiling the barrels of his rifles, seeming amused, incredulous and appalled at once. "For you, Eloise," he said, a tinge of sarcasm in his voice. "For you, my love."

CHAPTER FOUR

Months later in the autumn Eloise and Jonah were on the island strolling along the beach while their children were playing in the dunes. She watched anxiously as the last sign of civilization, the ship, vanished into the horizon, obliterated from sight both by distance and the approaching darkness.

"We're alone now," she said.

"For one month until another ship returns," said Jonah.

Eloise glanced toward the center of the island where all five slaves were congregated around the only tree on the island—their forms even darker now in the remnants of light.

"You trust them?" she asked.

"Who?"

"Shaka and Jake—all of them."

"Of course. They were chosen because of their trust-worthiness."

Eloise remembered that night when she saw Shaka in the hollow standing at the pulpit while cutting that bird from its bindings, some prophetic but wild and animalistic look on his face as he claimed, "Witness the nigger Jesus." Months later her father informed her that Shaka had been converted into a reliable and zealous preacher of the Word.

But she still felt afraid of him. She also felt untethered like the cord that connected her to the rest of her life was unraveling and finally severing, leaving her lost and disoriented, feeling too vulnerable before the incessant grinding and droning of the elements.

Not having time before darkness to establish their camp, Eloise and Jonah retrieved some quilts and pillows from one of the crates left on the beach below. As the round and unblemished moon rose above the mainland seen in the distance, she called her children over and not even bothering to change their clothes, they all nestled into one of the troughs of the dunes, swaddled in quilts, her children on one side of her, her husband on the other, all of them sheltered from the wind in a sort of white, moon-stained bowl.

Her children fell quickly to sleep. But she stayed awake gazing into the heavens above: The sky was starless and clear while the moon, which she could not see anymore, was penetrating its light into the darkness. Crickets chirped low and amiably above the churning surf. To her surprise Jonah gently grabbed her hand and when she turned on her side, he cuddled with her.

"This is Eden," he whispered to her, "like I said."

She was silent. For once her fear subsided. She could feel the heaving of Jonah's lungs next to her and when her breathing fell into rhythm with his, she sensed that the island itself was breathing as though alive and sensed too that this trough in the dune was the gentle and beatific palm of God holding them gently above the water.

"Maybe you're right," she said. "Maybe this is Eden."

Maybe God has at last, she thought to herself, brought her broken and wounded family to this island to find peace and wholeness.

Soon Jonah turned onto his back, pulling his arms away from her. Again she faced upward watching the interplay of silver and shadow on the sea oats on the crest of the dune. She could hear him breathing now, not smoothly as before but almost snoring, taking long, laborious breaths as though he was working too hard to simply breathe. As many times before she sensed about him what she could not explain: some kind of sadness, not ordinary grief, but something so powerful and overwhelming that it threatened to destroy him and their family. As her fear returned she imagined the palm of God slowly closing around them then squeezing and lowering them into the seawater below—and holding them there as they struggled to rise again to the surface before they drowned.

God is merciful and Christ is everywhere, including that wilderness of water, she reminded herself while fading into sleep, cuddling closer to her children but away from her husband.

CHAPTER FIVE

Eloise awoke at dawn, peeling her body away from her children who remained asleep. She climbed to the dune above her and with her back facing the gulf, she saw the sun rising above the broken, disjointed cluster of mangrove islands that seemed to merge into the mainland farther in the distance. Stretching out from the island was one sandbar rising only inches above the water at low tide, covered with swarms of flittering, chirping seagulls. Jonah was already walking across the island arousing the slaves who were scattered about from their sleep. Without even bothering about breakfast, they went to work building their camp.

While Eloise helped Nomaw in the organizing of the kitchen, Jonah supervised the others with the remainder of the camp. Unaccustomed to working under Jonah directly, the slaves seemed subdued under his command while moving slowly but consistently—the hymns which usually accustomed their labors were silent. As the heat mounted then subsided in the afternoon, they worked onward motivated only by knowing that once their chores were finished they could languish around as much as they wanted. To the east of the tree they raised two tents facing toward the mainland, one for her and Jonah and the other for their children, on some of the only flat land on the island aside from the beach. Behind them in some nice, small trough sheltered by shrubbery, they built their latrine, one hole suspended above another dug into the sand.

To the west and closer to the gulf, they raised one tent for the slaves. On the fringes of the shade from the tree—that huge, almost incongruous tree out there amidst nothing but dunes, shrubbery and cactus—they built their kitchen which consisted of one table, some crates for storing food and the firepit and pots. Moored on the beach were their rowboats which they intended to use for fishing and exploring.

After camp was established in the afternoon, Jonah called everyone under the shade of the tree. Speaking in short, staccato commands devoid of any nuance, not looking at anyone but rather off at nothing, Jonah outlined the protocols to the slaves for their camp: Fresh water was allotted per day, otherwise they could drink as much rainwater as they could collect during storms. They were not to use the latrine but the gulf to avoid befouling the island. Pear and Nomaw were responsible for the kitchen and tending to their tents; the men were responsible for fires and rowing the boats and for cleaning game and fish. He concluded by admitting that there was not much work or activities for them on the island so for most of the day they could "just slack around."

"Slack," said Jake, looking anxious. "What you mean—slack?"

"Do whatever you want."

Jake looked perplexed. "But I aint knowed how to do that."

"Just take naps, go fishing and swimming."

"I caint do that. I heard about some slaves that one day got some slack. They just sat under this tree all day long, not doing nothing, just sitting and looking at things. For long they got so stiff they caint move and drool started trickling out their mouths. They shrunk, withered away and was dead—all cause nobody aint cracked his whip."

Eloise was fascinated but disturbed by Jake. On the barge down from Mobile, Jonah explained to Eloise after she asked him that Jake was chosen because he had been around forever, coming to Alabama with Whiteoak all those years ago, and that he had contributed more pickaninnies to the coffers than any other slaves on account of his ferocious, age-proof virility and his way of charming

Negresses. He deserves to come, concluded Jonah. She also knew that because of his status, Jake was given the leeway to indulge his passion, spraying words from his mouth like minnows from the maw of a bass—in this case, the bass being his lifetime of anguish. Was he being serious or comical, straight or sarcastic, or subversive?

"All this slacking makes niggers funny. So don't give me none. Give me some extra chores, digging holes maybe. And if you see me napping, come whack me upside my head."

"Perhaps this arrangement is working against your natures," said Jonah. "But I'm not intending to supervise you much here so you best take care of yourself, Jake."

"And if I don't?"

"You gonna catch my ire."

"Thank the Lawd," said Jake relieved. "That'll keep a nigger busy for sho."

"Most of you were chosen for this trip because you're good slaves," continued Jonah, "not likely to cause us any problems."

Jonah continued to explain that the slaves were responsible for preparing their own food, either together or by themselves. They were to get their usual pone, pork and greens as long as they lasted. And something extra: salt, honey and spices. And all the fish and game they could kill. They could even use the boats when available for fishing.

Surprised by his generosity, Eloise concluded that Jonah for some reason wanted to give the slaves some kind of respite from their lives of eternal toil and deprivation. But what then would emerge from them, she wondered? What behaviors? What secret resentments or hatreds, what fallow dreams or dashed hopes? Since remaining more committed than ever to converting the slaves to Christianity, she resolved that she would use their freedom to help them find the light of Christ.

CHAPTER SIX

Over the next few days Jonah was gone from the island before Eloise even awakened, out fishing in one of the rowboats with Shobuck. After her breakfast of porridge and dried fruit was served by Nomaw, Eloise noticed that the other slaves seemed rather lethargic, lolling around on the beach and escaping the heat by dipping in the waves—except for Jake who walked around all day anxiously begging for chores.

When she gave him some, he started to admonish the other slaves. "Done told all yawl. Without toil, yawl bones is rotting and drool is coming out your mouth. Yawl best save yourselves."

But by the afternoon when the sun was scorching the island, even Jake was sitting on the sandbar without his shirt, half awake and lethargic, as the waves gently lapped about him.

One day after Shaka removed his shirt to bathe in the gulf, she was shocked to see the scars: the bulging, black matrix of wounds that were like straps containing the secret and invisible rage she instantly imagined inside of him. She was afraid as soon as she learned that Shaka was coming on this trip, which was not until they were already floating down the river. But when she asked Jonah why he chose Shaka, he only said because he was well behaved and handy with tools.

"But those scars," she asked him later. "Where did they come from?"

"Don't know," said Jonah too quickly.

"Did you whip him?"

"No."

"Aren't you afraid of someone damaged like that?"

"No."

But she was afraid. His limbs were thin but sinewy, making him look scrawny but with tight, well-defined muscles. He did not lumber along like the other slaves but rather moved with this graceful, light-footed gait. Ethereal but vicious, she thought, perhaps like that bird he held captive that time.

Soon after she saw Shaka in the dunes with his arms folded over his chest, muttering something she could not hear as he watched the the cormorants, the long-winged, ever-present birds soaring way overhead with the clouds. But when she called to him to ask him what he was doing, he only said he was praying.

"To whom?" she asked.

"To Jesus," he said.

The next day the island was deluged with rain, sending all the slaves into the shelter of their tent. The sand afterward was erased of all blemishes and footprints, smooth like paper, while the gulf continued to churn and send swells cascading into shore, all the louder now for the absence of the wind. Unperturbed by her watching them, Jake and Shobuck used shells to sketch lines into the beach which Pear then adorned with seaweed, shells, bits of driftwood, dead crabs, until staring up at Eloise were birds.

"My God," said Eloise.

But she was not afraid. She loved all the birds around the island, especially the sandpipers that ran along the wake of the waves, their thin, flickering legs moving so fast that they vanished from sight, while stabbing their beaks into the sand to eat something also invisible. And she loved the pelicans that always drifted with the wind in an echelon, their wings hovering barely above the water while at times flying upwind, ascending higher into the sky before folding their wings and diving beak-first to retrieve fish from the gulf like ethereal acrobats. And she loved the herons that fed along the beaches and sandbars at dusk, standing so still as to seem lifeless as the water lapped along their talons before instantly stabbing their beak into the water to impale some crab or minnow. Devoid of any other animals that might threaten them, the island was a haven for birds which were everywhere, below and above, soaring, walking and crying into the firmaments. She understood that the slaves were as inspired by these birds as she was. Regardless she remained curious and even concerned that on this strange and churchless island all of this could drift away into some primitive practice of animal worship.

But one day later around midmorning—all of these events happened when Jonah was away, she noticed with concern—she saw Shaka pointing into the sky as the other slaves, except for Nomaw, congregated around him to look at this one large, eaglelike bird with brown and white feathers soaring above the gulf, calling, "Eeeeeek... eeeeeek...eeeeeek," before swooping down into the water, talons first, and yanking a fish from the waves. The slaves watched all of this, not saying anything. Eloise afterward walked to Pear and asked her casually why they were watching that bird like that.

"Cause they angels, Missus. Shaka says they is and we ought to learn from them."

"But learn what?"

When Pear seemed to not know the answer, Eloise told her that those birds were not angels, that people most of the time could not see the angels.

"Yessum," said Pear shortly, without conviction. "Whatever you say."

Emerging from their lethargy the slaves increasingly devoted most of their time to rowing the boats into the gulf, casting nets to collect minnows for bait and then trolling lines behind their boat with baited hooks like Jonah taught them. At low tide they walked along the beach collecting shellfish. At twilight they built fires from driftwood and roasted fish over the fire until the skin was blackened and after the fish were allowed to cool in the sand, they took the entirety of the carcass in their hands, peeled back the skin and gorged on the steaming, lubricious slithers of fish inside and sucked on the bones. They were liberating themselves from starvation, Eloise thought, after years of subsisting on the minimum. Within days they looked more robust and full; their faces, once gaunt and almost bloodless, became fleshier.

Later into the night they sang hymnals—some of which her father had taught to them but some that sounded alien to her ears and she suspected that they originated in Africa. Sometimes she could hear Nomaw raising her voice angrily as though chastising someone while Jake erupted into guffaws which for reasons she could not explain always made her feel mocked and even ridiculed. After putting her children to sleep one night, she wandered down to the beach to stroll along the shore, pretending that she was not attentive to them while trying to hear the gist of their conversation. But she could not and as she moved closer to their fire, she noticed that they lowered their voices.

All of this was not much different from their behavior back on the plantation, she thought, especially on Sundays after church when they were given whiskey. But still she remained concerned so later that night she came to her husband and asked if he would take Shaka with him in the boat in the morning.

"Why?" he asked.

"He makes me uncomfortable," was all she revealed.

Early that next morning after Jonah had left for the day, she dressed in one of her gowns—the one she brought to wear in the captain's quarters on the steamship—and festooned her neck with one large golden crucifix. Concerned that the slaves on the island were straying from Christ, she decided to hold church which she would control herself for the purpose of steering the slaves back to Christ.

"Is we going to town today?" asked Jake, as she walked over to the slaves to announce that they were holding services that morning.

After his first visit to Whiteoak, Eloise's father had continued his grandiose fanfare through the plantation before congregating inside one of the barns, which was momentarily transformed into a church, to conduct his services—where the slaves sang hymns accompanied by fifes and fiddles, learned scriptures and listened to a sermon given by her father. Most of the slaves, terrorized by hell and desperate for hope, were converted easily.

When her father needed to return to his own church, he chose one of his minions to lead the services—a partially educated and freed black from town. She continued to attend mostly to make sure the slaves stayed on track while sitting in back trying to stay invisible—the only white person in the building. With her father gone the slaves dispensed with any show of constraint and intellectualism, expressing their torment or joy through singing, dancing and shouting. During the sermon the minister could hardly say anything for all the interruptions and shouts coming from his congregation. At first she was shocked, not even sure that they were in fact worshipping the Lord. But then she thought: Were they not singing about love and salvation? Were they not showing more enthusiasm for God than anybody in her own church? Maybe their behavior was somewhat distasteful but she concluded that although He might wear another mask, God was alive in that barn and taking hold in the hearts of that congregation.

Eloise was most comfortable conducting Bible study for the slaves who worked for her in the mansion because they, apart from adapting the manners of the whites, also performed their chores without the need for her to reprimand them, thus creating relationships that overall were pleasant and free of friction. As she read to them from the Bible around the kitchen table, they seemed amazed that she could convert all those markings on the pages into those strange words and glorious stories. They became believers without any sense of skepticism, seeming to magically understand the nature of Christ—his love, humility and fear—and accept Him into their hearts. The schism between master and slave, white and black, dissolved as they all became one in the body of Christ—sometimes even taking communion together. Instead of preaching that God wanted the slaves to honor and obey their master, she evaded this issue altogether and the slaves, not wanting to make things awkward, decided to not pursue the subject. After some weeks of these meetings, she tested their memories which were amazingly accurate then sent them out to spread the Word to those in the fields.

On the island Eloise wanted to attempt to instate the same Christian authority over the slaves that she had back at Whiteoak. While Nomaw came along Eloise walked to the beach and at the foot of one of the dunes, constructed a church by drawing a cross into the sand which she then adorned, with some help from her children, with shells, driftwood and seaweed—she then placed stumps and chunks of dried, sun-bleached coral to serve as seats beneath the arms of the cross.

After Eloise called the slaves over, they sat on their stools and she above them on a chair before the crucifix. She was relieved to find that the slaves seemed docile and appreciative of the church she created for them. After leading them in some hymns and reciting the Lord's prayer, she read from the Bible the verses she selected the night before. " 'We know that whosoever is born of God sinneth not; but he that is begotten of God keepeth himself, and that wicked one touched him not.

" 'And we know that we are of God, and the whole world lives in wickedness.' "

"Amen," said Nomaw. "All yawl wickeds hear that?"

" 'And we know that the son of God is come, and hath given us an understanding, that we may know Him that is true, and we are in Him that is true, even in his son Jesus Christ. This is the true God, and eternal life.

" 'Little children, keep yourselves from idols.' "

"Lawd, yes," said Nomaw, "stay away from Shaka."

" 'For false Christs and false prophets shall rise, and shall show signs and wonders, to seduce, if it were possible, even the elect.' "

Eloise defined idols and said that some people who are under the spell of the devil use deception to make others believe they are holy so they will follow them.

"You can usually identify these people from their idols," she continued. "I have seen slaves fall under these spells and they are bound for the fires of Hell unless we save them. The way of Christ is not always easy but usually full of sacrifice, pain and denial. But false idols and prophets encouraged others to believe that the way of righteousness is quick and easy, full of pleasure, not suffering."

Jake raised his hand but she ignored him and continued to talk until he asked earnestly between the pauses in her words, "But how does you know?"

"Know what?" she asked.

"Who be false?

"What do you mean?"

"I mean I got all excited when your Paw was preaching about praying to the Lawd. So I got down on my hands and knees and prayed, 'Oh, Lord, how you doing, nice to finally meet you after this long while. Wished I'd talked to you sooner but I aint knowed you was up there. Sho I is low and sinful, not much different from any old beast but I was wondering if my wifey, the one with the crooked teeth, was in heaven with you waiting for me to join her. Lord, I know you aint talk regular most of the time so just give me some sign so I got some hankering to die or live and someday know some crumb of happiness again.'

"I done waited. Nothing happened.

"I done waited some more until the moon rose. Nothing happened.

"Then some mouse scurried across the floor. What the hell does that mean, I wondered?"

"The ways of God," said Eloise, "are not always revealed to man. God sometimes chooses not to answer our prayers."

"But God aint never answered my prayers. Then just to see, I started praying to God about all sorts of things. God, I pray that Massa might retire my ass. I pray that some rabbit might get stuck in my trap so I aint got to eat pone, grease and worms for dinner again. I pray that Sally might want to get with me. But he aint never answered any of them.

"For long I figured the reasons whities got everything, and niggers nothing, is cause yawl know all the tricks of praying. So I spied on you while you was praying, looking at how you kneeled, held your hands, moved your mouth, even remembered some of your fancy, tongue-wrenching words. So I went home again and copied you. 'Behold, Oh Lord, sanctify my soul. Exalt thou to heaven. Therefore thou shall love the Lord, thy God and deliver me from temptation. And may it come to pass that my back aint ache anymore, that my chilblain goes away, so this nigger can get some sleep tonight, Oh sanctified One.'

"But he aint done nothing."

"I prayed all the time," said Pear, "when I was little that God aint never carry me from my mammy. But God aint hear nothing. Is that cause I is sinful and God don't love me, Missus?"

"Our prayers are answered in heaven, not on earth," said Eloise.

"So how do I know?" said Jake.

"How do you know what?" asked Eloise agitated.

"If my prayers is answered in heaven."

"Cause you'll be in heaven."

"Unless I'm dead."

"Or unless you in hell," said Nomaw.

"Shit, woman," said Jake. "Hear me through on this story. Some nigger come to the tree to plucket the fruit."

"So," said Nomaw.

"But there aint any fruit. So why he gonna come back?"

"You think," countered Nomaw, "God done born you with a hoe in your hand to ask questions like this?"

"Do you think I ought to worship this Jesus just cause the whities say?"

"Yes," said Nomaw.

"So the whities can dupe my ass all over again?"

Nomaw seemed unable to respond.

"I reckon we ought to ask these questions. Otherwise you might as well worship my ass. At least you can see it."

"We need to stay on the point," said Eloise: "false idols and prophets."

"That be my point," said Jake. "How do I know who is false if I caint reckon who is real? I aint got any truck with Jesus. I just aint never seen him. I talk to him but he don't never talk back. He aint never done nothing for me. I sho catch the spirit some of the time. But all I need for that is some whiskey and fiddles."

Pear and Shobuck were nodding their heads in agreement with Jake while Nomaw was looking at the ground and shaking her head.

"You gots to have faith," said Nomaw.

"What's that?" Jake asked.

"Believe in things you cant see," said Eloise hopefully.

"Cause they aint there."

Eloise wanted to talk but was left dumbfounded.

"And this Jesus is white, right?" Jake continued. "Aint nothing wrong with white folks unless you is black folk."

"Jake," screamed Nomaw who was looking at Eloise, seeing the disappointment and fear in her eyes. "She's trying to help you."

Jake was suddenly silent as though Nomaw knocked the words from his mouth—but only for one moment. "Sorry, Missus, I's just wanting to get some schooling on this Jesus."

All the other slaves were now looking at her intently as though seeing her—her fears and vulnerabilities—for the first time. She felt exposed and rose suddenly from her chair without speaking and rushed away through the dunes then slipped inside her tent, stuffing her head into her pillow to muffle her weeping.

Later that afternoon, while lying inside her tent staring at the canvas above, Eloise questioned if she should tell Jonah of her concerns about the slaves. Thus far she had chosen not to say anything to him—for good reason. She was not convinced first of all that her concerns were warranted. Secondly she was not sure that Jonah would react appropriately. For months now he had been acting strangely. Before coming to the island Jonah continued to work as usual from dawn to dusk, determined to prove he could manage his empire without his father. And productivity was increasing and he happily claimed credit but her father was encouraging the slaves to continue to work hard so their master would not have any reason to deny them their religion. Not participating in the rebirth across the plantation, Jonah was seemingly irrelevant now for although he thought he was in control, her father actually was wielding more influence over the slaves, so Jonah seemed like an expired ruler still wanting to sit on his throne long after the revolution had usurped him.

He seemed untethered but lost like some oxen suddenly broken free of its yoke only to discover that it did not know how to roam free anymore. He continued to sneak out into the woods without any warning and stay for several days, probably living in caves, hunting game and gathering crab apples and muscadines and huckleberries. Of much more concern were the rumors she heard from her father who had in turn heard them from some slaves, that Jonah was frequently observed around the slave quarters at night and early in the morning, not doing anything but spying on the slaves sometimes while they were in coitus. Reportedly he had once barged into one of their dances, drunk, flailing around with the others until the music and the dancing stopped cold and Jonah rushed off into the forest as though suddenly aware of himself.

When coming to the island, Eloise reconsidered the possibility that they could revive their marriage but after that first night when they slept in the dunes together, she forfeited all hopes. She had envisioned picnics in the dunes with him while reading to him from the Bible while he devoted time to his children. Instead all that energy and obsession that once went toward work at Whiteoak was turned toward hunting and fishing.

After inviting him one night to stay on the island the next day to spend time with his family, Jonah said restlessly, "I got to hunt."

The moon was not yet risen so darkness surrounded them, accentuated by the gentle swashing of the unseen gulf.

"But this trip was supposed to be for our family. And this island—it's so beautiful, so majestic."

"We still have time for that. But I must hunt."

"But why? We have plenty to eat."

Eloise remembered how Jonah returned in the afternoons, blood stained and foul smelling, his boat loaded with the bloodied and discolored carcasses of once beautiful fish and birds: seagulls, herons, ducks, crabs, raccoons and even porpoises—those gorgeous, friendly creatures who played in the wake behind the steamship. After rowing for him all day the slaves looked beyond exhausted, rising from the boat so stiff that moving was painful and sometimes when Jonah was walking away from them not even thanking them for their labors, they looked at him—in a way that she rarely, if ever, saw back at Whiteoak—with hatred. Not interested in his kill, the slaves usually just rowed the boat offshore and dumped the carcasses back into the gulf.

Jonah was gazing into the darkness, not responding so Eloise asked again, "But why must you hunt when we have plenty to eat?"

"Because something's out there," he said turning toward her, his face changing in the glow of the lantern.

Except for his bursts of temper, Jonah was almost always rational although blinded by the limitations of his thinking. But the way his face looked now, she knew he was speaking from another more frightened, more imaginative part of himself.

"Something's out there," he repeated.

"What do you mean?"

"That's looking for me, and I for it."

"But what is it?"

"Something," said Jonah, looking into the darkness beyond her, "that I must kill."

"You're frightening me."

"Don't worry," he said, although she was not sure he even heard her, "I will kill it." He rose from the table and headed toward the beach, fading away into the darkness, saying, "I will kill it. Before it kills me."

Eloise felt she entered into the mind of Jonah and sensed that out there, in that expanse of tangled roots clustered with barnacles, of vicious reptiles, ethereal birds, dead Indians and fish shimmering in all the colors of the rainbow, in all that nothingness of deep and turbulent water that shifted with the pull of the moon and the endless nudging and swirl of wind—that something out there was coming for them.

No, she could not trust Jonah, Eloise concluded while rolling onto her side and embracing her pillow to her chest. He might possibly see the slave's behavior as something deviant resulting from the introduction of Christianity onto Whiteoak. He might exploit her fears as an excuse to abolish the practice of any religion, including Christianity, while they were on the island. He might even react cruelly toward the slaves and punish them which aside from breaking her heart, might cause the slaves to react rashly in this lawless wilderness. No, she concluded, rising from her cot while feeling more confident with her own powers, the slaves were in fact striving for the divine and Jonah knew nothing about that so she would keep her concerns secret for now.

Later that night after the failure at her church, Eloise was waiting on the northernmost beach where nobody ever came because the shore was covered with rocks, coral and seaweed, when she saw Nomaw coming toward her, drawn in the by the lantern. Nomaw sat down awkwardly across from her on the ground amidst a smooth, rockless splotch of sand. Her breathing was shallow and quick and she smelled unpleasantly. She raised her head; blanched by the lantern, her face jutted outward from her shoulders looking stomped upon, flat, close to dissolving into one dark and formless puddle except for the strain that seemed to hold her features intact. She wants to be white, thought Eloise sadly, rejects herself for her blackness. Eloise felt all the more guilty for asking Nomaw to do what slaves considered forbidden: expose the secretive, inner world of their communities. But she consoled herself with the thought that Christ knew neither color.

Nomaw never spoke unless first addressed by Eloise but now she blurted, "I'm wearied with toting this burden by myself. But I'm afeared yawl might punish them for things I say."

"I promise that won't happen," said Eloise.

"Is you gonna tell Massa?"

"Not yet."

"Are you going to tell any of the other slaves that I spoke to you?"

"Of course not. I will not betray you."

"But you already have."

"How so?"

"You cast me down to live and eat with all them darkuns from the fields as soon as we left Whiteoak. I worked hard my whole life to elevate myself but you done got me using the ocean for my outhouse while Shobuck is laughing at me. You think that makes me trust you?"

"I'm sorry," said Eloise. "I thought you would never feel insulted to live amongst your own kind."

"They aint my kind."

"I see. After we leave the island, I promise that I will never put you in that position again."

"All right" said Nomaw. "At least I might be doing them some good—keeping them from getting too lost into their heathenism.

"I been trying hard to school them on the Bible. But Jake for one don't take well to Jesus. He liked Whiteoak better before Jesus arrived to steal his hooch, women and song. Now he gots to worry about hell."

"What about Shaka?" asked Eloise.

"Most of the time he don't say much. But I know he done hexed them, cast spells on them."

"What kind of spells?"

"Ones that make them think they is birds."

"Birds? What do you mean, birds?"

"I mean they believe they is birds—at least some of the time. For long they gonna start dropping shit from the sky. They all acting now like he's their...what's the word, Missus?"

"Their prophet," said Eloise.

"Yessum."

"And Pear—what does she believe?"

"She was raised on another plantation where she was allowed to learn about the Gospel. And her whole life she prayed for her to never get sold from her family. But when they put her on the block, she turned against Jesus and now she's open to the conjuring of Shaka. Besides, they got some kind of fever between them. I scolded her about Shaka but she caint hear me cause of the thumping of her heart. And for long he gonna pluck her blossom and she'll be gone forever.

"And you oughten to know too," continued Nomaw, "that Shobuck is bitter cause yawl done cast him in the fields while he was thinking he was bound for other work. And Shaka is fathering that boy now, whispering things to him—what, I don't know—while slapping him around sometimes to keep his anger under control."

"What do yawl talk about around the campfire at night?"

"Shaka gets everybody to talk about their childhoods before they was toted off into them fields."

"Are they worshipping something, Nomaw—something other than Jesus?"

"I don't know—maybe the devil. I heard some rumor that, even after your father came to Whiteoak, Shaka was holding his own secret midnight services out in the hollow. He had some apos... pos...how do you say that word?"

"Apostles," said Eloise.

"Yessum—his apostles—some of the craziest, most ignorant field hands around—coming to join him."

"Was anybody now on the island attending those meetings?"

"Naw, Jake won't go unless they is serving whiskey."

"But what were they worshipping out there?"

"What I heard once was that they believed that when Jesus was hung on the cross, with his arms stretched, he was a bird soaring into heaven."

"So they think Jesus is a bird?"

"I don't know. But just the other night Jake did ask Shaka if he was worshipping anything.

"When Shaka said he was, Jake wanted to know his name. Was it Jesus, Ezekiel, Moses or Mr. Duck?

"But Shaka just said they gonna know his name soon enough."

"Soon enough," said Eloise. "What did he mean by that?"

"I don't know. But as soon as hearing that, I started to worry something awful about all them. Before they was just acting strange but I figured we all soon be back at Whiteoak, toiling away, your father scaring the conjuring from their soul. But I started to worry when Shaka went on to say that soon someone was coming."

"Who?" asked Eloise.

"Shaka never said. Just said 'He' and once 'My father.' But he said they best be prepared."

"Prepared for what?"

"He didn't say. When Jake asked him if this someone was bringing the whiskey, Shaka just said they aint gonna need whiskey no more."

"Who do you think is coming, Nomaw?" asked Eloise.

"I don't think nobody is coming. But if someone does come, them niggers is going to ruckus like you aint never seen before."

"What do you mean?"

"I don't know what I mean. I just sense it."

They sat in silence, Nomaw again staring at the ground, Eloise listening for any sounds but hearing only the wind and waves. They were captured inside the light of the lantern, isolated from the depthless, churning mystery around them—like some firefly roaming around through the dark lost and without any destination, its lamp turning on then off while casting its dim and lonely glow only onto one tiny, infinitesimal part of the universe that it could comprehend.

"Shaka scares me," offered Nomaw. "But he don't mean any harm. They just aint scared and hungry like they was back home, so their minds is just roaming around looking for hope."

"I sense the same thing," confirmed Eloise.

"Don't hurt them. Guide them," said Nomaw, rising on her thick, trunklike legs before she was even dismissed.

"I will," said Eloise, rising next to her. "With your help this night, we can now turn our attention to saving them from whatever madness is overcoming them."

Later that night Eloise lay in her cot in her tent. Across from her Jonah was on the verge of sleep.

"Have you ever heard of slaves worshipping animals—rabbits, coyotes, birds—that sort of thing," she asked.

"Happens all the time," he said. "Comes from Africa. While ago this one Negress claimed she was raised by lions back in Africa. Everybody was afraid of her—thought she could cast spells on them. So we started to use her to our advantage to scare some slaves into submission. We gave her some chickens for her services and she was much obliged."

"Oh," said Eloise, noticing that Jonah was not at all curious about her question. She soon heard him snoring, slow and lumbering as though trying to purge something from himself. Considering his answer, though, she pondered the possibility that she and Nomaw were over-reacting due to their ignorance about field slaves. Maybe all of this was just make-believe, games of the imagination.

When on the verge of sleep later, she looked around at the tent: bubblelike, made from delicate, easily-severed material that fluttered and shifted with the breeze. What were the slaves doing now down on the beach around their fire, she wondered? Was Shaka casting spells on them? Pulling them back into the wild, primitive heart of Africa, transforming them into heathens while talking in low, muffled tones about revolt? Exhuming the memory of Nat Turner? She imagined them skulking around outside the tent, adorned with feathers and stained with blood, brandishing knives and spears fashioned from tree limbs and conch shells while slicing through the thin, gauzelike fabric of the tent, Jake sputtering all sorts of blasphemies and obscenities about Jesus while coming to sacrifice her to the forces gone rampant in his mind.

I cannot succumb to fear, she thought. She had after all been afraid of slaves in one form or another throughout her life. Even now on the island she was reticent about acting, having attempted only one service thus far that resulted in her running away flustered when Jake challenged her. But sensing that the slaves were searching for something not threatening but divine, she resolved that for the future she would not act fearfully but bravely and even talk to Shaka directly herself.

CHAPTER SEVEN

The next morning Eloise awoke hearing Nomaw shouting in the distance, "Get hold of yourself, Jake."

Inside the tent was hot. The sheets, damp with her sweat, clung to her skin. Startled by those words, Eloise strained to hear more: for once the wind and water were motionless, allowing her to hear the wordless and rhythmic chanting in the distance and again Nomaw shouting angrily, "I said get hold of yourself."

Eloise looked toward Jonah's cot, seeing the sheets disheveled, knowing that he and James, their oldest, were gone fishing for the day. Rushing outside the tent she looked toward the sandbar jutting bonelike into the gulf where the slaves were walking around in a circle chanting while Nomaw was standing outside of them. Between them in the middle of the circle was a captive heron—one of those tall, spindly birds, bluish-gray. While screeching the bird was poking its sharp, daggerlike beak toward the slaves and leaping upward only to get pulled earthward by the tether strapped about its leg.

In the distance, way out over the greenish-gray, mist-shrouded gulf, she saw one storm cloud—one huge and gray mass causing the winds to lightly shift about as though wandering around looking for something.

Josh wandered over to Eloise, rubbing his eyes, pointing toward the slaves. "What are they doing?"

"Nothing," Eloise said. "Just walking."

"Where's Father?"

"Off fishing, as usual."

Eloise dropped down next to him, held him in her arms. "We'll be all right, don't worry."

"May I play with them?"

"No, stay here with me."

The slaves continued to walk around in that circle and Nomaw sat down on the sandbar, wearied. Eloise waved her over but she did not come, just sat there nodding her head.

Gathering some courage Eloise turned to Josh. "You must stay here by the tents. Do not get anywhere near the slaves."

As Eloise walked toward the sandbar, Nomaw met her not far from the slaves and stood there sweating in that searing and sodden heat, fidgeting and shuffling her feet. Something already felt strange to Eloise about her presence—like their relationship was suddenly transformed after all these years—lacking any sense of subservience.

Trying to appear as unruffled as possible, Eloise said, "Lo and behold, Nomaw, what's wrong with them?"

Nomaw fidgeted.

"What's wrong?"

Nomaw stared into Eloise's eyes for the first time since they ever met, not maliciously but only suspiciously as though trying to understand something until Eloise diverted her eyes.

"There aint much wrong except what you see," said Nomaw.

"And much is wrong about that?"

"Yessum."

"Where'd they get that bird?"

"Shaka caught it this morning."

"Caught it?"

"Yessum. He been out there nearly every morning lying below the sandbar without moving, only half his face out the water so he can breathe. When that bird come along Shaka jumped out of the water and caught the beast by its leg, wrapped his arms around its body so it caint fly away or cut him with his beak. Then he tied it down."

"Them other comes down and forms this line and like they in communion while Shaka gives them some minnows to eat raw off the bone. Then they started walking around the bird in this here circle like some crazy Africans straight off the boat. They is hexed out their minds, Missus. They don't know who they is, where they is, or nothing at all. Watch this."

Walking toward the slaves Nomaw grabbed Jake by his arm and yanked him out of the circle. Jake momentarily lost his balance, stumbled toward Nomaw and stood there long enough for Eloise to see the vacuous but not unpleasant look on his face.

Nomaw reared back and slapped him hard across his cheek, saying, "Get on out, you devil. Get on out."

Jake did nothing except for shooing her away with his hands but not violently, then walked back into the circle and resumed his course.

Nomaw walked back to Eloise. "See," she said. "They is gone."

"Surely you can do something," Eloise said.

"I tried just about everything including praying but Jesus aint much help right now. They aint never listened to me no how." Then she just started walking away before she was dismissed while saying, "But Missus, you might do something. You might break the conjuring."

"Come back here, Nomaw," Eloise said but she ignored her, moseyed over and sat on one of the dunes by herself, just seeming to not care anymore.

Eloise was left by herself outside that circle, feeling uncertain. But remembering her resolution to help the slaves from the night before, she walked anxiously closer to the circle as their pacing and chanting intensified, the looks on their faces wilder and more menacing. She felt she was outside some dome of glass encasing them and, although unable to touch them, she felt that inside was some alien, incomprehensible reality separate from everything she ever knew. But to her surprise she was not afraid.

"Stop it," she said.

But they continued to twirl even more intensely.

"Please, stop." But they did not obey, nor even seem to hear her.

Eloise was suddenly infuriated, shouting, "Yawl stop this now."

But when they ignored her this time, she jumped into the middle of the circle next to the bird and started shouting—she was not even really aware of what she was saying—something about hell and damnation and Jonah whipping them when he returned to the island. But nothing changed except they were moving even faster, running so fast that she found herself trapped inside their circle unable to escape, dizzy with the motion.

After raising his arms Shaka screeched—some horrible, wild, inhuman sound. He tilted his arms from side to side, up and down, his body now seeming light enough for him to levitate above the ground.

The others began to move similarly to Shaka but with variations. Jake lifted his knees high off the ground, roosterlike, jerking his head around and clucking. Shobuck looked confused, trying this and that as though searching for his identity. But Pear soared close behind Shaka with that same light and graceful motion.

Although afraid Eloise felt, in some strange, unknown place in her soul, mesmerized by the beauty of their dance—and felt that something in her own soul was moving with them.

She started to back away from them closer into the middle of the circle but felt this sharp, prodding pain in her back and turning around, saw the bird, almost as tall as she was, thrusting its beak at her. She ran forward and collided with Shobuck and both of them were knocked to the ground.

On her hands and knees while looking down upon him, she asked, "What are you doing?"

Shobuck looked startled, not even seeming to recognize her. "What we doing?"

"Yes."

"Flying."

"But why?"

"Cause we's free."

"Free?"

"Free like the birds."

Rolling away from her Shobuck jumped to his feet. The impact of their collision apparently caused the slaves to break their circle because now they were running up and down the sandbar, each weaving his own pattern.

Coming in her direction was Pear soaring gently and gracefully down the length of the sandbar not far from the edge of the water. Josh was chasing her from behind while zigzagging back and forth with his arms supended like wings, laughing hysterically, jumping periodically from the sandbar as though trying to take flight.

"Oh my God," screamed Eloise and suddenly she was running to catch him.

When her heart started pumping powerfully in her chest, something inside of her packed tight and inscrutable burst and she felt suddenly that she was flying, free and blissful, mesmerized by all around her. The sky and sand and water became more vibrant and alive—but seemed to consist of the same transparent and ethereal substance. Overhead birds were soaring through the still and gray firmament but their wings, catching rays from sunrise, were glowing like sparks of fire. Everyone and everything now seemed unbound and liberated from the pull of the earth, hovering in some glorious and expansive heaven. Her son was still ahead of her except now he looked more beautiful than ever before. The strange and beautiful thought crossed her mind that this is the way Jesus felt when he walked on water.

Then some large, black, earthly mass slammed into her, pinning her to the ground, saying, "Missus, Missus."

She was looking at Nomaw, her flat face staring at her, both breathing heavily. She didn't know where she was, who she was or why she was on the ground. "What happened?"

"You was conjured like the rest of them. Shaka done got you—and it can happen to anybody lessen you know some tricks."

"Where's Josh?"

"There he is," said Nomaw.

Josh ran past them and they jumped to their feet, chasing after him. When Nomaw lurched forward to heave herself at him, Josh swerved and slid through her clutches while laughing hysterically—and continued onward. After Nomaw again heaved herself at him, Eloise managed to snag one of his arms and running as fast as she could, swooped him off the ground into her arms and ran away from the sandbar into the dunes.

Once getting back to their tent, Eloise called back to Nomaw and when she came up the dunes, handed Josh over to her, saying to hold on to him. Eloise went into the tent, wrapped Jonah's jacket around her shoulders then searched around in one of his trunks until finding one of his rifles. Utterly determined, she walked out of the tent and stood atop the dunes above the sandbar and aiming the rifle over their heads, fired as the shot almost knocked her backward.

Everyone stopped instantly—just seeming dazed like they did not even know their whereabouts, some even collapsing onto the ground while staring around listlessly.

They all eventually gazed at her, still not entirely comprehending until the gravity of their actions seemed to settle upon them—and they all looked away sheepishly.

Eloise went back to the tent, checked on Josh and Nomaw and after reloading the rifle, sat down outside her tent waiting for Jonah to return. Much to her distress Jake soon walked toward her. Alert for trickery she cautiously hid the rifle under the quilt she retrieved from her tent while sliding her fingers around the trigger. Jake stopped in front of the tent at a respectful distance, his eyes avoiding hers.

"Missus?"

"Yes."

"This here Negro's offering his services."

"Services...for what?"

"I's aching to help with something. With all that ruckusing earlier—you know niggers aint meant for such—I was feeling strange, untied so to speak. Looking for toil to bind all my bones back into place."

"I can't think of anything. So run along."

"Yessum."

For hours the slaves just lay on that sandbar, their bodies caked with sand, their flesh pale and ghostlike until the tide started to rise. Shaka then untethered the heron which lazily and slowly flew away. The other slaves then rose and waded into the water, the sand washing away from their bodies as though they were enacting an ablutions. Then all returned to normal as though their dancing was just some cloud of hysteria momentarily passing over the island. Nomaw and Pear walked toward the kitchen to assume their chores while Shobuck went into their tent.

Later in the afternoon she saw Jonah's rowboat approaching the island with James, her older son, sitting in the bow. Filtering through thin, mottled clouds, the heat of the sun pressed down against the gulf which unable to muster any strength, lay flat and still as though too tired to move. Once reaching the beach Jonah and James were greeted by Jake and Shobuck who helped them haul the boat farther onto shore. While James then wandered away in another direction, Jonah walked toward the center of the island and settled into his chair under the tree.

Eloise called with a weak and wavering voice, "Josh."

"Yes, Mother."

"You may go your way now."

After Josh bolted Eloise relaxed and eased her clutches from the heavy, sun-warmed rifle. She was now terrified that the slaves were succumbing fully to the control of foreign idols or false gods—or at least some mysterious and demented part of their own imagination. She was afraid for them but for her family most of all. She hated the notion but was forced to admit that the slaves did not fear her and therefore she could not control them, so she was dependent upon her husband to reinstate order on the island before something awful happened.

She walked into her tent, leaned the rifle against her cot then sat on the stool before her dresser looking into her mirror. Her face looked exhausted. Her hair was the color of sea oats but tangled and clumped and dirt-stained like roots yanked from the earth. Her eyes were blue, pale and liquid. Weak, she thought. She unbuttoned the jacket she wore—the one she borrowed from Jonah amidst her panic—and allowed the lapels to fall to her elbows. Underneath was her nightgown which, saturated with sweat, clung to her skin around the heave of her bosom. Her odor was pungent—the reek of fear. From the basin on her dresser, she grabbed her sponge and squeezed as water, blood-warm and oily-feeling, seeped into her hair and down her neck then between her breasts, causing her flesh, once numb, to come alive. And she wept.

She could not seem confused or hysterical when talking to Jonah, she knew, for that would only allow him to dismiss her and try to prove that her fear was unfounded. And she could not either question his authority or competence for he was not able to confront even the possibility of his flaws. She also needed to be calm and objective—just explain the facts and try to encourage him to take action to neutralize the threat from the slaves without hurting them either. Appeal to his instincts—and she believed he had them—to protect his family.

She walked from the tent into the light. Filtering down through the haze, the sun above, lackluster and cloying, heated the threads of her jacket until the collar chafed around her flesh. Flaccid waves, tinted with froth, sloshed into shore. She grabbed another chair from the kitchen, walked into the shade of the tree and sat down next to Jonah who was already asleep while sitting upright in a chair leaned back against the tree, exhausted from rowing and fishing all day. His face was dark from the sun, various levels of skin were exposed on the tip of his nose, salt caked about the sides of his eyes and mouth, making him look like some creature from the sea stranded on shore while desiccating in the sun. She again pulled the jacket back from her shoulders to cool off then reached into his lap and caressed his calloused hands which shimmered with fish scales.

"Wake up, Jonah."

Opening his eyes Jonah looked startled, stared at nothing then looked at her breasts. He coughed, clearing phlegm from his throat. "Yes?"

After she told him that she needed to talk to him, he leaned his chair onto the ground, hunched forward and asked, "About what?"

"The slaves are acting strange and I'm worried now for the safety of our children."

"What happened?" said Jonah forcefully, looking over at the slaves cleaning his boat on the beach below, anger flashing in his face.

"All this started perhaps months or years ago but culminated this morning."

"What did?"

"I know this sounds strange but I think the slaves are worshipping birds."

"Worshipping birds?"

"Yes," said Eloise. "Birds."

Eloise then told Jonah the whole story about the slaves and the birds, starting with her experience of encountering Shaka in the forest then all the way through the events on the island which culminated that morning. She told her story so calmly and lucidly that she felt she was entirely convincing but when finishing the last of her words, Jonah responded in a way which she was not expecting.

"You've nothing to fear. Most of these slaves, including Shaka and Jake, were chosen for this trip for their fealty. They're harmless. You still seem to operate on this misguided notion, gotten from your father or the abolitionists, that slaves are the children of God, equal with ourselves with the same desires for freedom and autonomy. For that reason you assume that we oppress and torture them and they harbor secret resentments and rages. But all that is nonsense. These slaves are content with our management, dependent upon our guidance. As such they're as endeared to you as you should be to them. Yet you want me to believe that they're dangerous?"

"Yes, possibly," said Eloise.

"My rule is not based upon tyranny and fear. The weak want to be managed by the strong—thus the relationship isn't conflictive but harmonious and in some cases based on mutual affection. And you know that."

"But..."

"Quit torturing yourself with your thoughts."

"But you acknowledge," said Eloise, "that to control your slaves, you must use force. So you must sense the rage smoldering in their souls. You must suspect that slavery is cruel and against the wishes of God. And you must suspect that by removing their supervision, you're unleashing something that might prove dangerous."

"They're angry only occasionally—same as our children. Most of the time they're thankful, especially now, given this respite from the endless toil and hopeless deaths of their lives to rest on this island."

"Endless toil that—"

"Hush, Eloise," said Jonah gently. "You forget that most churches, except that house of derelicts lorded over by your father, judges the institution of slavery not only acceptable but morally necessary to guide the souls of Negroes toward Christ. So concentrate on that."

"I will," said Eloise at last, "and I am. But please grant me this, that you will watch the slaves carefully and take at least some action."

"But why, Eloise? To soothe your irrational, fabricated fears?"

"But Nomaw also sees what is happening."

"But she's as isolated from the field hands as you are—even more so almost. She knows nothing of them. You're just being hysterical—too much heat, your mind is not occupied. You're like all women. You alter reality to conform to the whims of your emotions."

Anger flared inside her, her shoulders pinching tight. But to keep from reacting she paused and breathed. She glanced across the island at the slaves, at Jake and Shobuck now bathing in the gulf after having washed down the boat, at Nomaw and Pear tending to their chores in the kitchen. They were all acting as normal as ever.

Who are these people, she wondered? She was around them for much of her life but still they remained elusive and strange.

"But you're the one altering reality, not me, Jonah," she retorted, her voice sharp but not angry. "Everyone around you, most of all your slaves, are afraid of you. So their behavior and comments are designed to avoid your wrath and punishment so they kowtow to you with 'Yessas' and 'Nossas,' all the while hiding other parts of themselves from you—the dangerous, subversive parts. In the end all you hear from others are confirmations of your viewpoint, driving you from the truth, enmeshing you into your illusions. Making you blind. People who are feared are ignorant. Consider that at Whiteoak my father conducted a crusade to convert your slaves to Christianity without your knowledge—at least for some time. And the same is happening here, except Jesus isn't at the reins.

"Out here, where the Negroes are removed from all that made them slaves—fear, hunger, oppression, the constant regulation of their lives. Out here, where all the checks and balances of our society—government, religion, law, even your own sanity—are gone. Out here, Jonah, you see only what you choose to see that confirms your interpretations of reality, leaving you as the capricious tyrant of your own ethereal but disturbed utopia. And slowly under your blind rule, these slaves are all bounding toward madness, changing into something that could prove threatening to our family and yet you do nothing.

He glanced from her. A momentary, disturbed look of knowing plagued his face, perhaps revealing that on some level, however removed from his awareness, he too feared his slaves, sensed some troubled, intractable aspect in their souls, understood that her story contained some credence.

"Are you finished?" asked Jonah sadly, not looking upward.

"Soon they'll come into conflict with you. And they won't listen to you or me but only to Shaka."

"Shaka," he said, glancing at her. "This great, subversive, albeit paranoid cabal is being administered by that idiot Shaka who's as docile and brainless as a bovine?"

"Another example of your blindness. He's not brainless. He only wants you to think he is."

"I've known him since we were children."

"But not after."

"How do you know all this, Eloise," asked Jonah, agitated, "while keeping your mind buried in books? Do they teach you about governing darkies in the Bible?"

Stumped by his question she stepped back, her courage waning. "Because...because...," she stammered before becoming silent.

Why did she seem to understand these slaves so well, she wondered? Her experiences with her father helped some. But she was forced to admit that she also identified with the Negroes—with their frustration and secretiveness—because all of them were oppressed by the same man, her husband. And through their dancing they were beckoning her into her own freedom. Christ in heaven, she thought, offended by the notion, maybe I am insane.

"I don't know," she said at last.

"You don't know?"

Her soul felt as unmoored and fleeting as the island itself, her interpretaion of events like dreams as insubstantial and protean as the clouds passing overhead.

"Won't you please help me protect our family?"

Jonah suddenly changed and emerged from his confusion and frustration, seeming smug in knowing that she was reduced into confusion and doubt. "For your sake," he said patronizingly, "I shall provide them with that guidance. To alleviate your fears and to prevent you from ruining our vacation."

Jonah waved and whistled toward the slaves out bathing in the gulf, shouting, "All yawl over here now."

They looked toward him curiously. Nomaw soon roused them toward the beach and they trudged toward the tree, strangely buoyant and excited. Upon arrival they glistened with water and their clothes clung about their flesh, smelling of seaweed and salt. While Jonah stood from his chair, she saw that Shobuck was glancing at her furtively, his eyes mischievous.

"We here," said Jake.

Whether by calculation or not, Jonah was silent. The slaves seemed nervous; their feet twitched in the sand. Now and then she noticed one of the them quickly and almost imperceptibly glancing at her and she felt that she was somehow part of their conspiracy and that through these glances, they were questioning whether she had betrayed them.

Jake seemed disturbed by the silence so he asked, "What you wanting, Massa?"

"We came to this island to live in peace," said Jonah, sternly, factually.

Jake yawned. "Sho we know all that."

Some of the other slaves nodded their heads with nervous but desultory and somnolent confirmations.

"But yawl's dancing is upsetting that peace."

"That hoedown aint nothing," said Jake. "We just dancing about the place so excited that we done gone deaf. We's sorry about that, Missus."

"But the Missus and Josh was with us too," interjected Shobuck.

Eloise flustered with shame.

"What did you say?" Jonah asked angrily.

"She wasn't with you fools," said Nomaw, "but trying to save yawl from the devil."

"Miss Eloise said that your dancing was out of line," continued Jonah loudly, "and even worse, yawl did not obey her orders."

"We was deaf," said Jake.

"I don't care," said Jonah. "You go deaf again and you will pay. And if any of you are caught worshipping birds again, then you will face the whip. Fifty lashes."

Eloise just realized that she had unwittingly unleashed the potential for cruelty on the island and without forethought she walked from the gathering and toward her tent while hearing Jonah in the background issuing commands to the slaves while some tinge of anger entered his voice, obviously in reaction to her uncanny and fey departure of the scene. She was so confused, so exhausted with the futility of her efforts, and so disturbed by her own feelings, that she could not maintain, nor even care to maintain, the semblance of something normal. She only wanted to disappear into the tent and pretend that none of this had happened and fall into sleep.

CHAPTER EIGHT

In his dream Jonah lay with her. They were on their sides, his chest pressed against her slender back, their legs entwined, one of his arms reaching over her shoulder and cradling her breasts. He was in some place devoid of history and suspended from time, sheltered from the judgments of men. In the vague and unrevealing light, their flesh was colorless, neither white nor black. She was the nameless distillation of all women. After sliding under the cleft in her buttocks and undulating with her, he imagined he was about to impregnate her womb with some child who would be born into another world more gentle and loving. But before the act was culminated, he was abruptly and violently pulled from her.

He awakened, gasping. Whatever sundered him from the woman was still present, out there beyond the waves, malignant, stalking him.

He lay on his cot hoping to sleep to make the feeling vanish. The waves lolled into the shore, their noises amplified amidst the silence, echoing from the walls of darkness.

He knew he must go forth.

Peeling the sheets from his body, he groped around for his clothes, dressed, went to the bureau and scribbled this note to his wife.

"Fishing. Took Shaka and James. Will return after noon."

Walking toward the door he saw Eloise asleep on her cot, swaddled in pale, skinlike sheets, seeming mummified and even beatific and he wondered if she existed in that same lascivious, sheltered place which both of them could not inhabit when awake.

Outside the sky was streaked with thin, translucent clouds where in places moonlight filtered down to the earth, casting some faint, almost indiscernible glow across the white, domelike dunes. The air was still, not hot or cold. After Jonah lighted the lantern sitting outside their tent, a yellowish, wavering bubble of light emanated outward into the darkness. He walked to the slaves' tent and seeing the flap open, stepped inside while seeing their bodies spread across the floor, all indiscernible to him, wrapped in their covers like mysterious and unborn mammals still coated in membranes.

"Awake, Shaka," he said.

Shaka raised his head and looked toward the source of the light. Seeing Jonah, his face illuminated like some celestial but malignant orb. "Yessa."

"Going hunting," Jonah said.

"Reckon we is."

"Listen carefully to my instructions," said Jonah. "Fetch me a bucket, boy, and fill it from the sump over yonder, west of the kitchen. I want lots of fish heads, tails, guts, any kind of wretched, stinking flesh you can find. Now hurry on."

"Yessa."

Shaka rose from his mat and dressed. Penetrating through the canvas the light from the lantern was fading until darkness once again enveloped the tent, but Shaka could still detect the identities of the bodies sprawled across the floor. Jake was sleeping next to Pear, his body curled inward, his legs tucked into his stomach, one of his arms touching her shoulders as though he was groping for comfort in the anonymity of sleep. Shaka buttoned his shirt all the way to the top and walked outside the tent.

Feeling his way through the dark, he moseyed over to the kitchen and after fetching one of the buckets, walked over to the sump where he filled the bucket using the shovel next to the hole. He then walked toward the light of the lantern, toting the bucket. But he stopped at the crest of the dune and hesitated, seeing Jonah down on the beach.

Two evenings earlier after Jonah announced that he would whip any slave seen again worshipping birds, Shaka was about to fall asleep in the dunes when he heard Nomaw wandering around, whispering his name, lantern in hand. After he called back at her, she came over to him. Bending close to the ground she said, her voice full of warmth and concern—an almost motherly tone which he had never heard from her before— that Miss Eloise was wanting to see him.

With his knees rising to his chin, Shaka perched on the side of the dunes, trying to formulate his thoughts. With his heart thumping in expectation, he saw Nomaw again emerging from the darkness, her heavy, earthbound body aglow in the lantern. Eloise was behind her. As Eloise came close to him, he looked ahead listlessly to avoid her eyes although he noticed that she wore layers of thin, white clothes as though she needed protection from something, while her golden crucifix dangled from her neck like some kind of harness pulling her gently but onerously downward. She sat across from him also on the steep of the dune. Nomaw sat below holding the lantern which illuminated the inside of the dune like one large, white porcelain bowl.

"Sorry to wake you, Shaka."

Never before had any whitie ever apologized to him about anything, thought Shaka. Ever since she saw him down in the hollow, he felt exposed and defenseless around her and lived with the fear that she would expose him to her husband. She already had to some degree although not enough for him to become alarmed. By apologizing to him now, he felt even more exposed as though she knew, unlike her father and the legions of other whites, that underneath his mask he was something more than he wanted them to know, not just some thoughtless and obedient darky.

"Yessum," he mumbled.

"Before we left, Shaka, my father spoke highly of you."

He thought he heard in her tone of voice something uncommon for whites: reticence and even quaking like her voice was struggling for definition. She feared him, he thought. Breathing deeply and relaxing, Shaka felt powerful: wild, feral and incomprehensible, beyond the grasp of her mind, beyond the scope of her unmoving and invisible God scribbled in the pages of books.

He nodded his head, shrugged.

"He hoped that someday you would preach."

"Maybe," said Shaka, repulsed by the sound of his own voice.

"But I'm concerned too."

Shaka sensed condescension in her voice: something unreal, almost dreamy.

"Concerned that you have become lost in the ways of darkness and are shepherding your sheep into barren and dangerous pastures."

Shaka said nothing.

"All these birds and rituals, they're not Christian. I don't understand. What are you doing?"

Instead of lying as usual, Shaka wanted to tell her the truth. But he hesitated.

"She asked you a question," said Nomaw. "Now answer her."

Shaka ignored Nomaw, knowing that she would never order him around unless Eloise was present. He said finally, "Just following the spirit."

"How do you know that spirit is Christ."

"It just feels that way," he said, turning slightly toward Eloise, still not looking at her but somehow wanting to touch her in some way.

The image came to him of Eloise chasing after her son during their dance, her face losing its collection of itself and dissolving into the elements around her. He realized now that she went into heaven if only for one moment and found the freedom which she too was seeking.

"But your feelings can lead you astray. So God gave us the Bible for direction and instruction."

But now she is trying to deny her truth, thought Shaka.

"I been trying to tell him that," said Nomaw. "Almost them same words."

"Yes," said Eloise, her voice arrogant but lifeless. "You cannot just trust your feelings."

Shaka risked saying nothing.

"Yes," she said, as though trying to convince herself, her voice becoming weak. "We cannot trust our feelings." She looked at him furtively as though wanting his confirmation. "You understand that, don't you?"

"Answer her," blurted Nomaw. "She's trying to help you."

"But I caint read," said Shaka, feeling disgust but not for himself.

"That's right," said Nomaw. "He caint read."

"Yes," said Eloise, "he caint read."

"I told you he wasn't all that bad, Miss Eloise. He just needs some educating."

"Oh yes," said Eloise, "I can help him with that."

Nomaw and Eloise were now laughing anxiously, their bodies still tense but animated. Ignoring Shaka as though he did not matter, they were chatting away about starting Bible studies the next day for all the slaves. They would pray and sing hymns and Eloise would read directly from the Bible so that Shaka—and the other field hands—would know the word of God—their voices escalating into a pitch of whispered excitement and misguided relief.

Shaka smoldered in anger but tempered himself by knowing that they were laughing in ignorance. So he just remained quiet, comfortably fading behind his mask yet again.

When rising to leave, Eloise looked at Shaka directly and said, "You'll be there in the morning?"

"Yessum."

Looking away from him too quickly, Eloise then turned and followed Nomaw up the crest of the dune. At the top she stopped and while the back of her head was lit momentarily from the lantern now vanishing with Nomaw, creating some blurry, unformed, quickly fading nimbus, she turned toward Shaka and whispered loudly down to him, the worry back in her voice.

"He will, you know. I cannot control him. He will whip you. And none of us, not me, not you, not even the angels, can stop him."

Not waiting for his response, she turned and left.

In the morning Shaka arrived for the Bible study at the make-shift church carved into the side of one of the dunes. Only three of them attended on this day: Shaka and Nomaw on one side of the cross with Eloise in the front, Bible in hand—all of them perched somewhat uncomfortably on pieces of driftwood and smooth, sun-whitened coral.

Shaka sat properly on the piece of driftwood, his back straight, both of his hands resting uniformly on his knees. As instructed he sang and prayed and memorized verses from the Bible, amazing the others with the precision of his memory while they praised him as though he were some pony learning tricks. But he never expressed any enthusiasm or appreciation and he noticed that his impassivity was draining and even confounding both of them. Once their excitement passed away, they seemed to understand that his demeanor was a form of protest.

The next day Pear attended along with Shaka. But simultaneously she seemed to try to please both Shaka and her mistress. But in the end she expressed mostly worry and confusion.

The day after, Jake moseyed over soon after they said their opening prayer, look of consternation on his face. "Miss Eloise, why you done given me up for hell while delivering all these other niggers. Aint I done gnashed my teeth enough? And wailed? And begged? Aint I got some chance, some tiny, gnat-sized chance, to get into heaven?"

Eloise invited Jake to join them on the condition that he not interrupt her unless he raised his hand first. But Jake immediately began to raise his hand after everything she said, this sly but confused grin on his face but she ignored him. And when they moved into the praying and singing, Jake expressed such loud, if not obnoxious, enthusiasm that Eloise was not able to control the mood and tempo of the service. Becoming increasingly nervous and confused by the reaction of the slaves, she finished early.

During this time Shaka tried not to draw any attention to himself and waited patiently for this attempt to convert him to pass. But in the evenings while away from the eyes of the whites, he continued to work his magic amongst the others, teaching them stories he heard from his mother about Africa, always goading the slaves onward to see their lives differently. One night without any premeditation, he said, surprised by his own words, that he was not going to church in the morning.

"You aint going?" said Jake.

"No," confirmed Shaka before walking away into the dunes, hearing Jake saying behind him, "I aint neither."

The next day he watched calmly as Eloise and Nomaw arrived for the service and called for the slaves to join them and watched too when nobody came.

For some time Eloise and Nomaw sat patiently with their hands upon their laps, praying as though Jesus might magically make all the slaves appear until Nomaw, losing her patience, stood up and blurted toward Shaka, "Yawl best get you ass over here. Or Miss Eloise—she's gonna...she's gonna do something to you."

But Shaka continued to watch them patiently until both of them started to ignore the others and held their own service, singing and praying and begging that Jesus might forgive the sinners not present that day.

Shaka expected punishment and reprimands to be administered once Jonah returned. But when Jonah did appear later that afternoon, he never seemed to even consult with his wife. Around the fire later that night, Shaka expected him to appear at any moment, rifle and sword at the ready to make them disband. But nothing ever happened and when the skies became cloudy, Shaka soon retired for the night inside the tent with the other slaves. Hours later in the darkness Jonah came for him at last.

Standing at the crest of the dune with bucket of dead, rotting fish in his hands, Shaka looked warily down upon Jonah searching for some clues regarding his intent. While sitting on the bow of one of the boats, Jonah was coiling rope. Scattered across the beach were supplies: jugs of water, baskets of food, paddles and some clothing. Leaning against the thwarts of the rowboat were a rifle and sword which Jonah needed for hunting, Shaka thought, consoling himself. But were they really going hunting? Or was he falling into some kind of trap where Jonah intended to exact some kind of punishment upon him or even kill him or possibly just scare him further into submission for not attending those services?

Shaka was afraid.

Further afraid too because Jonah was acting so rashly and capriciously of late. Like his father before him Jonah was usually consistent and methodical and acted as though his darkies could never disturb nor ruffle him in any way. But when his father died Jonah became unbound and acted strangely toward the slaves, sometimes being rash and cruel and provocative without cause, other times strangely magnanimous. Shaka felt for this reason he could not predict how Jonah would behave anymore.

Shaka thought maybe he was overreacting, that they were merely going fishing as many mornings before. But he remained wary.

He began to stare hypnotically at the lantern down on the beach. The light was an omen. Filtering through the glass encasing the lantern, the flame seemed bleary and astigmatic like the vision of Jonah: incapable of seeing the truth. And Shaka was veiled in the darkness beyond the grasp of the flame.

He walked to the beach carrying the bucket at his side while the lantern turned his flesh yellowish and sickly until he stood before Jonah, assuming the pose he had mastered after years of practice, his face listless, his muscles flaccid. Not seeing him at first, Jonah turned quickly, startled, peering anxiously and randomly into the darkness.

"Goddamnit, boy," Jonah mumbled, disturbed. "Don't be creeping up on me like that."

"Sorry, Massa."

Shaka did nothing at first but soon spoke. "Yessa, reckon I did—spooked you, I mean. Sometimes I surprises folks. But I aint meaning to, Nossa. I reckon that lantern needs some cleaning, that wick some trimming so the light can shine on the darkness."

"Hush, Shaka. Don't have time for your gibberish," said Jonah, continuing to coil his rope. At the end of the rope was a ball made of wood and below that one large, menacing hook—the likes of which Shaka had never seen before.

"Sho," said Shaka, feeling more comfortable now.

But he resumed his pose until Jonah at last turned to him and asked, his voice irritated, "Are you just going to stand there like some mule?"

"Nossa, if you aint wanting me to."

"We going hunting," said Jonah.

"Reckon we is."

"Don't you want to know what we're hunting?"

"Yessa."

But Shaka was silent again, just standing there.

"Well, aint you gonna ask me then?"

"Ask you what, Sir?"

"Goddamn," said Jonah. Then he paused, looked toward the dark, mildly heaving ocean and said, his voice seeming distant and afraid, "Something's out there, something big—and we're gonna kill it."

"I reckoned on that."

Jonah walked toward the tents then returned moments later and Shaka was relieved to see that he was carrying his son James who, swaddled in a quilt with his face somnolent and bewildered, climbed into the bow next to one of the thwarts and dozed again into sleep.

After packing the supplies into the boat, Jonah spoke without looking at him. "Shaka, man the oars. Do as I tell you and quickly."

Jonah stepped over the gunnels and walked carefully to the stern and sat down. After nudging the boat into the water, Shaka also climbed aboard and settled into one of the seats, dislodged the oars from their locks and with one stroke, sent the boat drifting into the gentle and amorphous gulf.

"Onward, toward the mainland."

"Yessa."

But while rowing Shaka could not see the island behind him, nor the mainland ahead of him. Instead of penetrating into the dark, the lantern incarcerated the boat in its circle of light—similar, thought Shaka, to how Jonah encased those around him in his demented vision. The moon was gone and even the stars were cloaked behind the thickness of the atmosphere, enshrouding the boat in darkness from all directions.

Shaka was soon disoriented, not knowing the direction of the mainland or even the island and he stopped rowing, the boat now otiose in the small, ever-rising swells. "I caint see nothing, Massa. We's lost out here."

"Look yonder," said Jonah, pointing to the horizon, "to that smudge of light in the distance. Follow that star to our prey, Shaka."

Looking behind him Shaka did see one star almost orange in color hovering low over the horizon and he headed in that direction as the wake next to the boat curled into a thin, pale lip.

Sensing something out there, Jonah hunched into his seat and stared into the darkness, feeling exhausted already but too disturbed to rest. He had the feeling since coming to the island that something was stalking him. But whenever he wondered what that was, he felt as though his intellect was gazing upon the surface of the water, not able to see what was hidden beneath in some murky and bottomless part of his mind. They were in reality hunting for a shark: He had heard about them for years—how they thrived in the waters around Florida while feeding on blood and rot and occasionally people. But somehow he knew too that he was hunting for something more, something out there that wanted to destroy him—something that he must kill before it killed him.

To keep his mind lucid, he began to outline the dangers of this trip. Amongst the maze of the islands closer to the mainland, they could become lost and adrift for days and drain the last of their water and eventually die from dehydration. Or they could run ashore onto a shoal of oysters and destroy their boat. But really he only feared this thing which he was pursuing.

Surrender, retreating back to the paralysis of his tent, was not acceptable.

Jonah watched Shaka in the middle of the boat continuing to row with his smooth and black skin barely distinguishable from the night around him. Shaka was graced to exist in such ignorance, Jonah thought, to be confronted with danger and yet continue to follow his master blindly and unquestionably like some cow being led to its slaughter. He seemed so dull, so obtuse, so devoid of will. How could his wife fear someone like that? Regardless, he felt compelled to speak to honor his wife, however absurd her needs.

"Listen here, Shaka."

"Yessa."

"The Missus said you didn't show for church yesterday." Jonah snickered, amused by the irony of reprimanding one of his slaves for not attending church.

"When?"

"Yesterday."

"I caint sing, Massa. I caint sing at all."

"What's that got to do with anything?"

"The Reverend said if you caint sing, the Lawd aint gonna respect you."

Jonah thought it was indeed like Eloise to feel threatened by some slave who does not attend church, not from disobedience but from superstition,

"I don't care what the Lord thinks. If the Missus is telling you to come to church, then you go. You understand?"

"Yessa."

Jonah was silent for some while. Suddenly he started thinking about birds which for some reason had been on his mind lately; he recalled the thick flocks of squawking blackbirds like the ones that migrated to Whiteoak to roost in the trees around the fields in such multitudes that with one shot from his rifle he could drop several to the ground and blanket the warm, midday sun in blackness. Strange creatures, he thought, like visitors from another world. He imagined himself in the midst of one those flocks as though surrounded by some fog, the panicked creatures fluttering their wings as they maliciously pecked him on his head and ears and even on his eyes, as though trying to feed on him from some kind of starvation that he caused them. The more he fought, the more they seemed to attack.

"The birds, Shaka," he found himself blurting. "What about those Goddamn birds?"

"What birds?" said Shaka slowly.

"The Missus said yawl was bird crazy, hexed by them, something like that. Worshipping them, drawing pictures of them in the sand, talking to them, dancing around with them—all that kind of nonsense. What the hell's that all about?"

"Nothing much."

"For all I care you could do whatever you want with these birds, even roll around in their shit. But the Missus—you got her all worried."

"We aint meaning any harm."

"Whatever the case I aint wanting to deal with this further. So anymore of these birds, fifty lashes. You know how many that is?"

"Plenty."

"I aint used that whip in some time. But fifty, you hear."

"Yessa."

Jonah shifted his gaze to James who was still asleep, his face appearing peaceful and even cherubic amidst the foreboding. He loved his son, wanted to protect him, to grasp and embrace him, shelter him from the imminent, lurking adulthood that would soon envelop him and make him callous and cruel.

James was too pampered and spoiled by Eloise, making him weak and innocent, too mothered to endure the world manfully. James of course was still young but Jonah could not help but think that he would always be soft and frail. How could he ever expect one of his sons to manage the plantations some day if both remained under the sway of his wife?

Jonah felt righteous for stripping James, however underhandedly, from the clutches of his mother and carrying him into this world of nameless, womanless darkness and forcing him to face and disembowel this thing. James soon stirred from his sleep, pulling the quilt back from his face while looking around, peaceful but bewildered, as though not entirely awake while lingering in some place that was undefined, unborn, not yet revealed.

James looked toward his father, asking, his voice gentle and sweet but afraid, barely rising above the ripple of the wake and the creak of the oars. "Where are we?"

"Somewhere—I don't know."

"Are we lost?"

"Not really."

"Where's Mommy?"

"Where she belongs, safe on the island."

"But...but...," James stammered, his words quaking, fear entering his soul. "What are we doing out here?"

"Stalking."

"Stalking?"

"Yes, son."

"But what are we stalking?"

"I don't know. Something evil."

"Evil?"

"I only know that we must stalk this thing, son, find it, kill it."

"But I don't want to."

"You must."

"But why?" His voice was more imploring than curious.

"Because," said Jonah, though staring not at his son but into the darkness, his voice sounding cataleptic and even alien to himself like some entity possessed his mind. "Because that's our purpose in life. We're all slaves beholden to forces."

"But I'm afraid," said James, stifling his tears.

"You can live with fear," said Jonah. "But not cowardice."

"But..."

"Hush."

James wrapped himself back into his quilt and whimpered softly and shamefully.

Mesmerized by the rhythm of his rowing, Shaka stared over the gunnels where the light from the lantern lay flat and yellow upon the surface of the water like some puddle of urine. What was down there that Jonah wanted to kill? With all that stuff in the boat, they were indeed hunting for something real—something huge, judging from the size of the hook. But what sort of animal? Shaka was struck by this thought which he did not understand, that Jonah was actually stalking him.

I am his prey, thought Shaka.

Jonah suddenly said, "Halt the boat."

In front of them something was rapidly approaching the boat. Shaka paddled backward to slow the boat down while hearing the floor of the bay covered with seaweed brushing against the boat until their movement ceased altogether. They were still. This was strange, thought Shaka, not seeing any land, nor any dirt or rocks—only roots slithering upward from the water in pale, yellowish light, creating some impenetrable and serpentine thicket climbing upward with dark and greenish leaves. The land was repulsive, uninhabitable, smelling of bird shit.

"Row along the mangroves here, heading in that direction," Jonah said, pointing to starboard. "And you, James, watch from the bow. Shout if you see any shoals so Shaka can steer around them. And search for the river that bleeds into the gulf."

"I don't like this place," said James now alert in the bow.

"And you'll like this place less if we sink. So do as I say."

Paddling to starboard Shaka carefully turned the boat parallel to the land and as they moved along the shore, he could see that the roots of the mangroves were stained white with the scat of the birds roosting in their limbs above. While Shaka tried to discern their shadows and shapes in the glow of the lantern, one bird would occassionally get spooked, ruffle its wings and launch into the darkness above as the noise reverberated loud and unsettling in the darkness as though that land was only fit for fleeing.

"Shoal ahead," James said from the bow.

Shaka circumnavigated the shoal which was covered with shells then resumed course. But he felt the current under the boat pushing him seaward and watched as the mangroves receded from the light. They were, Shaka realized, in the mouth of a river. The water was turbulent but silent, forming rifts and eddies, and filled with splotches of froth, seaweed, flotsam and other forms of offal from the land. Occasionally slithers of minnows, reflecting silver and blue in the lantern, leapt from the water and vanished while other creatures, resembling spiders with long, calcified legs, floated under the boat. When commanded by Jonah, Shaka turned into the current and rowed as powerfully as he could. But relative to the current he could not discern whether they were moving at all until seeing the banks of the river enclosing around them, surrounding them in mangroves. After rummaging around in the stern, Jonah jabbed the hook into one of the bleeding and rancid fish while its entrails slithering from its underside.

As the river narrowed and the current became swifter, the boat began to stall. Jonah dropped the bait over the side and as the current tugged on the rope, the leader and the cork followed—all of which the water swallowed apathetically. As though using the rope as his tentacle to explore beyond his vision, Jonah allowed the cork to drift to the fringes of the light. Out there, where sky and water were of the same substance—darkness—the cork vanished.

As Jonah commanded Shaka turned the boat into the current and drifted downstream. Jonah looped the rope around one of the blocks nailed into the stern, placed gloves on his hands and sat poised and ready for the strike. Shaka rowed only enough to keep the rope taut against the stern and to keep the bow headed downstream. All was silent and still except for the rapid and nervous breathing of James crouching low into the bottom of the boat. Jonah occasionally dropped chum from one of the buckets over the gunnels. Once the banks of the river retreated, causing the current to languish, Jonah pulled the rope into the boat. Again Shaka strained into the current, up the mouth of the river where they drifted downstream again.

They repeated this process over and over until everything became monotonous and boring and until James once again swaddled himself into his quilt and fell asleep in the bottom of the boat. In the stern Jonah remained intent upon the rope.

James soon awoke in the bow, looking irritated to find himself in the same place, blathering, "There aint any beasts out here but what's in your head. Aint nothing out here but water and bird shit."

"Watch your tongue, son. Don't speak like that in my presence."

James again pulled his quilt over his head. Once the boat reached the estuary again, Shaka paddled back into the current. The rope then suddenly jerked tight against the block, rising from the water like some snake in midstrike, the noise yawnlike as the hemp stretched under the weight. The boat jolted. As the stern dipped toward the water, Shaka lost his balance and toppled onto the floor, the oars jerking from his hands but he scrambled back onto his bench within moments and retrieved his oars, lifting them from the water.

"Oh God," shouted James. "What's that?"

Jonah was crouched with his back curved, allowing the rope to slide through one of the blocks. The buckets of chum spilled during the strike, miring Jonah in this festering and rancid puddle of entrails and fish heads.

All of the nameless, haunting fear once imprisoned inside his soul, it seemed to Shaka, was at last liberated as Jonah proclaimed over the rope grinding through the blocks and over the smooth, polished flow of the wake, "Come you beast. For you are mine."

The boat was moving faster than the current, pulled it seemed by the unseen and incorporeal hand of God, moving toward revelation. More enthralled than scared, Shaka realized that he was in the presence of something both powerful and awful.

Seaward with the current, they continued to move. Once

stretched tight across the water, the rope gradually began to sink directly into the gulf close to the stern. While continuing to grind through the block, the coils of rope were shrinking until the end was at hand.

James once again implored desperately, "We caint kill this. Cut the rope. Cut it now."

"Shut up, you coward," blurted Jonah.

James soon touched Shaka on his back and crouched toward him, whispering in his ear, his voice veiled from Jonah by the sound of rope grinding through wood. "I know what yawl think."

"What?" said Shaka, surprised.

"I know what yawl think."

"About what?"

"About him you call your master."

"We don't think nothing."

"Yes you do. But you're afraid to say. You think he's crazy."

"Who?"

"Your master."

Was he just talking from fear? wondered Shaka. Was he angry toward his father? Had he penetrated into the world of Negroes? Heard something from his friend Shobuck? Or was he trying to manipulate him? He could not tell.

Shaka knew his words could backfire on him in the future so he parried. "He just behaving like Massas tending to behave. Sho we fear him and we should."

"Coming out here in the middle of the night to kill this thing? He aint supposed to behave that way. He was bitten—that's what Shobuck says— bitten by a coyote back at Whiteoak, right in the ass. He's rabid. And he'll kill us all."

"I aint got nothing to say," said Shaka, turning from him.

"Yes you do," said James, retreating to the bow and sitting on the floor, sullen and afraid. "I know you do."

As the coils of rope continued to shrink, Jonah looped another hitch around the block to increase the drag, slowing the outflow of rope. But since the end was still approaching rapidly, Jonah was forced to stop the outflow altogether by tying the line to one of the cleats. The hook held fast instead of jerking from the maw of the thing. Although the current was now weaker farther from shore, the boat moved faster through the water, outward into the infinity of the ocean.

"The beast is slowing, crippled by my yoke," said Jonah. "See that, James. I'll soon drive my sword into his heart."

James was silent.

Time, though lost in the darkness, continued to pass same as always. But what time was it, Shaka wondered. He knew not when he was awakened: whether before or after midnight, nor how many hours had passed since they boarded the boat or hooked this thing. All his benchmarks for time—the sun and moon, waking and sleeping, the process of his chores—were nonexistent, making time as abstract as the force at the end of their line, as abstract and undelineated as the darkness around them, as though all was merged into one vast, inscrutable eternity.

Jonah remained clutched to the rope as though hanging from some cliff, his gloves tattered, his hands covered with blisters and bleeding, his face stuck in one leatherish, almost calcified squint. Silently almost rhythmically, he mumbled and taunted the beast. After the boat continued to slow then languished, Jonah pulled in the slack to keep the rope taut and soon reversing course, the boat began to move toward the cork, toward the thing. Jonah became more manic while mumbling sounds which Shaka could not decipher but which seemed to cajole the beast in some way. Shaka sat still on his bench with all his senses alert, his heart fluttering in his chest, waiting for this thing to emerge.

"Reveal yourself," Jonah extolled. "Bow in obeisance before your master."

On the outskirts of the glow they espied the cork moving slightly, almost beyond detection like some waning and hesitant portent of doom. A revelation struck Shaka which was sudden and at first incomprehensible: That despite his fear he identified with this beast, with its darkness and power, its invisibility. He hoped this thing would defy Jonah and deprive him of his power. But, worried, Shaka noticed that the cork while nearing the boat became skittish and nervous like some small and helpless animal getting ushered to its slaughter.

Jonah silently fed the rope through the blocks back into the boat, anticipation evident on his face, speaking in hushed but urgent tones. "Load the rifle, son."

"But..."

"Prepare your weapon."

"But..."

"Do it now."

Holding onto the gunnels James moved toward the stern where he retrieved the rifle from its case on the floor. His hands trembling, he poured the powder into the barrel then the ball and finished with the ramrod. He then held the rifle, which seemed enormous and awkward in his hands, before his chest while sitting on the same bench as his father.

"It will come soon and I will kill it," exulted Jonah. "And I shall be free at last."

Ahead the cork was captured in the glow of the lantern yards away from the stern, the rope at times tugging against the boat. The cork then moved straight toward the boat without any forewarning, gaining speed and momentum as though coming to assault them.

"Oh shit," said James.

"Holy Father," shouted Jonah, his voice feverish and panicked. "God help it now."

Time stopped, became eternal. And they just sat gawking at the cork. But before colliding with the boat, the cork disappeared under the water. The rope went slack. Shaka peered over the gunnels and saw to his surprise that the water was clear. Shafts of light from the lantern, refracting outward, probed into the blackness. Suspended across infinity was the visage that shifted through the lens of the water, specterlike, not of the same substance of earth. It was monstrous and black with small, barely perceptible wings.

"Fire," shouted Jonah.

But James seemed paralyzed while peering over the gunnels holding the gun limp in his hands.

"Kill it."

Off the stern the cork surfaced while moving away from the boat.

"Fire your weapon, Goddamnit," Jonah shouted.

James trembled.

Although the cork was too far away to warrant a shot, Jonah continued to shout at his son almost hysterically. "Kill it, boy."

Something deep and woeful was jarred in Shaka. He gazed over at Jonah, the edges of his mouth caked with salt and spit, his cheeks covered with entrails. He resembled Whiteoak in all of his grotesquery. Shaka also felt something for James—something he never felt for whites before, something he could not identify. Compassion? Sympathy? He wanted to protect the boy from his ancestors.

While holding onto the rope with one hand, Jonah slapped his son across his face. James dropped the rifle, lost his balance and fell overboard while clinging onto the gunnels with his body half submerged. The rope that once lay limp in the water then became taut and rose into the air then yanked against the boat; then as nails groaned and unfastened from their thwarts, one of the blocks was yanked off the stern, unraveled from the rope and thumped into the water. Violently the boat jerked downward with the impact, almost tipping the gunnels under the water. Shaka again fell to the floor but once scrambling back to his seat, he grabbed James by the arms and hauled him back into the boat. Oblivious to his son Jonah remained in the stern bracing himself against the back of the boat, hunkered down low as the rope dragged over the gunnels. His gloves torn to tatters, his hands raw and bloody, he moaned painfully. As the pile of rope raced from the stern, specks of blood and entrails flung through the air, splattering his face.

"Get up, you cowards," he shouted. "Take the rope and hold fast."

James scrambled into the bow away from his father, crouching low on the floor but Shaka returned to his seat and grabbed the rope and braced his legs against the thwarts in front of him. Once the rope came tight, Shaka gripped hard at first, the fibers grinding into his hands as the rope slowed. But while continuing to grunt and moan, he began to ease his grip, gradually at first to avoid detection then altogether, so that most of the force from the rope was exerted on Jonah.

"Sho pulling hard now," said Shaka between gasps for air.

As dawn approached behind them, the bubble of light created from the lantern was fusing into the sunrise. The gulf now mirrored the atmosphere: gray and glassy except for the ripples radiating from the boat. Feeling he was expanding from some kind of imprisonment, Shaka looked to the north at the island where three of the slaves were standing atop one of the dunes looking toward them.

"What the hell are they doing?" mumbled Jonah, looking in that direction.

"Just looking at things," said Shaka, realizing that they were probably seeing the boat pulled by this enigma in the water. As the boat kept moving seaward, the figures on the dunes disappeared although the island remained visible.

As the rope continued to grate over the gunnels, the coils in the stern were almost all gone. Jonah slowed the drag as much as possible, mumbling again before shouting over his shoulder, desperate, "Tie off the end of the rope, Shaka."

Though understanding at once, Shaka parried. "What you mean, Massa?"

"Tie off the end."

"Of what?"

"Tie the end of the rope onto something."

"I see what you mean."

"Then do it."

"But where am I gonna tie this thing?"

"Anywhere."

"But I caint drop the line to tie the knot."

"I'll hold the line, you idiot. Drop your line now and bind the end around your bench," shouted Jonah, enraged.

"Yessa. I can sho try that with your permission."

While releasing the rope, Shaka worried that Jonah might detect that he was not applying any tension. But Jonah said nothing. Shaka scrambled forward into the stern, seeing that only several yards of rope remained. Jonah gripped the rope tighter in his hands, grimacing in pain, his gloves shredded open so that the blood saturating the rope now came both from his hands and the chum.

"I done got the end," Shaka said. He moved backward and looped the rope once around his bench. "How am I supposed to do this?" I aint never learned to fasten ropes before."

"Tie the goddamn knot, Shaka. Help him, James."

"I don't know how," said James.

Shaka held the end of the rope, pretending to tie the knot. When the coils were about gone, Jonah dropped the rope then leapt sprawling over his bench toward Shaka who obstructed him by feigning that he was too startled to move. Jonah shoved Shaka away and grabbed the end of the line but the rope pulled taut and leapt from his fingers. Jonah hurled himself at the end as though chasing a snake while the rope slid over the gunnels and dropped into the gulf then vanished under the surface.

Staring at his hands, Jonah shouted: "We lost the thread, James... we lost the goddamn thread...into the oblivion. God the fucking Father, we shall be haunted now until the end of time."

As Shaka crawled back onto his bench, Jonah turned quickly as though realizing something and glared at Shaka: on one of his cheeks was a thin, wispish line of entrails. For the first time since that day they forever parted ways as friends, Shaka looked straight back at Jonah, unwaveringly, until Jonah turned away, looking confused, mumbling. "You best learn to tie that knot so I can hang you with it and forever wipe that smirk from your face."

CHAPTER NINE

Perched on the fronts of his feet while squatting around the fire, Shaka was mesmerized by the smoldering of the embers glowing then fading from sight almost like they were breathing.

Shaka told the other slaves scattered around the fire about his trip with Jonah from the night before: about the dark and winged spirit that pulled their boat across the ocean and defeated Jonah in the end. When the breeze stirred some of the embers, flames erupted, casting Shaka with warmth and light as he pointed beyond the reach of the fire into the darkness toward the churning of wind and water and said, "Washaka's out there now speaking through my voice."

Pear and Shobuck looked into the darkness—as though expecting to see something.

"Who is this Washaka," asked Jake, looking across the fire at Shaka, a tinge of anger in his voice. "Does he be like Jesus? You caint see him? You caint hear him? And even the coon dogs caint smell him?"

"No," said Shaka. "You gonna see him. You gonna see him soon."

Shaking her head Nomaw skulked away from the fire but Shaka followed her and moments later watched from some distance as she headed toward Jonah's tent, bulbous and glowing and flowing in the breeze, then walked inside.

"Thy will be done," said Shaka.

When moseying through the dunes back to the fire, he realized that through this betrayal Nomaw was actually liberating him; exposed to all, he could now remove his mask and reveal his identity to everyone. The bridle that once controlled him, stalled him, oppressed him, was relinquished. Something flowed along his spine almost imperceptibly as the schisms inside of himself began to dissolve. Now the wind did not brush against him but rather moved with him like he too was the wind itself.

Once arriving with the other slaves, Shaka threw into the fire another piece of driftwood, dry, smooth and gnarled, while sparks shot into the darkness and wafts of smoke roiled the sky. Flames soon erupted onto the wood and rose above the embers, thrashing in the wind, the flesh of the slaves becoming luminescent and wavering while struggling for definition from the darkness. Their souls, thought Shaka, were like those flames, momentary visions in nothingness, instants in the eternity of time, existing inexplicably.

"You must now know the truth," said Shaka. "You must know why you are here."

In one burst of the flames, he saw the other slaves looking at him, confused.

"All these days, and all these years, I was hidden from you. But now you shall know me."

"What is you talking about?" said Jake.

Shaka began talking about how in his childhood he was traipsing through the forest back at Whiteoak. Over his shoulder he carried his prey from the hunt: squirrels tied onto pieces of twine. He loved the sensation of blood still warm from life seeping through his shirt and coagulating around the base of his spine. Next to him was Jonah whose face appeared wild and pale in the faint, almost indiscernible glow of twilight.

Cupping his hand around his ear, Shaka stopped and said, "Listen."

"To what," asked Jonah.

"Hush."

The air was cold and inert. The shafts of the trees rose black and regnant from the earth and the leaves above, withered from the chill of autumn, began to rattle in their branches. Then came the wind tepid like their breaths. Once the wind died the sounds came again: moans and wails.

"What's that?" asked Jonah.

"I don't know," said Shaka. "Come on."

They bolted in the direction of the sound, emerging from the forest at the back of the slave quarters where the dirt under their feet was packed and frozen into the consistency of stone. They stopped, panting and discovered the place from where the noise was coming: the window devoid of glass that seemed to eruct warmth and color.

"What's that noise?" asked Shaka who then jumped to attempt to look through the window. But he was too short so he flung his squirrels onto the dirt and said to Jonah, "Get down on your hands and knees."

"For what?"

"So I can stand on your back."

"You're too big to stand on my back," said Jonah.

"Naw I aint," said Shaka.

"All right then," said Jonah, dropping to his hands and knees under the window.

While leaning against the cabin, Shaka climbed atop Jonah and gaped into the window. Inside along the side of the building was the fire, sparks shooting and flames leaping into the room toward Jake who stood gnawing his fingernails while looking sheepishly toward the bed where the Negress named Bertha was hunched between the legs of his wife. Sprawled across the bed, his wife had her legs arched and spread apart, exposing her belly that swelled into a giant black and shiny mound. The flames of the fire seemed to curl around the inhabitants of the shack then flush onto Shaka, onto his chilled, chapped flesh like some belch from the throat of life.

"Uuuuww," Shaka hummed.

"What is it?"

"I caint reckon."

"You caint reckon?"

"There some woman in there—her belly's swollen."

"Swollen?"

"Looks like some melon's growing inside her. Some woman's fiddling around between her legs."

Bertha moved from the bed while flames fluttered from the fireplace, shining upon the crotch between the legs.

Shaka hummed with his lips closed, "Uuuuuuww."

"What is it?"

"She's tore apart down there."

"Is she hurt?"

"Sho she's hurt, she's screaming."

The wound moved then opened. "Uh-oh," he said, resigned and baffled. "This here's too strange. Something's coming out that wound."

"What's it look like?"

"Like rotten fruit."

"Maybe it's the melon."

Shaka saw that it was round and black and smeared with mucus and blood. "It aint fruit."

"Then what is it?"

"It's still coming."

"But what is it?"

Bertha moved toward the bed, blocking the view.

Under his feet Shaka felt Jonah trembling with anticipation, asking, "What is it? What is it?"

But Shaka continued to stare, wondering until Jonah moved from under his feet and he started to fall until grabbing the edge of the window and hanging in midair. After yanking upward to look into the window, he saw Bertha pull a tiny, grotesque baby from the insides of the woman. A serpent was fastened to its belly. He slipped and fell to the ground, crumbling the bones of squirrels under his back.

Jonah stood on his knees above him, desperate to understand. "What was it?"

"They yanked some baby from her," Shaka said before becoming silent and afraid amidst the painful and violent wails of the infant. He soon rose from his back and ignoring Jonah, bolted through the shacks and beyond into the fields delineated with rows of withering, defoliated plants, resembling skeletons slouching in obeisance toward the big house. He turned onto the porch of his home then barged into the door, throwing his string of squirrels onto the floor.

His mother, Maw, was inside the shack sitting by the fire, slumped, her spine bowed like some sapling that grew not upward but crosswise, curving toward the ground, forcing her into her permanent picking posture. She was cooking turnips and pork, stirring the pots with a stick. She obliviously stared into one corner of the room, her eyes vacuous and flickering while gesturing with her hands and chanting words or sounds that Shaka could not understand. She was communicating, Shaka knew, with the souls of her dead relatives from Africa. She dropped her stick onto the floor and guffawed as if chunks of her lungs filled with sputum were spewing from her mouth.

Dripping to the ground, his sweat was as cold as sleet. He walked into the shack and closed the door. "Maw," he said.

But she continued to guffaw, ignoring him. Shaka feared sometimes that she would never emerge from her hallucinations, leaving him alone on the plantation, homeless and unmothered.

His fear culminated until he sputtered, "Maw... Maw...Maw." She turned her head and seemed to totter on the edge of her vision, appearing uncertain and lost momentarily until with some regret she emerged from her world but not completely, her mind remaining cloudy and muddled.

She looked at him askew, registered his presence and spoke, "What you want, baby?"

"I seen something."

"So?"

"Something stranger than I seen before."

"What's that?"

"Delia was hollering. This baby come out from there," said Shaka, pointing to his crotch.

"She was about due."

"What do you mean?"

"You aint schooled about that, huh? But I reckon you about that age."

"For what?"

"Come here, baby."

Shaka came over, sat in front of his mother in the only other chair in the shack.

"Babies come from their mothers."

"They do?"

"Just like animals."

"Like animals?"

"We rut to make babies—the man gets with the woman. Aint you seen some of the goats and horses doing that?"

"You mean humping on each other."

"Sho."

"You mean I was made that way."

"Sho you was."

"Who done all that to you?"

Maw looked startled then smiled strangely. After looking toward the corner and nodding, she turned toward him with her eyes focused on him but also elsewhere, some place that Shaka could not see or even imagine.

"They always said that when you was asking, you was ready to know. Your father did all that to me."

"Who's that?"

"He aint what you think he is."

"But who is he?"

"He aint regular—that's for sho." By inhaling she seemed to suck much of the air from the room and pull him closer to her, sweeping him into her world. "I met him coming over here from Africa. Not long before them slavers done stripped me from my family when I wasn't but thirteen and shackled me into the bowels of their ship. Along comes this storm romping like death. Down in the dark we caint see or move, we caint stand or nothing, all we can do is lay on our sides, manacles shredding our wrists and ankles, wood grinding against our flesh. Our misery cut beyond the flesh, of knowing you caint even hold the shit seeping out your body. We was already starting to die.

"Then we heard the birdman."

"Who's that?"

"Our Lord, Washaka."

"That's like my name."

"And that's how come you're hearing this story. Back in the ship I recollected the story told in our villages about this birdman, Washaka. They said he was a child destined to free us from the slavers. But one day that Washaka was captured by the slavers and he too was chained onto the ship. But the gods helped him bust from the manacles and soar across the water back to his home. After while came stories all over Africa, about chilluns busting from the ships and soaring to their villages. Mothers searched the skies for their babies."

"So that's who you heard during that storm?"

"We heard the call of freedom. We all cried on the boat, sho scaring them white folks. And cause none of us can speak the same language, that cry became our voice, weaving together our hopes. I felt my spirit rising from my flesh. Though my body was about ruint, my soul was soaring with our savior.

"That dawn after the storm the water was calm. The whities opened the hatch and took some of the slaves dancing on the deck. Them Negroes was expecting on something. I heard the drum beating above, the manacles rattling, the feet thumping on the ceiling above slow and smooth like the whities wanted. Them above then started rattling their manacles on the floor, harder, faster, chanting now, making their own music. The whities shouted but they aint stop, naw. Wild and African came the music now until the ceiling about broke. Then we heard Washaka calling above the ship and we all called back, our voices rising like bird songs. And then they was scrambling, struggling and shuffling on top the deck. But I could hear the calls of my people as they rose to meet Washaka. Gun was fired. The hatches was shut." Maw slammed her foot on the floor. "But the whities was too late. Them was gone to Africa."

"How you know they wasn't shot dead and left in the water?"

Maw thrust from Shaka as though his words were blows then lurched toward him, pointing her finger into his face. "Them aint dead. Them in Africa."

"They soared to their homes," Shaka said. "But you were left shackled. That don't seem fair."

"For the longest I strove to reckon on why he done abandoned me. And later I knowed the truth."

"When was that?"

"When the Washaka came here to this shack. And told me that my suffering aint for nothing and that I was sent to this cruel, cold land cause he wanted me here."

"For what?"

"To deliver you, Shaka."

"To deliver me? I'd rather get born in Africa."

"But you don't understand."

She leaned back in her chair, swaying, wrapping her arms around her shoulders as though cradling her breasts and spoke gently. "Back years ago I was asleep over on that bed when hearing this flutter of wind, soft like the wings of ducks. I done woke, seeing this bird, naw this man, some kind of giant, black angel made of feathers and flesh flying through the window and landing on my bed, the moon silver on his wings. Don't know how but I knew that birdman was from Africa. Don't know how but I knew the reason he come, feeling the hunger, the yearning. And he come on over here, folded me into his wings slow and gentle and he come up inside me, then on up into that beating under my chest and on up, way on up, into my soul. Then Washaka," she yelled, propelled from her chair. "Freedom struck my womb like lightning. And that was you, Shaka."

Shaka tottered on the threshold of her dreams, trying to imagine but wanting to disbelieve. "You...you mean..."

"Your father aint man. Your father is Washaka."

Shaka stared at his body, at his arms and legs in disbelief. "Is I some kind of bird?"

"Yes."

"But I aint even got any feathers."

"But your soul is bird."

"My soul? What's that?"

"Something you caint see."

"But I caint even fly."

"Not yet. But someday. Before leaving Washaka said you was to save our people. Someday when you was ready, he gonna return back here and fly with you and all our peoples back to Africa, for the exodus."

"What?"

Maw was silent. Clasping her hands together before her chest, she bowed to him and looked at him adoringly, almost subserviently. Shaka felt afraid and alone like his mother was abandoning his reality, pulling him imploringly into those empty corners where her ancestors lived.

"I aint the messiah of nothing. And I aint going nowhere. But staying in this shack and eating turnips."

Her expression was unfazed. "No, baby, you going to Africa."

"No, I aint."

"Ponder."

"I aint wanting to ponder."

"But you're so different from the others."

"Naw I aint."

"Yes, you is. For one you aint raised like them other chilluns. All chilluns want freedom but their folks done beat the urge from them until they is weak. But I raised you to not fear or obey nothing, to roam across the rivers and forests even beyond the plantation without answering to anyone. Other chilluns learn to toil for whities but I teach you to toil for yourself, to fish for bass and crappies, to hunt for rabbits and coons, to garden for turnips and corn and whatnot. You can already live from the land without help from nobody.

"I love you cause you is free. And you the strongest and smartest child around these parts."

Disturbed and baffled, Shaka rose from his chair and retreated toward the door, wanting to escape. But Maw continued to look at him reverentially, saying, "Too late now to change your fate." When Shaka reached the threshold of the door, she said, "You caint tell anybody about this, Shaka. The whities will fear you and kill you."

Shaka walked across the threshold and shut the door on Maw. Darkness streaked the heavens which were devoid of moon and stars and static with cold. He walked along the rows of cotton paralyzed between identities, between dreams and reality, the known and unknown. He slowly raised and spread his arms into wings and in his soul he felt some flutter of knowing, some hint of inspiration, while his feet moved along the earth. But when on the verge of believing in the possibility of flight, he froze with doubt and dropped his arms, holding to his nexus of the earth.

Soon he arrived in front of the birthing shack. Through the window and cracks in the boards came the wailing of the infant, as though terrified of awakening into slavery and came too flames from the fire inside that, clouded with dust and rendered heatless by the cold, shone dimly and almost invisibly on the congregation of slaves. Leaning into the side of the shack, one of the slaves beat a drum which was carved from a log and failed to resonate but thumped flat and rotten. Some other slaves shuffled their feet along the earth, random and clumsy, tapping their toes at times but their movements were lethargic and riddled with dread, as though their legs were stiff and their toes blistered as though they could not generate any excitement for the life of a child born into slavery. Some children not yet yoked to the fields darted around oblivious to what was happening. Shaka meandered to the door of the shack where the father, Jake, was standing and expressing the dread and ambivalence of the others. Shaka tugged on his sleeve.

"What you want, boy?" asked Jake.

"Who's my father?"

"What?"

"My father—who is he?"

"Maybe you aint got one to feel sorry for you."

"But who?"

"I aint know. You around this place like rocks and stumps. You aint born like the others. So get on, leave me alone. You as strange as Maw."

"But Jake."

"Get on."

Shaka then moseyed from the shack and around the legs of the slaves, feeling like some ghost unable to penetrate their world. He recognized one of the women on the plantation who was friendly with Maw. He reached upward and tugged on her skirt.

Once she failed to notice him, he jerked, causing the woman to blurt, "Stop that." She swung and looked, finding Shaka. "What you want?"

"Where I comes from?"

"What you mean?"

"I mean like that baby in there."

"Pondering on that, is you? I reckon Maw done told you her story, huh, about Africans and all that. She aint one to want to raise her baby into slavery, reckon she sooner kill you than see you picking in them fields. Maybe she's right. Anyhow, Maw aint swell with you. One day you up and cried and there you was, Maw toting you around, you sucking on her dried teat. I reckon she found you in the forest, dropped there by some slaves heading north for freedom. You're a foundling as far as I reckon. But I aint reckoning that much."

"I aint what you say," said Shaka.

"Maybe you aint. Who knows? At least you got some room for figuring."

Shaka walked from the woman. He paused outside a circle of children about his age and touched one of the girls on her shoulder.

When she ignored him, he reached over and pinched her ear while she turned and screeched in anger, "Whaaat?"

"Where do you come from?" he asked.

"Shaka? You weirdy," the girl said with disdain. The other children giggled.

"Where do I come from?"

"We all come from the hollow of the log. But I reckon you come from the bottom of the swamp. Get on, weirdy, back to your spooky mother."

The drumming stopped and everyone became silent and still. Off in the distance walking from the big house and toward the congregation was the master of the plantation, Whiteoak, encircled by some pale and sterile ring of light glowing from the lantern in his hand, his movements stiff and ungainly. Once arriving around the congregation, Whiteoak walked toward the shack and without speaking handed to Jake a bundle of clothes, then he walked from the shack and stood on the margins of the congregation, alone and tall, reigning over the ambivalence of the birth like some warden expressing nothing but his misguided and futile sense of duty. Shaka meandered into the circle of light toward Whiteoak and tugged on his long, blanched arm.

"Who's my pappy?"

Whiteoak fidgeted.

"Where do I come from?"

Whiteoak glared down upon Shaka.

"Who is I?"

Whiteoak ignored him, said nothing while Shaka continued to tug on his arm undaunted, saying, "Where do I come from?"

Then Whiteoak just walked off, leaving Shaka by himself in the dark. The wailing of the birth at that moment passed on to the outside of the shack where the infant, not swaddled but naked, was handed to Jake who raised the child in his hands, lackadaisical and indifferent, to show the other slaves who almost succumbed to some kind of expression but mostly remained silent and still. Whiteoak clapped his hands; it sounded like boards hammered together.

He was different from the others, Shaka realized about himself. He wanted to be part of them but could not: to them he was strange and wild, the son of the spooky woman who saw things that did not exist; to him they were not alive, just domesticated animals, caught and fed by the white man—devoid of all the feelings inside of him.

He traipsed through the slaves and the cold, lambent flame to the margins of the fields where he stood shivering. Ahead of him were the rows of cotton which could someday become his prison and torment. But above were the heavens, cold, still and black, free from the grasps of all men. Rising from the ashes of fear and bewilderment, he felt this sense of impending and joyous birth—feelings which he knew the other slaves were too afraid to experience. He moved through the fields along the rows as blood pulsated through his veins and as warmth overcame the cold. Then he tore across the rows of cotton violently ripping his pants, breathing rapidly while somehow understanding that he was flushing through some kind of womb, reborn not as slave, nor man, but as bird. As the struggle in his mind dissolved, he euphorically curled his arms upward to resemble wings while the pull of the earth relinquished him from its grasp, and he soared through the fields on wings like a hawk, shrieking, feeling the spirit of his father inside of him.

Toward the middle of the field, he tipped his wings and circled toward the forest while the euphoria began to drain from his body and the pull of the earth grasped him in its clutches once again. He searched through the forest and found a tree, a black oak, twisted and gnarled and draped with dead, flaky leaves. He stopped and grated his hands along the trunk through grimy, coarse bark and leaping, grabbed onto a limb then climbed upward where the limbs flexed under his weight. He perched in the branches, roosting, folding his wings into his chest. Below in the distance was the river; while the ripples on its surface shone like flickering, silver scales in the moonlight, it wound through the forest and although vanishing from sight at the horizon, he believed now that it flowed...

"Onward, way onward, to Africa," said Shaka, finishing his story.

All the while Shaka was so absorbed in the telling of his story that he did not even look at the slaves but now he saw them through the dim, reddish glow of the embers, their bodies receding into the dark but their faces visible. Both Pear and Shobuck were gazing adoringly at him, breathing calmly.

"You mean," said Jake, speaking the moment another flame erupted from the embers, "that you some kind of nigger Jesus."

"I'm your savior," said Shaka calmly with his head upright, his hands dangling at his sides, feeling detached from himself.

"And we suppose to believe that."

"Yes," said Shaka, struggling to sound convinced.

"I knowed this whole time," said Shobuck, "knowed Shaka was gonna carry me away from them fields."

"And carry me back to my family," said Pear.

"Naw," said Jake testily. "I remembered what happened. Your Maw aint swell up. You was born too early before your brains got right. So now you caint understand nothing, not now, not ever. You bound to talk filth and lies for the rest of your life."

"I'm your savior, Jake," said Shaka, his face now fierce. "Believeth in me or perish."

"Goddamn, Shaka," said Jake. "I aint ask for this. I just liked them birds, liked dancing around with them. I aint wanting to perish, naw, and I aint really wanting to fly neither—dangerous up there for some bent, fool nigger like myself who caint see straight no more."

"You shall overcome your fear. Or you shall perish."

"Get...get...get hold of yourself, Shaka," stammered Jake. "We aint wanting any trouble here."

Flushed with rage and galvanized, Shaka sprung toward Jake and almost collided into him before swerving away from the fire and leaving the others behind and wandering along the beach into the darkness where he could not even see himself anymore. His body now a conduit of doubt and fear, he felt himself separating from the night around him. He could not help but remember the time when they came to carry him into the fields and he ran away and climbed yet again to the top of the tree as the hounds barked below and trusting all to Washaka, he jumped...and fell hard upon the ground almost injuring himself irrevocably. Might that happen again?

More than anything, he feared falling once again under the lash: not the pain but the violation of having your own body invaded by another man. Yet was he not heading again for that fate? And again his life was not under his control. Washaka instead was prodding him deeper into his own fate beyond any point of return, almost beyond his own ability to imagine and believe, way onto the margins of reality. At times he tried to cloak and hide and resist but always Washaka came for him yet again to prod him onward. But he knew that once he was exposed, very soon now, he could only escape further pain and anguish by shedding his earthly carriage so he could attain the sky.

"I tremble before Thee, Washaka" he said. "Do not abandon me but carry me to my home."

Something gently took his hand and tugged upon him. Shaka swung around violently and could barely see Pear smiling at him hesitantly. He wanted to grasp her, to embrace her delicate and untainted body, to kiss and disrobe her, feel her dark and unspoiled blossom—lose himself in her warm and real flesh to escape the impending horror of his imagined fate. But thinking that his desire would weaken him, he resisted the temptation, stood rigid and impassive.

"Come on," she said, continuing to tug.

Relenting Shaka followed her through the troughs and crests of the dunes, the sea oats brushing against their legs, and down to the beach on the other side of the island where sand crabs scurried militantly about their feet. They stood upon the shore amongst seaweed, shells and pieces of polished coral. The breeze was gentle and the gulf was smooth and the waves caroused upon the shore like messengers from more promising lands. Her feet sunken into the wet, shifting sand, Pear faced toward Shaka. Out beyond her, in the faint, barely detectable glow of starlight, the horizon was almost invisible—water and air merging together into darkness.

"He's waiting out there, aint he?" said Pear. Untying the strap behind her shoulders, she disrobed, standing naked. Her flesh was as smooth and unblemished as the gulf, the void between her legs seeming to pull him inward to the sea behind her.

Shaka breathed rapidly.

"Let us go," she said.

Pear turned and moved hesitantly into the gulf and as the water rose all the way to the cleft of her buttocks, she was surrounded by a nimbus of glowing froth. But when she turned then stopped moving, she and the froth dissapeared and he heard from the direciton of her shadow. "Is you coming?"

Shaka awkwardly doffed his shirt, unbuckled his belt and allowed his pants to drop to his ankles, exposing his tumescence. He moved sheepishly into the water, his legs beneath him seeming to melt into the substance that bubbled and glowed around him. He stopped next to Pear, his waist submerged in the water. He was afraid of venturing even deeper into the sightless, weightless void of unknowing but he was always confronted with that same fear throughout his life—and confronted too with the knowledge that if the fear stalled him, caught and claimed him, he would be doomed to a fate of illusion and apathy. Diving forward he swam under the surface and opened his eyes, barely able to discern the pale, rippled bottom slanting down from the island like some cliff falling into an abyss. He punctured the surface, needing air, inhaling.

He dove again and swam away from the island until the bottom below disappeared, until he was swimming in the ever-flowing, boundless nothingness upon which everything—his body, this island, and even the earth—were momentary forms always changing. His flesh dissolved into the water around him until he became sentience alone out there, boundless, graspless, free of all except the need for air.

He saw the blurry and dark form enshrouded in light that

moved toward him then came into focus as Pear, resembling the incarnation he saw beneath the boat while shifting through the lens of the water into something greater and more mysterious than her flesh alone. The light now rippled upon her body like the scales of flickering and spooked minnows. Puncturing the surface together they gasped for air and dove again while swimming around each other, flesh skimming along flesh.

After surfacing she swam back to the shore and slunk onto the beach where she settled, supine, suspended between land and water and while Shaka stopped at her feet, she opened her legs. Shaka wanted her; she was there for him as an offering. The waves lapped between her legs as he smelled the scents of salt and seaweed mingling together. He crawled on his hands and knees and stood between her legs on his knees, looking at the rapid heave of her lungs beneath her breasts, at her startled but euphoric face.

No, he thought, he did not want to be their savior. Nor blessed with the power to fly. Most of all he did not want to be bound and whipped again for as long as he lived. All he wanted was to live in the open peacefully, the rhythm of his life established by the sun and moon, not the clanging of the overseer's bell. All he wanted was to raise his own fruits and vegetables and hunt his own game as his mother taught him, not to toil endlessly to make his master rich. All he wanted was to love this woman, Pear, and to have children with her—to enjoy the pleasures and challenges of life to which all men should be entitled.

Why must I suffer? Why must I suffer to have freedom?" he wondered.

Standing at the tree above them, Jonah watched the two dark, almost indistinguishable figures on the beach, watched as Shaka lowered himself onto her between her legs. Jonah sipped from his glass of whiskey, the sour, sweet hot fumes drifting into his nostrils, the liquid settling feverishly in his gut. He was ashamed of his arousal, the swelling in his crotch but watched them anyway as Shaka undulated on top of her, satisfying his desire like any beast.

He sipped again, trying to douse the frustration he felt because one of his slaves was getting what he coveted.

Before, while watching them swimming in the gulf, he had sensed the conflict of the island—the struggle of the tiny, delicate mound of sand to survive against the forces of erosion and oblivion: the roots of the tree gripping into the sand to stave off the wind and water. And he also sensed the beast out there stalking him. He could not fathom why they were not afraid especially because Shaka saw that beast last night, experienced its power, its violence. Instead they swam around almost ceremoniously like they were anointing themselves or paying homage to something.

Below he could hear the girl barely whimpering, her legs flailing off to the sides, her arms embraced around Shaka as he continued to undulate on top of her. Feeling at once disgusted and aroused, Jonah began to remember some of Shaka's behavior from the night before, the cryptic comments, the evasive actions and the snickering when the beast finally escaped. It almost seemed like Shaka and the beast were in some kind of communion with each other, feeding each other, both visages of some force determined to destroy Jonah.

They were friends as children, Jonah acknowledged, although that thought rarely if ever entered his mind; Shaka was even spared the fields to play with him. Perhaps for that reason Shaka tended to despise his own kind back then and was not docile and fearful like the other pickaninnies but spirited, mischievous and competitive, all traits that died quickly for slaves. Understanding that he was somehow supposed to be more capable than the Negroes even in his childhood, Jonah was always trying to prove his superiority but because Shaka was one year older, Jonah always got outsmarted and outrun and outhunted and even on occasion outboxed, making Jonah feel confused and incompetent—feelings that were only soothed by his admiration for Shaka.

Below Shaka began to undulate more quickly until suddenly he stopped, placed his arms underneath the girl's shoulders, brought her close to him and collapsed on top of her. He rolled over next to her, both of them now staring at the stars above.

And what about birds? Jonah could not deny that either. Shaka suddenly one day refused to shoot birds, not even the ducks down on the river. On several occasions Jonah discovered Shaka off in the woods by himself making birdcalls while hidden in the branches of some tree. But Shaka was always evasive when Jonah inquired about his behavior—and he concluded back then that it must have something to do with his strange African mother who was always seeing and talking to things that were not real.

Shaka and Pear collected their clothes then walked up the beach while holding hands before vanishing somewhere off in the dunes. Jonah was left pondering the question now burrowing into his mind: What happened to Shaka, that strange and spirited boy, after that awful and bloody day when they separated ways never to be friends again but only master and slave in the future? Did he cease to exist? Become brainless like the rest of them? Or was he somehow still alive out there hidden from sight, playing fox and still winning? Jonah sniffed from his glass, the vapors flushing his mind, while he tried to neutralize that strange and taunting worry.

"Where is that boy, now?" he said aloud. "Is he still out there?"

Was he giving the slaves too much slack, he wondered, and allowing for the unleashing of something just plain odd, if not wild and dangerous? Was it possible that at the moment he lowered his guard and showed the slaves some generosity, they were devising against him instead of feeling appreciative?

"Damn," he said, pacing around the tree. "What's wrong with me?"

The paranoia of his wife was gnawing into his mind. Why was she so worried about these slaves and their hoodoo? Despite recognizing some credibility in her thinking—after all, slaves do at times turn—he was adamant about hectoring her with his confidence mostly so she would just leave him alone. Truth was, by allowing the slaves their freedom or the illusion of their freedom, he felt some burden relinquished from his soul, allowing him to feel magnanimous—something which for him was rare—while watching them trolling the waters for mackerel, bathing in the surf, singing around their fires at night. He felt kind, he was forced to admit, and he liked that. Ever since his childhood, he felt choked by Negroes and figured he was just damn wretched tired of managing their lives and just wished they could leave him alone. But now it seemed his wife was ruining all that—just because of her fear. He drank again, one long, swift swallow that finished the glass, the burn coming into his nostrils like an inhalation of fire. In the distance Shaka and Pear were climbing atop one of the dunes and as he watched them, dark and barely visible figures disappearing behind some sea oats, he felt fear swelling from that place where the liquor burned in his gut.

By the fire he saw Jake and Shobuck sprawled in the sand without any cover, already asleep—just out there exposed to rain, bird shit, crabs and bugs without any concern in the world, he thought, envious of their complacency. But now he could not find Shaka and Pear anywhere and that bothered him, made him angry and he thought of prowling around, looking for them, finding them, saying, "What the hell yawl doing? Making me some more niggers?"

He moseyed back to his tent, slipped inside the flap and without disturbing his wife, placed his glass on top of his trunk, removed his clothes except for his underwear, thought of loading his rifle and placing it under his cot but felt foolish about his fear so he just lay down in bed, not sleepy, wondering about the whereabouts of Pear and Shaka in the dunes, sneaking around outside of his reach and even outside his comprehension.

He was still aroused and although hearing the delicate, almost melodious snores of his wife, he could not avoid the temptation—did not even try, in fact—to imagine himself inside of Pear while she straddled his hips, not sitting there like his wife, moving only slightly and soundlessly while barely seeming to enjoy herself but rather bucking wildly, her hands gripped into his shoulders, her face vacuous but euphoric, her breasts misted with the sweat of her exertions, her nipples protruding like delicate and lubricious thorns. Now even more aroused, he considered going over to his wife, pulling the sheets back from her, sliding her gown above her buttocks and penetrating her while she was asleep to just get rid of the urge. But after imagining her waking furious and disgusted with him, he resisted and just to be able to sleep he freed himself, vigorously moved his hand over himself, completing the deed as quickly as possible. He shamefully wiped the mess onto the sides of the tent.

Lying back on his cot he saw nothing, heard nothing but the elements grinding away at the island. While falling into sleep, entering momentarily into this calm but lucid state of mind, he wondered what was happening to himself. He was haunted by vague, disturbed feelings all his life but ordinarily kept them subdued under his tight, rational mind. But not anymore: His feelings were consuming him now, drowning out his ability to reason, to know the real from the unreal. Paradoxically, it all seemed more real than anything in his life and for that reason he wanted to succumb to it, even into the fear and rage, because feeling something was better than feeling nothing at all.

Soon he faded off into sleep while sensing Shaka and Pear wandering around out there. Later in the night he awoke partially but thought he was dreaming when hearing the patter of the raindrops on the top of the tent and when seeing the distant but muffled explosions of light emanating through the canvas—and thought he was dreaming too when in one of the flashes of lightning, he saw a penumbra of wings silhouetted on the sides of his tent. He lay there exhausted, too tired to comprehend and while turning away from the image, he moaned—the sound low, somnolent and prehistoric.

CHAPTER TEN

"Not again, Shaka."

Jonah was awakened by Eloise's voice sounding panicked in the distance. A cloud of mosquitoes was buzzing around his head and one of them landed on his cheek, its legs thin and lashy, and pierced his flesh with its beak. Abruptly emerging from his sleep, Jonah slapped himself, smearing the insect and his own blood across his face.

He pulled the sheet over his head, hoping to fall back to sleep. But he heard his wife again outside the tent, sounding agitated. "You remember what he said, Shaka."

Yanking the sheet off his body, Jonah sat up and put on his trousers and walked outside the tent bare-chested, looking toward the direction of her voice. Hovering above one of the dunes in the north, he saw some huge black inverted wings strapped onto a staff driven into the sand. Below the staff were Shaka and Pear circling around the wings, flapping their arms about like birds.

Near them was his wife still in her bathrobe, beseeching the slaves. "Stop before he comes over here."

Jonah perceived some kind of harrowing, vast stillness all around him and for one moment he felt removed from his body, from the series of reactions and counterreactions coursing through him, floating in some peaceful and detached state of perception alone. Above the atmosphere was streaked with a mottled, lifeless skein of gray. The gulf was smooth, not even rippled, while occasionally one swell lolled toward the island, mounted into a wave and broke gently upon shore. After the storm from the night before, the sand across the island was unblemished, resembling gauze, not yet tainted by the touch of man. But the mosquitoes continued to fly around his head, one now landing on its thin and lashy legs and stabbing its beak into his neck.

"Must I do this?" he uttered.

After returning to his tent and loading his rifle, he marched across the dunes toward the wings, his feet punching holes into the skein of wet and crusty sand as though he were wounding the earth.

Eloise headed in his direction and then paused before him, trying to block his way, saying, "Please do not hurt them."

He just maneuvered around her and soon arrived before the wings. He gazed at the slaves as they sprawled their arms and danced silently around the shaft, oblivious to him, their faces looking mesmerized.

Jonah stepped close to them, shouting, "What in the hell are yawl doing?"

But they seemed not to hear him.

"Get hold of yourself."

After they did not even react to him, he held his rifle away from his body in one hand and with his other, grabbed Pear by her arm and yanked her away from the wings, her body feeling surprisingly light. Shaka swerved toward Pear and clenching both of his hands together, raised them above his head and came down hard on Jonah's arm. Caught by surprise Jonah released Pear, reeling painfully from the blow. Shaka lurched toward him menacingly but with his hands dropped to his sides and with his neck extended so his head seemed almost disconnected from his body. Shaka clenched the muscles in his face, squinted his fierce eyes and violently thrust closer to Jonah's face.

"Eeeeeeeeekk."

Jonah stumbled backward but, regaining his balance, took the barrel of the rifle into his right hand, came forward and rammed the butt into Shaka's thigh.

Collapsing, Shaka stooped over at the waist, cradling his thigh in his hands, breathing rapidly while Pear came around to his side. Then both of them raised their arms and started coming toward Jonah who backed away, pulling his rifle into his shoulder, raising the muzzle level with Shaka's chest, the thought flashing across his mind: don't kill him. They diverged away from him as Eloise suddenly came toward him, throwing her arms over the rifle and shoving the barrel into the ground.

Jonah pulled the rifle from under his wife. Then he swung around toward the slaves who were turning around, coming back at him again. He aimed at Shaka's head but before pulling the trigger, pointed the sight off to the side, the bang resounding through the atmosphere like some kind of altercation of time. Jonah then grabbed the barrel in both hands, cocked the rifle behind his shoulder, ready to swing.

Suddenly still, Shaka looked over at Pear to make sure she was not injured. Then he said to Jonah, "You've come for me."

Jonah was not sure how to answer.

"To deliver me to my father," said Shaka, looking not at him but at something above Jonah.

"Your father? Who the hell is that?"

"You will know soon enough."

Jonah went silent, felt the blow of grief. He felt dizzy, struggled to maintain his composure, said mostly to himself, "Forgive me, I must whip this boy."

"No, Jonah, you don't have to," said Eloise who was standing next to him now.

"But I warned him," said Jonah.

"Fifty lashes," said Shaka.

Now on her knees, Pear started to weep.

"You don't have to," said Eloise.

"He was warned," said Jonah.

Walking to Pear, Shaka placed his arms under her shoulders,

gently helped her to her feet and ignoring Jonah, walked calmly toward the tree with Pear following behind. Keeping his rifle tucked under his shoulder at the ready, Jonah followed behind with his wife. Jonah was perplexed that Shaka wanted to be whipped and even coercing him into fulfilling his promise—almost like Jesus succumbing to Pontius Pilate. But Jonah also realized the danger: He could not control Shaka if he was not afraid of the threat of pain.

"That's right," said Jonah. "Get along there."

Jonah felt removed from himself again as their feet punctured footprints into the smooth, rain-packed sand. Shaka stopped ahead, turned back toward Pear, whispered something to her then she walked off toward the kitchen.

"Where you going?" asked Jonah.

"To get some twine," she said.

"For what?"

"For Shaka."

The other slaves—Nomaw, Jake and Shobuck—were coming toward them now and Jonah told them to stay out front, motioning in that direction with his rifle.

"He done caught you playing with the birds again?" asked Jake.

Shaka said nothing.

"Aint that so, Massa?" said Jake.

"Yes," said Jonah.

"And now you gonna whip him."

"Yes."

"Just like old times, huh?"

When they all arrived at the tree, Jonah felt disassociated from his body like he was fazing out of existence. Before the tree Shaka turned and faced the others, looking toward the broken and jagged coastline in the east where the sunrise was eclipsed behind clouds. Though the island was obscured by shadow, some light escaped from the fringes of the clouds and reflected radiant and golden on the surface of the gulf. Birds too were now stirring, piercing the silence with their calls, some flying above the gulf in the light, their wings ablaze like sparks of fire.

Shaka reached above his head and grabbed hold of one of the tree's limbs and broke it off. While shredding the leaves from the limb, he said to the other slaves while nodding toward Jonah, "Don't blame this man. He knows not what he does."

Once all the leaves were removed, Shaka held a knobby and withy dowel slightly thicker than his thumb, and he handed it over to Jonah. Pear reappeared while walking toward Shaka with the twine in her hand. Shaka pulled his shirt over his shoulders and turned toward the tree, exposing the black, intestinelike matrix of scars across his back. He placed his arms around the tree, embracing its girth.

"Bind me."

"I caint do that," said Pear, shaking her head. "So he can beat you."

"Would you rather him?"

"Naw."

"Bind me now," said Shaka.

As Pear walked around the tree, Shaka pressed his cheek against the bark. Afraid now, knowing the pain was coming, he wanted to flee. But he remained still. He wanted to weep for his pain, for the cruelty inflicted between men, for the violence inside of Jonah. But he remained impassive. Slowly severing from the world around him, he retracted inside of himself except for the feel of Pear—her hands, not yet calloused from the plow, gently wrapping the twine around both of his wrists and pulling his arms together. Once his hands were bound, she stroked the top of his hands, whispered that she loved him then all sensations of her vanished.

Jonah spoke, his words muffled and distant, coming from another realm. "Goddamn you all. I never asked for this, never wanted to inflict any of you. I succored onto you this break from the endless toil and tedium of your lives. And now you repay me with ingratitude and defiance. You wretched and spoiled children. Damn you all. One," Jonah counted.

Shaka's chest slammed into the tree. Air gushed from his lungs. His muscles clenched then relaxed. He was looking through some darkened, obscured tunnel at Jake who was in one of those rare, almost unimaginable moments of muteness, his lips sealed tightly across his teeth like his words, unable to escape from his mouth, were about to rupture biliously inside his stomach.

"Two."

Welts slithered into his skin like some searing, parasitic worm.

"Three."

Blood threaded down his back. He could not speak the words in his mind: Weep not, brethren. Weep not for I leave this low and mean earth to live in the heavens.

"Four."

Another worm seared through his flesh. He saw Nomaw dropping to her knees, genuflecting. "You promised not to never whip this boy."

"Five.

Shaka heard some clamorous, turbulent chorus—the voices of slaves asking for salvation, begging to be released from their suffering.

"Six."

Keep me, oh Lord, from crying out and begging for mercy.

"Seven."

"Just like old times, Massa?" asked Jake. "When Whiteoak done kilt you. Kilt all the nigger from your heart. Kilt you as dead as himself."

"Eight."

Shaka hollered and pulled spasmodically against the bindings to escape, to drive the pain from his body. All around him others were crying and weeping.

"Ten," counted Jonah.

Shaka yanked again against the bindings and hollered.

"Eleven."

He pulled again but weakly.

"Twelve."

Urine trickled into his trousers.

"Thirteen."

His bowels voided.

"Fourteen."

The clenching and releasing of his muscles, the gasping and gushing of his lungs, began to cease. His body stopped responding to the pain.

"Fifteen."

He hung limp. All the slaves around him were hushed.

In his childhood at Whiteoak, Shaka was returning from the river, looking toward the fields of cotton that green and dotted with plumes, resembled inchworms hunching toward the horizon. The sun above shone dull and vicious and sucked the rain from the earth, creating flames of steam like translucent smoke that obscured the atmosphere above. Appearing through this miasma came Maw with hoe in hand, low on the earth, tatters trailing from her dress, departing the fields before all the other slaves. Yet her gait was dignified and purposeful as though now she was now and forever trudging from the whities toward Africa. Shaka ran and greeted her, curious to know why she was leaving the fields before the other slaves and together they walked into their shack, into the shade. After dropping her hoe on the floor, Maw walked across the room and collapsed into her bed flat upon her back, her body pooling upon the quilt like a mudpuddle, supported by the structure of thin, brittle bones poking into her skin. Sweat leaked through her clothes. Stuck into a squint from the sun, her eyes were transfixed upon the horsefly that buzzed above her head.

Shaka clapped his hands together, squashing the bug then kneeled over her, asking, "Why you coming home early?"

"Cause I's tired."

"Tired of what?"

"Tired of toiling. Tired of living."

"But aint they gonna come and get you?"

"If they is, I aint gonna get up for them."

"Maybe Washaka's coming for you."

"He aint coming for some time. I's too old to fly anyhow."

"You aint too old."

"Sho I is. But don't worry. I's gonna get my freedom the only way I can."

"How's that?"

"Dying. Withering into dust and blowing away."

"Dying? But where is you going?"

"Back home."

"But you caint leave me here alone."

Maw continued to stare, sighed, and spoke as though bored by his worry. "He wants you to live alone like the holy folks in Africa. Your Father wants you to suffer."

"Please don't die." Shaka pawed her hand.

"You gots to endure your suffering and your loneliness. At dawn the overseer's coming for you to take my place, to grind your bones into the dirt. Work them fields, Shaka, know the misery of slavery and let the pain strengthen your heart. Niggers will come to suck you into their families, into their weak, soul-numbing love. You'll crave their friendship and their women. But their love's fake and cherishes the worst in you—the thief that steals your spirit. Them is your enemies."

He stroked her hand, not even listening to her. "Please don't die."

"But you caint bend to them, naw, nor kill your hankering for freedom. Endure your suffering until the day of our salvation. Love none but yourself and your Father and the same that lives in others."

"Please."

"Look to Africa."

"But I..."

"I caint stay in this place. I's expecting on dying in peace, Goddamnit, not with your whining. So hush."

She shut her eyelids then her face went blank and her head tilted to the side. She seemed dead except for the slight but strained heaving of her lungs. Above her head dogflies buzzed, waiting like buzzards for their prey but he defended her flesh from their bites.

Outside the window the light became orange and thick. She soon began to chant with her eyes still closed, the tone doleful but serene. The spirits were coming for her, he realized, and he tugged on her arm as though pulling her away from them, hoping to break her trance. Maw jolted then lifted her head from the bed while straining her neck muscles, her expression blank and foul, encapsulating her experience in this world.

She spoke. "It's all right, baby." She collapsed back on the bed, her lungs deflating.

"Maw...Maw..." Shaka grabbed her face, shook her.

After cupping his ear between her breasts and listening into that still, flat chamber, hearing nothing, he clenched his fingers into her flanks and buried his head into her stomach like some leach sucking the remnants of warmth from her body, weeping spasmodically and merging his tears into her sweat. The crickets began their electric and persistent chorus amplifying his weeping outward into the forests and fields. In the distance he heard the singing of the slaves, their voices lower and even more morbid but merging into the chorus of the crickets and his own weeping. When looking out the window, he saw that the ether above was not dark but bestarred with the random, wavering flickers of fireflies that stored and distilled the remains of light for their nocturnal, clandestine duties. He saw the slaves returning from the fields, low and beaten on the earth with hoes and shovels over their shoulders, and he hoped they were bounding for his shack to show their respects to Maw and to alleviate his loneliness. Instead their voices and songs passed and waned then silenced altogether as doors opened and shut, but not his, until the chorus of the crickets returned even louder now into one shrill, hypnotic wail that made his own weeping seem unheard and ignored by everything that ever lived.

Nobody would grieve her death but him, he realized, nobody cared about him, and her greatness amidst slavery would remain ignored. Shaka then heard the noises of the evening—the laughter of children and the crying of babies and the chopping of firewood. As the noises began to wane, he pressed deeper into her stomach, searching for life but increasingly she was becoming cold all the way to her bones and stiffening too. And all his senses and feelings retreated away from life; and his soul flushed from his body and disintegrated into nothingness.

His door was suddenly and forcefully opened, exposing the overseer glowing with light from his lantern, and chewing tobacco, saying, "Where's that wench? Absconded from the fields? Begging for the whip, is she?"

Lifting his head Shaka tried to choke his sobs.

"What you doing, boy?" Casting light through the shack the overseer walked toward Maw and placed his finger upon her neck. "Up and roasted to death. Now I gotta dig her a hole. How absurd—if Whiteoak wants burials for his slaves, then he should dig those holes himself." Then he looked at Shaka. "You dig holes, boy?"

"I aint digging nothing."

"You aint, is you? She worked beyond her usefulness, if you ask me, to spare you the fields. Whiteoak agreed, I suppose, so you would play with his son. But those days are over. Come dawn you hit the fields, starting with digging her grave." The overseer walked from the room and slammed the door.

Shaka remembered the cemetery for slaves on the far side of the fields: He imagined Maw's tombstone carved from logs, inscribed with the scribbles of white men and encaged by that square, white fence. He could not allow her remains to be trapped eternally into this world.

The image of the river flowing onward to Africa flashed across his mind. In the darkness he slid his arms under her armpits and cradled her head onto his chest then yanked her from the bed, causing her to flop on the floor, thudding and shaking the boards, and pulled her across the room, hearing splinters snagging into her clothes, and out the door. Outside the magnitude of the darkness, devoid of boundaries, was stunning. The crickets raised their pitch into a frenzy like some chorus of scavengers feeding upon his anguish by taunting him with the discord of their song. While he dragged her carcass into the forest, something snapped in her shoulder and one of her arms separated more from the rest of her body but stayed adhered into its socket by skin and muscle alone.

At the bank of the river he dropped her. From above starlight sieved through the atmosphere and distilled into particles of moisture, creating a gossamer glowing above the river. The black and oily water curved around the bend and eddied along the bank, forming whirlpools that swirled into the depths. Shaka grabbed her shoulders again and pulled her through cottontails to the shore where they sank into effluvium. With the mud rising to his knees, he stripped her clothes from her carcass, starting with her boots then moving to her blouse, the rotten threads ripping in his fingers until she lay prostrate and naked. He then pulled her into the river, disinterring her from the silt until the water rose around his waist and Maw, flowing from his arms, seemed to almost disperse then disintegrate into the current. Once in the middle of the river, he held on to her by her shoulders and cradled her head and stepped into a whirlpool. Feeling the suction of the current pulling imploringly toward the depths, he sank under the water and resting his cheek upon hers, relinquished her shoulders and in exalted anguish felt her flow away from him into the river that flowed onward through the land of slavery stealthily and mockingly and undeterred into the ocean beyond and onward still, to Africa.

While under the water sensing that his flesh was also disintegrating, Shaka flowed with the current, opening his mouth to taste the rotting, musty flavor of the river. When his lungs ached for air, he pushed from the bottom, puncturing the surface. After swimming toward the shore, he trampled the cottontails and ran blindly and wildly through brambles to his shack. There he stripped from his clothes and lay in bed, swaddled in quilts, foreseeing nothing in his life before his exodus but the strain of reckoning with violence and loneliness.

In the midst of the night Shaka was awakened by a tapping upon his door. While he arose and sat in his bed, the door hesitantly opened to reveal the girl who smooth, dark and nude, with breasts and hips blossoming into womanhood, stood in the doorway, smiling sheepishly while raising her hand and motioning with her finger for him to come toward her, saying, "Come on, Salamander."

Shaka peeled back his quilt and, naked and entranced, walked to the door and curled his fingers around her palm and together they tiptoed into the night that blushed with light and that licked around their loins like invisible tongues and they meandered through the forest upon the warm, sodden earth. They soon arrived at the bank and looked over the river, the surreptitious, molten graveyard.

Shaka kissed her, sliding his tongue into her mouth. His hands dropped along her pelvis as the bone softened into her buttock. As they sat down onto the earth together, he placed his arm around her back and laid her upon the ground and nestled between her legs. She guided him into her and while moaning slightly and befuddled she sucked tight and snug around him like piglets upon the teat. Bliss pulsated above anguish, counterbalancing death with life, resurrecting his mother in the visage of this girl. He imagined his spirit soaring toward his homeland and while thrusting, cried, "Washaka," and spurt his seed. Pain and pleasure, birth and death, were as intertwined as their bodies. Then he collapsed onto the girl, rolled onto his back and stared at the stars in silence while believing he had found the remedy to his loneliness, the incarnation of his mother.

But she intruded, reminding him of his isolation; her voice was pale and viscous. "My motha say that you and Maw is crazy, worshipping demons from Africa. She say that you bound for the whip—that you be that sort of nigger. That I caint touch you or nothing or even look at you."

The night soon erased the impact of her words.

"But around you, Shaka, I feel free like all the whities is gone from the earth. And when you come up inside of me, then don't know what happens. Love, I reckon."

"That's Africa you feel," said Shaka.

"Sho wished I felt that Africa all the time. I caint hardly tolerate the rest of the day."

"But soon we gonna fly to Africa to live forever."

"Forever? You and me?"

"Sho."

"That sounds good." She sat up from the ground and wiped her fingers between her legs then smudged them across his belly. "African juice," she said, rising to her feet and meandering into the forest toward her shack.

"Sixteen," counted Jonah.

The pain now was constant. Time was unbroken except for the numbers.

"Seventeen."

After deadening all his reflexes, the whip was boring into his mind.

"Eighteen."

He was lost, disoriented.

"Nineteen."

He only knew pain without will or purpose, without meaning.

The morning after Shaka buried his mother, dawn oozed from the night like something wounded. The door slammed and, alarmed, Shaka jerked awake to see the giant and malicious overseer stomping into the shack and walking toward the empty bed with Jake shadowing him.

Throwing the quilt onto the ground, he uttered from his coarser and separate realm, "Goddamn. Where is she? Eaten up by coyotes?"

He stomped on the floor with his foot, rattling the boards of the shack. Shaka jumped onto the floor and gathered and donned his clothes, crusted with mud.

"Where is she?" asked Jake.

Buttoning his shirt, Shaka gaped.

"Boy, I said, where's that wench?"

"Where's the wench?" followed Jake.

Shaka felt that these people around him were not real but

spooks like his mother told him. But they looked real. He tottered between realities, between night and day, black and white.

He ventured forward and shouted as though he were speaking to the overseer from another world. "Whitie?"

"What, boy?"

Shaka was surprised the overseer responded. "Whitie?"

"What?" the overseer shouted.

"What, fool?" mocked Jake.

"Where's the wench?"

"Where that wench?" said Jake.

"Gone to Africa."

"To Africa?" said the overseer.

"Where's that?" said Jake. "Around Mobile?"

"How'd she get there?" asked the overseer.

"I done carried her."

"Massa," said Jake. "This here shack's strange and haunted. Maw yanked Shaka from some hollow in the woods and now she done vanished with the wind. They's spooks, these folks."

"Shut up, Jake. Niggers got buttholes for mouths."

"Buttholes for mouth and scat for brains."

At last the overseer looked at the mud caked on Shaka's clothes. "You dumped her in the river, didn't you? You done saved me some heap of trouble."

"Now we aint got to dig," said Jake.

"Reckon not."

"She gone to Africa," said Shaka.

"Whatever, boy. You sure got some strange notions about things. But the fields—the sun, sweat and bugs, your aching back, bloodied fingertips and swollen, chapped feet—that'll teach you to think like the rest of them."

"Pain, Massa, pain," said Jake.

"Pain," agreed the overseer.

"My mouth aint all the time the butthole, huh, Massa?"

"I reckon there's some truth to that, Jake. Now to your school, boy," said the overseer, walking toward the door.

"I aint going," said Shaka without moving.

"Uh-oh," said Jake. "He's needing some instruction."

"Come on, boy," said the overseer nonchalantly.

"Naw." His words felt weak and probed wanly toward the overseer.

"He aint right in the head," said Jake.

At the door the overseer placed a black leather glove over one of his hands, apathetically. "Choose now between obeying my words...or my might. Either way, you obey."

Behind the overseer Jake was waving for Shaka to come, a concerned, worried look across his face, his mouth mimicking the words, "Come on, come on."

Shaka was worried but suspected that he was somehow protected, that all of this would vanish before him like some sort of dream until the overseer lurched forward, reared back and swung his gloved, semi-rigid hand across the side of Shaka's face, dropping him to the ground.

"Get up, boy, and come along."

Shaka sat stunned on the floor, wiping some scattering of tears from his face, feeling all around him becoming intensely, undeniably real. The overseer above him was now removing the glove from his hand and glaring down at Shaka, seeming disgusted with himself.

Jake looked anguished, almost on the verge of tears while his words cleaved apart from him. "Now you done knocked some sense into him." But all the while he motioned for Shaka to come.

Shaka stared back at Jake and fixated on him and not thinking, nor feeling, rose to his feet and followed them out the door into the sodden, salivating dawn, into another form of rebirth more vile and troubling.

The overseer mounted his horse. "See them fields, boy. Your life's as narrow as those glebes of cotton." He yanked on his reins and kicked with his heels, trotting between the rows on his horse behind which Shaka and Jake jogged, panting, until arriving at the edge of the forest where the overseer removed some baskets from the back of his horse and spoke without dismounting. "Jake, you know your job."

Once the overseer galloped away, Jake sighed then placed his hand gently onto Shaka's shoulder. "Sorry about Maw. Nobody knew she died all of sudden so none of us came over and paid our respects. I knowed you feel lonely."

Shaka said nothing.

"But she's sho nuff gone now and aint never coming back. She done sheltered you from the fields while keeping you from us others and taught you some strange notions about things. But aint none of them real and if you aint understanding that, you gonna suffer. You got some taste of that this morning.

"Them rows of cotton are like cages," Jake continued, pointing around the fields. "Above them rows is the hot, scalding sun. To the sides is the whip. Below aint nothing but dirt. Understand? Africa aint out here. This picking aint nothing—aint bad or good, aint this or that. It just is. And you caint escape that, not now, not ever."

Shaka hazily sensed the omnipotence of the white man. Imitating Jake, he lifted his basket from the ground and walked along the row, bent at the hip, carefully pinching his fingers between the husk to remove the plume of cotton which he then dropped into his basket.

"Good, Shaka. They always said you was smart."

Shaka was quiet.

"Obey the rules and life is alright. We come out here, pick for the whitie, retire to our shacks at night to be with our families and friends."

"But I aint got any family or friends."

"But all that's gonna change. Folks is afraid of wild niggers like yourself. Carry on with this picking and forget about Africa and you'll make heaps of friends and one of them wenches too might take some shine to a strong and obedient fellow like yourself. And whenever you's lonely, you come yonder to my shack and sit around the fire."

"Really?" said Shaka.

"Sho. Come for vittling tonight. The wifey expecting to cook up some pig ears for dinner." Jake rose from his slump and popped his vertebrae. "You all right there, Shaka," concluded Jake, placing his hand on Shaka's shoulder.

Feeling grief and relief welling upward from his gut, he wished Jake was his father, someone real and present, not mythic and unseen and lurking only in the future. "I…I aint never had any family but Maw. I aint never..."

"Maw's dead," said Jake gently. "You're part of my family now."

Shaka felt calm and peaceful. Before, he was forever trudging forcefully away from something but now he felt he could rest and exist in this reality. While previously viewing the other slaves disdainfully, as ignorant and cowardly, he felt now that he had secretly envied their simple lives and pleasures, their communities and their sense of belonging. He flowed into the redundancy of his work and the burn of the sun.

For some time they worked in silence. Rising higher above the horizon, the sun began to scorch Shaka and wrench sweat from his body. Not yet noon, his back was aching and his impatience with the drudgery of the task was percolating into anger. He stepped away from Jake, turned his back and pissed—golden, rancid, burning like molten sunshine. Then he returned to his picking.

Jake asked, "How's your back and fingers?"

Shaka tried to focus.

"Don't fight, think or question, just sweat all the trouble from your mind. Once the sun gallops across the sky like some spooked horse, the whities will coil their whips away and we can nestle into our shacks."

Shaka looked across the fields toward the gang of slaves who were slumped in the fields in the distance like weary bovines. With his tolerance waning, he tried to imagine working in this manner all day and all week except Sunday for the remainder of his life, all his dreams sweated away into the dirt, his life nothing more than this endless and stooped march up and down these rows of cotton driven ever onward by the fear of the whip.

While picking one of the plumes, Shaka snagged his finger on the husk and spouted angrily toward Jake, "Why teach us to live this way?"

Jake scratched his scalp frantically. "Cause there aint nothing else. I done seen all them fools who think they's too wild and strong for slavery, seen their bloodied backs, their withered souls, their weeping mothers, seen them killed or sold from their families. Accept your fate—the only fate that exists—and save yourself some heap of anguish in the future."

"Accept your fate," repeated Shaka over again obsessively as though trying to block the words now coming clearly into his mind. "Niggers will come to suck you into their families, into their weak, soul-numbing love. But that love is the thief that steals your spirit. Them is your enemies."

Maw's prophesies was coming true, he realized; he was already attempting to displace Washaka with this weak, cowered surrogate to escape his loneliness. He wanted to run but could not, feeling paralyzed by the thought that maybe slavery was inescapable, maybe Washaka was not real, maybe Maw was crazy. But the thought was so intolerable that when some butteflies fluttered from some flowers blooming amidst the weeds, Shaka dropped his basket and overwhelmed with the desire to escape, sprawled his arms and tore through the glebes, chasing the butterflies.

"Come back here," shouted Jake, a tinge of terror in his voice. "There aint gonna be any pig ears for you now."

Shaka ran not along but across the rows of cotton, shredding his pants. About midway through the fields he lost the butterfly and bounded into the forest where he found the old, sacred tree that in the past had showed him his path to Africa. After climbing through the limbs and perching in the crown of the tree, he saw the river before him but not the lake which was cloaked in some thick, flat haze. He stayed there for some time, too afraid to run farther, too afraid to return, feeling paralyzed. He heard barks before long then saw the hounds bolting across the fields on the same path as him, wild on his scent as they entered into the forest and started within moments to claw irately on the trunk below him, barking viciously.

He waited for his body to shrink and for his arms to sprout feathers. But nothing happened. The overseer shouted angrily from the ground. Driven not by faith but terror, Shaka rose from his perch and scuttled out onto one of the limbs of the tree. He jumped. Gravity relinquished. He flapped his arms and screeched.

"Twenty," counted Jonah.

Nothing.

"Twenty-one."

Darkness.

"Twenty-two."

Oh, Father, why have you forsaken me?

Shaka opened his eyes while fingers poked painfully into his ribs. Surrounding him, imprisoning him were white, wooden walls. Above him stood a man, tall and thin and gaunt, whose face was scarred above his eyes. He was not in Africa, he realized, but caught by Whiteoak. He tried to move but pain jolted in his ribs, paralyzing him. Whiteoak walked away from him into the corner of the room, his footsteps knocking across the floor and huddled with the overseer.

"Fell from the tree?"

"No sir. He jumped."

Silence.

"He's not broke yet. They think he's spooked. On account of him playing with your son and all, he aint indoctrinated."

Silence.

"A whipping alone will work on this boy now."

"Wait," said Whiteoak.

"Yes sir."

"But have him report to the fields soon."

"Yes sir."

"Don't let him run."

"Run? Not barefoot with cracked ribs."

Was he betrayed by his father, thought Shaka? No, he was not betrayed; rather Washaka did not even exist except as some figment of his dreams—dreams that disappeared in the light of day. Jake was right—nothing existed for him but to eat, to sleep, to march up and down those rows of cotton for the remainder of his life, calculating all his action to avoid the lash while trying to eke bits of happiness from his misery—until his mind was stupefied and content. And all this even seemed preferable compared to the anguish of striving for something as invisible and powerless as the wind.

But even without Washaka he would never serve the white man. He crawled from the bed and jumped onto the ground. Pain jolted his ribs, which served not to paralyze but drive him into some feral, violent state. Naked except for his pants and barefoot, he walked toward and opened the door.

The slaves outside were slouching along the glebes toward their shacks, the glow and thickness of the sunset shellacking their flesh like honey. Shaka slipped out the door and bolted through a garden, trampling plants. He crawled through some boards into a coop, caught one chicken, wrung its neck and as it spasmed in his clutches, he then crawled again out of the coop and ran quickly along the edge of the fields. Under the cover of the trees, he trotted toward his shack, the pain in his ribs now fading but still goading him onward into a more fierce and determined state of mind.

He crawled into his shack from the back window, landing awkwardly on the floor. Before him he saw someone white on the periphery of his vision. Shaka instinctively charged forward slamming him into the wall then pinning him to the floor, clenching his hands over his throat before realizing that Jonah was beneath him. But he did not release.

"What you want, whitie?"

"What the fuck you doing?"

"Did Whiteoak send you to get me?"

"That bastard don't send me nowhere."

Shaka did not see his friend, only the color of his skin, the augur of cruelty to come.

"I heard your mother died. I was waiting on you."

Shaka released his clutches but still sat limply on top of his friend, looking ahead at nothing.

"He took my mother away too," Jonah said. "I thought you might…I thought you might…I just wanted to see you, is all."

Shaka wiped the tears from his eyes. Then he sprang off Jonah and stood above him as Jonah scrambled to his feet.

"Whiteoak's on my ass," said Shaka. "I gots to get out of here."

Shaka rummaged around his shack and from under his mattress pulled a spear made from a sapling stained with blood, an arrowhead at the top held fast by strands of leather. Also from under his mattress he pulled then donned some kind of contraption around his shoulders that resembled wings made from bones and feathers.

"I caint stay with you no more," he said, crawling through the window.

As Shaka bolted through the forests along the river, he realized that Jonah was following him. Shaka stopped, turned, and jabbed his spear toward Jonah who dodged to the side barely missing the arrowhead.

"Get away from me," Shaka said.

"I want to get out of here just as much as you."

"But you aint even know where I's getting?"

"Where is you?"

"Some place where they kill whities like you."

"Where about's that?"

"Beyond the water, Africa," Shaka said boldly, his eyes widening.

"I can take my chances."

"Then how is I suppose to run from the whitie with the whitie?"

"I don't know but my mother was a whore."

Shaka did not know the meaning of the word "whore" but he liked Jonah's desperation. "I reckon they might tolerate the sons of whores."

Shaka gazed into the hazy and darkening atmosphere. He

maniacally thrust his spear upward, wanting to pierce the clouds to see the heavens beyond. But as pain thrust through his ribs, he screamed in agony and when seeing Jonah looking at him as though he was deranged, Shaka said, "I aint waiting on you."

He ran again along the embankment. As the remains of light drained from the atmosphere, making all dark and amorphous, the pain in his ribs drove him through some portal where everything became incorporeal, almost unreal, while he felt this sense of animalistic and tumultuous euphoria as though he were an eagle with crippled wings flying above a mire, painfully enraptured in flight but terrified of falling.

The moon soon sank into the horizon, sealing the forest in darkness so that his cadence became irregular. At last he stumbled upon some logs and landed upon a cushion of mulch.

"I caint get on no more," he said. "We gonna stay here."

Jonah collapsed by Shaka, panting. Shaka scrambled down to the river, collected some rocks then returned to build a fire circle. After piling twigs into the circle, he removed some matches from a groove in his spear. Moments later flames erupted and leapt onto the pile of twigs until they were surrounded by the flames that reached through the night like some palm laden with heat and merged their souls into this quavering, uprooted world.

Jonah plucked the feathers from the chicken, skewered the carcass then began to roast the meat while Shaka continued to feed the flame. Jonah removed the bird from the flame and stabbed the other end of the limb into the ground to allow the meat to cool. He then removed the bird from the stake and ripped the carcass down the middle, handing one of the halves to Shaka. They gnawed through the layer of singed and black flesh into the oily and white meat within, some of which was cooked, some raw, their faces smudged with grease and warmed by fire.

Once the bird was devoured Shaka stared vacantly into the flames. As the chirping of the crickets rose into a cloying and discordant crescendo, he felt the pulsing of the pain in his ribs amidst the infinity of the dark and menacing forest around them. He moved closer to his friend, almost within touch, wanting to feel the comfort of his body.

"Are we really going to Africa?" asked Jonah stupefied

"Sho we is."

"But there aint nothing out here but woods and more farms up the way."

Shaka looked over at Jonah, his whiteness taunting the foolishness of their quest. "Cause you caint see Africa. But I reckon I can fix that."

Shaka lurched toward Jonah and grabbed him by his collar and ripped his shirt from his back.

"What the hell you doing?" asked Jonah.

"You caint go to Africa looking white. They gonna kill you."

"Kill me?"

Shaka then grabbed Jonah and ripped his trousers from his legs until Jonah at last freeing himself from Shaka, stood naked and pale in the firelight, anomalous amidst the blackness of the night. He smiled oddly, amazed with his nudity. Shaka then reached toward the fringes of the fire and grabbed some charcoal which he crumbled in his hands and smeared over Jonah, starting with his feet then moving to his waist and chest until Jonah himself, liking the experience, began to rub the charcoal into his face. In the end he stood negroid, widening his nostrils, grinning.

"They aint gonna kill me now," said Jonah.

"They might. Your heart still beats with the blood of your father."

After grabbing his spear Shaka grabbed Jonah by his hand then sliced the arrowhead over his palm, making a gash that oozed satiny, purplish blood. Afterward Shaka did the same with his own palm. Then he pressed their palms together, allowing their blood to intermingle and flow sacramentally into the veins of each other, solidifying their bond.

"We brothers now of flesh and blood," said Shaka.

"Sho nuff," said Jonah wanly.

"They aint gonna kill you."

Breaking the adhesion of their blood which had begun to coagulate, they separated their hands and stood for the moment, awkward and uncertain. Darkness settled over the fire and shrouded over their bodies and they settled onto the ground, lying close to the fire to feel the remnants of warmth. But as the night seemed to suffocate the fire, the flames changed to embers and the crickets encroached with their version of annihilation. Shaka felt the coming of fear and crawled closer to his friend, nestled close to him and slid his wounded hand into Jonah's hand and together, scab upon scab, they vanished into their last and only refuge: sleep.

"Twenty-three," counted Jonah.

Oh, Father, deliver me unto you.

"Twenty-four."

Deliver me unto you.

"Twenty-five."

Deliver me, Oh Father…

"Twenty-six."

Unto you…

"Twenty-seven."

Father…

"Twenty-eight"

Deliver me…

"Twenty-nine."

Please.

In the morning Shaka awakened with his head falling from Jonah and thudding upon the earth. He opened his eyes into dawn, seeing only ashes in the fire-circle and dew beaded upon the foliage. When hearing hounds barking in the distance and bounding toward them, he jumped to his feet while feeling the pain in his ribs. Surveying his surroundings he saw Jonah across from him, still naked and looking panicked while trying to rub off the ashes that made him look less negroid but more ghostly.

"Run!" shouted Shaka. "Run!"

Shaka scrambled toward the river and turned. The hounds approached, barking and encircled him while nipping at his flanks so his only escape was the river. Behind the hounds arrived horsemen, brandishing steel and leather with rifles toted over their shoulders, seeming nonchalant at first but quickening to the chase.

While moving toward the river, Shaka heard shouted over the din, "Get away from him."

"What the hell is that?" one of the horsemen said.

"Aint that Whiteoak's boy?"

"I reckon. They said he done run off with the slave."

"Reckon he thinks he's nigger."

"I've seen stranger things around these parts."

"Reckon we ought to show him what being nigger is like?"

Shaka saw Jonah coming toward the horsemen holding the spear cocked behind his shoulder, his body resembling something that just crawled from some hole in the earth. When the horsemen startled and turned their horses from the river, Jonah heaved his spear which landed lamely on the rump of one of the horses before falling to the ground. But that horse reared and whinnied and upset the other horses. Amidst the confusion Shaka slunk into the river and drifted with the current under the water, opening his eyes into fetid and murky green. A gun fired, muffled by water. As his lungs ached he emerged from the surface of water where gasping for air, he saw men running along the bank and one man down the stream crossing a sandbar to the other side. Shaka realized that escape was impossible, that he was surrounded on both sides of the river. Another gun fired. Lead whooshed through the water above his feet. Again he dove even deeper into the river until reaching the bottom, touching silt, reminding him of the decaying body of his mother.

Words emerged in his mind. "Your father wants you to suffer."

His father did not want him to be desperate and afraid, wanted him to endure his suffering and loneliness manfully. Pain was his path to salvation, his minister in flight. He ceased to struggle, hovered over the bottom limp and peaceful until the edge of the sandbar rose under him. Hands locked around his arms and yanked him from the water, the pain sharp in his ribs. Remaining limp he was carried toward the bank dangling in the air and dumped onto the ground.

"Got him."

"I was reckoning on shooting the shit. Until like them good niggers, he lay over and flop."

Arms rolled him onto his stomach. His hands were jerked behind his back and cinched with rope then his legs too. His body was lifted and laid stomach down across the rear of one of the horses behind the saddle. The horse began to trot, each cadence pummeling his ribs like fists and soon cut from the trail into the forests until arriving on the road that led to the gates of the plantation. After the horsemen dismounted at the end of the road, Shaka was untied and muscled from the horse and thrown upon the ground into caked mud and fecal dust. The patrolmen guffawed. But silence truncated their laughter. While the horsemen rode from the plantation, Shaka sensed the presence of Whiteoak like something impending and regnant. Fingers stabbed into his armpits and dragged him toward the barn where he was tied to the black, resin-coated gibbet with his hands above his head.

When Whiteoak walked from the barn, Shaka craned his neck toward the fields. Hoards of slaves headed toward the barn then gathered around the gibbet, congregating in groups devoid of individuality as they stood on the dust, apathetic and silent and motionless, gazing into the atmosphere listlessly. Amongst the crowd was Jake leaning into the barn, lacking his usual expression of knavery while looking at Shaka without any hint of regret or even acknowledgment. They were all subdued by Whiteoak, mimicking his mien as vassals of his reign, waiting intent but bored to pilfer the spirit of Shaka into subservience.

"Salamander."

"Huh," Shaka mumbled. He turned his head, seeing his girlfriend in tattered and filthy clothes.

"Why you hanging on that thing?"

"I don't know."

"Jake said you run away."

"Sho."

"Where was you running?"

"To Africa."

"Without me?"

"I was gonna come back and get you."

"Now you caught by the patrol."

"I let them catch me."

"Sho you did, Shaka." She became sad. "Oh, Shaka, you bound... Oh, Shaka...they about to..." She was interrupted by hooves clanking upon the ground.

He craned his neck but could not see so he turned toward her. Dread was on her face. "Who's that?" asked Shaka.

"That's your friend Jonah. And he with Whiteoak," she said beginning to weep.

"That's Jonah?"

"That's him," she said, shuffling from the gibbet.

"What's happening?"

"Oh, Salamander," she said while tears beaded under her eyes. "He got the whip."

"The whip?"

"He gonna whip you."

"But he's my friend."

"Not anymore," she lamented between choking on her sobs. "My motha said that I shaint mind with you, that you just wrench my heart. But I didn't listen cause all them others—they wasn't like you. And now look, she's right. I'm sorry but I caint bear this."

"Don't leave me," whimpered Shaka.

"It the truth...I caint leave you...But I caint stay with you neither." She retreated from the gibbet, turned and ran into the fields, vanishing from sight.

"Maw," he shouted, weeping openly now. "Maw."

He struggled against the bindings, writhing and shaking

and hollering, hoping the words would exact magic. "Washaka... Washaka...Washaka." But the bindings stayed intact until his muscles were exhausted and his throat hoarse and his motion absorbed into the hot, fetid stasis of the atmosphere.

Leather hissed through the air, thumped on the dirt. Again the leather hissed, slapped his back but the blow was weak and the pain was tolerable.

Then the blow was hard and jarring.

"Jonah, please don't," Shaka shouted as he craned his neck to look behind him while waiting for the next blow.

Hissing, leather slapped his back.

"Jonah, please don't," said Shaka weeping while looking around at the other slaves for sympathy but they failed to change their expressions or acknowledge his words, remaining impassive and bored, making him wonder whether he spoke at all.

Hissing, leather slapped his back. But once the whip recoiled from the gibbet and Shaka recovered from the blow, he heard Jonah behind him whimpering then wailing and collapsing into the dust and thrashing the whip about as though inflicting the pain upon himself until that noise too was absorbed into silence. The hooves of horses then clanked away from the gibbet.

Shaka believed the whipping was finished until seeing his girlfriend coming from the fields while weeping and pointing behind him, saying, her words barely audible from that distance, "Whiteoak got the whip now. He gonna kill you."

Limp in the bindings, Shaka waited in terror.

"Thirty," counted Jonah.

"Deliver me unto you, Father."

"Shut up, boy," shouted Jonah.

"Thirty-one."

The pain was subsiding.

"Thirty-two."

He was numb.

"Thirty-three."

His flesh was just a shredded, blunted carapace, his mind obscure.

"Thirty-four."

Shaka turned his head and in the distance saw the slight, almost indistinguishable horizon separating the gulf and sky—both of which seemed to consist of the same substance, varying only by shades of blue. Suspended there were the wings which black and inverted were soaring untethered from the pull of the earth.

"Thirty-five."

Shaka relinquished all—pain, time, desire and hope—and dropped into that chasm devoid of earth.

"Thirty-six."

"At last Father."

"Thirty-seven."

Routinely, mechanically, Jonah raised the branch above his head, cocked his arm, released the tension, splattering the branch into Shaka's back—in the same fashion as all the other blows, without thinking or feeling. Now he did not even notice that Shaka was not moving or flinching but hanging there limp.

"Please stop, Massa," said Nomaw, her voice now hoarse. "He aint moving no more."

She grabbed Jonah around his waist to try to stop him but he twisted from her clutches, stepped back and kicked her. Jake lurched forward and snarled but before colliding with Jonah, he dropped into the sand next to Nomaw who lay there on her side, weeping, blood oozing from her mouth.

"Thirty-eight." Jonah again cocked his arm while hearing his wife shouting behind him.

Alarmed, he turned his head and saw Shobuck running toward him while hollering and wielding a small rusty knife in his hand. Jonah quickly sidestepped then extended his leg and tripped Shobuck who stumbled and fell to the ground. Then both of his children, James and Josh, ran past him and descended upon Shobuck and beat him with all their might across his back and legs with the poles they held in their hands. Skin was tearing in places and Shobuck was crouching and whining and trying to defend himself with his arms while thrashing toward them with his knife.

His children were shouting between shrieks of violent, nervous laughter, "Beat the nigger. Beat the nigger. Beat the nigger dead," tottering between the world of violence and play.

"Oh, God," Jonah said. "What have I done?"

Past and present merged inside of him. He was the boy before his father, and the father before his sons, locking them all in the chains of violence. He turned around to look at the body hanging from the tree, motionless—seeing the blood, welts and cuts and underneath he could see the darker, membranous flesh that was thrashed years before—the scars of then and now, the pain of generations merging into one moment. Like some filthy and gaseous cloud, masses of mosquitoes buzzed around Shaka's back frenzied on the vapors of blood.

Jonah stared around the island which remained the same: The gulf was calm, the sand was unblemished and the sun was eclipsed behind the clouds, shadowing the island amidst the radiance of the gulf. All he could hear was the squawks of gulls flocking around the island and settling on the sandbar, chorusing the violence with their anxious, piercing cries.

"Who did this," he asked?

"You did," said Jake.

"No," said Jonah, looking down at the branch in his hands, at the scabs of white sand congealing atop the blood. "Father made me do this."

His gut swirled. He buckled at the waist and heaved. When vomit seeped into his mouth, he pinched his lips to block the flow and after the excess trickled from his lips, he swallowed.

CHAPTER ELEVEN

Standing alone on the dune, Eloise touched the feathers of the black inverted wings which seemed to radiate something both hallowed and fearful across the island, making her feel the presence of both death and hope. She was ashamed but also intrigued that they somehow reminded her of the crucifix.

She noticed within moments that the wings were coated with mud and ashes which fell away to the ground with some scraping to expose the feathers underneath as pink—as bright, glaring pink. Before she assumed that these wings were probably from some bird which Shaka captured—one of the herons from the sandbar—but having never seen any large, pink birds around their island, she began to wonder.

Dropping to her knees she stroked her hands along the staff under the wings. Toward the bottom the wood was still covered with bark—pine bark—while the remainder was stripped bare. Because the wood was still oozing with sap, she concluded that it was probably cut within days.

The island of course did not have any pine trees and from what she gathered, the cays in the distance did not either; they were all covered with mangroves. She concluded that the wings were not made from materials found even close to the island. She gazed toward the mainland, the coastline full of swamps and reptiles—an awful, dark place, she imagined.

"Who's out there?" she said aloud. "Who left these wings?"

She thought of destroying the wings or at least laying them down on the ground to prevent them from manifesting their power but she resisted, felt the need to allow them to continue to work their spell over the island.

She trudged through the sand over to the slaves' tent. She was surprised to find that out front Nomaw was laying her head in Jake's lap while he wiped the blood from her mouth. They turned their heads, ignoring her.

"Are you all right, Nomaw?" she asked.

Nomaw didn't say anything.

"May I help you in some way—bring you some water, something to eat?"

"On account of your help, Missus," said Nomaw, "I just about got Shaka killed. So just leave me alone."

Eloise had never been addressed so disdainfully by any Negro either at Whiteoak or at her father's church. In her own soul she felt their pain—the anguish of having all of their humanity suddenly stripped from them.

"I never wanted something like this to happen. I was trying to help. My heart was broken twice, once for Shaka and once for my own husband."

"But he aint done nothing," interrupted Jake.

"Who?" said Eloise, confused.

"Shaka. He aint done nothing but catch the spirit. Aint that what your father wants? But now we getting whipped? Problem is, yawl whities preach Jesus but we all know that you worship that fellow in hell."

"Jesus is my savior."

"Then he aint ours."

"I need to know something, Nomaw," said Eloise hurriedly, trying to thwart her tears.

"Leave her alone," said Jake, wiping the sweat from her forehead. "On account of her rattling her mouth, she got some of her teeth knocked out. Served her right, I reckon."

"I need to know where those wings came from."

"We don't know nothing about them wings," said Jake. "They come all over the place, in the sky and in the water, on that dune over there."

"But did Shaka put them there?"

"So Massa can whip him? Them wings just there like the wind."

"Like the wind?"

"Yes," said Jake.

Eloise then stepped inside the tent where Shaka lay on his stomach, the blood on his back congealing into scabs. Pear sat next to him and while swatting away the swarm of mosquitoes, looked at Eloise briefly, her face twisted with agony, then looked away hatefully.

"Get out of here."

"I'm so sorry," said Eloise, trying to restrain her tears. "May I…"

"Leave us alone."

"Please just tell me first where those wings come from?"

"I don't know," she said.

"Shaka didn't leave those wings?"

"No," said Pear. "Him did."

"Him—who's that?"

"You gonna know soon enough."

"What do you mean?"

When Pear did not respond to her question, Eloise backed out of the tent and not restraining her tears anymore, ran toward her own tent. After composing herself she walked inside and saw Jonah sitting on his trunk with their children next to him, their ankles bound with twine, Jonah wrapping his arms around their necks and pressing their heads into his sweaty and hairy chest while covering their eyes with his hands like he was trying to shield them retroactively from what they saw by the tree. Not resisting, the children just sat there like trapped and blinded animals. Not even looking at her as she entered, Jonah stared ahead listlessly at nothing, sweat beaded on his forehead, his emotions seeming paralyzed in conflict like men of equal strength and skill wrestling with each other.

Eloise gently removed his arms from around their sons' necks, untied them and walked with them outside the tent and sat them down in the sand where she could still see them from inside.

Into their baffled faces, she said, "Yawl stay here, you understand?" She then walked back and sat close to Jonah on her stool, her back turned toward her children to block their view and her voice.

"How did they get free?" asked Jonah angrily.

"Who?"

"Our children."

"You mean when you were whipping Shaka?"

"Yes," said Jonah.

"I kept them in their tent to keep them from hearing—even covered their ears and sang songs to them. But they heard everything—the slapping of the whip, the wailing and weeping. When they questioned me about what was happening, I lied to them by telling them that you were playing rough-and-tumble with the slaves in the same way that they sometimes played with Shobuck. And in their own confused and traumatized minds—it's probably hard for them to acknowledge the violence of their father—they believed me.

"Becoming concerned that you might actually kill Shaka, I stepped outside the tent to see what was happening and when coming back, I found our children were gone—evidently having escaped right about the time that Shobuck decided to launch his attack upon you. Ironically, if they had not chased after Shobuck, he probably would have stuck that knife into you.

"So blame me not," concluded Eloise, her voice strong, "for the behavior you promote in your children."

He spoke awkwardly like he was forcing himself to reveal his thoughts. "I just don't want them to become like me."

"Then don't act that way. You didn't have to destroy Shaka like that. You didn't have to ruin the remains of goodwill that exist on this island. Even your own father claimed that all deviancy should be managed as gently as possible."

His mood quickly changed again. "Don't talk to me about my father. I warned that boy, told him his due for his transgression. His behavior not only broke the rules but also flaunted his defiance in front of everyone. And my father would never in this situation back down from force—would whip that boy even closer to death as an example to the others."

Flummoxed, she said, "I've never suggested that you're not as good as your father."

"And consider your own caprices," said Jonah. "Yesterday you tell me to reinstate order on the island. But once that happens you condemn me for my actions."

"I never persuaded you to use that whip— would never encourage you to destroy the mind and body of another man even to protect our children. Not ever. Do not shirk your blame onto me."

"But none of this would have happened if you had not provoked me."

"Only something worse," she said. "And probably to you."

The conversation stalled as they looked away from each other with disgust. She knew she would never see him the same again, perhaps never experience those moments of fleeting, almost inchoate love. Even now she could hear the hum of the whip, his voice clicking off the numbers clocklike, his arm mechanically cocking and releasing in the same fashion as he sometimes made love to her. She realized then what she was always trying to deny: that she loathed her husband, his capriciousness, his need for power, for still remaining dragooned to his dead father. And even the love she sometimes felt for him was based on pity—as Christ loved the infidels, the destitute, the odious of the earth.

"You were my wife once," said Jonah. "Now you constantly undermine me. And the result is that our system—our family, our slaves—are falling into chaos. After being introduced to Christianity by your father, the slaves have become uppity and subversive as we predicted, not knowing their place anymore in the echelon of command. Even you—and now our children—do not know their place. Nature is not that cruel but tamper with its processes and you ignite its fury."

"Will you ever look at yourself, Jonah? Or will you continue to shirk your vices onto others and make them suffer?"

The stench of their bodies was fumigating the tent in the heat, making them repellant to one another. Eloise looked over her shoulder at their children who remained where she put them, dazed in the sun.

Eloise studied Jonah who was still slumped with his head almost between his knees like he was thinking. She hesitated about telling him what she discovered earlier that day about the wings—after all, he was not worthy of her trust or even her respect anymore. But she acknowledged that her family—from which she now excluded Jonah—was at threat not only from the slaves whose anger was mounting but possibly something other as well. Maybe by telling him about the wings, she could force his attention elsewhere, allowing her to try to assuage some of the tension with the slaves to prevent them from turning on her family.

So she told him what she discovered about the wings and about her conversations with the slaves—while to her surprise Jonah listened intently as though he had already somehow drawn the same conclusion as her.

"I suspect the slaves are lying or not revealing all of the truth to protect Shaka," said Jonah.

"Or perhaps Shaka's lying to them so they believe they're telling me the truth," said Eloise.

"And why would he do that—lie to them?" asked Jonah.

"If he did somehow leave those wings, perhaps he isn't telling them so they'll believe that something's out there coming to redeem them. He can control them better that way."

"But if he did not leave them but knows who did, then maybe he just doesn't want them to know yet."

"To know what?"

"I don't know."

Jonah was pressing his fingers into his temples and sometimes cradling his head forcefully in his hands as though trying to contain something. While rocking back and forth, he said, "The preponderance of the evidence suggests that those wings were not left by Shaka but by another source."

"Then who?"

Eloise tried to read Jonah. But he was looking at the ground, rubbing his temples.

"Someone out there," she said, pointing toward the mainland. "Maybe someone who doesn't want us here. Someone dangerous. Perhaps someone who is in contact with our slaves, controlling their minds—maybe even from the beginning."

"Something submerged," blurted Jonah, not looking at her, jolting every muscle in his body. "Something malignant."

Startled by his reaction, Eloise slowed down to try to bring him back into reality. "But who, Jonah? Nobody lives around here."

"I've known something was here ever since we arrived—known that something was out there. I've been trying to kill it ever since."

"But who, Jonah? You think it's escaped slaves? Natives? Even you told me that this area was known for harboring convicts and pirates."

"No, its something more," Jonah said, sitting up suddenly with his eyes wide.

"What do you mean?"

"I don't know," said Jonah sounding strange and haunted. He rose from his trunk and paced about the tent. "If it's still out there—and I sense its presence—then I will find it, capture it and kill it."

"But maybe it doesn't need killing."

"Yes, it does," said Jonah. "It has stalked me from the beginning."

"You're more superstitious than the slaves." Eloise sat silently as Jonah paced about the tent, realizing that she was yet again inadvertently releasing some sort of madness inside him. "Perhaps we should proceed calmly, very calmly. And devise some sort of plan for protecting ourselves."

"But my plan is already designed."

"What plan?" She paused, watching as he rummaged around the tent, his movements becoming mechanical again. In his trunk he found his rifle which he loaded, stuffing more lead and powder in the pockets of his pants. He then found the same jacket that she wore the day before made from heavy black wool with shiny copper buttons. Grimacing in the rancid and stultifying heat of the tent, he pulled the jacket over his sweaty, bare torso and closed the buttons all the way to the top.

As he walked toward the door, she said desperately, "Where are you going?"

"To prepare for his return."

"But whose return?"

As he marched from the tent toward their sons, into the blaze of the sun, she saw the terror on his face.

CHAPTER TWELVE

"I will stay with you forever," Pear said.

Shaka lay inside the tent—for how many days he did not know—flat on his stomach, his cheek pressed flush against the rough, straw mat separating him from the sand below. When opening his eyes, drifting into some vague and hazy awareness, he saw only darkness and heard only the swashing of water, not even sure he was alive, maybe dreaming, maybe dead—nothing seeming real except for the sensation of pain pressing down upon his back.

Stay with me, Father. Please stay with me.

Pear was gently turning him on his side, putting the cup to his mouth; he tasted broth: salt and bones and seaweed. "We gonna find our home in Africa next to the river and sow our fields with barley. I can see you hunting in the forest, bringing your kill home to your family. We all sitting around the fire with our chilluns, roasting the meat, eating the greens and corn from our garden. We're free, Shaka, free."

Sometimes his back felt numb; maybe his back did not exist anymore, he thought. But slowly the pain would build in intensity until he was gritting his teeth and clinching his fingers into the sand, straining for breath. But the pain remained on the fringes of his consciousness—something like the way rain sounded on the outside of his tent.

How long, Father, how long?

The pain began to seep into his soul, almost undetected.

Why have you left me, Father?

When he was on the verge of crying, the pain would suddenly subside, quenched by something mysterious inside of him and his back would become numb again.

I caint feel…caint feel…nothing.

She was laying something damp on his back, smelling of seaweed. "This will keep the bugs away. This will heal your wounds."

Please leave. I aint wanting anyone to see me this way, wounded and broken by the wrath of another man. Please leave, leave me alone.

"You's healing up fine."

Leave me alone, girl.

"Soon we going to Africa."

He could feel the pain of Jonah, that angry and violated boy, seething into his back—could feel his anger and arrogance and pain wounding him for the remainder of his life.

Why did you allow him? Why did you allow him to hurt me?

Another woman was inside the tent. Shaka closed his eyes, turned away from her, laid his other cheek flat on the mat, staring at some bug lumbering across the ridges of straw.

Leave me alone. I aint wanting to be seen this way.

"Leave us alone."

"I'm sorry for what he did to you," the other woman said, weeping.

"He aint saying nothing to you."

Please leave me alone.

"Please forgive me for bringing this upon you."

"Leave him alone."

"I will pray for you every day."

Why you allowing this woman, his woman, to see me this way, Oh Father?

Later he awoke numb on his back, opening his eyes into light which even when filtering through the canvas, was too bright and intrusive. On hands and knees he crawled outside his tent then stood and walked behind some stand of sea oats and peed something the color of rust that smelled of poison even over the salt and seaweed.

Turning around and blinded by the light, he stood outside the front of the tent and not from hope or desire but apathy, he looked down on the four other slaves who were digging trenches into the beach and tossing the sand into the gulf, seeming to help the water dissolve the island into oblivion. Above them was their master, the man with the whip, rifle slung back over his shoulder.

You're stupid and weak, brethren.

They stopped digging and wiped sweat from their brow and looked in his direction, some pointing their hands as though amazed.

You deserve to suffer. As I have suffered.

Shaka shook his fist angrily at them. Exhausted with the effort, he turned and walked back inside the tent, wanting to disappear back into the shade. The girl was again at his side—she was always there—taking his hand and leading him back into the tent like he was some old, cantankerous man too futile to threaten anyone. He lay on the mat again and placed his forehead directly on the straw, closing his eyes.

"He seen you, Massa did."

Why have you let him see me this way?

"You aint needing to scare folks like that. Just lay here, baby."

When the pain came again, rage erupted from his gut—the ever-present, always-clamoring rage at God for borning him into shackles, at his mother for abandoning him to the overseer, at the whities for dragooning him every day of his life, at other slaves for their acceptance and cultivation of their bondage, and even at himself for always striving for freedom but ending always in defeat and pain. Usually this rage was contained and managed, funneled into his ambitions or alleviated in wild, violently euphoric flights through the forest at midnight. But now the rage spread from his gut throughout his body.

Rage and pain, aint they the same, each fueling the other?

Gripping his fingers deeper into the sand, Shaka saw himself standing over Jonah who was beaten and bloody and barely conscious beneath him. After cutting through his breastplate with his machete, Shaka drove his hands upward into his diaphragm and ripped his heart from its carapace, holding it now in front of Jonah's face as the life faded from his eyes. He could feel the blood running down the sides of his arms.

Give me the strength, Oh Father. Give me the strength to do what you will not.

Rising from his mat he walked outside and headed across the island.

"Where you going?"

To kill.

The girl was gently pulling him back into the tent. He felt weak and unable to resist and he was lying back down inside the tent, placing his cheek against against the mat. Not his own fear nor his own weakness but something not understood kept him lying there and breathing hard, his life but one omniscience of pain.

"Back at Whiteoak we gonna find ourselves some shack all to ourselves. You aint got to work in them fields. You can build things and I can work with Nomaw. We got to prove that we aint trouble, that we can behave ourselves. At midnight we can go back into the forest by the river, just the two of us, and pretend that we's free, free, baby, like we always wanted."

Leave me alone.

Closing his eyes he turned his head, not wanting to see her.

Leave me alone.

He sunk even more deeply into the earth, heavy with shame and while fading away into sleep, he thought, I aint me. I aint me. I was never even born.

He awakened, hearing a gunshot booming across the island. He opened his eyes—only saw heat filtering through the canvas of the tent. After turning his head he placed his cheek flush with the mat, seeing that nobody was inside the tent with him except for the mosquitoes buzzing above his back, scavenging upon his blood as though he were already dead.

I aint me. I aint me. I aint even alive.

His back became one constant, dull ache. Not able to either resist or avoid the pain, he succumbed to exhaustion, the sort that was not soothing but that held him down against his will and suffocated him. His rage was like demons without any place to settle—nothing to inhabit or remember or regret—and were thus exorcised from his body. For hours—how many he could not say—he faded into sleep while awakened at times to the sound of a gunshot, momentarily startled, feeling the heat of the overly bright and intrusive sun scalding his back.

I aint nothing. I caint hurt or kill.

In his sleep he was swimming from the river, emerging onto the bank soft with effluvium and loam, naked except for the cloth around his loins, feeling the warmth of the air. Ahead was Maw, his mother, watching him while sitting amongst green reeds swaying in the breeze. Her face was free of strain, serene yet vital. Shaka walked toward her but she did not come to greet him but stayed, not moving.

Are we home?

She smiled.

Shaka looked into the atmosphere at splotches of bulbous, white clouds blocking the sun, holding the earth captive in shadow. But the clouds drifted away and the earth became light, revealing the clarity of the water and the verdant plains stretching into the horizon.

Are we home? he said again.

Again she smiled and as the clouds drifted over and away from the sun, he saw her face changing in shade from dark to light, from black to…

Mother.

He writhed now on the mat, rubbing his forehead on the straw, wanting to scar his face.

"Why have you forsaken me?"

"I aint forsaken you, baby." Pear was holding his hand, rubbing the back of his head.

Leave me alone.

"You never talk to me or listen to me. You don't even care about me," Pear said weeping.

I caint love you. I aint nothing to love.

Pray to nothingness.

Once the light faded into the color of fire, he drifted toward sleep again, hoping not to dream.

Burn me, burn me, flame, and blow my ashes into the wind.

He awoke to someone touching his arm. Opening his eyes he saw knees crouching next to him and without turning his head, strained his eyes upward to see the man he remembered as Jake towering above him, smelling pungent, his face strained and agonized.

"I caint tolerate to see you this way."

Shaka settled his eyes back down, looking at his knees.

"We needs you something awful."

I don't need you.

"They done ruint you, aint they."

"He aint wanting to hear you now."

"But he's gonna hear me now."

"Leave him alone."

"Listen here, Shaka. Massa done gone rabid. They know you aint leave them wings up yonder so he all afraid of something he call the beast. He marches around all day with his sword and rifle, wearing some black suit with shiny buttons, from one corner of the island to the next—then he stops and loads his rifle then shoots at them wings on the hill. His wifey—she want even let her children from her sight. Most of the time she walks around holding them too tightly about the wrist. She scared of everything—of us niggers and even her own rabid husband.

"And he got all us niggers in his army running drills. We done chopped down limbs from that tree to fashion into spears, sharp and blackened in the fire—then we all get in lines and charge like we trying to stab this beast. And on the beach he got us digging deep, long trenches that we supposed to cover with sheets and things—then with sand—so that when this here beast comes around, he gonna fall in the hole and we gonna stab him to death.

"We is sore, Shaka—naw, we is angry. Even Nomaw, who gots to dig with us, aint liking them whities no more—her heart all broken for knowing she nigger like rest of us. And Shobuck is churning in rage—and if aint for me keeping the harness on him, he like to start sticking that spear where it belong—up Massa's ass.

"Jake," said Pear, "he aint wanting to hear this. He aint hardly alive."

"We aint liking this bondage, especially being nigger soldiers for the white general, especially ones that whips you, Shaka," said Jake. "We's carrying forward with our work. But underneath we is alive. We is ready and we is looking for hope. And we is looking for you to come out of here and lead us to freedom."

"We aint expecting on freedom," said Pear. "We aint wanting any trouble. We loves each other—that's all we need. We going back to Whiteoak to live in our own shack."

"You fooling yourself, woman. And you trying to fool Shaka."

"We got love. We can have our own chilluns."

"Chilluns," said Jake. "What you mean? You wanting to born more niggers into his hands—that fool out there that think he George Washington.

"Woman, let me tell yawl my story about my wifey and my chilluns, so yawl aint gonna trick yourself into thinking you got something back at Whiteoak—but borning chilluns into stupid and anguishing lives."

"We aint wanting to hear," said Pear.

"Save yourself some lifetime of misery," said Jake "and listen to my story. After all my days of toil and sleep, pick and eat, hoe and fuck, one day as mean and tired as any another, everything done changed when my woman done dropped my son. I carried him squirming in my arms onto the porch to show all the other niggers gathered around my shack and when holding him above my head, I felt something I aint never felt before—pride. My son aint gonna be like them other wearied, stupid-looking niggers gathered round my shack. And he aint gonna be like me neither, bent and weak, eager to shovel shit for some splash of whiskey. Naw, he gonna be stronger and faster and smarter. He gonna know how to look at paper and talk inside his head and he gonna ride horses and drink the finest of whiskeys. He gonna boss around all them chipmunk-eating, goat-fucking niggers that don't know nothing."

He talks so loud. Why is he shouting at me?

"He gonna make his Paw proud like you gonna make me proud, Shaka.

" 'His name is Jake,' I said while holding him on the porch.

"About that time Whiteoak comes trotting over from his little old dog-trot and hands me some pile of cotton. Little Jake, I thought, done got him some pretty clothes. My wifey done dressed him and handed him back to me and when walking out onto the porch holding him above my head, I noticed that he was wearing the same kind of clothes as myself and every other goat-fucker out there.

"Whoa, this boy aint gonna lord over nobody," I thought. "Naw he aint even gonna lord over his own ass.

"The baby was wailing like he done figured some things out for himself. I cradled him in my arms, looked into his little, angry eyes. This here baby, he aint mine or my wife's neither. She aint even my wife. Naw, this here baby belongs to Whiteoak same as myself, same as all them niggers, same as any mule in the field."

"That baby was hollering now. Maybe he aint wanting to be born no more?

" 'Shut-up,' I said. 'Shut-up before Massa whips you.'

"But when he just kept on hollering, I was wanting to choke his little baby neck so he caint whine no more. I was wanting to drop him on his head, stomp him in the dirt, fling his head upside some tree. I was wanting to shove him back up my wife's cunta hole so he can crawl out another.

"I tried not to romp with my wife, tried to leave her barren and seedless. She always wanting to snuggle with me, but I said, 'Get away from me woman. I aint making Whiteoak rich.' But I caint stop, not even for one week and before long I done spewed enough seed to fill our whole shack with babies. They was crawling all over the floor looking for something to eat, smiling and giggling and shitting and pissing all over the place so when coming home from the fields, I gots to watch my step. I tried not to love them, shooed them away like stray dogs, saying, 'Get on outta here. I aint got any money to buy your ass.'

"But I loved them, loved them all—more than anything. Already some was running around in the woods, wild as beasts, playing with salamanders and turtles and trapping little rodents and bringing them back into the house. How they asked questions about things: What does birds eat? How comes they was fire? Why is the overseer mean? But some caint even walk—they just crawled and upchucked and peed on my leg, giggling. When the chill come rattling our bones, we'd all heap together in one bed under our blankets for warmth. Sometimes I stay awake at night—just to feel their little bodies against mine, their breathing, their warm, smooth flesh—knowing them was the finest moments of my life."

Leave me alone.

"Love's like fungus, Shaka. Recollect how you be walking through the fields, seeing some cowshit all growed over with mushrooms. Loves like that, growed from misery like mushrooms from shit. That's how come, I suppose, whities never know love. They aint never knowed shit."

Shaka turned his head away from Jake, placing his other cheek flat on the mat, not looking at his knees anymore. But he felt his presence all the more pungently, something large and powerful hovering over him and speaking too loud, wanting something, needing something as though with each gasp of air he was sucking Shaka and the remnants of his energy back into himself.

"You know why I loved them, Shaka?"

Leave me alone. I don't care.

"Cause they were alive."

But they cannot stay alive.

"But you know why they was alive?

"Cause I aint educated them with the whack like I learned from my folks back in Virginia.

"If forgetting my chores, my folks go whack.

"Steal some apple from Massa's tree. Whack, whack.

"Talk shit about whities. Whack, whack, whack.

"Run away in the woods. You like to get something broke.

"By the time I headed for them fields, I done got some bunches of dents upside my head.

"I also done got me the diploma. Know what it said? "Dumb nigger."

But you learned the peace of ignorance.

"But I caint whacks my own chilluns cause I loves them too much.

"One day I come home from the fields, the leaves crackling under my feet. Inside the shack was ablaze with the warmth of the fire, pork fat simmering, turnips boiling, some corn sludge piping in the pot. All my chilluns runs and wraps their arms around my legs and pulls me to the ground and piles on top of me, yanking on my ears, sticking their fingers up my nose, one of them even trying to choke me.

"The door slams.

" 'Look what I got,' my oldest says.

"All my chilluns just stop, looked toward the door.

"There was my oldest, Jake—the one I wanted to drop on his head—holding this chicken still jerking around, its neck just broke.

"My stomach was gurgling. I could see that bird roasting and simmering over the coals, me holding some pan underneath to catch the grease. I could see myself chomping on the meat, tossing the bones to my chilluns for them to gnaw.

"Aint he powerful? I thought. He done got us some meat.

"He was proud of himself. Some of my other chilluns was now next to him, wondering why that dead chicken was still jerking around. Then some of them started acting like the chicken while rolling around on the floor, jerking and squawking and kicking they little legs.

"The grin fell from my face. 'Where you done got that chicken, boy?'

" 'From the coop.'

" 'What coop?'

" 'Whiteoak's coop,' he said, his own grin now falling from his face.

" 'Aint you got any sense?'

" 'Sho I does.'

" 'Wifey,' I said, turning toward her, 'aint he got any sense?'

"But she aint said nothing, just stood there, stirring the pot, baby sucking on her teat.

" 'Don't you know nothing about stealing chickens?'

" 'I know that chickens taste good.'

"I studied on that boy. He was tapping his foot on the floor, acting restless like some live animal you just found in your trap. All my other chilluns aint acting like chickens no more but looking at me.

"The truth done whacked me upside my head. I caint whack my chilluns cause I loves them too much. But now they aint educated, not even aware of the always-watching, leather-fanged snake in the grass. They aint even know that Massa whips his niggers for stealing chickens. I saw my boy on the gibbet straining against his binds, the overseer walking forward with the whip.

"You done failed, Jake, I thought, as I imagined the overseer cocking that whip behind his head.

"Whack him…whack him hard.

"Jake, you spurt-loving cunta hog. You uneducated baby-wrestler. You done raised some bunch of ignorants.

" 'Shutup,' I shouted.

"But nobody was saying nothing but staring at me with their shiny and spooked eyes like they aint never seen me before. One of my chilluns was already hiding behind something.

" 'I's Jake, the Negro,' I said, 'here to educate yawl's asses.' I jumped toward my son who seeing it all coming, done flung his chicken away and starts darting around the shack with me chasing after him, flipping over tables. But I done cornered him before long and was moving toward him and he was breathing fast and putting his hands up with his fingers open like he was trying to protect himself.

"I wanted to take him in my arms, hold and love and protect him forever. But I knew I could not, not ever, not from the whitie, not from nothing. So I just closed my eyes and started swinging and slapping him while his little arms and tiny head jarring around. For long I was hitting something hard and opening my eyes, seen that I was slapping the wall cause my son done slipped away from me again.

" 'Come on back, boy,' I said. 'You aint educated yet.'

"I was running all over the shack, swinging my arms at all my chilluns, some scattering away from me, some of them hiding behind they mother.

" 'Yawl Goddamn ignorant forest chilluns,' I shouted.

"Then I whacked one hard.

"Whacked him for all them times I aint whacked him before.

"And whacked another for being wild.

"Whacked another for not knowing her place.

"Whacked another so he know that he aint nothing but fungus growing on shit."

Shaka turned his head, looked upward at the man towering over him, feeling like one of those children trying to protect himself.

Don't hit me, Father. Please don't hit me.

He felt their pain and confusion and fright as they scrambled around the room to dodge the rage of the father they loved.

Why are you hurting me, Father?

He felt his anger and denial and resignation passing away into sorrow. He was weeping inside, not having the energy to expel tears.

Please don't hit me.

"I was weeping. Tears streaming down my cheeks," resumed Jake. "But I felt powerful too. I started stomping around, throwing chairs and kicking the table over and flinging pots against the wall. Some of my neighbors was watching all the commotion from the porch and I just stomped on over and whacked they asses too.

" 'I's Jake,' I shouted for everyone to hear. 'Lord of this here shack and yawl best lie down at my feet.'

"I was gonna bust from the roof, flinging boards and shingles all around and walk on down the row, the earth shaking while all the animals and birds was fleeing away from me. I was gonna find the overseer drunk in his cabin and whack his ass into smithereens. Then I was gonna stomp on down to the big house, rip off its roof, find Whiteoak there eating some drizzle for dinner and whack his ass into one bloody pile of meat and bones.

"*Whack*! I done felt upside my head.

"I dropped to the floor feeling dizzy and blood was leaking from my scalp. My wife was standing over me and my chilluns was grabbing around her thighs. All around the room was junk thrown about and beans and turnips splattered against the walls and that dead chicken that aint jerking around no more. And all my chilluns was crying and hollering, rubbing they arms and legs. In my wifey's hand was some log, cocked back and ready to swing again.

" 'Get hold of yourself, nigger,' she said.

"After that, whenever I come on home from the fields, my chilluns aint run and hugs me or drags me into some wrestling. They just hide behind their motha, wrapping their arms around her thighs or run outside to play with their friends or cover themselves in blankets like they was cold. Cause from that day on, I was handing out diplomas.

"Aint finish their chores. Whack.

"Steal some of Massa's apples. Whack, whack.

"Talking trash about white folks. Whack, whack, whack.

"They all got dents in their heads.

"One day I hear one of my sons saying to his sister that he was down by the river trying to catch him some fish when he see this riverboat coming along with some Negro steering the boat down the river wearing this fancy hat. My boy started running along, waving.

"That old captain waved back at him.

"My boy done waved until that boat done passed the bend. He aint knowed I was listening. And he said to his sister that he aint never wanting to be like me, some shit-talking, whack-happy field hand but he wanting to be like that riverboat captain."

I feel your children inside of me.

Not from his own desire nor from his own power but from something larger and deeper outside of himself, Shaka wanted to help them break from their bondage.

But I am broken.

"I caint whack my son that time. I caint even say nothing—just felt hurt inside. By the time that boy reached the age, he aint wanting to sail nowhere but only to hoe, pick, spew and sip.

"My chilluns was some of the most educated in them parts. Aint none of them ever caused much trouble or been whipped. None of them, neither, run their mouths like me cause I aint never given them the chance. 'Yessa' was some of the first words they ever spoke. And when coming to the fields, they aint had any complaints. They is what Nomaw calls 'Gooduns,' hardworking, friendly and obedient— and I hate myself for making them that way.

"By the time you come around, Shaka, they knowed I was the best around for easing bucks down into their shackles. But you was too wild for all that.

"My chilluns done growed, built their own shack, found they own wives and done born they own babies to make Whiteoak rich. Aint none of them got any scars on their back and some of them is even working around the big house or driving the darkies in the fields or hammering and sawing like you. At least they aint like me, digging and hoeing themselves into their own grave. And all of them is whacking they babies like their fathers before them and their fathers before that, going all the way back to when our grandfathers left Africa.

"When thinking about all my chilluns scattered across Whiteoak, I feel ashamed for leaving one galloping, seed-spewing chain of ignorants behind me. And Pear and you too Shaka—you aint wanting to make the same mistake."

"We just want to live," said Pear.

"But you aint doing that back at Whiteoak.

"I aint done nothing in my life worth some heap of shit except for dancing with you and them birds, Shaka. You done showed me something—some glimpse of my soul—and I aint never going back to myself. Give me freedom or give me death.

"We know you're hurting, Shaka, like some duck blown from the sky and flapping around at Massa's feet. But you aint dead yet. And I done known you since you was little—you done gotten whipped, fallen from trees, seen your mother die but after all this, something still lives inside of you. God, freedom, Africa—I aint even know the word for it—that carries you beyond your pain.

"Pear, this man aint going back to Whiteoak to become your house nigger.

"You rest up, you heal your wounds, you find your God again and you come out this tent with freedom on your mind, Shaka."

Jake was rising above him now and walking toward the door, disappearing from his sight but he stopped and said, "But if freedom aint on your mind, then you just skip the pain of living, lay down in darkness—and die."

Shaka turned his head again to place his cheek flush on the rough, straw mat and stared into the darkness—for how many hours, he could not say. He listened to the wind ruffling the canvas and the drone of the waves and the slow, strange chirping of the crickets.

You've taken away my darkness, Father, and left me as nothing.

Turning his head again, he lay his cheek flush on the mat and saw Pear lying next to him. He placed his hand in her palm.

So I can become.

He could sense the yearning for freedom of all the Negroes in the land—and each was calling to the other and to God and to all the forces under earth and while fading into sleep, he thought: I am the wind. I am the water. I am the earth. And I am nothing.

In his dream Shaka was moving through smoke and flame, multitudes of drums pounding and people chanting unseen all around him. He was not flying or standing but was merely suspended. Someone he could not identify was moving toward him; his body was the color of clay and was adorned with wings. Together the two of them danced to the drumming while bent at the waist, lifting one foot at a time from the ground while raising their arms into the air while experiencing the power and mystery of their manhood and freedom. Somewhere on the fringes was another man obscured in smoke and naked while gazing upon them but not participating in the dance. Shaka moved closer to this man and, through the smoke and flame, he saw—and he looked again—the baffled and mystified face of Jonah.

CHAPTER THIRTEEN

Several nights after the whipping, Eloise heard an uproar—voices of surprise and excitement—from the beach where the slaves were congregating to eat their dinner. She ran over to the tree and saw the slaves encircled by the luminous, orange light from their fire that thrashed about with the gusts of wind blowing from the roaring but invisible gulf. They were all on their knees gaping into the darkness beyond the fire except for Jake who was standing and wielding a flaming limb in his arm torchlike—all of them waiting with bewildered but eager expectations.

Coming from the darkness was something fast and swooping. While hurtling toward the fire, it was caught motionless and soundless like some faint and barely perceptible tear in the fabric of night, the flames glistening and quivering golden across its black and changeling surface, before it landed on the other side and vanished again into the darkness. The slaves gasped, then hushed.

"Shaka's up. Shaka's up," Jake shouted, waving the torch now victoriously,

Shobuck started to lilt and gyrate around the fire.

Everything seemed unattached, the island floating upon the surface of the heaving and roiling gulf, the fire thrashing in the wind as things faded capriciously in and out of reality.

Again Shaka darted from the darkness and as soon as emerging into the light, his shadow leapt from his body and flitted huge and menacing across the sand as though his soul was thrust from his body. While Shobuck carried on with his dance, the others crouched before the shadow while Jake drew his torch back with his face full of wonderment. At the fringes of the light, the shadow collapsed back into Shaka, all its power and strength distilled into that bony and ectomorphic frame, waiting to come forth yet again.

Collapsed on the ground, imprisoned within the thick, corporeal husk of her body, Nomaw screeched something that Eloise could not understand. Jake dropped his torch and with Pear and Shobuck started to gyrate around the fire, their shadows also exploding from their bodies and projecting onto the beach like great, chaotic and vengeful birds.

Bang. Sparks skittered from the fire and the smell of gunpowder and flint lingered in the air. Eloise was momentarily deafened and startled by the noise. She heard Jonah.

"Next one of you I see running around is dead. Dead, I say." He was next to her, she realized, now reloading his rifle.

Shaka did not reappear from the darkness and almost immediately the other slaves dispersed from the fire. Later that night Eloise found Jonah inside their tent where to compensate perhaps for the chaos in his mind, he kept his belongings with a persnickety and militant neatness as though he had enlisted himself into his own military. He was sitting on his cot polishing the barrel of his rifle by candlelight with his black wool jacket, which he wore ever since whipping Shaka, buttoned tight about his neck. Even in the cool of the evening, his stench was immense, fogging the air around them. Otherwise he was groomed and shaven with his hair slicked back from his forehead. Beyond using any guile now, she spoke directly, trying to look into his eyes which were flitting about nervously.

"Are you all right?" she asked.

"Fine," he said. But he was not all right, she realized. She spoke almost hopeless with her ability to sway him in any way. "Treat them delicately. They're seething with anger. Nomaw too. We're alone here. By inflicting too much oppression and pain upon them all at once, I'm afraid you might cause them to revolt, perhaps even violently. At my father's church I've heard Negroes say that once men experience freedom, they can never revert back to slavery. They're not slaves anymore but people."

"They're not slaves? What the hell do you mean by that?"

"Just that. They've changed."

"Whatever they are, they best behave like slaves cause I aint gonna treat them any different. Don't worry your mind. I got this under control. This meeting's adjourned."

While he headed out of the tent for his nightly patrol of the island, she said, "I won't continue like this, Jonah, not forever."

He kept walking until she raised her voice. "Can you hear me?"

He turned toward her, his face ruddy and flushed from the heat.

"I won't endure you forever," she said sternly. "Do you understand?"

His face was listless.

"I'm warning you."

While walking away from the tent, he said, "You shall see, Eloise—indeed, you shall. I'll capture the beast. And reclaim my kingdom."

Later Eloise extinguished the candle and lay on her cot. What could she do to keep herself and her children safe, she wondered? She had already collected everything she could find that could be used as weapons—knives, forks and axes—and hid them in her tent. She tried to remain communicative with the slaves and occasionally brought them water as an act of goodwill while they were working in the trenches and still offered to help with Shaka in any way. But they were not responsive and even disdainful. They performed their chores but otherwise made it clear, even Nomaw, that they neither liked nor respected her.

What could she do about her husband? Wait until he fell asleep, steal his guns and hold him captive while she tried to manage the situation on the island? That seemed far-fetched and beyond her capabilities and would undoubtedly leave her exposed to the slaves and the possible intruder all by herself. For the moment she decided to remain an observer, hoping all was in the hands of God.

While on the cusp of sleep but startled into alertness by any sound not made from wind or water, Eloise imagined Jonah out there looking for something to kill to make his madness subside while Shaka soared through the darkness unseen and undetectable by any eye.

The next morning when the slaves came to the trenches, Shaka appeared of his own volition, grabbed one of the shovels and saying nothing, began to dig. Again he was shirtless, the scars on his back still swollen but encrusted with scabs, the veins of his arms and legs bulging from his skin like worms feeding on the remainder of his flesh. Hunched over his shovel he was so weak that he struggled to dig and then dispose of his load and afterwards would rest his weight against the shaft or lean against the side of the trech, squinting while looking towards the gulf. Perhaps his determination was admirable, she thought, but to what end? He just seemed damaged, worthy mostly of their compassion—just like some racehorse now turned to pasture, rendered forever worthless by crippling his leg in the heat of competition. Even before midday he retired to his tent, disappointment evident in the faces of the other slaves.

Later that night Eloise was keeping watch over the island while Jonah slept inside their tent. In the faint and murky light, she saw who she believed was Shaka, Jake and Shobuck in one of the boats rowing away from the island. Were they going fishing? But at this time of night? Once some distance from shore, the boat, which was just barely visible now, stopped—she heard the splash of someone jumping into the gulf then silence then someone emerging, splashing and gasping for air. Two others then did the same. They soon returned to the island and she watched as the three dark figures settled into sleep across the dunes while lying supine and bare to the heavens.

She could not even fathom the meaning of that.

When reappearing again at the trenches in the morning, Shaka was stronger than before which in turn seemed to inspire the other slaves. But why would he inspire them to work, she wondered? Before Shaka arrived they worked as slowly as possible, their movements sluggish and purposeless but now they seemed purposeful—and yet defiant in some strange way.

Around twilight that same day, all the slaves but Nomaw went down to the beach and Shaka and Shobuck netted some fish just off shore—a bucketful of small, silvery minnows. They then formed a line and as each one approached, Shaka quickly disemboweled and beheaded one of the fish then ritualistically tapped each slave's shoulder and fed them on the flesh and bones. While they ate the fish raw, Shaka preached to them while gesticulating with his hands as though delivering some kind of communion.

Later that evening she watched as Jake lay down on his back next to the fire while Pear and Shobuck pinned his arms to the ground. Shaka swabbed his hands with cloth then reached into the fire and grabbed a piece of long, narrow metal—one of the spikes they used for their tents, the tip glowing orange and emberlike. When Shaka stood over him and pressed the blazing steel into his flesh, Jake arched his back upward, hollered then relaxed. Shaka repeated this process several times until Jake endured the pain impassively without even moving, lying there like something wounded with his chest heaving. Later he rose from the ground, stood in the glow of the fire, looking down menacingly at the crude and jagged set of wings singed into his flesh.

She smelled the stench of her husband who was standing next to her, rifle slung over his shoulder, watching them too. "What do you suppose," she asked, "is the meaning of this?"

He said nothing.

She had heard of zealots from many religions using torture to drive themselves closer to God, to help them overcome the limitations of their flesh. Was that their purpose? Or were they preparing themselves for something? Were they trying to intimidate her and Jonah?

The next day during their break for lunch, Shaka stood behind Shobuck with a branch in his hands—the same one that Jonah had used to whip Shaka. Repeatedly Shaka beat him with the dowel; she could hear the slap against his flesh although it was not hard enough to break the skin. All the while Shobuck stood still and not flinching until he raised his head and looked directly at her and Jonah with this muted but rageful euphoria on his face as though challenging them in some way.

Jonah headed toward the slaves with his rifle slung over his shoulder, nonchalantly. But the whipping did not stop. Eloise cupped her hand around her ear, straining to hear but all she heard was Jake, saying, "What you gonna do, whip us?"

CHAPTER FOURTEEN

Eloise sat under the tree in the shade with the Bible on her lap and the crucifix festooned around her neck, both brandished to protect her from the increasingly disturbing and mysterious behaviors of the slaves. On the beach below Jake, Shobuck and Shaka were buried to their waists in the trenches, throwing sand into the gulf with their shovels. By now they all wore the symbols on their chests: The rough, darkened outlines of wings which they had singed into their flesh with hot, glowing metal in the evenings around the fire—strangely contrasted to the chaotic, wormlike scars on Shaka's back, which were slowly healing. They were all in pain, she realized—from the salt-infused, stifling heat, from their blistered hands and aching muscles, from being driven unmercifully by Jonah, from having their hearts trampled and their hopes denied yet again. But they were not crippled. Instead they seemed driven by some kind of fierce, focused and even jovial energy while hovering above their pain like dark and damaged angels flying over their own hell.

While Jonah kept watch during the evening, Eloise spent the night with her children in their tent usually curled around Josh but she was not able to sleep well, remaining afraid of the slaves and of whatever it was out there that had left those wings. Perhaps most of all she was afraid of her husband. Every sound, outside of the drone of wind and waves, alarmed her. Today she was exhausted and anxious as usual and intermittently dozed off into naps filled with strange, fast-paced dreams.

Below, Shaka raised his head and called toward the others. Along with the ceiling of hazy and white clouds, the wind was blowing from the mainland and pushing compact and furious waves into the shore. Shaka pointed at the flock of pelicans flying into the wind like fish swimming upriver in an echelon, their progress slow and laborious but unrelenting. One of the birds ceased its struggle, tipped its wings and abandoned the flock while flitting away into the open and everlasting expanse of the sea while Shaka tracked its flight with his eyes. All three of them climbed from the trenches, set their tools upright in the sand and just stood there, not speaking, only waiting, Shaka out front, Jake and Shobuck flanking him.

Something was about to happen. Eloise pulled the pistol from the bag next to her. She called her children who came over and sat next to her. Nomaw was over in the kitchen but where was Pear? After returning from his march around the island, Jonah stopped on one of the dunes close to Eloise but, once seeing the slaves, did nothing except stand there looking immovable and inalterable with his boots entrenched in the sand and his clothes somehow static amidst the wind like the statue of an indomitable but archaic general now beyond his time.

But Jonah soon marched toward the slaves and she realized that he might be falling into some trap which would endanger them all. Suddenly she found herself thinking that she had never caused the slaves any harm, only he did, that only he deserved their malice. Maybe they would not kill her and her children. Maybe they would just kill him, yes, just him—and get rid of all their problems.

"Thy will be done," she said, gripping the handle of the pistol.

Shaka stood on the beach flanked by Jake and Shobuck, watching as Jonah marched down the dunes with his rifle resting against his shoulder and his sword dangling at his side. In the distance the echelon of pelicans continued to head toward the mainland but the lone, wayward bird was way over the ocean drifting toward oblivion.

Even after all these days Shaka still felt withered and damaged and feverish from the whipping. His throat ached whenever he swallowed; and the scars and scabs on his back burned in the heat. As Jonah approached, his heart beat faster and his lungs ached for more air. In the silent panic of his mind, he wondered if he was like that bird, veering away from all that was known and heading into nothingness.

He wondered how his life had become distilled into this one, suicidal moment. When recovering from the whipping back in his tent, Shaka was at first confused by the presence of Jonah in his dream. Why was Jonah watching him, he wondered, as he danced with the other strange, winged man? In his childhood Shaka knew Jonah was searching for freedom from his tortured and fast-encroaching future. Maybe as an adult, after all these years, Jonah was still looking. Amidst that fire and smoke Jonah was perhaps yearning to understand the dance of freedom that was occurring all around him, possibly even inside his own heart.

When emerging from the tent, Shaka knew he could not fear Jonah, nor obey him, nor ignore him but rather only guide him toward his own freedom.

"Why is you concerned about his freedom when you aint even got your own?" asked Jake one night. "Aint he the one that just whipped you?"

Jake and Shobuck also argued for ambushing Jonah and Eloise in the middle of the night, holding them as their prisoners to keep them from hurting or controlling them ever again. Shaka could not counter their arguments, nor alleviate their fear and anger, only said that he knew what must be done.

Jonah was now standing before Shaka down on the beach, looking at Jake and Shobuck who were flanking him. He looked large while breathing hard, his cheeks twitching, his stench overpowering them like some kind of weapon.

Shaka glanced into Jonah's eyes then down at his body. He sensed misery imprisoned behind that jacket, grief and fear sealed off and festering. The image crossed his mind of Jonah removing the jacket like he was relinquishing himself from some yoke made from memory and befouled instinct.

"What yawl doing?" asked Jonah.

"Nothing," said Shaka, holding his gaze.

Jonah deflected his eyes. "Your break's over. Get back to work." Abruptly, preemptively, Jonah turned and walked back up the dunes but then stopped and turned around. "I told yawl to get on back to work."

"We aint getting back to work."

Jonah walked back to Shaka and stood close to him. "Yawl get on back, I said."

"No," said Shaka.

Inside his mind Jonah heard voices, the refrain: The beast is coming…The beast is coming…The beast is coming… He struggled to maintain his concentration to speak over the voices. "Get on back to digging, boy… Function, you hear me? Function, like I say."

"No."

Jonah felt convulsed by rage as specks of spit flung out his mouth. "Aint I done beat you enough, boy?"

Shaka said nothing at first. But once Jonah calmed down, he said, "Yes you have."

The beast is coming…The beast is coming…

"So obey my command," said Jonah.

"We aint ever obeying you again."

Jonah became still. Something inside his mind was collapsing, chaos encroaching. They aren't functioning…They aint functioning…They aint functioning…

"We's intending to be free," said Shaka.

"Free? Aint none of us free," said Jonah. "We're all beholden."

Jonah then turned toward Jake whose gaze was easier to tolerate and said over the voices inside his head, "We go back a long way, Jake. Aint I always treated you right?"

Jake said nothing, just looked at Jonah like something was wrong with him.

"You know we got to function. You've seen what happens when

we don't function. You and Shobuck step back from Shaka and return to work, let me handle him."

Jake did nothing.

Jonah became dizzy, almost lost his balance. He stepped away from the others. The beast is coming...The beast is coming...The beast is coming for me...

The slaves moved toward Jonah while maintaining the distance between them, looking at him with some perverse but almost benign curiosity.

"Do yawl understand your actions?" asked Jonah.

"Yes," said Shaka.

Broke...they done broke. The yoke is broke.

"What yawl think? That the son of some whore caint handle some bunch of niggers gone askew? All right, off to the tree, all of you, for another lashing." Jonah tilted his head and moved in that direction, keeping his distance from the slaves.

But nobody moved.

"All right then," said Jonah. "Jake and Shobuck—yawl haul him over there."

They did nothing.

"Well, then, Goddamnit," said Jonah. "I can haul all of you over to that tree, one by one."

After nothing happened Shaka stated the obvious. "Three of us. And one of you."

Jonah studied the wild, animalistic and resolute look in their eyes, then the scars across their bodies; they are not afraid of pain, he thought. Cannot win against all of them, cannot expect to survive.

"The beast is coming," he uttered out loud. "The beast is coming. Can't you see that?"

The slaves looked startled and perplexed.

"Yawl must function. Function. Protect us from the beast."

But they did nothing.

He felt the rifle in his hand, the black, warm weight tugging on his joints. Violence. Death is my command. Death is my power. Kill the niggers, kill the niggers, kill them dead

He raised the muzzle upward. "I don't need to fight you," he said. "I can just kill you."

"But you won't," said Shaka firmly.

"Yes, I will," said Jonah.

"No, you won't," said Shaka.

"Why?" asked Jonah.

"Because if you shoot me," Shaka said, "they will cut you."

Jake and Shobuck reached behind their backs and pulled knives from their belts. Jonah noticed that Shaka was looking anxiously toward the tree.

Jonah imagined himself as his father pulling the trigger and killing Shaka then drawing his sword and severing Jake's and Shobuck's arms from their bodies, their faces shocked as they looked at the stumps of their arms gushing blood and their knives lying harmlessly in the sand—then at him, their master, incredulous and awed by his ruthlessness.

But he did nothing except redirect the rifle at Jake and probe for weakness. "Drop that weapon, Jake, and come over here. You aint wanting to die for the sake of birds."

Jake now spoke, all the sarcasm gone from his voice replaced by gravity. "Some fellow once said that all men is created equal. And I aint tolerating your shit no more."

Jonah then aimed at Shobuck, raising the tip to his forehead. "You want to die today, boy?"

Shobuck still held his knife ready to attack. But when looking into the muzzle, the muscles in his face twitched and tears rolled down his cheek. The knife went slack in his hand.

"All right now," said Jonah. "Just step over here. I won't punish you."

Shobuck diverted his eyes. "No."

Jonah sensed the ghost of his father next to him prodding him on. Go on and kill them, son. Act fast before they have time to react.

He pointed the rifle at Shaka, saying, "I will kill you."

Shaka paused and looked into Jonah's eyes. "But would your mother want you to?"

Jonah looked away from Shaka. The rifle in his hand, suddenly becoming heavy, dropped about one inch while his mind reeled then lapsed; his childhood became distilled into that one compact question.

After witnessing the birth of the slave in the shack, Jonah rose from his knees and, ignoring Shaka, bolted through the shacks into the blackness and vacuity of the fields then toward his cabin that, seen low and beaten in the distance, was slightly larger than the shacks of the slaves but just as crude. After coming around to the side of his home, Jonah entered into the kitchen, leaned his rifle against the wall while throwing his quarry upon the table, the skulls of the rodents knocking against the wood. Huddled by the fire in the corner was the Negress named Thelma, her dark, flattened face glowing orange and warm in the firelight while she stirred peas boiling over the fire with a stick.

She looked at him, sighed then said, "Don't throw your meat around like that. Give it to me, over here."

Jonah handed his sling to Thelma. "I seen something strange," he said.

"What's that?"

"A baby coming out this woman."

"Yawl shouldn't be watching that."

"It gots me to thinking."

"About what?"

"About where I come from?"

Thelma looked at him searchingly. "Do you know where you come from?"

"From there, I suppose," said Jonah, pointing toward her torso.

"All these years, Jonah, and we never told you, not even your father," she said dolefully. "While I reckon it aint my place to say, I think its time for you know. When you were born, I wasn't even around these parts."

"What do you mean?" said Jonah.

Thelma hesitated and listened through the cabin for his father but, hearing nothing, she grabbed Jonah by his shoulders and nestled his head into her stomach as if trying to pull him inside of her. Jonah inhaled her scent, the sweet, singed, effervescent smell of pork fat and smoke.

"I love you like my own son," she said, becoming grave and morose. She paused and looked into his eyes but became stiff as if she were rejecting him from her body and Jonah pulled away and stood before her, unable to look into her eyes. "We oughten to have told you this long time ago. But I aint your mother."

"Sure you are," he said.

"I'm black. I caint be."

Jonah groped around in his mind, feeling the world becoming chaotic and unreal. As far back as he could remember, Thelma always acted like she was his mother, feeding him, dressing him, tucking him into bed at night with cookies and milk—same as Maw cared for Shaka. Whenever attending picnics and barn raisings with other white families that lived scattered across the frontier however, he noticed that the other children always came with their mothers while Thelma stayed at home.

"But...," he stammered, trying to deny the truth. "But you aint any different from other mothers around here."

"I is black, Jonah, and you aint."

"So?"

"Black and white don't mix."

"If you aint my mother, then who is?"

"Nobody knows for sho except your paw and he aint saying, not now anyhows. But I done heard some rumors from Jake who said Whiteoak was visiting some whore who lived back in the woods in this shack. Jake said the lady was fine except that most of her fingers was lopped off, making her hand ruint, nasty to behold. So when the men came to visit, she just lay back and buried her hand under her pillow and let them commence with their mean and wicked business. Anyhows Whiteoak figured that she was gonna make some decent stock for breeding. So he was sneaking across the river in the dark, coming back at midnight. Some say he was singing like he in love or something. Anyhow, this woman for long come swollen with child and she shacked up in this here cabin with Whiteoak until one day out you come, just like that baby yawl saw tonight.

"Jake said she stayed here in the cabin for some time, suckling you to her teat until she vanished back into the woods. Whiteoak bought me in Montgomery about that time to care for you. Jake said that she done came back from the woods once with her hair all messy and her clothes tattered, claiming that she loved Whiteoak, that she wanted to be his wife and to mother their child. But Whiteoak just stood there like the dead, leafless tree that he is, saying nothing but that he aint want some old, whorish hag raising his child, that she best get along like they planned. She done got her money and aint nothing left for him to give her, except some whacking about the head.

"After some time she don't come around no more. Her heart broken, she caught a boat down to Mobile, shooing away somewhere to carry on with her whoring."

Jonah felt uprooted from all that he knew and flung against his will into some world more confusing and demented. Most of her story, however, just wafted across his mind, incomprehensible to him, so all he envisioned in the end was that his mother was some creature of the woods—some chimera of woman and animal.

"What's a whore?" he asked.

Thelma looked surprised then worried. "If your Paw knowed I done told you all this, he might take the lash to me. So please don't tell him nothing. Besides, in town one day, I heard some folks saying that your maw just up and died once you was born, leaving Whiteoak forlorn and lonely forever and unwilling to marry another woman. So nobody knows where you came from. I just reckon that some angel delivered you hereabouts. So I could love you."

The door into the cabin flung open and his father barged into the room, his face featureless in the dark, his frame tall and gawky and draped with an overcoat and top hat.

Thelma became stiff as she whispered, "Please, Littlemassa, don't tell your father what I said. Don't tell him nothing."

Whiteoak came into the kitchen and sat at the table across from the hearth and doffed his hat while the flame exposed his slender and handsome face, except for where his flesh was mutilated above his eyes, mottled in hues of pink and brown with clumps of hair sprouting sporadically from his scalp.

"Yessa, Massa, dinner about done," said Thelma.

Jonah crossed the room and sat rigidly next to his father, not speaking. Thelma came across the room carrying thick, pewter plates covered with mounds of pone and peas stewed in pork fat. On top were the roasted, brown carcasses of squirrels. Spoons poked out the side. She returned later with cups full of buttermilk. She retreated backward and sat at the hearth, seeming to disappear.

Whiteoak scooped the pone and peas into his mouth methodically and vigorously, not stopping to talk, until his plate was empty, then he gnawed and sucked the scraps from the bones of the squirrels, gulped his cup of buttermilk, stood from the table, tossed the bones into the fire, grabbed one of the lanterns from the kitchen and disappeared into the night again.

Thelma rose from the hearth and sat at the table next to Jonah who sat there defeated and forlorn like he just lost a competition against his father, while slowly and pathetically swallowing spoonfuls from the mound of food, not from hunger, but as though obligated to somehow finish the event.

Once Jonah finished his meal, Thelma took him by the hand and using a candle to guide the way, they walked across the room to the corner to his bed. His mattress was calico, stuffed with cotton and hay, elevated only slightly from the ground. While she straightened the quilts he undressed and then donned his pajamas and crawled into bed. As the candle wavered in the dark and cast shadows throughout the room, he sat in his bed and she gave him some cookies to eat. While the quilts around his body, once cold and stiff, infused with heat and became soft, he looked into her face and saw anguish.

"Why does he hate you?" he asked.

"He don't hate me none. He's just ashamed. Ashamed that this fat, old, tired nigger pretending that she's the mother of his child.

"But he loves me too cause he caint find nobody else to love, he so ugly and cruel that regular old white women don't want him. And he loves me cause I love you. But he caint admit that, not even secretly, cause that would make all us niggers people same as him. And he caint tolerate that."

"Does he love me?" Jonah asked.

"He loves you more than you gonna ever understand. He loves you in the way that he don't love himself. Before coming down here, I was up in Virginia where the whities live in mansions and dress in bright, dainty linens. And the slaves aint got to work until they is dropping dead from weariness. Whiteoak has somehow got that in mind for you—that someday once he done growed enough cotton to damn near kill all his darkies, he gonna build you one of them big houses and buy you some fancy, golden chariot so you can parade around with your wife and live the life that he too ugly and mean to live himself. So you's the one that makes his dirty, wearying toil in them fields worthwhile.

"But the day is dawning when you is expected to become like your father, not to love Negroes but to rule them—and cruelly too. When that day comes I pray you gonna remember Thelma and treat me well and not turn your cheek from me and care for all your slaves as best you can."

She sighed and strained to rise to her feet and moseyed toward the kitchen, the glow from the candle fading with her while Jonah slouched under his covers and burrowed deeper for warmth. Hearing Thelma in the kitchen eating the leftovers from their dinner while humming some hymn under her breath, he closed his eyes and tried to remember his birth, the time when he slithered from the insides of that disfigured, maternal whore. Yet when tracing his memories backward, visualizing himself becoming smaller, he seemed to vanish into nothingness before reaching his birth, so it seemed that he did not exist back then at all except in the stories told by others.

Jonah awoke later in the night. From around the kitchen he heard the noises: the slow, barely audible breathing and the rhythmic squeaking, which he had heard almost ritualistically every night for as long as he could remember but which he was always too tired and scared to investigate—the noises that in the morning were forgotten like some dream buried too deep in memory to be recalled. But this time, drawn by something nascent and instinctual in his body, he slipped from his sheets, feeling the cold bite into his skin and began to slide his feet across the worn, polished boards of the floor, probing with his hands like tentacles in the dark to avoid bumping into the furniture. Ahead, jutting outward from the kitchen, was the lean-to where Thelma lived. Jonah peeked through the curtain that separated the lean-to from the cabin.

The ceiling above was covered with sticks that were laid across boards; cold and metallic moonlight filtered through the slats. On the floor below was Thelma sprawled across her mattress, her legs arched upward over the bed. Naked in the cold, quivering tendrils of light, her bosom was collapsed across her chest, sagging into her armpits. Between her legs was the backside of some man which Jonah realized was his father with his pants draped about his knees. His ass was luminous and white and thrust back and forth into Thelma while the indentations in his buttocks clenched and released mechanically. Both of them were silent, nothing was uttered and even their breaths were muted as though they could deny that the act was happening in the silence.

Gradually the thrusts became quick, hard and erratic until it seemed like his father was driving Thelma through the mattress and into the earth. Jonah moved to one side of the partition so he could see them from the side while they were entwined. Once the motion became frenzied and climactic, Whiteoak pushed himself from her and slithered from her insides and rose into the darkness like some mutated, leafless sapling then spewed his pale and congealed sap all over the black and quivering pool of her belly. Once

Whiteoak maneuvered from between her legs and pulled his pants around his waist, Thelma turned on her side and pulled her knees toward her chest and covered her body with her quilt.

Without looking at him she penetrated into the silence, speaking low and fatigued and bitter. "I thought we was done with this."

Whiteoak said nothing.

"I should testify about the evil lurking in this house," she said. "I should scream, wail and weep to keep you from treating me like your whore. But I caint. Cause if I did, you gonna sell me away from my baby, leaving him alone and unmothered in your cruel world."

Whiteoak turned from Thelma and peered through the partition, seeming to see Jonah through some tear in the linen but his eyes revealed not recognition but only suspicion. Jonah retreated toward his bed where he crawled under the covers that were still warm from the heat of his body and pulled the quilt over his head to protect himself from the strangeness and horror of his house. Moments later he heard the footsteps of his father hard and etched in the puncheons of the floor while coming from the kitchen then stopping and seeming to hover over his bed for a moment, listening and probing before continuing and ending at the corner of the room where his father slept.

Breathing quick underneath his covers while his heart palpated in his chest, Jonah remembered what Thelma told him about making babies. What he just witnessed was somehow like that. But he knew something was wrong: they did not seem to love or even like each other; their eyes did not twinkle around each other and Jonah suspected that they were not making babies in there—but some kind of violence.

While falling again back into sleep, Jonah imagined some vision of his birth. Instead of seeing the wild and wretched whore, he saw Thelma sprawled across her mattress with her legs spread. Crouched before her was his father whose face was not scarred but unmolested and even handsome and whose hands were pulling him from Thelma's insides. While his head then his shoulders and legs emerged into the world, his father lifted him joyfully into the air and as the blood and mucous was wiped from his flesh, Jonah recognized his own face, his own eyes, his own hair, recognized all except the darkness of his own flesh.

On the island as Shaka probed into his eyes, Jonah felt violated and invaded like Shaka was seeing that part of his soul not even revealed to himself. He tried to turn away, could not, felt his resistance draining from his body, almost lowered the rifle. Shaka softened his face as his eyes somehow became larger, deeper, more transparent, somehow opening into some larger, more inclusive reality.

He spoke. "Once we was the wings of the same bird."

"I never wanted this." Jonah wondered if his words were inside his head or spoken. "Only came here to find peace, to give yawl peace. Yet you forced me. You forced me to raise my hand."

"No," said Shaka. "He did."

Several years later in the summer, Jonah and Shaka were returning from fishing on the river with poles slung over their shoulders, holding slings of bream, bass and catfish in their hands. Off in the distance slaves were working in the fields, the thick, morose sun seeping through the haze in the atmosphere and shellacking their flesh with sweat. Close to the slaves was his father on horseback, the brim of his dark and broad hat hiding his face.

While walking sluggishly in the heat, Shaka turned toward his friend, his eyes glinting and devilish and said, "Have you spurt yet?"

"My sheets was wet in the morning."

"Cause you peed in your bed."

"It wasn't pee."

"You still need some help."

"Help with what?"

"Spewing."

"Gross" said Jonah. "I aint queer."

"I aint neither, fool," said Shaka. "Just meet me at the river swing at sunset."

"Why?"

"You gonna find out."

Jonah walked away from Shaka toward his cabin. When walking inside he saw Thelma as usual sitting at her table while shelling peas, sweat heavy and beaded upon her brow. He as usual threw his string of fish on the table before her, blood, scales and the slime smearing into the boards.

Irritated in the heat she said, "I aint your regular old nigger. Fetch them fish to where they belong, back on the water shelf. So they aint rot and stink up the place."

But Jonah left the fish on the table, ignoring and testing her. Lately he had come to disdain her authority, all authority for that matter. Though he was acting upon nothing but his instinctual and adolescent desire for independence, she was powerless to rectify his behavior because they both understood that despite her position as his nanny, she as a slave was powerless to control him. Instead of resisting him Thelma set her peas aside on the table and began to carry the string of fish toward the porch. But struck with guilt Jonah grabbed the fish from her and completed the task and returned to the table and sat next to her.

When she reached over to hug him, he felt her bosom rubbing against his face and felt too what he suspected but wanted to avoid: the bulge in her belly. This thing inside her he envisioned as defiled and deformed, something that would wail upon leaving the womb and continue to wail throughout its existence. Repulsed he pushed himself away from her while also feeling overcome with guilt and confusion.

"I know what he does to you in the middle of the night," he said, unable to resist the temptation to reveal the secret at last.

Thelma looked blank then fearful before saying as nonchalantly as possible, "What you talking about?"

"I know he comes to your room."

"He don't mean no harm, your father. He just needs someone to love and hold him."

"What goes on in there, that aint love," Jonah said, pointing to her lean-to.

"I tries to love him. Tries to tolerate him anyway."

"And I know you got one coming in your belly," said Jonah. "And he aint gonna like nothing about this house."

"You's wrong about that. This child inside here," she said, touching her womb. "He gonna make our family whole. Cause now Whiteoak caint sell me, caint tear me away from you, cause now I gots to take care of another of his children."

Jonah looked at her harshly and incredulously and walked out the door. Sinking to the horizon and filtering through the haze, the sun was orange and dull like the yoke of an egg. Jonah hiked past the quarters then to the end of the fields where he cut through the forest and soon arrived at the swing by the river. The crickets were beginning their shrill, electric chorus, heralding the reign of twilight throughout the forest—all punctuated by the deep and ponderous solos of frogs. Once scorched and oppressed by the sun, the earth was relinquishing its heat, causing mist to rise upward into the atmosphere into a sodden, hazy, almost illusionary world of light and form. From this emerged Shaka, smiling.

Jonah suddenly felt awkward and ashamed. He did not know what to expect, only that he must learn to spurt. "All right then," he said. "Let's get on."

"Hold there," Shaka said pleased with the suspense and power he wielded over Jonah. "Quickness scares the quail, spooks the deer. Gots to move slow and silent like the hunter."

"All right," said Jonah.

"To make this work you must obey me," said Shaka. "And keep quiet."

Jonah nodded his head but felt suspicious.

"Follow me."

They traipsed upriver from the swing, moving under huge,

ancient trees and weaving through brambles of honeysuckle and blackberry which at times snagged around their ankles, eliciting whimpers and curses. Before long Shaka stopped behind one of these trees, using the trunk to shield their bodies from the river. Some ways below them and farther upstream, amidst the thick, impenetrable underbrush hugging the river, was a beach covered with loam and pieces of driftwood and shells.

"Sit tight for a while," said Shaka.

"For what?" whispered Jonah.

"Hush."

They waited silently. The remnants of light in the atmosphere were stored in the specks of pollen and dust and particles of moisture that descended toward the river. Something started to stir on the beach below which Jonah thought at first was some kind of animal—a deer or coyote or bear perhaps—but soon saw that it was a Negress some years older than himself standing on the beach gazing silently over the river while inhaling the scents of the atmosphere. She untied the string wrapped around her neck and her garb of calico, tattered and brown and soiled with dirt, fell to the ground around her ankles, exposing her slick back, her curvy hips, her slender but rounded buttocks—exposing the feral and nubile beauty normally cloaked behind the garbs of slavery. She waded into the river as the water rose around her to the cleft of her buttocks. She turned toward the shore, exposing her breasts that looked like nocturnal, moon-stained flowers. Then she sank into the water all the way to her neck so that only her head stayed above the river.

"Off with the clothes," whispered Shaka, turning toward Jonah.

"What?"

"Off with em."

"Huh?"

"This is your chance."

Jonah pulled his shirt over his head then sitting on the ground, removed his shoes and his pants. When standing again he thrust outward and spearlike like some animalistic and crazed antennae, feeling embarrassed but staring wantonly at the girl.

Shaka slapped him on his ass, giggling, saying, "You's ready for sho. Now sneak down there real quiet and wade out into the water. Start rubbing yourself down there, real soft and nice. Then get with that girl. And you gonna spurt for sho. And she gonna like that."

"What you mean, 'Get with that girl'? "

"Just get with her," said Shaka.

Sheepish now and even afraid but rapturously drawn to her, Jonah waited for the girl to turn and face outward over the river, then he wove through the underbrush onto the beach, standing with the loam massaging his feet. Out on the river she faced away from him while water bugs settled onto the surface, creating dimples while the maws of bass and bream broke the surface here and there feeding upon them. Silently he slid his toes into the river and moved toward her, feeling the bottom at times hard with rocks then at times soft with effluvium like some kind of strange, lascivious flesh.

Exposing her breasts she swirled toward him while staring at his penis which was still above the water and eagerly aiming toward her. She looked into his face, startled. She could not escape and swim back toward shore without passing over him, Jonah realized. So she stood still. The water swirled around her while Jonah moved toward her, not violently, not thoughtfully, only with the desire to touch her, to feel her, to love her.

Once his torso sunk below the water, he began to rub himself, his arm above the surface moving rhythmically while some strange but rapturous sensation mounted throughout his body. As his hips convulsed and spasmed uncontrollably, the girl looked at him not with fear but with disgust and then with curiosity. He closed his eyes while succumbing to the feeling of euphoria and thrust forward while his soul imploded. Opening his eyes he looked into the water and below his navel saw sinewy and pale filaments drifting away with the current.

"I spurt," he said. "I spurt," he shouted.

The girl then escaped past him, grabbed her clothes on the beach and vanished into the forest.

Shaka laughed hysterically in the bushes and again Jonah felt embarrassed and even shameful, thinking that maybe he was tricked by his friend for some unknown purposes. But once the laughter faded, leaving him alone, he lay on his back and floated on the river, peace and clarity coming to his mind while feeling his flesh mingling with the water and becoming part of the flow and swirl. He gazed upward into the darkness falling across the land while specks of light sieved through the atmosphere. He felt that through at last spurting, he had crossed some kind of boundary between black and white, that somehow through loving that Negress in that one moment, he had breached the gap between his father and Thelma, healing the schism that inflicted his family. And once his brother now in Thelma's womb was born, his family would somehow become whole. The peace and bliss lasted until the river sucked a minuscule but noticeable amount of warmth from his body, until his skin separated from the water and wrapped around his soul like something cold, lifeless and reptilian.

Back on the island standing before Shaka, Jonah was looking at the ground but in his mind saw his mother, Thelma, her face above him as he lay in the warming quilts, the smell of cookies and smoke wafting in the air. He heard her voice.

"Be kind to us."

Jonah could not raise his head but still stared at the ground, hearing her words from his childhood.

"When that day comes, Jonah, don't forget me, don't forget Shaka."

Jonah glanced at Shaka—saw another image of him running ahead of him dodging along the trail as powerfully as any deer, Jonah desperately pursuing to prevent losing the one person who amidst the misery and darkness of his life, represented something good and noble, who could slip through the omnipotent and always-closing fingers of Whiteoak, and who might save Jonah from his own fast-approaching and embittering future.

The muzzle of the rifle dipped to the ground and Jonah stood there defenseless. He imagined himself falling before Shaka imploring for forgiveness for whipping him. Telling him he never meant to, never wanted to hurt him in that way, that he was always weak, still was, could not bear to defy his father. For one moment he thought the heft, the always-present, strangling heft of his guilt suddenly lifting from his back.

Instead Jonah retreated from the slaves, his rifle pointing toward the ground while Jake and Shobuck dropped their knives to their sides.

Shaka still stared at Jonah, saying, "We're the wings of the same bird."

"I aint gonna kill yawl. Yawl just leave us alone, you understand? Leave us alone," he said before turning and heading back into the dunes.

CHAPTER FIFTEEN

While walking into the dunes with his back toward the slaves, Jonah looked at the tree and saw Pear stepping slowly and cautiously away from where he last saw his wife and children. His rifle was in one of her hands, Eloise's pistol in the other.

He felt his soul closing. "The beast has come. The beast has come for my family."

His sword drawn he ran toward the tree while Pear, seeing him coming, turned all the way around and bolted in the other direction. What has she done? He imagined his wife and children scattered across the roots of the tree, their clothes stained with blood, himself stooped over them cradling their broken bodies in his arms and realizing that he loved them more than anything but failed to protect them. Instead he saw Eloise leaning against the tree, her arms wrapped around both of their children.

"You're all right," he said, relieved.

She smiled at him. "Yes."

Lying on his stomach Jonah lined Pear into the sights of his rifle while she ran toward the west. But, reaching over James, Eloise pushed the barrel of the rifle into the roots and in that instant Pear dropped from sight behind one of the dunes. Jonah fired anyway, the bullet skimming along the crest, spraying sand. Quickly he reloaded. Then he saw that all the other Negroes, even Nomaw, were running toward that same spot and disappearing from sight.

He is submerged, gone under yet again.

After Eloise took their children over to their tent and shuffled them inside, she came back and Jonah asked, "How in the hell did she get my gun?"

"While I was watching yawl below, she sneaked into our tent from the back and stole your rifle."

"But how did she know where it was?"

"Probably from tending to our tent. Anyhow, she then placed the rifle at my back and said that she was not wanting to hurt me but that I must give her my pistol. Not wanting to get shot, I obliged her."

"Now we're powerless, Eloise."

"But they don't want to hurt us. They only want their freedom."

"They tricked us. They are not to be trusted."

Soon they saw a small, white flag raised above the dune where the slaves were hiding and moments later Nomaw emerged holding onto the shaft and trudged laboriously toward them, shouting, "Don't shoot me. I gots this here flag."

When she arrived Jonah said harshly, "What do you want?"

"To talk for them heathens," said Nomaw.

"You mean Shaka?" asked Eloise.

"And the rest of them."

"What do they want," asked Jonah.

"Let me say this first. Them over yonder is pagans. They think Jesus is birds. Aside from speaking for them, I aint gots nothing to do with them. So when that ship gets back, you can hang them as high as you like but leave my neck unbroke."

"I'll remember your request," said Jonah. "Now what do they want?"

"Shaka wants to make something he calls the covenant with yawl."

"An agreement?" said Eloise.

"Yessum."

"What do they want?" Jonah repeated.

"They want you to know that they don't mean yawl any harm. Not unless yawl's intending to harm them."

"So why are they stealing my firearms?"

"Cause they was afraid you might not back down on the beach, thought you might scuffle, shoot one of them. And they figured that without guns you aint gonna boss them around no more."

"Do you believe that?" asked Eloise.

"Yessum. They's messed up for sho but they aint meaning to hurt nobody.

"But while here," resumed Nomaw, "they say they aint slaving for yawl no more. Aint digging your trenches, cleaning your latrine or rowing your boats. But they intending to eat your food, take anything of yours they want and move around as they please while leaving yawl whatever you need to take care of yourselves until your boat comes."

Jonah felt that fear, present ever since coming to the island, that the beast was somehow slowly overtaking the island. He imagined his father looking over him, scouring with disgust for his son who was forced to negotiate with slaves.

"But what about the intruder?" asked Eloise.

"The who?" asked Nomaw.

"The bearer of the wings."

"If we're defenseless, he'll destroy us all," said Jonah.

"Oh, him." Nomaw studied Jonah. "You don't understand, do you?"

"I alone understand," said Jonah.

"Maybe," said Nomaw. "But they aint afraid of him."

"They best be," said Jonah.

"But he's their savior called Washaka."

"What?" said Jonah.

"It's true," said Eloise.

Jonah looked gaunt while suddenly seeming to understand something. "They were the same from the beginning, their savior and my beast." Remembering their night of fishing, Jonah realized that even then he understood but could not acknowledge that Shaka was inextricably linked to that force hidden under the water.

"They are with him and they are coming for me."

"What do you mean?"

"They want to annihilate me."

"But they don't mean to hurt you."

Jonah said nothing, only knew that somehow he must stop this force—dragoon and fight it to the death. He imagined shooting and killing some giant black bird from the sky that lay in some heap of broken bones, ruffled feathers and blood before his feet while Shaka was now begging for mercy before him, saying, "Whatever you want, Massa." But while lost into his fantasies, he could hear Eloise talking to Nomaw.

"But that's absurd," said Eloise. "Their savior—something called Washaka."

"I told them that too," said Nomaw. "You wanting to know what they said?"

"What?"

"They asked me how come I believe in the savior who lives in the scribbles of book and talks funny but not in their African who lives in all the birds around here, lives in our own hearts, lives in the soul of Shaka most of all? And who will soon carry us home?

"I reckon they made some sense," Nomaw concluded.

"But there's but one God of all men," said Eloise.

"And they reckon they know him best."

"What do they expect to happen once the ship returns," asked Jonah loudly.

"Don't you see?" said Nomaw. "They aint expecting to be here. They's expecting to fly to Africa."

"With Washaka?" said Eloise amazed.

"But I can't let them," said Jonah.

"But that's all they want," said Eloise, "to be left alone so they can fly back to Africa with their Washaka?"

"Yessum, that's all."

"But they won't fly away," said Eloise.

"But they aint gonna reckon on that until the noose is tight about their necks.

"They's all," resumed Nomaw, "fiercely devoted to Shaka,

willing to follow him to their death. They could have ambushed yawl, held yawl captive or made you their slave. But they didn't, not cause of fear but cause they just aint got any truck with you. And cause Shaka thinks—although the others don't understand this—that yawl too need to find your redemption and freedom through Washaka."

Shaka knows, thought Jonah. But how does he know? How does he know that Washaka is stalking me?

"I will kill Washaka," said Jonah.

"Shaka knows you wanting to," said Nomaw. "But if you try, Washaka's gonna destroy you. He says you just have to open your heart—allow yourself to feel. He says you wrapped yourself in that jacket so you caint feel nothing."

" 'The earth will light with flames and the wicked will perish or descend into hell.' It's like the second coming, except the name is different," said Eloise.

"I reckon," said Nomaw. "So they wanting to know if yawl agree to the covenant?"

"That we leave them alone and they leave us alone?" said Eloise.

"Yessum."

"We agree with all of our hearts," said Eloise.

"But I will never surrender," Jonah said, "never lay down my weapons, not even in the moment of my death. My own slaves won't hold me captive. Their surrender, complete and total, is their only option. Otherwise, woe for them."

"No, Jonah," said Eloise, turning toward him and seething with anger. "You tell her different. I will not allow you to bring more suffering to this island. You tell her now."

"No," said Jonah.

"Then I—and my children—walk away from you."

"So," said Jonah.

"Then I want nothing to do with you."

"So be it. You heard my answer, Nomaw. You're dismissed."

Nomaw sighed and turned and walked away, shaking her head. As she trudged yet again through the sand, Eloise called to her.

"You tell them, Nomaw, that Jonah is on his own, that I agree to their covenant. Tell them that I—and my children—want them to be free."

"Yessum," said Nomaw turning, "I surely will."

Eloise then promptly walked away from the tree, not even speaking to Jonah then retrieved the children from their tent and headed toward the beach on the eastern side of the island, away from Jonah and the slaves.

"Come back here," said Jonah.

But she ignored him, clenching the children all the tighter about their hands. Jonah stayed for some time to the south of the tree while lying flat on his stomach, his rifle at the ready while scrutinizing the crest in the distance beneath which were the slaves. But he never saw anyone.

He felt safe for now but imagined the night when the slaves would blend unseen into the darkness while he and his family were cocooned within their flimsy, defenseless tents. So he resolved to build a fortress. With the tree behind him he turned the kitchen table over on its side, assuming the wood was thick enough to defend against bullets, then used some crates to fill in the gaps between the tree and table. With an axe he then carved an opening into the table, through which he could see and aim his rifle. The spears, which he retrieved from his tent, were arranged so that the tips were pointing outward with their ends buried into the sand before the table or wedged between the crates. Once finished he stepped back to look at his fort—the rectangle with spikes pointing outward like some kind of calcified and prickly crustacean.

Eloise wandered back from the beach about that time, looking rather relaxed with the children next to her. After looking derisively at his fort seeming to almost laugh, she grabbed some books from her tent and steered away from Jonah as quickly as possible and disappeared again with the children.

Jonah sat alone inside his barricade, sweating. He remembered the book about the life of his father; before dying Whiteoak commissioned some writer to help him record the narrative of his life. For months Jonah avoided reading the book, not wanting to exhume the ghost of his father but now he needed some inspiration to keep those nagging and obsessive voices from overtaking his mind. Jonah climbed from his barricade and rushed over to his tent and after rummaging around in the bottom of his trunk, found the book then ran back into the fort and began to read the first page.

"I was raised in Tennessee to parents who immigrated from Scotland, having their homestead back in a hollow in the woods, farming pigs to provide pork for those who were heading west for the frontier. Not taking well to my chores, I was already roaming the woods with my crew of roguish and motley kids, stealing fruit and livestock before retreating into the woods to camp in caves, hiding out from the rest of civilization, fashioning ourselves somewhere between outlaws and Indians. My father attempted to discipline me with the lash but one day, I, who was unusually tall and strong for my age, struck to defend myself and realized in the end that my father, who was short and stout like the animals he raised, was not the better at fighting. From that day onward, I was my own lord beholden to nobody—the only retribution was that if not finishing my chores, I was forced to sleep in the barn and scrap around for my own food, which was often the case.

"But one day my father said to me, 'I aint much of a man, been in this here mire for most of my life, knee-deep in slop, nostrils full of stank, saturating my hands with the blood of swine. Hog Man, they calls me. Pig Woman, they calls your mother. But we aint damn near swum the Atlantic to come over here and raise some heathen and outlaw for our son.

" 'We done heaped up some pile of cash from all them pigs. And whether you like it or not, we's intending to send you to that school up the way—already made arrangements with the headmaster. I aint stood in your way on much in the past but concerning your education, I am your father and you will obey me. You will become educated folk. You resist, I will turn you in to the law as the leader of that gang committing mayhem all over these parts. You run away, fine but don't never come back, not even to sleep with the pigs.'

"When attending the school, I was unrelentingly tormented and ridiculed by the sons of planters and lawyers and doctors for my rough, unstylish way of dressing, for my woodsy, uncouth way of talking, for my inability to match the others in learning. 'Oink' was heard frequently. I earnestly wanted to find success in that school if only to prove to my tormentors that I could outcompete them, though I was still far behind. The headmaster tried to defend me against their attacks and always suggested that by turning the other cheek, I was only making myself stronger. At his behest I prayed nightly for deliverance from my predicament. And daily my cheek was turned.

"But I was never delivered.

"Until one day outside of school on my way home, I had the fortune of encountering some of my tormentors who accustomed to the protection of all the codes and conducts of their society, were not prepared when my rage broke free from its cage of numb hope and righteous constraint and feigned belief and in short, I beat those boys, all three of them at once, in one burst of violence. Standing above them victoriously, their blood on my fists, I felt that at last the world was righting itself for the rule of order—the rule of the strong over the weak and cowardly—was reinstating itself. And I wondered if Jesus had ever known the pleasure of prevailing over the wicked in battle, would he ever have believed that he could call the angels from the heavens?

"From that day onward I never found need for Jesus and from that day onward, my troubles at school were much alleviated.

"After the completion of my schooling, my father, saying that pigs might drop pennies but that he aint never seen them shit gold, refused to allow me to stay on his farm and I was forced happily to find my way toward New Orleans where I learned the pleasures of women, some who were as sweet and aromatic as rainwater pooling in magnolia blossoms, and some who were as filthy as swamps, and where I learned to earn my keep through boxing and thievery and, when necessary, hard labor. Most boxers and thieves are driven by their emotions, of fear and need but I learned to tackle my endeavors objectively, calculatingly, methodically—never allowing myself to become vulnerable. In time I found much success in both but in time, that paradoxically began to make me slovenly and sloppy in my work.

"After nearly meeting my end with the law through some unplanned, drunken thievery, I decided that I was in need of discipline and chose to return to Tennessee to join Andrew Jackson and his militia for the purpose of killing Indians—sport which I thought might prove most extraordinary and entertaining. Most of the men in the militia were like me from poor backwoods farms and eager to escape the tedium of their lives. But unlike them, I was educated and already practiced in the art of combat and eager to elevate myself. I practiced vigorously to perfect my command of rifle and sword, both of which were not strangers in my hands and even affected some of the manners of the officers. However, as I always proclaimed myself proudly as the son of pig farmers, the other men came to revere me for being one of them but able to lead as well and once given my own battalion of pickets to lead, I was heralded as the Prince of Pigs."

All that day the slaves stayed hidden, never even showing their heads; they had evidently made some caches of food and water and did not need to come to the kitchen, thought Jonah.

During twilight the dunes were bathed in vague and pastel lights, the surface of the gulf calm and metallic and the darkness approached like something slow and predatory, smothering then asphyxiating the remnants of light, leaving Jonah alone in his carapace watching the outline of his body fading away while sensing the forces of anarchy around the island. Eloise soon returned and through the cracks, he could see her retrieving some bread from the cupboard and water from one of the barrels while their children waited back at her tent.

"Get the children inside here," said Jonah.

"Inside there with you?"

"They will come in the dark."

"We'll never come inside that thing with you."

"Get into this Goddamn fort now."

Jonah then broke through some of the crates and lurched toward Eloise, grabbing her arm but she twisted away from him and violently smacked his arm, causing him to break his grip.

"I'm not getting inside there with you."

"But I command you."

"What are you going to do," she asked, "shoot me?"

"Maybe."

But she just walked away from him back inside the glow of her tent where her children waited for her. Jonah suddenly felt all alone like his mind was sealed off, perhaps irrevocably, from all around him and again he returned his thoughts to his father.

"Soon I was called to war in Alabama which was hardly anything but wilderness during this time, full of lakes, creeks, wolves, lions, trees as wide as houses—and full of savages. The white men, mostly trappers and some farmers, were encroaching upon the Indian's territory while the government was offering every incentive to them to integrate into our way of life. However, tensions were mounting and soon the chief called Tecumesh ventured into the territory to rally the Creeks against the settlers and in the process, inspired one of their leaders into action, by the name of Crazy Medicine, who started the tribe of warriors known as the Redsticks—crazy, foolish sorts who believed that the magic of their leader protected them from death.

"One summer the Redsticks were traveling to Pensacola to trade for munitions and in route attacked the homestead of a settler then later sold her away. Upon their return with their horses loaded down with weapons, they were attacked by settlers hungry for revenge. Outnumbered, the Redsticks fled into swamps but counterattacked later and won the engagement—which led at that point to an open, full-bore conflagration. The settlers then retreated into a fort but the man in charge did not offer ample protection so that when the savages attacked, the women and children were slaughtered. Our militia was then at last called into duty. Unlike the other men who considered Indians on about the same level as rabid dogs or possessed demons and who thus were eager for the kill, I had admired them ever since my childhood and believed that their form of open and shameless savagery was preferable to our own rationalized, moralized sort.

"My battalion of pickets was elected to first cross into the wilderness to map the lay of the land and to locate the whereabouts of the Indians. On several occasions we indulged in skirmishes, shots fired on our part, their arrows whizzing through the air but, as commanded, we retreated as quickly as possible. But after one such skirmish one night, we traveled until complete darkness then, without building any fires or raising any tents, sprawled on the ground for some hours of rest before dawn, leaving one man awake to keep guard. But evidently we were stalked. In the middle of the night, I felt someone heavy on my back grabbing hold of my hair and at once, before even understanding what was happening, I felt the knife on my head and suddenly my hair being cut from my head. I bucked upward while the brave shouted victoriously, and threw him backward and landed on top with the force of my weight, leaving him stunned and gasping for air. I turned around and in the glimmer of moonlight, I noticed that he was not much older than fifteen. I unsheathed my knife and while he looked on somewhat incredulously, as though none of this could happen to him, I slit him open from below his naval to the bottom of his ribs, the euphoria of his coup fading from his eyes like light from a lantern, his victorious clutches releasing from my own thick, bloodied scalp, the smell of charred venison and fresh pecans wafted from his entrails like smoke from an oven.

"I and my men—or what was left of them—fought bravely but we were outmanned so I shouted for everyone to scatter. I spent the night under a ditch covered with fallen trees, too scared to even move for fear of alerting the redmen eager for my death and in the stillness, the pain of my wound steadily encroached—and all that it signified.

"In the morning I gazed at my reflection in a creek. My face and head was scabbed with blood and evidently the Indian in his excitement carved not upward but downwards toward my forehead, removing not only half of my hair but some part of my forehead as well. From thereon out I would be hideous to behold, forever ostracized from the finer, more sophisticated realms of society, incapable of fulfilling my ambitions. From thereon out my pulsing, electric urges would be satisfied only amongst besmirched street whores—if even they would take me into their arms.

"I placed the rifle under my chin while cursing my fate for showing me the kingdom of earth but barring my passage.

"What good is my life? How could I face the humiliation of this?

" 'Fire your weapon,' I shouted.

"But with my death but one twitch away, I could not snuff away the smell of the trees, nor the cries of the birds, nor the warmth of the air, nor the haunting and disturbing sight of myself reflected in the water—could not leave the cursed but beautiful life around me. I placed my head to the side of the barrel, lit the wick and felt the whoosh and bang of the lead passing next to my face, then cracking into the branches above my head. For one moment I died but I was resurrected and never thinking to pity myself again, I rose to my feet, the rush of life coming again but meaner and sharper and darker than even before."

Placing the book at his side, Jonah retrieved the lantern from the kitchen and, after lighting the wick, hung it above his head on one of the limbs of the tree. In the remnants of the sunset to the west, he saw the glow of the slaves' fire—his first evidence that they were still out there—as though he were a hunter in Africa looking over the plains at the fire of a distant, hostile tribe not yet contacted by the white man. Then he was hit again even harder by that pang of loneliness, realizing that for once his slaves were not even conscious of him, that he was irrelevant.

But they were all wrong, he thought. None of them knew that their lives were in danger from the beast lurking in the unknown, and that he alone was redoubtable, cunning and calculating enough to save them all. Yes, save them all. In the end he would know victory—just like his father.

He imagined himself now sneaking from the barricade, skulking around under the cloak of night with nothing but his sword, stalking the slaves then attacking them, slicing off their arms before they had the chance to wield their weapons, blood spurting forth as they hollered in terror, their faces showing surprise at his strength and cunning, while they dropped to the ground on their knees, bent in obeisance before him yet again. Yes, he would know victory just like his father.

Instead he stayed hunkered in his fortress as the glow faded from their fire until the island was dark except for his lantern casting its wan but steady circle of light into the vastness.

When overcome with his own loneliness, he called to Eloise in her tent to make sure she was all right and she called back, her voice weary, almost saddened with, "Yes, we're fine."

Jonah enviously imagined them inside the tent experiencing the safety and warmth that he never felt himself.

Soon she snuffed out her candle and he heard James and Josh say, "Goodnight, Father, goodnight."

Wanting to ward off his loneliness and the voices he sensed struggling to plague him again, Jonah returned to his book.

"Consequently, after my convalescence, I, incapable of imagining anything other for my life, directed all my energies into the heat of battle, into my only refuge for the forever angry and ugly and rejected—and when the lead and fire was all about me, I felt I was at home, eager to live, eager to die, most alive for having nothing to lose. And lo, I could exact my revenge against those who deprived me of my face.

"And my men came to dread my charge because under my command we always found the hottest part of the battle. The desire to conquer, to master, to intimidate, kept my heart beating in my chest, not gouged by my own sword.

"Soon the numbers of the Creeks were declining and the lot of them mistakenly gathered in one place, at Horseshoe Bend, an island almost circled in full by a river except for one narrow bridge of land. While some of our men swam or paddled across the river to prevent the Creeks from escaping, I volunteered to lead the charge across the bridge into the maw of the enemy. That day, my flesh was pierced, my blood spilled, to the count of five—once by arrow, twice by lead, twice by the shrapnel of our own cannons. But while many of my men fell around me, I for some reason refused to die, my wounds always but on my limbs. And that day, my hands were wrung deep in the blood of savages. And that day, the Creeks were fully defeated.

"Soon afterward they signed the treaty that ceded much of their lands, about half of the state, to our government, even though most of that land belonged to Creeks who were not hostile to the settlers.

"Afterward General Jackson called me into his tent and said, 'Your bravery and effectiveness was unmatched in this campaign. Now your enlistment is about to expire and of course you have the option of renewing or walking away.'

" 'I want to stay, sir.'

" 'But, son, you will be frustrated with your future in this army while serving under the command of men more accustomed to watching battles from the tops of trees and knobs. They will fear your style of fighting, especially against the Europeans and consider you too wild, too intractable and too eager for the fight.

" 'So you can stay on, the puppet of those who want to place you where the battle is hottest but most obscure, so they need not be there themselves.

" 'I know you have asked many questions about growing cotton and managing Negroes. That land down in Alabama—that flat, low-lying land with that dark, loamy soil—is good for growing cotton, the sort that works well in that gin created by that Mr. Whitney. Someone like you, smart, ambitious and fearless, you can grow some heap of cotton down there and make yourself the master of your own domain.

" 'You are entitled to claim the land in this state as your own. My recommendation is that you discharge with full honors and regalia and seek your fortune before others steal that chance from you.'

"After that I chose to slouch into the anonymity of the wilderness to lay my claims and to satiate my drives, not amongst society but amongst beasts, dirt and Negroes."

Jonah placed the book at his side while feeling inspired by the life of his father. I too have my enemy, the beast, he thought. As my father hid in his ditch, I hide in this fortress with danger all around as some of my troops have already fallen by the wayside. But I will fight this battle, I will win and my enemies shall fear me as the Indians feared my father. I am lord of this island, master of my Negroes—fearless in exacting my will. And I too will lord over the beast, dirt and Negroes.

But he felt exhausted and lonely within moments. Even the drone of the gulf seemed distant and even foreign to him, not able to soothe his mind. He began to hear what he thought were murmurs and whispers swirling around him, so close in volume to the sound of water that he thought he was hallucinating at first. He placed his rifle through the hole in the table and stared into the darkness, searching for movements and saw—or imagined he saw—something: flickers of dark taking form momentarily then flitting away into nothingness.

The beast is coming.

In another part of his mind, he was asking: Is this real. Is any of this real?

Coming closer the voices continued to swirl around him—then fused into one murmur that soon became a slow, undulating hymnal of words Jonah could not yet decipher.

He fired into the darkness, drew his sword and reloaded while waiting for them to attack.

But nothing changed except that the singing became louder, rising above the drone to consume everything.

"What do you want?" shouted Jonah.

The music came even closer, separate voices becoming audible before fading again into the hum. Jonah could now see them, four dark silhouettes of bodies out on the fringes of the lantern glow.

"Come on out, Jonah, from that low and dark place," Shaka said.

"So you can kill me?" shouted Jonah.

"So you can join the brotherhood of man."

"Go to hell."

"We would there, Massa," said Jake. "But how we all gonna fit in there with you?"

"Listen to my story about this boy," said Shaka.

"Tell us about the boy," said Jake.

"He come on down to Whiteoak—from where, nobody knew, delivered to a cruel and loveless father. But this boy wanted freedom and he found it in his friend, Shaka, and he wanted love too, and he found that in his Negro mother, Thelma. And she protected him from his father. And she taught him, oh my brethren, and his friend taught him..."

"What did they teach him, Shaka? What did his friend and mother teach him?" cried Jake.

"They said, 'Jonah, oh my son and oh my friend, when you put away your childish ways, when you's called to rule your empire—when all these souls stretching from forest to field are under your command, be good to your Africans, be good to them, leave your heart open to their love and set...and set...and set them...' "

"Free," bellowed Jake.

Jonah suddenly remembered that day in his childhood back at Whiteoak when he was returning from town where Thelma had sent him to purchase some flour and sugar so she could make his cookies. While Jonah was riding on horseback on the road to his house, he crossed paths with many slaves who ordinarily greeted him but today looked furtively and apprehensively away from him. He felt instantly that something was wrong.

Once arriving outside his cabin, he dismounted from his horse and ran into the kitchen but the room was empty and dinner unprepared. He pulled back the curtain, looked into Thelma's lean-to, thinking that maybe she was sick in bed. But she was not there. He searched around the cabin then raced outside toward the well then along the rows of the garden where he expected to see her harvesting vegetables for dinner. But she was not there. Mounting his horse he drove his heels into the flanks of the beast, driving him onward toward the slave quarters where he stopped in front of one of the shacks and dismounted. He walked along the row, peeking through the windows looking for Thelma, seeing nothing but the slaves recently returned from the fields and huddling around on the floor and preparing their dinners, staring listlessly at things, trying to recover from the heat and exhaustion of the day. When seeing Jonah many of the slaves grimaced and glanced away from him. At last he arrived before Jake's shack and peeking through the window, saw that the room was full of girls.

"Jake," he called.

Jake emerged onto his porch, his eyes still bloodshot from squinting in the sun. "What you want, Littlemassa?" he asked nonchalantly.

"Have you seen Thelma?"

"I aint seen her." He turned quickly to return to his cabin.

"But...but...but...," Jonah stammered on the verge of tears.

"I aint," said Jake. "I said I aint seen her."

About that time his wife Delia came onto the porch followed by their daughters who poked their heads from the doorway, their eyes bright and inquisitive, gawking and smiling at Jonah who was struggling to repress his tears.

"What you want, Littlemassa?" she said, her voice exhausted but compassionate. "You looking for Thelma?"

"Naw, wench," interrupted Jake. "Don't say nothing."

"Don't you reckon, fool," said Delia, "that we aint got to dump more on the heap of his sorrow by lying to him?"

"Then go on, woman," said Jake. "When you got the mind, I caint control that old spigot of yours."

"She done sold," said Delia, shaking her head. "That old nigger driver we call Pincher done dragged her from yawl's cabin this afternoon, clamping her down with manacles. I knowed. I seen the whole thing while working in the garden. She screamed for you, Jonah. Then she cursed Massa, saying that he done planted her womb with their child and he was selling her cause he didn't want nobody to know the truth. As she was dragged away in the wagon, she was hollering for you, Jonah, hollering cause she loved you, child. She loved you even though you is white."

Jonah began to shake and tears trickled from his eyes. Jake and Delia and their girls stared at him amazed like they could not believe that whities cried. But all Jonah wanted was someone to hold him, to draw them into their homes and care for him.

Still the others just stood there, awkward, until Jake said, "Now he knows what it's like being a nigger."

"Hush, fool," said Delia.

"I mean," said Jake apologetically, "that I was stripped from my mammy when I was about your age. And I reckon I done survived, barely though." Jonah peeked upward toward Jake who smiled, exposing the gaps in his brown, decaying teeth.

Jonah ran from the porch and into the fields, sobbing. But once the remnants of the light faded, he could not bear the darkness so he returned to the glow of the shacks and wandered around lost in misery and disoriented, listening to the sounds of infants crying, of the men in hushed and weary voices laughing and telling stories, hearing at times the sounds of sex and smelling the odors of sweat, smoke and simmering salted pork fat. Amidst his anguish he sensed their peace, that though they were too exhausted for anything but to fade toward sleep, they were allowed this respite from the fields to languish in the affection of their homes, whereas he could not find any escape or enclave from his cold and cruel father, from the morbidity and emptiness that he imagined would plague his life forever. He wished his flesh would somehow draw pigmentation from the night so he could fuse into the lives of the Negroes and vanish altogether from the world of his father. He stayed on the margins of their shacks, cloaked in the darkness until their fires extinguished and the voices waned into silence and until all that was heard was the twitching and mumbling of slaves in their sleep waking at times, gasping from their nightmares.

Too afraid to endure the darkness, he wandered back toward his cabin and walked inside. The darkness was pierced by one low, static flame from the candle and contrary to his hope, he saw his father sitting at the table alone hunched over some pile of stale and molded cornbread which he was dipping into a pot of pale, half-congealed lard. Jonah was tempted to retreat back outside but instead walked forward and stood before his father who stopped eating and looked uncomfortably at his son, crumbs dropping from his mouth. For once their eyes met and locked until Jonah looked away, disturbed.

Jonah spoke, his voice forced and high-pitched. "I know you sold her."

His father said nothing, looked down at his food.

Jonah blurted, "I know you fucked her. I watched you fuck her. And you sold her and my brother because you were ashamed."

Jonah started to walk away but suddenly seized by rage, turned and charged toward his father, up and over the table, swinging his fists and yelling and crying while his knuckles smashed into his father's skull, into his nose, his eyes, his teeth, into that pinkish and mottled mutilation on the top of his head. His father did not resist, did not defend himself but sat there tolerating the blows impassively. His rage exhausted, Jonah fell from the table and by accident extinguished the candle so the room became dark. On the floor he crawled around and once finding his bed slid between the sheets, lying there as numb as the dark except for the pulsating in his fists.

Moments later Jonah saw that the candle was reignited. In the kitchen his father rummaged around through the cupboard then outside around the well. Then his footsteps, knocking and scraping on the puncheons like furniture possessed by demons, moved across the floor toward his bed where Jonah hid under the covers. His father stopped by the bed and Jonah heard something being shuffled toward him; then the footsteps moved away. Jonah pulled the covers from his head and looked on the floor, seeing in the dim and shady light the plate of old, stale cookies and the glass of milk still cold from sitting in the well. In that moment Jonah realized that his father, in his awkward, lifeless manner, was also mourning the loss of Thelma who nurtured his child and brought love and care into their dark, tormented home and was also mourning the force in their world that caused humans to abuse and exploit each other, the force over which he lorded and under which he too served.

Back inside his carapace on the island, his rifle now cradled between his arms, his cheek pressed against the cold barrel, his hands gripped tight about his shoulders, as though he was trying to seek comfort from steel and powder, Jonah felt the words rising inside of him propelled by the nervous back and forth motion of his upper body and before thinking to edit himself, he shouted, the noise like some great, all-consuming exhalation, "But they left me."

"They left him," said Shaka, his voice now doleful and slower along with the hum of his choir. "They left him, my brethren. They left him all alone."

"With nobody but Whiteoak to tend to his heart," said Jake. "Nobody but the cruel, oh so cruel Whiteoak to mend his broken heart."

"Whiteoak took his mother away and he forced his hand against his only friend. And Whiteoak, he tooketh his son's soul away.

"And our boy stealed away from the memory of his mother and his friend and stealed away even from his own heart. And, oh my brethren, his soul was destroyed by the hand of Whiteoak."

"And our boy who used to play in our shacks and suckle on

the nipples of our mothers—that boy, whom we all loved, he went away," said Jake. "He done went away."

"And he kneeled down," resumed Shaka, "before his father, offered up his life, and he kneeled down too before the golden calf, and offered up his life. And they took him.

"But even when God took away his father," said Shaka.

"He still walked in sin," said Jake.

"And he hunted and killed all the creatures of the earth, and they came to defile him."

"And still he walked in sin," chorused the slaves.

"And God took away his slaves."

"And still he walked in sin."

"And even his wife turned away from him. And his children knew him not."

"And still he walked in sin."

"And now he swallowed himself inside his own fortress."

"And there he be," said Jake. "Buried in his own sin."

Jonah was holding his rifle even tighter now, the blood in his face warming the barrel. Liquid was coming down his chin but he did not know why. All he knew was that he somehow wanted to bury himself even deeper into his fortress.

"Oh Lord," preached Shaka, "the white man forged the sword and the gun to steal the black man from his family."

"When does the woe end? When does the suffering stop?" sang the other slaves.

"And the black man chopped down all the trees. And the white man ate the finest of meals. And the black man tilled his fields. And the white man…"

"Drank the finest of whiskeys," said Jake.

"When does the woe end? When does the suffering stop?"

"And when the black man wanted to be free, he was whipped or he was shot."

"When does the suffering end? When does the woe stop?"

"Come on out there now, Jonah, and make the suffering end…"

"And make the woe stop."

Jonah was not even moving now—just trying to fade away into nothingness, repeating over and over again, "He has come…he has come…he has come."

"Come on out there and make the suffering end.

"And make the woe stop."

The voices of the slaves merged again into one hum that wandered and meandered and rose and subsided like the undulation of swells while refraining: "When does the suffering end, when does the woe stop..."

One of the slaves would occasionally preach above the din to voice his own message, Jake saying, "Your whiskey is so fine and sweet that lessen you make the suffering end and the woe stop, I gonna drink it all by myself."

Heard over the slaves the drone of the elements that once seemed so distant and impenetrable now flowed into his mind so he felt inseparable from all around him and he lay his sword by his side, and he lay his rifle by his side and soon the humming of the slaves subsided altogether and before falling into the nothingness of sleep, he heard his son in their tent not too far away, saying, "Mommy…Mommy. Why are you crying? Why are you crying?"

Jonah awoke rigid and sore into daylight filtering between the cracks in his fort, his head throbbing, his mouth coated in something cottony and foul tasting. Beneath his jacket his flesh was merely numb. But inside his mind he felt chaotic and disoriented so, to settle and inspire himself, he once again began to read from the book about the life of his father. Randomly he flipped through the pages until finding a passage that appealed to him.

"Jefferson meant not that all men are created equal at birth for obviously we are all different, varying in strength, capacity and tenacity but that we should all be allowed to prove our mettle without the restraints of law or class—thus allowing for the weak to fall, the strong to rise, regardless of their birth so that the law of nature prevails. We are after all thrown into the arena of life and left on our own to better our neighbors ultimately to the death."

Jonah skipped some paragraphs and read, "Most men know their darkies from observing them from their verandas while eating their sugar cakes and cookies and sipping tea. But when first coming to Alabama I lived with them in their own sheds on the coldest of nights and even eased my loins inside their wenches. And I know them and I say Negroes are men indeed, the same as you and me, possessed of the same faculties of intellect (though some have minds more akin to bovines), the same instincts for power and submissiveness and undoubtedly their antennae to pain are just as refined as those whose skin is shaded differently. But they had inferior weapons and tools and are now systematically deprived of knowledge and power. You think Negroes are stupid; they will outsmart you every time. You think they are lazy—then imagine yourself in their shoes, forced to labor for the benefit of another man.

"Why do the mass of planters ignore this fact? Because of Jesus. If they acknowledged that black and white are essentially the same, then they would be forced to dismantle the institution to appease their Lord. But no, only by denying the truth do they feel justified in owning slaves. Hypocrites, the lot of them and poor, overly cruel managers as well.

"I say again, Negroes are men without guns. But if they ever get guns then you will be plowing their fields, cleaning their outhouses, frying their cornbread and they will be fucking your wife in the back of the shed. Always give them something to lose. Give them as much as you can to lose—and you will control them."

Jonah wondered if he underestimated his slaves, if he was blinded by his own ignorance and hubris. Yet the slaves, even though having guns, were not seeking power over him, nor forcing him to fry their cornbread or do their chores. They just seemed to want to be free of him.

When looking outside his fortress he did not any longer perceive the conflict between land and water, between the powers of edification and destruction, nor the beast lurking in the water waiting to destroy him. As he noticed the sun, shellacked by a mild and yellowish haze, reflecting off the surface of the water, he felt that the elements of nature were not fighting but caressing each other, delighting in their touch, in the friction of creation.

Shaka and Jake were fishing not too far offshore. On the beach his children were playing with Shobuck, all of them running and jumping into the languid, transparent waves while shrieking in delight then hurling globs of sand at each other and grabbing each other either to wrestle or just hug, their bodies quick and unrestrained with joy. Up from them was Eloise sheltered under her parasol while talking to Pear slowly at first with long, awkward pauses in between but gradually their conversation became more gently animated.

He does not lurk out there anymore, thought Jonah. He now rules the island. But instead of fear he only felt the sadness of acceptance.

"I am the Lord of my fortress," he said out loud, mocking himself. "King of my domain, regnant over all the men and creatures, and the cotton that shelters man from the north wind.

"I am Lord of nothing," he said. "Not even myself."

He smelled food. Just inside his fortress he saw that somebody had left him some food and water. Suddenly he was gulping water, dissolving away the foul taste in his mouth then gorging on chunks of cornbread saturated with molasses. Then he lifted the whole roasted fish to his mouth and with his teeth pulled the flesh from the bones underneath. Afterward, feeling sated and full and even tranquilized, he saw amidst the remains of his meal what at first he missed: the yellow cactus blooms which he held before his eyes, realizing that someone out there still cared about him.

He wanted to walk from his fortress but imagined himself in this newfound, alien world where all those once under his command were free, where even his own wife and children regarded him with fear and disdain, where he was exposed as a lonely and tortured soul and where all his stigmata, once held tight inside of him, was now revealed to everyone—where he was merely one man amongst many other men wandering through life searching for salvation. A world where all that he was no longer existed.

So he pulled his jacket closer about him and all through the day he observed that part of the world around him which was always there but which he never saw. He watched as Jake and Shaka excitedly pulled yet another fish into their boat then returned to shore where they were greeted by the other slaves and where they roasted the fish, all feeling the joy of laboring in the wilderness without his hindrance to provide for their own nourishment.

He watched too as they lolled around afterward and took naps while staring into the ether at the birds above them. Watched as Pear and Shaka waded into the gulf and held each other gently afloat amidst the waves. Watched as his own wife watched the couple in the water longingly before looking up toward him then looking sadly away when not seeing him. He watched as Jake approached Nomaw and bent on his knee, pointed toward the other couple in the water and pleaded for her to come with him. And watched as these men and women lived as they should, as God wanted them but in a way that he strove to deny them. He watched as they lived as he himself wanted to live but in a way that he strove to deny himself. He watched as the sun began to descend mysteriously back into the darkness from which it came, watched as his own footprints around his fortress slowly dissolved from existence in the wind. And watched too in the approach of darkness as one lone, prehistoric bird drifted with the breeze around in circles so high that it was unbeknownst to anyone except himself, while doing nothing but being.

He felt deeply ashamed for seeking meaning through power, for resolution through violence, for denying life the opportunity to express itself. Life was not what he thought. In this world, not the illusionary one created by his father, Jonah knew he was not powerful, not important, nor special or even talented—he was only his body, his thoughts, his feelings in that moment.

After the slaves congregated at twilight back at their camp on the other side of the dunes, Jake appeared walking along the beach in Jonah's direction; slung back over his shoulder was Jonah's rifle and strapped about his chest was the pistol. Jonah placed his rifle into the window of his fortress and set his sights on Jake while scanning around in back of him to see if anyone was attacking from behind.

Jake stopped at one of the rowboats, leaned the rifle against the thwarts then pushed the boat into the waves. After wading with the boat until his knees were submerged, he climbed aboard and rowed swiftly out beyond the waves. He rested his oars along the gunnels, grabbed the gun and stood on one of the benches while balancing precariously. By now all the other slaves were watching as Jake placed the butt of the rifle into his crotch, so that the barrel was projecting upward like some giant and iron phallus. He bucked his hips back and forth. The slaves laughed and jeered. He stroked the barrel back and forth and when reaching the climax, he drew one of his hands close to the trigger and, *bang*, the rifle fired while Jake was bucked backward and nearly fell over the gunnels before saving himself and landing hard on his butt in the floor of the boat. Still holding the rifle he stood up and waved to the slaves then bent over as though in agony while rubbing his thigh. He stood upright again, holding the rifle ceremoniously overhead then calmly and slowly tossed it overboard where it disappeared without a splash into the depths of the ocean.

Next went the pistol.

Jonah realized that all that remained within their grasp to allow one man to harm or dragoon another, besides fist, teeth and fingernails, was the metal now lying inertly and repulsively at his side. Since the slaves had ceremoniously disarmed themselves in his view, he did not have any reason to remain inside his fortress. Yet he knew he still could not leave but must stay consumed inside this thing, forced to confront the bare, not any longer deniable truth of his existence: That he was too ashamed, was always too ashamed since whipping Shaka as a child, to show himself to this world.

After arriving back at the island, Jake reconverged below the dunes with the other slaves, except for Nomaw who was now cooking in the kitchen not far from Jonah. The glow of the fire appeared over the dunes again. The noises coming from that direction were now celebratory; the slaves were beating on pots and logs like drums and singing and laughing raucously—again making Jonah feel taunted and all the more aware of his own misery. Appearing over the crest of the dune was Jake dressed like Eloise, wearing her red silk gown and her hat adorned with flowers while her crucifix was festooned around his neck. Jake swigged from the bottle of whiskey—Jonah's own whiskey—burped, looked toward the kitchen and shouted at Nomaw, "Meat, woman. Bring me meat."

"I aint your slave," shouted Nomaw.

"Yes, you is. You's my love slave."

"Hush, you old drunk."

Jake started walking over toward Jonah. "Hey, Massa—I mean, Jonah—is you still in there?" He swigged from his bottle. "Come on now, take your rifle and try to shoot me."

Jonah said nothing.

"You caint shoot me, naw, cause I aint nothing but wind and bunches of feathers. Bullets pass right through me."

"Maybe not," said Jonah.

"When you gonna come out that thing? You oughten to come on over here and join the feast of…the feast of… What's the word, Nomaw?"

"Emancipation."

"Sho, emancipation."

Silence is more commanding than words, Jonah remembered his father writing.

Jake then walked straight at Jonah, stopping at the end of the spears protruding out from his fort. "Aint I pretty?"

To blaze, with the insignia of my name, through life, thought Jonah.

"You oughten to come over and sip some whiskey. If none of the other lassies take up with you, you can dance with me. Even let you squeeze my teats. What you say?"

You are the god of your kingdom—revel in it.

"Oh, Massa—I mean, Jonah, Shaka say we supposed to call

you that now—I know what you need. Take some swig of this," said Jake, maneuvering through the spaces between the spears and handing Jonah the bottle through the window in the table.

Jonah grabbed the bottle and swigged, feeling that the voice, that ever-present, never-escapable voice of his father, might now fade.

"You stole this from me," Jonah said.

"Sho I did. And you stole all my chilluns, even my own black ass. So what you complaining for?"

Jonah sighed and said as though some new voice was aborning in him, "Maybe you're right."

"Wait for that liquor to take hold so you can break free from your prison. But give me my bottle back for now."

"No, Jake…I mean...you have plenty more, don't you," asked Jonah.

"Keep it. Sometimes when you aint got love, you needs whiskey."

The liquor now dazing his mind, Jonah asked, "How did yawl know I wouldn't shoot yawl?"

"I thought you was. I done told Shaka that I hoped he gonna be dead, not me."

"How did Shaka know?"

"He aint known, not really. Although he claimed the spooks told him."

"But…"

"He gambled."

"But why?"

"Bunches of us niggers knowed you since you was a baby, wandering around looking for nipples to suck. You come around my shack at night, chomping on pone, playing with my chilluns. When you was young, you was just like us. You loved us and we loved you. And we always hoped until that hope done run away, got lost and jumped off some cliff, that you was gonna be better than your father.

"And Shaka knowed you better than any of us. Yawl was both

strange, bound together in your aloneness. I reckon it's more complicating than this but I think Shaka just wanted his friend back."

Jonah stopped drinking.

"But Shaka," resumed Jake, "done said that Washaka came to him in his dream and told him not to fear you."

"I see," said Jonah.

They lingered in silence. "Caint I just get me another sip?" asked Jake.

"Here," said Jonah, handing the bottle over to Jake who swigged then returned the bottle.

"Who is Washaka, Jake?"

"I aint really know for sho. Maybe Jesus done busted out the Bible? Maybe he's our savior coming to carry us to Africa. Maybe he's the dream of Shaka's mother. Sometimes I think Jesus and Washaka is just words—sounds even—for something that come long before anything we ever knowed. Sometimes I think he aint nothing but our own hopes. But it don't really matter, it's all the same."

"The same?"

"Sho. Cause whatever you want to call him, you sho as hell knows him when he comes along."

"What do you mean?"

"You know him here," said Jake, thumping his fist hard into his chest next to the crucifix. "Not just in your heart but all over like you was struck by lightning."

Jonah felt sad.

"And you's coming to know him too, though he aint feel quite the same for you."

Jake left suddenly, walked over to the kitchen, smelled what Nomaw was cooking, pinched her ass, did not even attempt to shield himself from her slap and wandered toward the others, shouting, "Massa's coming on over. Coming to eat with the niggers for the feast of emancipation."

Jonah was alone in the darkness, wishing Jake would come and talk to him again. He sipped slowly from the bottle, coming to fully acknowledge the nature of what the slaves called Washaka and what others might call God, something that was both real and imaginary like the beast in the ocean, something that unmercifully destroys and unrelentingly creates, something beyond comprehension—and he knew too that all those forces were now seething through him. He had glimpsed this force throughout his life, even experienced it in his youth while hunting with Shaka but had denied it for years in his attempt to live for his father.

Lying on his back Jonah placed the jug on his belly and closing his eyes, strove to relax but felt some memory struggling to emerge. He resisted at first but slowly succumbed, allowing it to flow through and hopefully away from him.

He saw the ground of caked mud and fecal dust with splotches of stomped, withering weeds after he and Shaka were captured by the patrol. The footsteps of his father scratched toward him on the dust until stopping before the horsemen, saying nothing.

The voice of the patrol strove to break the silence, his voice awkward, hesitant, quaking. "Here's your little nigger boy, Whiteoak."

Then he laughed, his guffaws becoming idiotic until Whiteoak, either cloaking or blocking some portent of fury, seemed to strangle the laugher from his throat. Jonah soon felt the untying of the tethers around him then he was hoisted from the saddle and thrown over his father's shoulder and carried toward the back of the barn where he was dumped onto the ground in some pit of mud and dust, then doused with cold and limpid water, while his father used clumps of hay to grind the charcoal from him, exposing his pale and delicate and sterile flesh so that he was the same color as his father, transmogrified into something he despised.

Again Jonah was slung over the shoulder of his father and carried to their cabin where he was dumped inside on the floor; moments later he heard his father outside hammering the door shut with nails. Jonah crawled across the floor toward his bed and collapsed, too traumatized to sleep, so he just stared at the ceiling, sweating and panting in the humid and colorless heat, trying to keep his feelings on the fringes of his mind.

Sometime later in the day he heard someone prying nails from the logs and pulling the door open. Light seeped inside. His father entered bedecked with his hat and his draping, dusty clothes. Jonah rose from his bed and, realizing that he was naked, dressed and stood before his father, feeling drained of will, of any capacity to resist. Together they walked outside into the light and mounted a horse and galloped through the fields.

Soon they arrived at the barn and dismounted. The light in the atmosphere seemed imprisoned in particles of moisture that settled over the earth in this miasma of sodden, porcine heat. All was gray, dull and inert. Out in the fields Jonah saw a gang of slaves slouching toward the barn, the blackness of their bodies appearing to meld together in the atmosphere as though they, devoid of individuality and denied their humanity, were but some vague and dark cloud somehow swept along by the will of his father. They soon arrived and settled around the barn, not speaking, staring listlessly about, not knowing nor caring why they were called from the fields.

Jonah saw motion, quick and violent. Strapped to the gibbet—the black, oily, immovable shaft driven into the earth—was a Negro, his backside facing the congregation, his loins covered with one strap of cloth, his arms and legs pulled tight around the sides of the gibbet and bound with rope. He struggled against his bindings spasmodically—like an insect with nascent, half-sprawled wings attempting to soar from its bondage. But the energy was rapidly draining from his body.

Next to the gibbet was the overseer sitting on a bucket and holding a spear in his hand—Shaka's spear, Jonah realized. The slave bound on the gibbet was Shaka. Jonah was grabbed by Whiteoak and yanked forward—then some whip was thrust into his hands that uncoiled away from his body like some vile, parasitic worm. Jonah stood there limp, his shoulders hunched, holding the whip. He looked toward his father, confused.

And in one of those rare moments, his father spoke to him in that scratchy, hoarse voice of his, his face unflinching, his message seeming irrevocable and predetermined. "Get on, whip it, boy."

Jonah looked at the wretched, black thing strapped to the gibbet, knowing he must whip it, deplete it of life, make it succumb to the force permeating the atmosphere. If he failed to exact the deed, he knew his father would beat him for the act of malfeasance, beat him as bad as any slave from the fields. Jonah gawked around at the others who stared at him wearied and disgusted.

Jonah felt the urge to walk forth and unfetter his friend from the gibbet. But he was paralyzed with fear. He felt the urge to testify to the others that while he was the son of a whore, he loved the Negress Thelma as his mother. To testify that even his father loved Thelma and fucked her in the secrecy of the night. To testify that the brother he loved now lived inside her womb even as she was being sold in Montgomery. To testify that Shaka was his brother and his friend and that the blood of Africa pulsed through both their veins. To proclaim that all of them, black and white, were brothers enslaved to the same forces and they should, at last, resist and kill that force and flee along the shores of the river to that land called Africa.

But nobody cared, Jonah realized; they seemed to accept this whipping as though the deed was already done. At last he turned toward Shaka on the gibbet, seeing that even his own friend was now caught, incapable of escaping again, and Jonah lost all hope. Resistance was futile. All he wanted now was to avoid his own pain, to become like his father: insensate, indomitable, sustained by power, beyond the miserable, nigger humanity of this vassal before him.

Aiming for the gibbet he raised the whip above his head and missed, hit dust. He repeated the motion except this time leather slapped flesh. He repeated the motion. And he repeated the motion with the same redundant, mechanical, soulless movement of his father. Again and again, as though this clicking of movement would shield him from feeling the rest of his tortured and cold life. Once again he raised the whip but in midstrike his body just wrenched, seeming to implode, as he collapsed on the ground, his mind racked by forces he could not control or comprehend. He flailed in the dust, still gripping the whip and thrusting the shaft forward as though inflicting the pain upon himself. His sobs erupted from his mouth like bile and splattered across the congregation of bodies until beginning to evaporate into the squelching and fetid vapors of the atmosphere.

All these years later while weeping inside his carapace, Jonah realized that was the moment that his soul left his body—the same soul that ever since coming to the island, taunted him, evaded him, swallowed him and destroyed him before finally reclaiming him.

Eloise rose at sunrise, her children sleeping next to her in their cots. She did not any longer fear the slaves or even the intruder; indeed, she realized that God, in his own strange and mysterious way, had blessed her by granting her the emancipation of the slaves. So she slept well through the night and now felt rested while hearing the gentle lapping of the waves onto shore coinciding with the slow and expansive heave of her lungs. Without disturbing her children she rose from her cot, donned her robe and looked outside her tent at Jonah's fortress, anomalous and menacing amidst the placidity of the island like some lonely and dangerous creature had crawled onto shore from the depths of the ocean. All this time she had wondered about Jonah with some mixture of compassion, satisfaction and anxiety and feared that he might hurt himself and perhaps even kill himself when forced to confront the nature of his soul.

But she suspected that for him to emerge from that thing, he must reckon with something larger and more destructive and compassionate than herself. But now she felt overcome with worry bordering on panic. Before stopping to think she was standing before the spears calling his name and, when he failed to answer, she felt certain that he was dead due to her negligence. Then she was grabbing the spears and laboriously pulling them from the ground and throwing them to the side and now working her way toward the table and grabbing its edge and pulling it toward her, throwing it flat on the ground at her feet. Beneath her was Jonah lying amidst the roots of the tree on his side, his knees tucked into his stomach, a jug of bourbon tipped over and staining the sand, everything smelling of his stench and liquor. Lying helplessly at his side was his rifle and sword.

He drank himself to death, she thought. She bent on one knee before him and rolled him over onto his back so that he was facing upward. Cradling his cheeks between her hands, she looked into his face as tears beaded under her eyes, saying, "Jonah, wake up, wake up."

She was relieved to see him squirming around on the ground while scratching his fingers across his chest as though irritated underneath. She released his face.

"Thelma…Thelma," he said, his voice eery and childlike.

"It's Eloise."

"Thelma?"

"No, Eloise."

"I'm sorry."

"I understand," said Eloise softly, not resisting anymore.

He reached up with his arms, breaking slightly at his hips like he wanted to be hugged so she pressed him against her body.

"You left me," he said.

"I had to," she said.

"I'm sorry," he said. "I'm sorry."

"I understand, dear," she said. "We forgive you."

"But you left."

"Because I had to. But I've loved you this whole time. And I will never leave you again. I will never leave you again."

They stayed that way, she still holding his weak, collapsed body as though he was not her husband but one of her children until he faded again into sleep and she lay him back on the ground. Below on the beach she could see the slaves pushing the rowboat into the gulf as they looked in her direction.

Later Jonah awoke again. This time he opened his eyes and stared about blankly and bewilderingly—then bending at the waist, pushed himself up by leaning on his elbows. He looked around at the pieces of his fortress scattered across the ground and without expressing anything, laid back down and stared into the sky above. Slowly she reached forward to the top of his jacket and when he did not resist, she unlatched the top button then the second all the way below his navel. In one swoop she pulled the lapels back from his chest and stomach, exposing his skin covered with large, enflamed, white-crusted pustules.

CHAPTER SIXTEEN

Eloise slowly walked with Jonah toward the north away from the view of everyone. While he stood there passively on the beach, not speaking or resisting, she peeled off his jacket, removed his boots and unbuckled his pants which fell down around his ankles, as he moved only as she desired, giving his body over to her gentle command. Without blush or shame, somewhere between childhood and infirmary, he stood naked while the pale skin underneath his pockmarks contrasted sharply to the darkened, rust-colored areas around his face and hands. She removed her own dress, leaving only the slip underneath.

She held his hand and led him into the water, feeling as though she was washing away the past from both of them. The saltwater was stinging him but they continued to move farther from shore all the way to their waists, then beyond where they relinquished their weight onto the buoyancy of the water and floated. She wanted to embrace him like Shaka and Pear the day before but knowing that might be painful for him, she only held his hand and drifted momentarily disconnected from the harsh pull of the earth.

Soon they walked back onto shore. She retrieved some fresh water from the kitchen and came back to the beach and washed the saltwater off him as he kneeled before her. They walked back to their tent and once inside Jonah wrapped his loins with a towel and sat down on his cot and looked at the ground as she pulled back the flaps of the tent so the breeze would blow inside.

For the remainder of the day, giving the care of her children over to Nomaw, she stayed next to him. Once the slaves returned mid-morning with fish, she prepared his breakfast and was amazed to find herself feeding him like he was an infant: cutting the flesh back from the bone and spooning the fish into his mouth, giving him the last of their dried figs and apricots then some of the bright, red fruit from the cactuses on the island. Seemingly devoid of the will to live or even die, he never said anything, hardly moved, either lay back on his cot to sleep or arose at times only to sit and stare into the light outside the tent. She thought that all that he was—his memories, feelings, desires and strivings—were annihilated, leaving him raw and unformed like an infant who had not yet revealed his personality. And she hoped that the God who destroyed him would use his kinder, more creative impulses to recreate him.

After dinner was finished around dusk, Jonah was lying back on his cot. She thought he was asleep so when he spoke it seemed like he was emerging from another, dreamlike world.

"I always feel afraid when the night comes," he said, his voice not forceful as in the past but gentle, almost whispered, seeming to flow naturally from him.

After placing her book down, Eloise rose from her cot, sat down next to him and leaning forward, cradled his hand in her own. "Do you feel afraid now?"

"Yes. But once night comes, I usually feel better."

"Perhaps death is like that," she said. "We fear its coming but we find peace once it arrives."

"Maybe," said Jonah. "But Thelma—she always came to me this time of night and sat on my bed with me as though protecting me from my father. She would stroke my hair, lull me peacefully into sleep. But once she was taken away, I always felt afraid at twilight and sleep has come fitfully for me ever since then."

"Is that why you always worked well beyond sunset—then fell asleep in your chair next to the fire, eased into your dreams by bourbon?"

"I suppose."

"Your work always seemed like your way of escaping from yourself."

Jonah continued to lie back on his cot, seeming to talk not to her or even himself but something above both of them. She wished she could see him but knew he needed to shield his vulnerability from her.

Eloise succumbed to the longing to ask the question. "Why did you never tell me these things?"

"What things?

"About your mother, your father and Shaka."

"I was ashamed."

"Of what?"

"Of myself. I wanted you and our children to believe that I was strong and indomitable like my father."

"But why?"

"I don't know. Maybe to avoid feeling that I was nothing at all."

"Is that how you feel now?"

"I suppose."

Eloise pulled him closer to her. She looked into his eyes and felt disturbed, even jolted, by his gentle and hurt gaze. Something behind his eyes was dissolving into the larger, more complicated pool of his being.

"I don't know who I am anymore," he said. "Or what to do."

"I don't know who I am anymore either," she said.

Jonah almost smiled.

"Have you ever wondered why we were attracted to each other all those years ago?" asked Eloise.

"Should we wonder about such things?"

"Maybe. You always scared me some even back then. And I have always wondered why I loved you from the beginning—perhaps from the moment I received your invitation to Whiteoak. But the answer is obvious. We're the same in many ways.

"As with you, my mother was torn from me not by force but by death. And both of us were left to live with overbearing, zealous fathers, isolated from the rest of humanity. We were both lonely, both wanting to escape, to discover ourselves in the future.

"But we've always done that separately. Both hidden our fears and hopes from each other, retreated back into our past for guidance. But from now on I hope we have each other and our children. We can leave ourselves behind and walk into the light.

"When we're afraid, Jonah, maybe we can hold each other, share our fear and leave it behind."

Jonah was silent but the way he looked at her, sort of resigned but pleased, revealed that he understood. He was soon staring again at the ceiling. But while she was dozing off into sleep, she heard, "I'm sorry, Eloise."

"Sorry for what?"

"Sorry for hurting you and our children. Sorry for my cruelty, my neglect. Sorry for my life."

"You're forgiven."

Drifting back into sleep she did not for once feel alone in her family but sensed that Jonah was with her now, even in his sleep, merging his soul into hers. Would Jonah become the man she always envisioned, she wondered yet again? Would he become free of the influences of his father? Would he set other men free from himself? Would he father his sons, teach them to become gentle and brave? Would he hold her around the fire at night and look into her eyes when they made love? Yes, he would become all of those things because that, she knew, was who he was when he was free.

The next morning while she was on the beach with her children building sandcastles, Jonah came down and sat next to them and she was saddened to notice that her children cringed around him and turned their backs as though expecting some sort of blow. Sitting alone Jonah watched them for some time then moved closer to Eloise, placing his arm gently around her. The boys started to peek over their shoulders, looking hesitant but surprised and finally happy. They turned around toward Jonah as though inviting him back into their lives. Seeing that they were building forts into the sand with high, entranceless walls, Jonah kneeled down next to them, filled the mote in with sand and began to cut passageways into the fort until the boys, coming closer to him, began to do the same.

CHAPTER SEVENTEEN

Eloise closed the cover of the Bible. While sitting on the crest of one of the dunes, she looked toward the sunset: While shimmering through thin and wispish clouds, the sun, it seemed, was fighting against the approach of night but was losing the battle and slowly slipping off the face of the earth.

"Look at the moon," said James, sitting next to Eloise but facing in the other direction, toward the mainland. "We're going home soon."

Eloise turned around and saw the waxing moon limpid and pale in the sky above the horizon of mangroves. "Yes, our ship should return soon."

"But I don't want to leave. I like it here," said Josh sitting on the other side of Eloise, "

"I like it too," said Eloise sadly.

"It feels different here," said Josh.

"Yes," said Eloise, "it does."

"Will we still get to play with Shobuck back at Whiteoak?" asked Josh.

"No," said James. "Father's gonna shackle him down, send him back to the fields."

"Is he, Mom?"

"I don't know," said Eloise. "I hope not."

"And Father's gonna hang the rest of them," said James.

"But why?"

"For not obeying his orders."

"Is he, Mom?"

"I hope not."

"Me too," said Josh. "Me too."

"I never want to go back to Whiteoak," said James. "Not ever."

Eloise saw something flash—some instant, barely-discernible pulse of light. She saw the clouds south of the moon hovering above the horizon: billowing and gray, neutralizing the remains of light in the atmosphere. Way on the other side of the island, Shaka suddenly bolted up the sides of one of the dunes and launched into the air while facing the storm, his body a coil of smooth, quivering muscles broken only by the bright, feather-clad cloth around his loins. He seemed to levitate in the air before hitting the ground again and disappearing.

"Look over there," said Eloise, pointing toward the north to distract her children from Shaka.

"At what?" said James.

"Oh nothing," said Eloise. "I thought I saw some porpoises."

Imagining what the slaves must be thinking, Eloise felt some current of fear and expectation. Behind her the sun slid from the earth altogether, losing the battle against the night. All was now cast in shadow.

"Looks like we might get some rain this evening. So let's get yawl to bed," Eloise said, taking their hands and rising.

As they walked toward the tents, Josh asked, "Can't we sit with the slaves tonight around their fire?"

"Not tonight," said Eloise. "I think they want to be alone."

"But why?" asked Josh.

"Just because."

Inside their tent she tucked both into their cots. Kneeling on the floor between them, she took both of their hands and prayed. "Lord, tonight we open our hearts to you, trusting that what shall come is your divine will. And if we die before we wake, we pray our souls the Lord will take."

She rose onto her feet and as she was leaning to kiss Josh on his cheek, she heard some distant grumble of thunder. She sensed that Josh knew something was about to happen tonight—perhaps even understood what was about to happen. She also knew that he could sense her fear.

Then he smiled without any sense of restraint or doubt—only acceptance. "The storm is coming, isn't it, Mommy?"

"Yes. Promise me this, son."

"What?"

"That you stay here with your brother inside this tent unless we come for you."

"But why?"

"Just promise me."

"I promise."

Before leaving the tent, she said, "I love both of you."

Outside, the mass of gathering, ionic darkness drifted slowly across the surface of the moon, extinguishing its light.

On the beach that faced toward the storm, she saw Shaka and Pear throwing pieces of driftwood, rubbish, dried seaweed and boards into a pile to be set to flame. Beyond the dunes Jake and Shobuck collapsed their tent which was then hauled over and thrown into the pile. Although the air was calm and even eerily motionless, blackish-green swells came from the direction of the storm, formed into waves and curled gradually before swashing into shore.

She walked into her tent. Jonah was inside flat on his back, naked except for the towel wrapped about his loins, the rash on his upper body having now receded into clusters of ruddy bumps. Although the tent was nearly dark, he was holding a Bible before his eyes—the placement of his page revealing that he was reading from the New Testament.

As soon as hearing her, he placed the Bible to his side and rose to sit and looked at her in a way that she longed for her whole life and, evidently sensing something on her face, asked, "What's wrong?"

"There's something you need to know."

"What?"

Eloise sat down in the chair next to him. Thunder grumbled off in the distance.

"The Negroes believe that Washaka comes with the storms," she said. "When Shaka's mother, Maw, was in the middle passage, she claimed that she first met Washaka during a storm that roiled their ship. Shaka claims that he could feel the spirit of Washaka during storms back at Whiteoak. And those wings were left the night a storm passed over our island."

"They believe Washaka is coming tonight?"

"They believe that lightning and Washaka are related," continued Eloise, "that Washaka like Zeus will harness the power of lightning, literally send down bolts to strike them, convert them into birds so they can fly across the gulf to emancipate all the slaves back in Alabama."

"They believe that?"

"Their religion is not written in books, nor established with dogmas and creeds or even beliefs. They're creating this world around them like playwrights writing themselves into life. At any moment the scene might change. But to answer your question, yes, they believe all that fervently."

She heard the sound of an axe being driven into wood outside their tent. In the near darkness she could see the expression on Jonah's face—so different than anything she had seen before—of amusement, curiosity and profundity all at once.

"What do you think we should do?" he asked, seeming not yet aware of the chopping.

"We must not interfere unless we're threatened," she said decisively but she stopped breathing while waiting for his response.

"All right," he said.

Eloise breathed again.

"What's that chopping?" he asked.

"The slaves are chopping everything into firewood. I think they're probably working on our table or some of the crates now."

"But why?"

"I don't know for certain. But I think they believe that for them to pass into this other realm, they need to destroy all that remains of this one—all that oppressed or hurt them or reminds them of their past."

"I understand," said Jonah. "I've had visions lately of burning Whiteoak to the ground."

"Maybe we should."

Jonah did not respond.

"We should also consider something else," she said sadly.

"What?"

"While you were hidden away, Shaka visited with me. I was sitting on the beach under my parasol when he appeared rather suddenly from the dunes wearing nothing but that strange, feather-clad loincloth. I could see up close those wings singed into his flesh. I wanted to leave but stayed put anyway until he was sitting upright and sort of regal outside the shade of my parasol, looking at me. He's not that fawning, cowering slave anymore, which I think was nothing more than an act anyway—but confident and open. I believe strongly that this man is divine, holy in some way but also dangerous.

"He confirmed what Nomaw already said, that when Washaka comes, they'll leave with him while we remain behind. He said too that if Washaka believes that we'd ever again enslave another person, he'd destroy us in an instant. But if we open our hearts, we shall be transformed—resurrected, to use his words.

"As he was leaving, I asked him if he would ever harm any of us.

"He stopped, turned around abruptly with these precise words, 'I've known harm. I caint wish such on nobody without losing my way.' "

Even in the darkness Eloise could see from the slant of his face that Jonah was studying her, looking concerned and incredulous too. "You believe all that?"

"I neither believe nor disbelieve," she said. "But I know that divinity resides in the souls of these people. God lives in this beautiful, mysterious and unadulterated land so close to the rhythms of the universe, of the movement of wind and water—all of Him, not just the glimpses we get back in our churches. We're living in God.

"In Biblical times, in barren, sandy places like this one, God was fully present. Seas were parted, angels were seen, men spoke to God and He spoke back. Maybe I am so mesmerized by the strangeness of this place and by the sounds and the light that I have lost my discernment but I believe that something miraculous could happen here tonight, not for us, but for the Negroes—for those poor, displaced people who have suffered so long at our hands but kept their hearts pure. Do not they deserve salvation?

"Do not they deserve miracles like the Israelites?

"Even back at Whiteoak you heard God calling you here to your Eden where you knew that, freed from your multitudes of distractions, you could not escape Him, would have to tangle with Him—and become baptized yet again, first by fire, and now maybe by love."

The tent was nearly dark now. Light pulsed vaguely and thunder grumbled moments later.

"Those men and women are alive with God—with whom they call Washaka. They're makers of his word. And I believe God will be revealed here tonight in some way for everyone."

"Revealed?"

"Yes. And we should open ourselves to his revelation with all our hearts. Celebrate the freedom of the slaves as well as our own."

All was silent except for the swashing of the swells and the incessant, energetic chopping of the axe. But through the canvas she could see the faint, orange glow of their fire outside already beginning to strafe the past into ashes.

Jonah was silent: She felt he understood her but could not articulate his feelings.

"Run along," he said, at last, "and get the children. I need some time to prepare."

"Prepare what?"

Jonah was silent again.

"To prepare your weapons?"

"Only as a precaution."

"I understand but once you step outside that tent leave all of your fear behind. And be with love."

"I will," he said earnestly.

Eloise stepped outside into the darkness. Toward the mangroves the moon was cloaked behind the swelter of clouds on the horizon while only the hint of day remained in the other direction—one thin, bluish streak of light fading into darkness. All the slaves down on the beach were congregated around the fire which was steady in the absence of wind but rising upward in long, slender flames. Jake and Shobuck were hacking everything into fodder—pieces of the table, shreds of their tent, Jonah's old spears. The fire suddenly thrashed sideways away from the direction of the storm, causing Jake and Shobuck to holler and jump away, laughing. Eloise felt the breeze, light, cool and alive, striking the side of her face like something with intent.

She hurried inside her children's tent.

"Mommy," said Josh, "I knew you were coming back."

"Come with me," she said.

In the dark she felt their expectant, nervous hands grabbing onto hers and they walked together toward the tree—the glow of the fire now visible.

"Mommy," said Josh.

"Yes."

"He's coming tonight, isn't he?"

"Who?"

"The one Shaka speaks of."

"How do you know about him?"

"Shobuck told us. He said he was gonna leave us."

"They do believe their savior is coming tonight."

They soon arrived at the tree where they could see all around them. Jonah came toward them with a tarpaulin in his hands. With Jonah on one end and Eloise on the other, with their children in between, they sat down against the tree and Jonah covered their legs with the tarpaulin. Jake and Shobuck below had resumed their tasks of reducing most of their community into fuel for the fire, the hacking of the axe now seeming to be in dialogue with the occasional, ever-louder sounds of thunder. Shaka and Pear were building the fire using ever larger pieces of firewood as the flames thrashed about in the wind over their heads, propelled by cool, storm-driven winds. Away from the fire, Nomaw sat alone on the beach, watching.

"Mommy, can we go say goodbye to Shobuck?" asked Josh.

"Yes, can we?" asked James.

Eloise glanced over at Jonah who nodded his head. "I suppose we can."

They rose from the tree and she held their hands and they walked through the dunes toward the fire. As though entering someplace sacred, they slowly walked into the light from the fire, mesmerized by the huge, sprawling flames above their heads, the pop and crackle of ashes.

"We came to say goodbye," said Eloise before any of the slaves noticed them.

But when they walked even closer to the fire, Eloise felt suddenly ridiculous as the slaves glared at them, eyes fixed and uncomprehending, as though they had never seen them before—like someone from another world suddenly intruded into their home.

"We came to say goodbye," said Josh, walking over to Shobuck while James followed him.

At first Shobuck looked shocked and confused. He looked at Shaka for guidance and after seeing him nodding his head, Shobuck smiled and said, "I suppose I won't be wrestling with yawl no more."

"No," said Josh.

"Are you really going to Africa?" asked James.

"Sho is."

"Then goodbye," said James. "Maybe we can come see you sometime?"

"Maybe," said Shobuck.

Eloise walked forward and took their hands once again but Josh, breaking from her grasp, ran over and embraced Shobuck who looked surprised momentarily before embracing him back and lifting him off the ground. Josh squealed in delight. Afterward, Josh again took his mother's hand and together they stepped back from the fire.

"May you know God's grace," said Eloise.

"We already knowed it," said Jake.

"May you know his salvation," said Eloise.

"So long, Miss Eloise."

Before turning her head she saw Shaka close to the fire. Behind him was the blackness of the gulf where the swells heaved forward from infinity, refracted orange and yellow in the firelight before churning into froth and collapsing into shore. Shaka was smiling at her, looking spectrelike through the smoke and flames that roiled and distorted the air before him, an avatar of something she could only glimpse but never understand.

They nodded at each other. She turned and walked with her children into the darkness of the dunes as the energy of their fire— and her intense, almost irrepressible pull toward it— relinquished its hold on her.

When crawling back under the tarpaulin under the tree, she resigned herself into knowing that her life was not with the strange, mystical world of the slaves but there with her husband and children.

Once finishing hacking everything into fodder, Jake left the fire but returned moments later carrying the black inverted wings over his shoulder. After dousing the wings with wax from some candles, they then mounted them before the fire facing toward the mainland.

The slaves then circled around the fire, staring into the flames that thrashed even higher and dwarfed them. Eloise could sense that all their memories and sense of self were burning away so they were becoming expressions of the greater, more elemental energy of heat. From his waist Shaka pulled off his loincloth which he then pitched into the fire. When seeing Pear about to do the same, Eloise pulled her children's heads into her lap to shelter their eyes but then changing her mind, released them so that they could see all the slaves now standing nude before the fire.

Flashes of white, not yet defined into bolts, exploded upward into the towering, bulbous clouds—and thunder followed even louder now. The tree above was shaking and thrashing in the wind, the leaves one continuous rattle and rustle and Eloise could even discern movement in the thick trunk. But the storm was moving northward up the mainland, not toward the island.

They were walking around the fire in one circle, their faces staring into the flames, their pace perfectly matched to each other. In the nude they looked gorgeous in the firelight, transformed into something more primitive and mysterious. Eloise could vicariously feel the caressing of the heat, wind and sand on her as though she was down there with the others.

Although nobody spoke, Eloise felt her children pressed against her body while holding her hand. She watched the Negroes circle around the fire, for how long she could not say, hypnotized by the repetition until words and interpretations and even expectations passed away—leaving only sensation.

But as the storm continued to move northward, not toward the island, her children were becoming restless, asking, "Where's Washaka?"

"I don't know," said Eloise. "Maybe he comes only in our dreams."

The slaves continued to pace and the children soon pulled the tarpaulin over their heads and fell into sleep. And Eloise felt the nudge too toward sleep and tried to resist until…

She awoke with something gripping the back of her neck. "Wake up, Eloise," she heard Jonah say.

Opening her eyes into blackness, she heard nothing but the sounds of water thrashing into the shore and pattering on the tarpaulin. Her face felt wet and cold and water leaked down the back of her neck.

"What?" she said.

"Something's out there," said Jonah.

She looked to where the slaves had been before but only saw the embers of the fire glowing. Fire suddenly exploded in the middle of the air and assumed the form of wings inverted above the beach.

"They must believe that someone is out there," she said.

"I believe there is," said Jonah.

"But I caint see them anywhere. Are they gone?"

"They're waiting in the dunes."

"For what?"

"You'll see."

"Where?"

"On the water when the lightning strikes."

"Wake up, children," she said while shaking them.

The wings collapsed, burned briefly on the sand then vanished. They waited in the darkness for the longest of times, not seeing anything. Lightning at last struck over the water in front of the mainland and in that second of light Eloise looked through the shards of shimmering, silver rain to find the horizon. Thunder struck almost simultaneously, concussing and compressing the air. But in the final instance before darkness, she saw something on the gulf: not large or grandiose but small and unidentifiable, something either floating on the water or hovering above it.

"What's that?" asked Josh.

"I don't know," said Eloise.

"Is that Washaka?"

"I don't know."

Eloise's sense of boundaries and perception changed in the darkness so she felt not contained within her own flesh but dissolved into the elements. She felt lighter, not attached to the ground, almost incapable of telling up from down.

A bolt struck in the gulf like the jagged and electric finger of God. The thing was coming toward the island and floating on the water, not above.

"What's that?" she asked.

Nobody answered.

Josh was gripping her hand tightly. The rain was thick and wind-driven. Her hair was soaked as water streamed down the sides of her face and obscured her vision. During another crack of lightning, she saw the figure even closer to the island in what appeared to be some kind of canoe floating where the swells mounted into waves and collapsed on themselves.

"Here he comes," said Josh. "Here he comes."

Eloise stared at the beach in the darkness where she thought the figure would land so she would see it during the next strike of lightning.

The world became light—refracted through layers of rain. Washaka was on the beach, looking manlike while gazing into the dunes, his body long and gaunt and wingless.

The world became dark. Birdcalls came from the dunes all at once, a cacophony of chirps, shrills and eeeeks. But soon was heard only the high and ethereal shrill of the osprey—one call coming from the dunes, another coming from the figure down on the beach, both seeming to grope and reach for each other.

The world became light. Washaka was standing on one leg and slouching forward, arms raised upward as though he was about to launch into flight.

Shaka and Pear came running down from the dunes toward the beach, calling, "Eeeeeek… eeeeek..." They raised their arms when coming closer to Washaka and in that instant when they were about to fly, they vanished…

Into darkness.

"They flew away, Mommy," said Josh. "They flew away."

"My God," said Eloise. "It's so beautiful."

Washaka was still calling ospreylike down on the beach, piercing above the turmoil of the water.

The world became light. Washaka was still poised for flight while searching into the dunes with his eyes. But where were Shaka and Pear? She searched desperately across the beach for them then into the gulf and finally into the sky above. But she did not see them anywhere. On the periphery of her vision she saw Jake and Shobuck sprinting down from the dunes, making all sorts of bird calls and when coming closer to Washaka, they raised their arms then vanished…

Into darkness—as though her own eyelid was closing.

"I saw them," said Josh.

"Saw who," said Eloise, squeezing his hand.

"I saw Shaka and Pear."

"Where?"

"In the clouds."

"You saw them?" said Eloise.

"Yes, Mommy, in the clouds."

Osprey was still heard on the beach calling, "Eeeeek…eeeeeek," over and again as though beseeching the others to run for the sky. Though steady the rain was already dwindling and the waves were not rolling into the shore with the same force.

From the dunes she heard Nomaw calling, "Where is you, Jake? Where you done gone?"

"Eeeeek…eeeeeek…"

"Don't leave me here by myself. Come on back and gets me."

"Eeeeeek…eeeek…eeeeeek…"

"Is that you, Jesus, yonder on the beach? Or is you the devil?"

"Eeeeeeeeek."

"I don't know who you is—but you aint like Jesus."

"Eeeeeek…eeeeeek…"

"I aint going with you, birdman. Quit calling to me. So long, Jake. So long, Shaka, Pear and Shobuck. So long."

Another bolt of lightning struck silently somewhere over the mainland without any thunder. Down on the beach Washaka was still poised for flight, looking yearningly toward the dunes.

The world became dark. Thunder grumbled slowly from the distance as the storm headed farther north.

Washaka continued to call, "Eeeeeeek....eeeeek," over and again.

Maybe he was calling for her and her family, thought Eloise. She imagined them all running down from the tree as the earth released its grasp, feeling some jolt, sudden and electrical, as they soared upward into the roiling and wet winds and looked down upon the island during the next strike of lightning, seeing their home receding away into just another minuscule fragment of nature. But when the birdcalls faded away so did her hopes for heaven.

The lightning was gone for the moment. All that remained in the utter darkness was not rain, nor wind but only the occasional cascade of the waves into shore, and the feel of her son shivering and clinging to her side to gather warmth, saying, "Is he gone now, Mommy? Is he gone back to Africa?"

"I suppose he has," said Eloise, beginning to realize that she had just witnessed some kind of miracle.

"They've all gone back to Africa?" said Josh.

"I suppose they have."

Moments later, wanting confirmation about what they just witnessed, Eloise said, "Jonah."

"He's not here," said James.

"What do you mean, he's not here?"

"He left some time ago."

"When?"

"Sometime after Jake and Shobuck flew away."

"Where did he go?"

"I don't know."

James crawled around to the other side of his mother so that she was now between both of her children who were cold, damp and shivering while burying themselves under the tarpaulin and nestling into her sides. They waited like this for minutes, maybe hours, Eloise could not tell. She could still see the muffled, upward-exploding flashes from the thunderhead in the distance but the light shone upon their surroundings only enough for her to realize that Washaka was not any longer on the beach. As the storm continued to move away, the moon above, though still enshrouded in clouds, leaked enough light for her to discern the outline of the island, the water, the tree, the undulation of the dunes. But she did not see any people, not Jonah or the birdman or anyone else.

Long after her children fell to sleep and long after she too succumbed to cold and shivers, light rose flat and gray above the mainland as though the sun was gently placing its tentacles back onto the earth and pulling itself into the night. Swells continued to roll along the smooth, unrippled surface of the gulf and collapse into shore. The sand was rendered smooth but pocked by the rain while the sea oats were stooped over with moisture, their golden, seeded tops nearly touching the earth as though genuflecting on some sort of altar.

Where was Jonah? she wondered. As a colder, more ordinary form of consciousness settled over her, she began to wonder about the events from the night before. Did he fly away? she wondered, incredulous at her own consideration of the question.

She roused her children from their sleep, looked James in his eyes and instructed him to stay there at the tree. After completely covering them with the tarpaulin so they would fall back to sleep, she stood and managed to hobble toward her tent, although stiff with cold. She discovered to her amazement that one side of the wall was sliced into shreds by what she assumed was a knife or sword. Their belongings inside were ransacked: pillows thrown about, chests turned over, their cots ripped down the middle.

"My God," she said, panicked, while looking around the island for signs of danger.

She ran back toward the tree but after seeing her children were safe, she trotted back toward the tent. She looked around the tent in circles and after finding some tracks to the north, she followed them while scanning around her for any signs of danger, contemplating the multitude of scenarios of what could have happened—but nothing made sense.

Within moments she saw what she once thought was Washaka on the beach below. While facing upward toward the dunes, he was holding a bow cocked back and ready to release an arrow. She bent down and continued to move toward him but he suddenly saw her and pointed his weapon in her direction.

From somewhere to the side of her, she heard, "Get down."

She dropped to her stomach on the ground and rolled behind a clump of sea oats. To the side of her but closer to the birdman was Jonah hiding behind some knob of sand, his sword at his side, the rifle trained directly on the figure below. He could easily kill him, she realized.

"We mean you no harm, sir," Jonah said. "Please surrender your weapon."

The man said nothing. He was tall and gaunt with gray and straight hair dangling around his neck which was festooned with strands of shells, bones and teeth while his loins were wrapped in some tattered, leather pelt. He looked ancient but vital—like something that was extracting energy from the forces of erosion around him. Although he was the man from the night before, she realized conclusively that he was not Washaka but an Indian.

"He aims to kill us," Jonah said.

Jonah only had one shot in his rifle, she realized; by the time he reloaded the Indian could have already attacked. But Jonah clearly did not want to hurt him.

"You're within my sights, sir," said Jonah. "You don't have a chance. So drop your weapon, tell me your purpose and you are free to leave."

"My purpose is kill you," said the man.

"But I won't allow that to happen," said Jonah. "I will not surrender my ground if you move. I shall be forced to fire."

They all stayed in this position for some time as the grayness of dawn gave way to brighter, more colorful light. Birds now were arriving, some of them feeding in the water behind the Indian.

"I cannot let him escape, not yet, for fear he might return with others," said Jonah. "And I cannot let him see the other slaves because he may inspire them to turn against us. If he attempts to move, I must down him…I must."

"The slaves?" said Eloise mystified. "What slaves?"

The Indian moved away from Jonah.

Boom.

Jonah's aim was true. The top of the bow was shattered; the strand of leather once holding the tension dropped. The Indian threw the bow onto the ground but did not retreat. Instead he drew his sword and waited.

"Come here, Eloise," said Jonah.

Eloise ran to Jonah who was reloading his rifle while keeping his sword at the ready. "If I should fall, Eloise, you do not have any other choice but to kill him to protect the children. Kill him, I say, kill him if I fall."

Eloise took the rifle from Jonah and trained it on the Indian's chest, following his movements, determined to shoot if necessary before Jonah was wounded; after all, had Jonah not given the Indian the chance to disarm peacefully? Jonah then stood, drew his sword and walked down to the beach. The Indian charged without any hesitation, swinging his blade at Jonah who deflected the blow. The Indian continued to attack clumsily. But Jonah merely defended himself until his opponent, unable to swing his blade without losing his balance, began to exhaust himself. Then Jonah came at him hard and fast, not attacking his body but trying to knock the weapon from his hand.

The Indian hollered, part birdcall, part war cry—and in an explosion of energy that Eloise never expected, attacked again with all his might, swinging wildly at any part of Jonah's body. She almost fired. But when the Indian swung downward, Jonah stepped aside as the sword struck the sand, causing the Indian to lose his balance and bend over at the hip. Jonah then stepped forward onto the sword and with the flat side of his own blade, smacked the Indian on his wrist, causing him to release his sword altogether.

Lurching forward the Indian grabbed Jonah around the waist, trying to tackle him to the ground. But Jonah raised his arms into the air, his sword pointing upward then drove his fists and the butt of his sword into the man's back, causing him to lose his grip and stumble forward. Jonah kicked upward, driving his knee into the Indian's chest. While the Indian was gasping for air, Jonah drove him to the sand, jumped on top of him and pinned him to the beach, placing his knees on his arms.

"I need rope," he shouted.

Shaka was soaring on the updrafts from the storm with the billowing and electrified clouds all around him while Pear was flying at his side, looking gorgeous with her wings extending from her shoulders. Jake and Shobuck were following behind, looking fierce, intent and warriorlike. They were flying over the gulf back to the homeland where they would soon swoop down and shoot lightning from their fingertips toward their brothers below still held in captivity who, once stricken, would rise to join them in multitudes like flocks of blackbirds headed back to Africa.

"They done got Washaka," Shaka heard from above.

Feeling the cold and damp seeping ever deeper into him, Shaka held onto that image of liberation until realizing, slowly and regretfully, that he must let it fade away.

"They's binding him to the tree," said Pear.

At last Shaka accepted his reality: He was rigid with cold and bruises in a puddle of rain and sand at the bottom of the trench which he and all the other slaves were forced to dig to capture the invader.

From above he heard Pear calling to him, "Come on out that hole, Shaka. It's warm up here."

He opened his eyes to look up the white, vertical sides of the trench, seeing her mournful but longing face looking down upon him. Beyond her face was the pale and blue ether where splotches of thin white clouds drifted and where flocks of birds flitted about looking lost and senseless. He did not any longer see signs, nor omens; he did not see the sky as a reflection of Washaka. He just saw elements indifferent to his plight—just air, color and light—and animals not much different from himself, darting here and there looking for something to eat.

The doubt was always there demanding to instruct him even in his moments of faith, thought Shaka. Was he not betrayed before when he fell from the tree? At the gibbet? He remembered what the woman told him when he asked about his origins: that he was not conceived from the lovemaking between his mother and Washaka but was the foundling discovered in the woods, the castaway probably of renegade or freed slaves. Yet by being trapped in his mother's troubled and bizarre delusion, he came to know the beauty and potential of his own life. And since that could not find expression in the reality around him, he had created his own reality—his own world where, if only in hopes and visions, he could find and love himself.

"I thought he was their savior," said Eloise, looking over at the Indian now bound to the tree. "How could I be so foolish?"

She and Jonah were sitting not too far away from the tree on one of the dunes overlooking the beach while their children slept inside their tent. The sun was rising above the mainland, banishing all nocturnal mysteries and shadows from the island. Blowing northward, as though trying to chase down the thunderhead, the winds were driving away the remaining wispy clouds. Everything across the island was devoid of occlusion or refraction but rather starkly and achingly bright.

Down below Jake stood next to the trench into which he fell the night before, shoveling sand back into the hole, looking toward them and shouting, "If aint for this hole, I be in Africa now sucking on melons and hunting me something to eat."

Not far from Jake, Pear lay above the trench looking down at Shaka.

"I believed too," said Jonah. "When seeing him on the beach with his arms outstretched, I felt something—hope and possibility,

I suppose—and saw things differently. The world became vast and infinite. It seemed completely possible for someone to fly."

"Something did happen last night."

"Yet we find that he came here to offer death not salvation. Your god—this God—is strange. Maybe he only knows cruelty."

Eloise looked away from Jonah. "I don't feel I know God anymore."

They paused in silence before Jonah asked, "Do you fear the slaves now?"

"They have conspired against you and for that reason they probably believe that you intend to hang them once we return to Alabama. They believe their lives are at stake so, yes, I think we've reasons to fear them."

"Perhaps I can avoid our predicament by telling them that I intend to set them and their families free once we return to Whiteoak, provided, of course, that they not cause us any harm before then."

"I believe you should on one condition."

"What?"

"That you will in fact set them free."

"I will."

Eloise saw sad, gentle resignation in his face. "Does that mean you intend to set all your slaves free?"

"Do you remember asking me when we were courting what I wanted from life?"

"I remember."

"And I said to get the hell away from Whiteoak."

"I remember that well. It made me love you."

"I still want to get the hell away."

"You mean forever?"

"Upon returning to Whiteoak, I mean to finish harvest, emancipate our slaves and sell the plantations."

She felt relief and happiness welling inside her. "But where will we go?"

"West," said Jonah. "To the frontier."

"West?"

"Provided that you agree."

"It's not Massachusetts. But I know you would never want to live someplace like that."

Eloise imagined sitting with her children on the porch outside their future homestead at the end of civilization, surrounded by prairie with colossal, snowcapped mountains in the distance, seeing Jonah riding in from the range on his horse, wearing chaps and some wide-brimmed, weathered hat on his head, a look of contentment on his face.

"I agree. We shall at last live our own lives."

CHAPTER EIGHTEEN

"Would you like some water," asked Jonah, holding the cup toward the Indian.

"I want nothing from you but your death," said the Indian, looking through clear, light-brown eyes at Jonah but seeming not to see him.

The Indian was as Jonah had left him some hours before, tied at the hands and feet then bound to the tree, standing upright. Because of his thin, light bones, the man did in fact resemble a bird, an egret that was stripped of its wings and feathers. Throughout the past hour, he had been staring into the heavens at the birds passing over him, and calling, "Eeeeeeeeek… eeeeeeek," as though appealing to the birds to rescue him. Occasionally the slaves would gaze over at him, confused but expectant, seeming to hope something would happen. But his head was down for the moment, his long gray hair falling in front of his chest and he seemed delirious with exhaustion.

"But you cannot kill me," said Jonah.

"The birds kill you," said the Indian, his voice hoarse.

"What birds?" said Jonah piqued.

"The birds," said the Indian.

Jonah decided to try another approach. "Why do you wish to kill me?"

"This my island."

"This is not your island but mine. I bought the deed."

The Indian looked at him blankly.

"I paid money for this island. Money, you understand."

"Money," said the Indian. "Money means nothing."

"Yes it does."

"You own nothing."

Jonah paused, confused.

"Dig," said the Indian.

"Dig?"

"At your feet—dig."

"Why?"

"Dig."

Though perplexed Jonah dropped to his knees and dug about one inch into the sand with his fingers.

"Deeper," commanded the Indian.

Using an old, sun-bleached shell to help him, Jonah dug deeper between the roots of the tree to about his wrists, then even deeper. When down to his elbows he hit something more solid—something white and slender, a bone he realized. He dug along the length of the bone then stopped and glanced at the Indian.

"What do you see?"

Jonah stood up.

"What?"

"A bone. The arm bone—of a man."

"Many more too," said the Indian. "From back before you remember."

"What are you saying?" Jonah stared at the Indian, perplexed.

"Whiteman stupid," said the Indian. "Look into ocean—see not fish, only his face."

"What do you mean?" said Jonah.

"Look," said the Indian, nodding toward the mainland. "The other island. Only trees. No sand, no shells."

"Yes," said Jonah.

"But this island by itself. Much sand, shells, birds."

"Yes, but why the bones?"

"My tribe buried here—my grandfathers, my father, my brothers, my children—all here."

"You mean that your tribe created this island, that this is your mausoleum, your graveyard?"

"Yes."

Jonah had read about burial mounds, even seen them in Alabama—places where the Indians buried their dead, stashing along with them things like pottery, clothing and weapons. Jonah realized at last why this Indian was enraged because he, Jonah, and the rest of his party, were intruders violating the cemetery of his dead family.

"Money?" said the Indian. "You not own my tribe."

"I see," said Jonah, not revealing his feelings. Now that he understood the source of the Indian's rage, Jonah began to wonder about the threat to his family. "Where's the rest of your tribe?"

"Murdered."

"All of them?"

"Yes."

"By whom?"

"By men like yourself?"

"You mean by our army?"

"Yes. You come back and shit on their grave."

"My people killed your people and now we have claimed your cemetery."

Both were silent for the moment until Jonah spoke again. "You came before, didn't you, left those black wings here on the island?'

The Indian looked confused.

"The wings before," said Jonah. "First wings."

"Yes," said the Indian. "My wings, yes. Hope you think me the devil and go from island. Later come back to kill you."

"Must you want to kill me?" asked Jonah.

"Not me. But they."

"Who's they?"

"My people."

"But I thought they're all dead."

"But not tonight."

"What do you mean?"

"You see."

Jonah imagined the evening before from the perspective of the Indian: He must have imagined that the Negroes rushing down to meet him, visible only in the strikes of lightning, were the souls of his ancestors who were flying away as soon as they disappeared into the darkness. The Indian had not yet come to understand that the Negroes below him were the same forms he saw the night before. He obviously believed that those spirits would return tonight to finish his task for him. Jonah was struck by the coincidence that both the slaves and the Indian thought the other was the vehicle of their redemption. But both were deceived.

"You saw the spirits of your ancestors last night?"

"You saw them too," said the Indian, looking at Jonah proudly, even snidely.

"I saw them."

Jonah considered revealing the truth of what happened the night before but ultimately withheld the information; he did not want the Indian to make any connections between himself and the slaves below. Besides, he figured that once that evening passed, the Indian would see that his beliefs were not real, only illusions—and at that point might be willing to leave the island peacefully.

"My fathers tell me our dead live in the birds."

Jonah understood at last the reason why the man continued to call toward the other birds.

"And your spirit," said Jonah, "where will it live?"

"In Osprey—chief of all birds."

"You were the chief of your tribe?"

"Me the chief. Many men die to save me from your people. Many die from diseases."

"Where did the others go?"

"Many go to reservations in the west."

"But you stayed here alone?" asked Jonah, still considering the safety of his family.

"I leave my home to live on water. Live or die, I not care—let the Spirit choose. I drift with tides—and human words leave me. And sleep in canoe—and human thoughts leave me. And birds and fish are my brothers—and human sadness leave me. Like my brothers I not save food for tomorrow—just ate what came my way—fish, seaweed, water from heaven. I not man anymore. Me like wind or rain, fish or bird, drifting with the wind and water.

"I hear voices from birds, mice and crabs. Their words beautiful, not unhappy or lonely or stupid like men. They talk to all things. And I wait for Osprey to catch me in his arms, take me away forever from your world."

Jonah wondered why the man was so eager to talk to him. He suspected that despite his claims the Indian was lonely and needed someone with whom to talk, even his enemy. Perhaps the Indian wanted Jonah to understand the destruction and suffering his people unleashed upon his tribe.

"Before the white man came," asked Jonah, "what was your life like?"

"Many years ago," said Osprey, "before your army came, one of your people—missionary—live with our tribe."

"You learned English from him?"

"We teach each other."

"He not hunt, fish, weave or gather plants. He not act like man or woman. All day he eat little, read from his Bible and talk to his hands. He never smile. Always mean to himself for sinning. But he teach us English, want to make us into him, into sinners that talk to somebody not there.

"One day we burn his Bible in fire. We stop feeding him. One night we drag him into the swamp and leave him there. Days later he find camp. We not feed him. He learn to fish and hunt, know what plants to eat. We not speak English with him. He learn our language. Somebody not seen not help him. He help himself. One night he make with woman. Next night, another.

"He smile much, eat much. Good hunter. He never go home. Change his name."

"Changed his name to what?"

"Adam."

Jonah's stomach pulsed, some coil of emotions seethed up his spine. He was baffled by the convergence of hopes and expectations on this island, between white, black and red—all coming to this island to search for salvation in their lives but finding only disappointment instead.

"Adam."

"You know that name?" asked Osprey.

"I came here looking for him," said Jonah, feeling kinship with this Adam who found salvation in this wilderness.

He imagined Adam's life amongst these natives, living always close to rain, sun and wind, drifting with the tides to search for fish and birds, not planning or calculating or hoarding, not always delaying gratification from one year to another but rather living from his heart and instincts: hunting when hungry, fucking when desirous, sleeping when tired, dancing when joyous, killing when threatened. Jonah imagined raising his children, not to dragoon Negroes and keep ledgers and learn fancy, convoluted and useless information from teachers but to read the tides and to know the habits of fish and game. And in the evenings, not to read books and hide away inside homes but to gaze in wonderment above at the stars without any desire to name, worship, fear or subjugate themselves to the unknowable all around them.

"Soldiers kill him."

"What?" said Jonah.

"Soldiers kill Adam. Rape his wife."

Jonah wanted to weep for these Indians, for Adam and Eve. But now that his own soul was cleansed, he wanted to weep most of all for his own culture—for the countless men and women intent upon dragooning and violating others in the name of progress or freedom or Christianity. But he could not weep, not now, not before this man who was intent upon killing him.

"I do not mean you any harm," said Jonah.

"Tonight we kill you."

"Do you understand me?" exclaimed Jonah. "I don't want to harm you."

"Tonight."

"You are free to leave here when you want. And when our ship returns and we leave this island, I will never return. We will return this island to you and your memories. Do you understand?"

Osprey stopped looking at Jonah.

"We leave," said Jonah desperately. "We leave. You have island back."

Once Osprey looked toward the sky, suddenly jolting with intensity, Jonah turned around and saw the flock of seagulls above their heads, heading upwind while gracefully waving their wings, expressive of some kind of divine but animal power. Despite their labors, however, they were not moving at all relative to the land but stayed fixed in one place, not conforming to man's need for progress, for man's need to escape the misery of their here and now, not conforming to man's overly eager and greedy interpretation of the other life around him.

CHAPTER NINETEEN

Later that same day while Eloise kept watch over the island, Jonah retrieved his father's biography from his trunk and walked to the beach facing the gulf and settled into the sand where he was about level with the small, pellucid waves lolling into shore. Earlier, while in his fortress, Jonah recalled skimming some section on Indians and now he opened to that page and read.

"I was given another opportunity to expand my empire through the manipulations of the Creeks, those little, ignorant savages who for whatever cause or curse of nature, were rendered haplessly feckless in protecting their own interests. Taking their land and even their lives proved as easy as catching turtles for my stew, yet their carapaces are as fleshy as our own. At that time they continued to own the elevated, sandy land in the southeast of the state, which in the past was thought to be unconducive for cotton but later was proven as fertile as the rich black soil along the rivers.

"Through some convincing, which I failed to understand, the Creeks were persuaded to sign a treaty which ceded all their lands to the state of Alabama on the condition that they be allowed to keep some tracts for their homesteads or, if so choosing, sell to whomever bid the highest. Even some of the brightest of the Indians seemed unable to comprehend even the fundamentals of our culture: That we own dirt and create laws to protect that ownership. Further, they are just plain wild and compulsive, living by urge and caprice. Knowing this, I figured that since they deprived me of my face, I would deprive them of even more of their lands—lands too which I figured would lie fallow and full of weeds under their management.

"So I loaded my wagon with hard, shiny money and cheap liquor and headed toward this region, bringing along with me one easily corrupted government official and my lawyer with contract and quill. Because of hearing that many of the Creeks were unhappy with the treaty and might band together and maraud senselessly against the whites, I also brought along several of my more trustworthy and behemoth slaves, armed to the hilt and hungry for battle, and I myself was not all that resistant to engaging in yet another quick, victorious battle with these people of the forest to relive my days of glory in the militia.

"But we did not encounter any resistance, the will, spirit and culture of these people now long since destroyed after they repeatedly were defeated and routed to lands farther on the fringes of our own culture. As expected their thirst for firewater was unquenchable. We moved from one homestead to another where the Indians had established miserable little hovels for homes and were already on the verge of starving, most of them not having the inclination and knowledge to make farms. We laced their lips with one ounce of our liquor and let them run their fingers through our money to make them excitable. (They understood nothing about finance: They were more impressed by the quantity of the money than the amounts printed on the coins; so we carried lots of pennies.) We then told them that if they signed our contact and abandoned their lands and headed to town with our payoff, they could spend their days eating whole sides of beef and potatoes covered with thick globs of gravy, quaffing the finest of whiskeys, dancing with whores and howling at the moon.

"We gave them enough whiskey for the week and enough money, if they were not cheated, to allow them to stay inebriated for months into the future by which time, if they returned, they would find my Negroes on what was once their land, slashing down the trees, churning up the soil, their hovels and tents either burnt to the ground or occupied by my darkies who would be willing to fight to the death to avoid sleeping in the mud on a cold, rainy night and would find too my claims to their lands now filed with the State of Alabama and bearing all the weight and force of our government.

"At that point, caught between their unwillingness to adapt to our culture and the unfeasibility of their own, and too far gone into debauchery and licentiousness to organize and save themselves, these poor but deserving fellows would mosey on their way yet to farther, more infertile reaches of our continent, either heading west or joining the Seminoles in Florida to live amongst the swamps and mosquitoes. Perhaps I was at last happy with my trade, half of my face for more of their land."

Jonah set the book next to him in the sand. He never bothered to feel much sympathy for the Indians until today but in truth, except for this man bound to the tree, he never really saw many real Indians, only the drunks and derelicts living in sheds in the backwoods, eating possums and wild plants. But when roaming around in the woods as a child, Jonah like his father—and, yes, even his father seemed to appreciate the virtues of savagery—fashioned himself as an Indian. Once after dining in some cave back in the woods on berries, crab apples and roast venison, he and Shaka smeared themselves with deer's blood, carved spears from saplings and resolved upon attacking Whiteoak for the purpose of killing his father to prevent civilization from overtaking the wilderness. At twilight they in fact invaded the plantation, hurling their spears at the overseer and some Negroes gathered around—then they rushed back into the woods. That night they built a campfire, planned their attack for the next day and slept covered with leaves and branches.

Jonah realized that even on this island he was seeking that same wildness and freedom—while dreaming of burning Whiteoak to the ground.

For some reason which he did not understand at first, Jonah recalled some experience back in college at the University of Alabama when he was out drinking at one of the taverns and this boy named Hoard told him that he was brokering deals for the girl named "Melons," some young local slave girl who was interested in playing "sipping the spigot" or "riding the pike" for pay.

Jonah followed Hoard to campus. Hidden by bushes they huddled around one of the buildings and after handing Hoard his money, Jonah crawled through the window into the room. Inside was dark except for one candle flickering shadows across the white, wooden walls. By the chalkboard, sprawled across one of the desks was Melons supine on her back, her legs dangling beneath her, her breasts hanging loose from her blouse while flopping and quivering around when she moved while something oozed from the dark, moundish patch between her legs. She looked barely removed from puberty. She was drunk, he discerned; her head rolled back and forth over the table while the blinks of her eyes were slow and long. She rose onto her elbows and looked at Jonah with some mixture of apathy, sultriness and belligerence.

"Get on with it," she said.

Jonah's desire was urgent, almost consuming, like some spate that he could not block. He imagined ramming himself inside of that runny, used pustule of hers and expurgating the urge from his loins. Take her, he thought, like his father took bodies, took land, used them for his advantage. But why was he hesitating? Across his mind flashed the image of his father years ago thrusting into Thelma, raping her. He became nauseated and heaved, almost losing his stomach.

Regaining his composure, he looked into the girl's face, distraught. "Why are you doing this?"

She cocked her head. "What do you think?"

Jonah shrugged his shoulders. "I reckon you like it."

"Un-huh. What do you think I like? Yawl's mean white dicks inside of me?"

"I don't know," said Jonah. "Why else are you here?"

"Cause that fat boy out yonder, he done make me. He said lessen I spread for you boys, he gonna get Massa to sell me from my family."

"I see," said Jonah.

His desire waned. He became impassive. "Get on out of here."

"Huh?"

"I said leave this place. Return to your family."

"But…"

"Now."

Once rising from the table, wobbling, the girl pulled her blouse around her breasts, slid from the table onto the floor and dressed. They climbed through the window together, Jonah lowering the girl onto the ground.

From the bushes Hoard appeared, grinning and grabbed the girl by the arm. "Liked her that much, did you, that you want to take her home?" he asked.

"I'm sending her back," said Jonah.

"Sending her where?"

"Back to her family."

"No you're not."

"Yes I am," said Jonah menacingly.

Jonah reached forward to take the girl by her hand. But when Hoard tried to push him away, Jonah sidestepped, causing him to lose his balance. Finding the channel for his rage, Jonah charged toward Hoard and punched his nose, feeling the cartilage crumple beneath his fist. Grabbing him around the neck, Jonah flung him to the ground and straddled him, pummeling his chest, his neck, his face, so full of rage and loathing that he was not in control of his actions. Seeing on the periphery of his vision the girl running away into the night, Jonah felt amidst his rage, or perhaps because of his rage, some sense of liberation from the tyranny of himself and his father, as though by giving that girl her freedom he succored freedom onto himself. And at last he felt alive.

Withdrawing from his memory of that event, Jonah, as though controlled by something outside of himself, grabbed his father's book in his hands. For all of his life, he worked at destroying the freedom and wildness of people on lands, including this island, that were stolen from the people whose way of life he most loved.

Jonah discovered himself tearing out the pages, one by one, then releasing them into the breeze that carried them seaward onto the shore and at that nexus where the gulf cascaded into the island, the paper was drenched then thrashed and while obscuring into the greenish and frothing water, flowed away from him into the infinity of the gulf.

CHAPTER TWENTY

"Nomaw, thank you for your years of service but you now have your freedom," Jonah said later that day.

"What you think I's gonna do with that? Starve?"

"You're free," said Jonah, "to make that decision yourself."

"From what I seen, freedom makes niggers crazy."

"Maybe that's not so bad," said Jonah.

"What you mean by that?"

"I don't really know."

"Can I stay on as hired help?"

"For as long as we stay at Whiteoak."

"Yawls gonna leave?"

"At some point."

"Can I come with you, of my own damned free choice?"

"Maybe," said Jonah.

"How much you gonna pay me?"

"I don't know."

"Can I eat what I wants, when I wants?"

"I suppose."

"And go to town whenever I damned well please? And spanks your children when they misbehave without fearing they gonna get revenge on me someday?"

As Jonah rose quickly to leave, Nomaw said, "This here freedom —maybe I's can learn to like it."

"I hope so," said Jonah, leaving Nomaw behind on the beach.

Jonah walked over to Jake and Shobuck who were shoveling sand back into the trench as they had been doing throughout the day. Once filling one section of the trench earlier that day, Jake walked to the top of the dunes and, mimicking the night before, ran down to the beach with Shobuck behind him as though practicing for some other chance at flight in the future.

"Ho dare, Jonah—I mean, Massa," said Jake. "I aint knowed what to call you no more."

"Call me what you will," said Jonah.

"What I calls you depends on hows you treats me—if you wanting to know the truth."

"Then I hope you address me as your friend."

"Me too," said Jake. "So who's that, friend?" said Jake, pointing at Osprey.

"He's an Indian," said Jonah. "Claims that this island belongs to him and his tribe. He wants us to leave—yawl included."

"He the one that left the wings that Shaka thought was Washaka's?"

"Yes. He told me that."

"How come he keeps making that noise?"

Jonah hesitated, not wanting to tell them the truth for fear they might imagine kinship with Osprey, but not wanting to lie either. "I'm not certain."

"Sho you aint, sho you aint."

"Jake," said Jonah, changing the subject as quickly as possible. "Provided you and Shobuck don't cause any harm to my family before we return to Whiteoak, I will emancipate both of you and your families."

"Say again," said Jake, not even smiling.

"Set you free—both of you free."

"What you mean, free?" said Jake skeptically.

"You won't be my slave or anybody's anymore."

"You mean I aint got to fly to Africa?"

"I suppose not."

"You mean I can get me some shack back in the woods in Alabama, grow my own turnips, hunt my own possums and bring my chilluns and grandchilluns with me?"

"Yes."

"Why didn't you tell me sooner?"

"Because I decided only recently."

"If I'd known that, I aint bothered with this shit about birds for one smidgen. I aint like em nohow." Jake danced around some on the ground, slapped Shobuck on the back of his head. "You hear that, Shobuck? The Kingdom done come."

Suddenly Jake stopped, scratched. "How does I know you aint lying?"

"I give you my word?"

"But you aint never given me nothing except some dirt to hoe."

"I do not have the right to take back my word. On my honor."

"What honor's that?" asked Jake.

"The only honor I have."

"What if I get you angry one day on the boat ride back, cause I done upchucked on your shoes? You gonna take that freedom back?"

"No," said Jonah.

"Maybe you's just scared," said Jake, "that we gonna get you tonight, makes you our slave so you be eating grubs, shining my shoes and plowing my fields."

Jonah said nothing.

"But when we back at Whiteoak and you aint scared no more, you might just change your mind."

"I won't," said Jonah. "On my honor."

"All right then, I might trust you if you tell me the truth this time. "Why's that fella up there making them noises?"

Jonah sighed. "The members of his tribe and his family are buried here. And he thinks their souls live in the birds."

"And he be talking to them?"

"He believes he is."

"He as crazy as us niggers."

Pear did not seem at all interested in seeing Jonah, ignored him when he sat next to her. He peered over the edge of the trench below at Shaka who was lying on his back, eyes closed, hands at his sides, all evidence of expression gone from his face as though he were inside his own grave.

"Is Shaka all right?" asked Jonah.

"He's all right," she said sadly, looking away from him.

"The man up there strapped to the tree," Jonah said loudly, hoping Shaka would hear below. "He claims this island is his and that if we don't leave—all of us—he means to kill us. I must therefore keep him in captivity until we leave."

Jonah then informed them that they were both free without any repercussions, provided they did not cause any harm to his family before they arrived back at Whiteoak.

But Pear did not respond—only said, as Jonah walked away, "He'll be all right, my Shaka," as though not talking to him but only trying to console herself.

For the remainder of the day nothing much happened. Jake and Shobuck went fishing in the afternoon while Pear stayed with Shaka. When not asleep Osprey continued to call across the island, "Eeeeeeeek...eeeeeeeek." Jake would pause from his digging, look toward Osprey and scratch his head as though trying to discern whether Osprey was calling for him. But in the end he turned his head toward the sky and called mockingly, "Cockle-doodle-do," before tucking his hands into his armpits and strutting around like some belligerent, oversexed rooster. Ignoring Jake, Pear continued to look anxiously and furtively toward Osprey as though simultaneously drawn to and repulsed by him.

CHAPTER TWENTY-ONE

As soon as the top of the moon rose above the mainland, Osprey roused from his dreams and shrieked, "Eeeeeek...eeeeeeeeeek," as though beholding something that would announce his redemption, his body squirming amidst the binds of the rope.

Yet nobody answered him, not even Jake, not even the real birds who were now roosting back in the mangroves. Jonah felt sad for this man who would never have the opportunity to recover what he lost and thus would forever hope for things that did not exist and call endlessly toward nothing but some figment of his imagination. Osprey was not even able to acknowledge the obvious, thought Jonah, that what he thought were his tribesmen from the night before were only the people below him. As the moon rose higher, seeming too close to the earth, Jonah thought the birdcalls in their meaninglessness were eerily, prehistorically beautiful.

Sitting atop one of the dunes, Jonah could see the specks of sand shifting around in the wind, forming ribs all around him and even molding to the contours of his own body. All those things that he once thought were stable and unmoving like earth and men were in fact always shifting, not any different from the waves in the sea except for their degree of timing and solidity. Even now he could feel the blood flowing into his head as though cleaning something out, each pulse of his heart causing his skull to shift outward and expand slightly.

He glanced northward to the horizon, looking in the dim but purified air for the billows of smoke that would augur the return of the steamship and along with it, civilization. He would greet that moment with some degree of relief—for at last everyone would be safe—but not any warmth for he knew that from thereon out his society—the only one he ever knew—would ridicule him for emancipating his slaves. Upon returning to the plantation, he imagined visiting the graveyard and telling his father that he loved him, always did, like someone loves the only drink of water in the desert, and that explained why he tried so thoroughly throughout his life to emulate him and seek his approval. But that he was not committed to the acquisition of wealth and power but to freedom and wildness and was willing to sever himself from all previous blood and social belonging. He imagined gathering his slaves around him in the fields one day with his family at his side and announcing that from that day forward, they were all free, free at last.

The bottom of the moon cleared the mangroves as the top of the sun sank into the ocean, withdrawing the last of its rays. The light changed from orange to silver. But as the moon reflected the light from the sun, the island reflected the light from the moon and resembled the moon in many ways: round and white with craters and suspended in infinity.

Below on the beach he saw dark figures, Jake, Shobuck and Nomaw walking toward Pear with candles in their hands. Once arriving around the trench, they sat down next to the trench where Shaka was still residing, having not risen once throughout the day. Nomaw then placed her arm around Pear.

Jonah was still wary about the slaves even after offering them their freedom because amongst other reasons, he heard from Eloise that Pear had actually talked to Osprey that afternoon. But now they seemed harmless.

Below, their bodies began to sway slowly. Emerging from the churning of the wind and the rattle of the sea oats was the humming of Nomaw and Pear. Emerging from the lolling of the waves, as they mounted and collapsed, was the deeper and more powerful humming of Jake, followed by Shobuck striving to match his depth—all infusing the indifferent and the humanly inalterable universe around them with melancholy.

"Tell us," sang Nomaw.

"Come on out that hole, Shaka, you aint dead yet," sang Jake, his voice commanding all around him.

"Tell us about the boy, Jake. He aint dead yet."

"Let me tell you this story."

"Tell us now. He aint dead yet."

"He come from nowhere, stashed away in the huckleberries by some niggers that don't want him."

"But he aint dead yet."

"And the babe called."

"And she called back," sang Pear.

"And she came and saved him from the coyotes and the panthers and gators and took him to her breasts."

Jake then sang about Shaka's mother who wanted to believe in things that were not real to save her son from the pain of reality. And sang too about Shaka's attempt in his childhood to free himself from slavery. And most of all he sang about their love for Shaka for setting them free from their own being, concluding with singing, "Come on out that hole, Shaka. Death aint calling to you yet."

"Death aint come for you yet."

Above their singing, Osprey called as though singing with them, the "Eeeeeeek...eeeeeeek," piercing into the night, still unheeded.

Jonah hummed along with them too. And he prayed—to whom or to what he did not know—that Shaka would live to discover the freedom that Jonah would grant to him.

Once their humming died down and even Osprey again faded into silence, the other slaves dispersed back into the dunes to sleep except for Pear who remained by the trench. Jonah rose too and walked back toward the tree to sit closer to his family but with an easy view of Osprey. He stayed awake for hours, reveling in the evening, watching the moon cast patterns of light upon the ripples and swells of the water and upon the slopes and crests of the dunes. He watched too as the herons on the sandbar not even moving sometimes before instantly driving their beaks into the water. How magnificent life must be for that bird—and he was struck by the oddity of his thought. Osprey would occasionally stir within his binds and call again across the island, the noise all the more acute against the calming seas, "Eeeeeek...eeeeeeeek," but nobody answered as usual, including Pear who was now asleep by the trench. Sensing all was at peace around the island, Jonah succumbed to sleep with his arms still wrapped around his weapon.

He was in another earthless world of smoke and flame, hearing chanting and drumming unlike he had ever heard before from the hands and mouths of multitudes of people. Amidst the smoke he saw Shaka and Osprey dancing together, chimera of man and bird, flesh and feather, arm and wing, their eyes open but not seeing things around them, both mimicking and guiding each other like rivals and brothers too as though communicating with each other. Everything started moving faster around him—the light, the smoke, the bodies of the others as he realized, astounded, that he was dancing with them.

Jonah awoke with something pressed against his neck, something lifted from his arms. He opened his eyes, staring into the moon: The world was still so calm and beautiful. But someone was holding a blade to his neck.

"Do not fight. Or I will kill you," said Shaka from behind him.

Pear stepped around in front of him, pointing his rifle at his chest.

Jonah felt sad.

Shaka pulled Jonah's sword from its sheath, saying, "We're leaving. And we aint wanting you to stop us."

"Eeeeeeek...eeeeeeeek."

Turning his head Jonah saw that Osprey was looking at him now. Jonah felt afraid but not for himself. "You're free to leave, Shaka, without my interference."

"I done trusted you—and God too," said Shaka, "too many times and I aint intending to make that mistake again."

"Do what you will with me, Shaka. Kill me, I don't care. Just don't hurt my wife and children."

"I aint hurting nobody, unless they get in our way."

"But Osprey. If he's unbound, he'll try to kill us all."

"He aint gonna kill nobody," said Shaka.

"He said he will."

"He just wanted to make sure you dies some more."

"But he thinks…"

"I know what he thinks," preempted Shaka.

Jonah was confused momentarily before understanding that there was more to all of this than he had realized. "Just please protect my family from him," said Jonah.

"Seeing this here situation, you aint got any other choice but to trust us," said Shaka. "So don't flinch while I tie your hands."

Jonah considered fighting but knew instinctively that violence was not the solution.

After his hands were tied securely in front of him, Shaka said, "When we get your wife and children, tell them to obey me."

Shaka and Pear stood and while keeping Jonah at some distance, they allowed him to rise to his feet and together they walked over to the children's tent.

When they arrived, Eloise said before they even touched the tent, "Is that you, Jonah?"

"Be calm and listen to me, Eloise. I'm held captive at gunpoint by Shaka and Pear. Do as they say and nobody will be harmed."

"Send James and Josh outside the tent, one at a time," said Shaka.

"All right," said Eloise.

After James and Josh walked outside the tent, looking more amused than frightened, Pear bound their hands behind their back.

Still dressed in her nightgown, Eloise walked out, saying, "Why, Shaka, why? We told you that you're free—both of you. Since God does not send you angels, you now think He has given you the right to raise the sword?"

"I don't care about God," said Shaka.

"Understandably he does not trust us," said Jonah. "He just wants to make certain that he leaves without our interference."

With Pear and Shaka behind them, their weapons at the ready, Jonah and his family walked in formation toward the tree where Osprey was still shrieking. On the way there Jake appeared from the darkness, heading toward them.

"Ho dare, Shaka. What you got going here?"

Shaka trained the sword on Jake, saying, "Stay clear, Jake—this aint your business. If you aint wanting nobody hurt, you best gather up the others and meet me on the beach below."

"All right then," said Jake, looking at Jonah. "You the one with the killing tools."

"Go on," said Jonah. "We're all right."

Jake disappeared. Once they reached the tree, Osprey became silent and gazed at them. Shaka and Pear walked around to the front of the tree, standing before the Indian.

"You see," said Osprey, craning his neck to look at Jonah. "They come for you."

"If you release him," Jonah said, "he'll try to kill us."

"He saw you," Shaka said.

"Saw me? What do you mean?

"He knows your heart."

"How?"

"The dream," said Shaka.

Jonah remembered the fire and smoke. "You mean…"

Shaka walked over to the tree, ready with the sword to sever Osprey's bonds.

"You mean that was real?"

"Aint nothing real but what you think," said Shaka, slicing through the ropes around the tree.

Frightened, Jonah watched as Osprey hobbled from the tree, almost collapsing from stiffness and exhaustion before Shaka grabbed him by the arm to help him find his balance. Shaka then cut the rope around his wrists and his ankles until Osprey was free. Breathing hard, Jonah stood before his family, his arms bound tight but his feet loose, determined to do all within his power to stop Osprey from harming anyone.

Osprey walked toward him and said, "You like Adam. Must be lost and scared. Die many times. But you find your way."

Osprey then turned and walked down to the beach.

As Shaka instructed Jonah and his family sat down by the tree facing the mangroves, Jonah now relaxed but baffled. Shaka then wrapped several rings of rope around them, starting at their laps then working all the way to their shoulders, then tying the rope around back.

When Shaka started walking away, Jonah called to him. "Shaka, the dream—what was that?"

"For many nights I dreamed you were there. And now you know too."

Shaka and Pear then headed down the dunes, shouting to the other slaves congregating below on the beach around the thin, strange man, "Washaka is free. Washaka is free."

Shaka sat next to Osprey down on the beach as the others gathered around. This was his only family, thought Shaka—all of them, Nomaw included—that he had ever known and loved. Their faces alive with moonlight, they were never more beautiful than now that they were shorn of illusions and living reality head-on.

"Are you sure that you aint wanting to come, Jake?" he asked.

"You think Massa good for his word?"

"I suppose. But you never know what mask men choose to wear."

"I done pondered on this until my brain done broke. But I done left back on the plantation some heap of chilluns who I aint never taught nothing but lies. And now they all just some bunch of ass-licking, snake-scared fools likely to squirt them out some babies who gonna believe the same.

"I reckon on heading back to find some land back in some hollow, way away from whities. We gonna learn to live from the land, to hunt, fish and grow turnips, and never bend before another man.

"But most of all they's gonna learn about you, Shaka."

"But remember to teach them that there's only one Washaka."

"Themselves," said Jake.

"Shobuck. Are you sure you're willing to leave your family to come with us?"

"They aint gonna understand any of this no how," said Shobuck.

"You want to come, Nomaw?" asked Shaka, smiling.

"I don't even know where you's going? Back in them swamps, with it?" she said, pointing to Osprey.

"Yes," Shaka said.

"Why don't yawl just come on back?"

"Cause even if we was sure about Jonah, we aint wanting to live surrounded by whities. We live wild out here."

"This whole time," said Nomaw, "yawl done broke my heart over and again. And this whole time, I thought yawl was deranged. But somewhere in the back of my mind, I wished I was deranged too."

"Then you can get deranged with me," said Jake.

"Lawdy," said Nomaw, blushing. "Maybe I ought to come with yawl to stay away from this fool. But too many snakes and bugs back there for me."

"All right then."

"But one more question," said Nomaw, pointing at the Indian. "Who's that?"

Checking to see if he wanted to answer the question, Shaka glanced over at Osprey who looked merely eager to leave.

"Is he Washaka?" asked Nomaw.

Still bound to the tree, Jonah watched as Shaka tied some rope around Jake and Nomaw.

"Why are they doing that?" asked Eloise.

"They're not going," said Jonah. "And Shaka doesn't want us to believe they are colluding with him in our capture."

Jonah then watched as Shaka left Pear behind and came back up the dunes, still carrying the sword in his hand.

"What does he want now?" asked Eloise.

"I don't know," said Jonah.

Shaka was now standing above them, looking feral and strong with moonlight at his back. Without grimacing but rather smiling as though inspired, he held the sword above their heads.

"Shaka, no," screamed Eloise.

Shaka just stood there for several moments as though some dark, unfinished part of him were reveling in his power over them. He suddenly brushed the palm of his other hand over the edge of the blade, blood oozing over metal.

"Raise your hands," said Shaka.

After Jonah raised his arms into the air, Shaka cut the rope between his wrists. Shaka then placed the sword before him and Jonah sliced the palm of his own hand over the blade until he felt the skin was cutting.

Then uniting their palms by clinching their fingers together, they intermingled their blood.

"I'm sorry," said Jonah, looking into the eyes of his friend.

"Be free," said Shaka.

"Be free."

Shaka turned, one dark, energetic figure running down the dunes, tossing the sword into the sea oats. Down on the beach he rushed toward the others waiting for him with one of the rowboats and Osprey's canoe at the ready. Osprey shoved from shore first, drifting in the small waves as he waited for them. Once Pear and Shobuck were on board, Shaka pushed the rowboat off the shore, waded through the waves and climbed on board himself.

Eloise watched as they paddled beyond the small but upward-striving, moon-drawn waves into the flat and calmer water beyond—just figures drifting toward the mainland. God—or at least what she thought was God—was much stranger and vaster and earthy than she had ever imagined, gracing people in ways that were beyond her comprehension.

Out on the water the boats were still moving quickly from shore and Pear was standing in the bow of her boat, her arms lifted into the air to form black, inverted wings. But as the boats moved miraculously into alignment with the moonlight, flowing upon the molten, silver pathway toward that Eden in the swamps, she slowly reversed the arch of her arms, pointing her fingers down, the wings metamorphosing from death into life.

CPSIA information can be obtained at www.ICGtesting.com
Printed in the USA
LVOW08*0000210614
391073LV00001B/1/P